BETWEEN YOU AND ME

By

Ernie Robertson

Ernie Robertson

To Yvonne
A good neighbor & friend

Copyright © 2008 by Ernie Robertson

All rights reserved. No part of this book shall be reproduced or transmitted in any form or by any means, electronic, mechanical, magnetic, photographic including photocopying, recording or by any information storage and retrieval system, without prior written permission of the publisher. No patent liability is assumed with respect to the use of the information contained herein. Although every precaution has been taken in the preparation of this book, the publisher and author assume no responsibility for errors or omissions. Neither is any liability assumed for damages resulting from the use of the information contained herein.

This is a work of fiction. Names, characters, places, and incidents either are the product of the author's imagination or are used fictitiously. Any resemblance to actual events or locales or persons, living or dead, is entirely coincidental.

ISBN 0-7414-4360-0

Published by:
INFINITY
PUBLISHING.COM
1094 New DeHaven Street, Suite 100
West Conshohocken, PA 19428-2713
Info@buybooksontheweb.com
www.buybooksontheweb.com
Toll-free (877) BUY BOOK
Local Phone (610) 941-9999
Fax (610) 941-9959

Printed in the United States of America
Printed on Recycled Paper
Published February 2008

This book is dedicated to my wife Pearl, and our children, Donna, Diane and Bruce. We have withstood the tests in the Ocean of Life; and have the strength to overcome any obstacles of the waves we have faced or will face in our life's time with each other.

Prologue

Knowledge is the beginning of wisdom. As Francis of Assisi once said, "Help me to change the things I can change, to accept the things I can not change, and the wisdom to know the difference." Who are they that can attain this? In reality, knowledge is only as effective as you put it to practical use. To have knowledge is to know the difference between fact and fiction, to know right from wrong. Knowledge is a process of learning in the span of life you have between birth and death. A person's success depends on one being satisfied, knowing what they have learned is still only a part of the whole. It is a wise person who never stops learning.

There were many relationships made in the past that would last a lifetime. Many times relationships made only for the present would diminish and fade away, such as the annual flower, blossoming for a year, and then disappearing in the fall, never to appear again. A telephone call, a picture, will bring back a memory, soon to find its way back to the forgotten era of the past. It was good while the relationship lasted, not something that endures forever. Promises of undying love made from the head not the heart, soon to fade away when relationships end, only time has the answer.

Friendships as well as relationships made in the past four years have rocky roads to travel at times, yet the deep rooted feelings of friendship, and love comes from the depth of one's being, and can withstand any trial or tribulation that may come. Friendship is like the perennial flower returning each spring, lifting its head out of the earth to reveal the beauty that will never disappear. So too, as the earth nurtures the flower, friendships are nurtured with love one has for another that lasts a lifetime, even if separated.

Introduction

The world will welcome the class of 1982. Friendship is like the perennial flower, even though the winter arrives, as differences come in relationships, friendships can last forever. Soon the graduates will leave their cocoon, each going their separate ways. Relationship: or friendship? Time has the answer.

It is spring, graduation time at Ohio University. Students of the graduating class are moving around the campus in and out of the dorms, congratulating each other. They share a beer or a soft drink, toasting the future. Even though drinking was forbidden on campus, this was the day the campus police looked the other way. Parties the night before and more to come the next day. Then the parting of the ways became certain when they say their good-byes.

Promises of those who fell in love these past four years were made on the seats of the stadium, or on the stairs of the different buildings. These students were oblivious of those who would step over or go around them, even trying to break apart those who were holding or kissing each other. Theirs were a commitment of the friendship and love to last forever. It was the promise made at that moment in time.

Jim, Scott and Kevin are three young men who met through playing sports, and having adjoining rooms next to each other. The past four years enhanced their relationship. Their sharing time together developed into a friendship with the hopes of it lasting forever. An extra room next to Jim's was used to entertain their friends. It was a gift from Jim's Father, when he gave one million dollars to the school. He came from California the son of a wealthy family. His Father, who owned a construction corporation, spoiled him.

His Mother had left the home when Jim was ten because of his Father's infidelity.

Jim was the star player on the football team in high school. During his junior year at college, his Father indulged him with a new Corvette. At first he had many dates, but eventually they became few because of his demand for sex from some of the female students.

Scott Drew came from North Carolina; his Father had been a Senator in Congress, powerful and influential in foreign affairs. He was looked up to by many of the business and political factions in the country. Many social bills were passed in Congress because of his influence. Scott grew up in the fast pace of the political life style, and desired to follow in his Father's footsteps. His Father was disappointed because he had decided not to go to North Carolina University, where he had graduated.

Wanting to ask Scott why he decided to go to Ohio rather then stay in North Carolina that was so close to home, he refrained, hoping that after a year he would change his mind. Scott admired Jim and the exciting life he was living because Jim often would lend him the Corvette to go on a date. In truth, Scott took advantage of Jim's good nature of lending him money. Scott played on the basketball team at Ohio for three years. He too had many offers to become a professional player, but refused, his heart was set to become a Senator and be involved in the political arena.

Kevin's Father had inherited a vast tract of land, raising cattle, grain, and enjoyed training the wild horses when available. Being successful, growing up in this unspoiled land inspired Kevin to go to college. After his graduation he returned to Wyoming to work and share with his Father in protecting his ranch from the poachers, who would destroy the land by drilling for gas and oil. Kevin played varsity baseball for the University. He also had many offers from the major leagues but turned it down

Different than Jim and Scott, he seldom dated while in college. He felt an obligation to Jim, keeping him from getting into trouble as often as he could. For some unknown reason, Jim admired and respected Kevin; looking up to him as a big brother. Yet as good as the offers to play professional baseball were, he knew that he was going back to the ranch in Wyoming.

Many times these young men would go to the local night clubs, to enjoy the swinging life that college students do. Dates with the female students were mostly double or triple, having to rent a car because the Corvette had two seats. Jim had the luxury of having a car, though he was willing to let Scott or Kevin borrow it. They refused at times knowing an accident would be too expensive to repair.

Jim would say, "Don't worry, if you have an accident with the car, my old man has plenty of money." In time their association became a relationship; and then developed into a friendship with the hopes of it lasting forever. Jim was physically large and strong. Many of the underclassmen admired and were envious of his popularity with the female students because of the car and his money. Jim thought money would solve any situation, until threatened with expulsion. In his senior year, his drinking habits lessened. He became a well-known football player.

Contents

Chapter	Page
In the Beginning – Alicia	1
Separation	16
Jim 1982 – 2002	21
Karen and Tiffany	29
Responsibility	37
Wanting a Child	43
Joyce	47
Trying Again	50
Mrs. McKane – Justin – Tiffany	52
A Child is Lost & Born	61
A Baby is Born	64
Discussions	71
Scott – 1982 – 2002	76
Carolyn and Grace	80
Jasmine	89
California	106
Commitment	111
Office Conversation	114
Jasmine and Philip	117
Kevin	123
Kevin and Katy	125
Children	131
Reunion in Ohio	135
Katy leaves Home	138
Shallow Love	139
Katy Makes Contact	142
Making Plans	147
Time Moves On	152
Jasmine's Graduation	157
Reunion Time	164
A Repeat	173
Guests Arrive	178

Carolyn and Robbie	179
Sharing Time	182
Karen – Alicia	187
Confession	191
Jim Sr. – Joyce – Eric	195
Heather – Chante	197
Eric	207
Jon & Suzy	210
The Past is Gone	214
Looking For Love	220
Discussions	227
Suzy's Plan	230
Confession	237
Vacation is Over	238
Dilemma	242
Once More	249
More Truth	253
Justin Calls	259
Katy's Advice	263
Dad and Daughter	265
Growing Up	269
Washington D.C.	272
Justin Calls Again	278
Truth Time	285
Reprimand	302
Where is the Boy	304
Finding the Boy	316
Right or Wrong	324
Presidential Plans	330
Tiffany is Missing	337
More Plans	338
The Oval Office	342
Missing Again	345
Kevin's Plan	351
A Change	353

In the Beginning

Alicia

Kevin had met a student in one of his classes. He had taken her out on a date, but thought better of asking Jim if he could use the Corvette the next day. Jim seemed to have been drinking, and so he decided to ignore him. Starting to leave the room he heard Jim, "Hold it a minute." With a slurred voice he asked, "How was your date last night? I hear she is one beautiful babe. Did you make out? Come on Kevin have a drink and tell me all about it."

Feeling the hair on the back of his neck rising, Kevin turned to make a reply but restrained himself. This type of conversation with Jim in his condition would lead nowhere.

After a few more unnecessary wise comments Kevin replied, "For your information she is one beautiful girl, you wouldn't know about her kind. In fact I'm seeing her again tomorrow. I need the Corvette to pack the grille, steaks and wine that are in the refrigerator. Is that okay Jim?"

Look buddy," Jim replied as he put his arms around Kevin's shoulders. "You know you can. Wait a minute. Get a date for me and we can go out together? We can let Scott have the car and we can rent one."

Kevin wanted this date with Alicia to become a long lasting relationship, but Jim is a hard person to change when he sets his mind to anything. Not wanting to hurt their friendship and knowing his quick temper he said nothing. The quietness gave Scott the time to speak. "Jim I don't need the car tomorrow.

I'm sure Kevin would like to be alone with his girlfriend. You know you want to be alone on any dates you have."

"I guess you're right. Now Kevin, I want to know how you make out." Kevin remained quiet.

The next morning Kevin picked up Alicia at her dorm. Driving down to the beach he found a place where there weren't many people. Having put on their swimsuits back at the college they ran hand in hand into the lake. They swam back and forth enjoying the coolness of the water over their warm bodies from the rays of the sun. Playful Kevin would push Alicia under then dive deep down and touch her.

"Just kidding," Kevin would say. Swimming for a while longer they headed to shore until reaching where they could stand. Kevin kissed Alicia, and with affection she returned it. This went on with each kiss getting longer as the feeling became one of pleasure. Kevin was excited wanting to explore and build on the situation as it was progressing. Afraid she might object to him moving too fast, he decided to pull away.

"Let's eat Kevin I'm starved." Alicia said as she lightly pushed him. He took the grille from the car and fired up the charcoal. Alicia spread out the blanket, set down the cooler and opened it placing the steaks, wine, chips and pickles on top of the blanket, leaving the salad they had bought inside the cooler. Sitting on the blanket they sipped the wine finishing the first glass. She poured a second drink as Kevin turned the steaks over on the grill.

Alicia starting to feel the effects of the wine and was concerned that she had been drinking too fast. Her head was getting heavy and she started to feel insecure as she spoke.

With a slight slurred in her speech she asked, "Are the steaks ready Kevin? I'm famished."

"They'll be done in a few minutes; will you make up the plates with the rest of the food?" When everything was ready they sat down to enjoy their meal. Finishing, they sat there looking up toward the changing of the sky, as the sun moved toward the west. They watched the sun mixing in between the clouds, designing myriads of colors, making for romantic moments. It was a game, trying to make different images of the clouds, seeing who could find the most.

Holding hands, they relaxed, moving close to each other. Kevin moved his hand from Alicia's. He started to touch her in places, making her feel uncomfortable. She wanted him to stop; yet; there was an exciting sensation she felt as she laid beside him. These were feelings she had known before on dates, as exciting as they were, she always pulled back. Wanting yet frightened; just as before, she pulled away.

Torn between the pleasures and fear she would lose control, decided it would be better to get up. "Alicia. Why are you frightened?"

"Let's go for another swim Kevin. I think we better be careful. Too much of the wine might cause me to forget myself. It's not you I worry about; it's me. The wine is getting to my head. I could do something and be sorry."

The warmth of the evening weather, and as the sky darkened came the glow of the moon. The gleaming brightness of the stars searching and waiting for a response to make a wish.

She was becoming more excited as Kevin continued to touch her. With his passion increasing and her emotions running high, she pulled him on top of her, as they both were satisfied.

Separating they lay quietly, the only audible sound was their heavy breathing. After a few moments, as Kevin held her tightly, she broke away, gathered up her clothes and ran to the car. Getting into the front seat she struggled to put her clothes on. "What's wrong?" Kevin called as he leaped up and raced towards her to find Alicia quietly crying.

Not wanting to touch her for fear it would compound the situation, he returned to pick up the blanket and grill, placing everything else into the cooler. Putting his shorts and shirt on he got in the driver's seat leaning over to her.

"Don't touch me." she stammered through her tears. Moving away he started the engine and headed back to the college. Thinking to him self as he drove, "She instigated it. One moment filled with fire, the next moment cold as an iceberg." He was at a loss for words, she was the one who ignited the spark after it had extinguished.

Arriving at her dorm, she opened the car door, fled up the stairs, never looking back. Kevin got out and ran after her, grasping the door handle it failed to open because it automatically locked when it closed behind her.

Not wanting to disturb anyone, he returned to the car. He was astonished at the sudden turn of events. "She made love with me, responded in every way." Waiting in vain it was obvious he would not see her tonight. "Is this the end of what he hoped was a new beginning?" With that thought, he drove away.

Racing up the stairs to the second floor, Alicia opened the door slamming it shut behind her. Crying uncontrollable it awakened her roommate and best friend Allison.

By the time Allison got out of bed and went over to her the only sound coming from Alicia was a subdued whimper, sounding like a hurt young puppy in pain. She lifted her up stroking her singing with a soft hum. In time Alicia quieted down nestling tightly to Allison seeking comfort. "What's wrong, what happened? Are you all right?" Holding her Allison tried to run her hands through her hair, trying to ease her shaking body and get her relaxed.

In time Alicia was able to talk "Why did I do it; he'll never want to see me again? I did something that was so wrong; why? We were just lying there kissing, when I lost control of myself." Again Alicia burst out in tears. "It was my fault."

"Alicia what could you do that was so terrible? If you want to talk I'll listen, no advice I promise. Did he hit you, abuse you in any way?"

Quietly Allison sat on the side of the bed wondering what she could do. After a few moments Alicia spoke.

"No, it was my fault. We went to the beach and had a great time. We had a cookout, went swimming most of the time. He would touch me in certain places gently, I would resist, and he would apologize. He didn't try a second time. I wasn't surprised because he isn't that type to take advantage of me."

"For heaven's sake Alicia, why didn't you tell him to take you home? You don't have to take that from any man. If you want, I'll tell him where he stands. You're too nice a person. The majority of the guys here are like animals."

"We laid down and started kissing, then holding each other very close and moving back and forth. It was a very romantic time looking up at the clouds as they changed colors in the sky. It was so exciting; I had never had such a fulfilling experience in my life. It was me who lost control. I became so excited I removed my swimsuit, and we made love. I forced myself on him." What will he think of me now?"

"Alicia, that's not love. It was nothing but having sex. I think you should go to the emergency room at the hospital to be checked out. You might have gotten pregnant."

"No, I'll be okay. This is the first time I've ever made love. My Dad always warned me how men want only one thing. I'm an only child. My Father said women should wait until they get married before they have sex. My Mother was never happy. I was born three months after they married."

"I still believe you should go to the hospital, but if you don't, that's okay with me.

Alicia, you have to know what to do so you won't get pregnant. A man has to use protection. Didn't your Mother tell you what happens if you have sex?"

"My Mother died when I was a teenager. My Dad gave me books to read, but back then I didn't understand. He kept me close to home. I had a few dates, and had to be home early. I can't remember any boy in high school ask me for a second date because my Father grilled them when we were going out. The few dates I had when they tried to get fresh I would scream stop it and they would take me home."

"Alicia, you're a twenty two year old woman, not a child. I find it hard to believe you went through high school and college, and never had an affair, at least one time. It isn't wrong, as long as you're careful. I can't believe you're a virgin. You must be the only one here on campus?"

It was a sleepless night for Kevin; he couldn't get Alicia out of his mind. He had been intimate a couple of times with a girl but never had he experienced before like what he had with her. Having sex with her was passion, an act of deep feeling. In the morning he made breakfast, and had a cup of coffee. Later he called Alicia's room, hoping she would answer the phone. When her roommate answered he asked to speak to Alicia.

"Sorry, she isn't taking any calls; by the way, what happened last night? You should be ashamed; this isn't like you. For heaven's sake, don't you get it? She's not taking any calls. Stop calling!"

"It's none of your business Allison, why would you ask? It isn't your concern. You know I would never take advantage of anyone." Kevin continually dialed Alicia's telephone number. Allison would pick up the phone; hear his voice and hang up. Not giving up, he tried once more and the message was clear.

In anger, he slammed the phone down, the sound waking Jim and Scott. Getting up from their beds and going into the guest room they saw him pacing the floor, muttering words they couldn't understand. Jim walked over to Kevin wrestling him down to the floor. "Well, well, she must have said no again."

"Jim, let me up, I'm relaxed and calm. You don't understand." Silence prevailed until Kevin said, "Come on Jim, let go of me."

Jim pulled Kevin up on his feet and slapped him. "I do understand! They chase after me, I have money, the car, and I show them a great time. Many of the girls I dated before have gone out with me again."

"Yes, only because of what you have, and what they can get. I feel sorry for you, you're a good guy."

The tension continued to rise between them, until Scott spoke up "Okay guys, cool it. We only have a few more days here before we celebrate our last time together. Remember we made a commitment to have a bash before we leave; then make our plans to reunite in twenty years and have another celebration to out do any we had before. Our plan is to celebrate tomorrow night at the club down town."

"Let's shake hands Jim, we've been friends for four years and hopefully will be for the rest of our lives. Let's put our hands together, to keep our relationship strong like we do after we've had a disagreement."

"You're right Kevin. We've been like brothers for some reason. I can't figure out why I like you so much. I must confess you have helped me out of problems many times in the past."

"Going to Alicia's dorm room would be fruitless, "If only she would let me explain. I'll go over and wait until she comes out." Kevin thought. Arriving at her door hearing voices, he knocked and was surprised when the door opened A tall older distinguished man stood there. Kevin was speechless and backed away. Finally he asked, "Who are you?"

"I know why you're here young man. I'm Alicia's Father and she isn't here. What do you want?" Before Kevin could respond, Alicia's Father said, "If you continue to harass my daughter I'll call the police and have you arrested. So get the message and disappear. I'm warning you."

Frustrated Kevin tried to push his way into the room to no avail. Her Father held him at arms length. Try as he might and as physically strong as Kevin was, he was no match for this man. "Sir, I just want to talk to her. We had a wonderful time." Glancing around the room he saw a closet door open.

"Kevin." Allison pleaded as she came into the room. Please, don't cause any trouble."

"Young man, the plans for her life are all set; and you're not a part of them, let's not have any problems. You had a good day yesterday; that was yesterday. Today it's different; now leave."

Kevin knowing it was fruitless to argue returned to his room. "So that's Alicia's Father. What did she tell him?

Maybe she said I raped her? No," he thought; "She knows she was the one who started it, and kept it going." He satisfied himself with the thought it was consensual.

Back at his dorm Scott asked, "Where have you been? Go take a shower and get ready. When the club closes we can bring the girls back here for an all night blast."

Going into the shower he saw a girl inside and called out to Scott. "Who's the woman in here? Where's Jim?"

"She's some one that Jim dated and he's bringing her to the club tonight. Her name is Carolyn; Jim's been out with her many times. In case you forgot, we have women living here in the dorm. I guess theirs were all taken so she asked Jim if she could shower here and he said sure. You know him; he figures this is his last fling here, why not go all the way. He told me his Father is waiting for him to come home and get involved in his business."

It was seven in the evening when they entered the club and noticed the owners had hired more policemen this year for inside and outside of the building to control any situation that might occur. They remembered the past years when the situation got out of control and the club was shut down.

Two women graduates; Chante and Heather joined Carolyn and the men at their table. A few students were out of control when they arrived and were quickly removed and taken to jail to sober up. Fights and arguments became frequent during the evening between some of the students. The owners of the club and the police found it increasingly difficult to keep things under control as the night passed. Local young men resented not being allowed to come into the building, and started fights. This was the first time the club was scheduled for a private party. They were soon removed from the club and taken to jail.

By midnight, Jim had become intoxicated and difficult to control. Kevin was concerned, knowing in two days they had to evacuate the rooms, leaving everything in order. Because of the mounting problems, the owners decided to close at one instead of two am. The problems increased and more police were called to stop this becoming a full blown out riot. Jim invited the women back to their dorm.

All the persuasion Kevin offered why they shouldn't have the women up to their rooms fell on deaf ears. "Yes," chimed Heather. "Let's make this an all nighter. It's too early to break up." Taking Kevin by the arm Heather pleaded with him, "Come on Kevin don't be a nerd. I'm yours for the night, who knows what the future will be."

Pulling Jim and Scott aside, Kevin pleaded, "We can't do this. We have to be out in a couple of days. The rooms have to be in top condition or we pay the damages. Let's leave it as it is now."

"Come on, this is our last party for twenty years Kev, don't spoil it. We're going to continue the party, don't be a spoilsport," Arriving back at the dorm the drinking continued.

In utter frustration, Kevin finally called out. "It's three o'clock, this is it. Let's call it a night Scott. Where's Jim?"

"I think he's in his room with Carolyn. Chante is waiting for me and Heather is waiting for you in your room. Go and enjoy, have a good time. This is our last party for years; don't spoil it now. No more classes, we're free. How can you pass up a girl like Heather? Many of the guys would give their life for a date with her."

Going into Jim's room he saw him pinning Carolyn down on the bed. "What are you doing? She's telling you to stop. What letter in the word 'No' don't you understand?"

Carolyn repeated again. "Please Jim, stop it! I want to go home, let me up! You're hurting me, I said no!"

Walking over to the bed, Kevin reached down grabbed Jim's arms and pulled him off of Carolyn, pushing him down on the floor. Trying to get Jim up became impossible for he was too drunk to comprehend what Kevin was telling him. Lying on the floor he looked up to Kevin and with a slurring voice he said, "This isn't a church meeting, it's a party."

"Thanks Kev for coming; he wouldn't stop. I've tried to tell him but he wouldn't listen. I've had dates with him before and controlled him. This time he's impossible."

"You idiot Jim! Get with it man, she could call this rape and then you'd be in real trouble."

Helping Carolyn up from the bed, Kevin told her, "You get the other girls and I'll take you back to your dorms."

"That's okay, I can stay in my Mother's apartment. You know she's a Dean here; she's gone home for the night and I have a key. Don't worry, I'm not going to make waves in Jim's ocean now, He has done a good turn in his past reputation of what everyone thought of him. He'll grow up after he leaves here I hope. Maybe you and I should have hooked up tonight. Perhaps some other time we can get together."

"I know Carolyn; we don't want him to leave the college with this type of a memory. I appreciate what you're saying. Maybe we can get together some day. We'll see."

"Scott, get Jim into the shower, and to bed. He's out."

Taking Kevin aside, quietly Scott pleaded with him, "Pacify Carolyn, My Dad had been a Senator for about twenty-four years in Washington. I'm planning to enter the political arena when I get home. She lives in Greensboro, North Carolina where I do. My Dad has great expectations for me becoming a Senator some day."

"Okay Scott, I'll try, but don't plan on it. She's upset at the present time. The trouble with you and Jim is, you think every woman is the same. They aren't, that's the way it is. They all don't want to go to bed with you." Thinking to him self he said, "I'm no one to talk, I tried to make out with Alicia, look what I got out of that situation. Now I've lost her, the one girl I hoped to marry. How will I ever find her to apologize?"

Driving the girls back to their dorms, they thanked Kevin. "I have to apologize for the three of us; it wasn't intended to end this way. We have plans to meet in twenty years to prove our friendship is forever, we're really not the kind of guys you saw tonight."

Still feeling some effects of all the drinking, Heather looked at Kevin and said, "Kevin sweetheart, I wish you had come with me. I waited patiently, and was disappointed. Maybe before we vacate the college we can get together. One final date for a farewell goodbye and it will be different this time. We're open for an invite to celebrate your reunion, if you would like. It would be hilarious to review our lives of the next twenty years."

"I'll keep in touch with both of you," responded Carolyn. As Heather and Chante left the car Carolyn turned to Kevin and quietly said, "They sure are the party animals especially Heather. She looks like she should be in high school. I heard she is a tease and sometimes goes too far in leading her date on, and then has to fight back against their aggression toward her. She'll get hurt some day if she doesn't stop."

At Carolyn's Mothers apartment Kevin shut down the engine turning to say, "We've had some good and not so good times. In reality Jim drinks too much, at times, and is over sexed. If you like I'll send you my address and E-mail. I'd like to have you celebrate our twentieth."

"That's a fantastic idea Kevin. When I get your address I'll keep in contact with you. I'll let the girls know, you do the same with the guys. I can hardly wait for the years to roll by."

Carolyn opened the door to leave and turned putting her hands on his face giving him a kiss. Startled for a moment Kevin pulled her back to him, to return the kiss he had received.

Breaking away, he sat there for a moment, surprised at him self, how much he enjoyed it. They sat breathless for a while. "Would you like to come in for a cup of coffee?" Pausing for a moment he said, "Why not." Reaching over to Carolyn again, he kissed her back with feelings as she responded in return. Suddenly the image of Alicia's face came into his mind.

With his body shaking, he held her at arms length. "Is something wrong Kevin?" It was only a kiss, but not the way Jim kissed her. "Come in and have a cup of coffee, it'll calm your nerves."

"Carolyn, I want to have that cup of coffee with you, but no, I better not. Thanks anyway for the invite. I shouldn't have done that; you see there is someone else and I'm having difficult trying to sort it all out. You're too tempting and I really must get back and get some sleep. We're having our last breakfast together before we head back to our homes. I think we would be sorry later on for what might happen if I stay. My head says to stay; my heart warns me not to."

"You've had enough of a hard time tonight. I had no right to try to take advantage of you. I guess I just wanted to share some time with a nice guy like you." Carolyn said.

"You're always there, when somebody needs you. I know the guys and girls have a lot of respect for you. I'd love to have had a date with you. Well, that's the breaks; maybe some other time in the future we can get together."

Disappointed, Carolyn opened the door of the car. "Good night." She said. Wishing Kevin would change his mind and accept her invitation. When she reached the top of the stairs Carolyn turned and came back to the drivers side of the car.

With the window down she reached in, taking Kevin's face with her hands, she kissed him seeking and hoping for what, she was not sure. Wanting Kevin to come in, she waited for his response, but there was no answer to her invitation. It seemed like an eternity before she broke away.

At the top of the stairs she turned, and called, "You can return that before twenty years. I'll be waiting."

"Carolyn, I'll be waiting to return it. Your place or mine, only time will tell." Thinking out loud, "What a fool I am, letting that invitation go. She's an attractive woman and she wanted me. The story of my life, never know when or not to do. I must be a fool." Deep in thought, he kept driving, until he realized he had driven fifteen miles from the college.

Turning the car around he headed back as the sun arose above the horizon, bringing the brightness of a new day; remembering this is the last day they would be together for twenty years.

Back at the college grounds, he stopped at Carolyn's Mother's apartment and seeing a light on in the window he parked the car. At the top of the stairs, he started to ring the bell, but quickly pulled his hand away. Sitting back in the car thinking, "Should I go in?" Alicia's face flashed across his mind. He saw a light on in the window and the curtain being pulled open. "No I can't, I shouldn't get involved," Starting the motor he hesitated, and then quickly put the car in gear and drove off.

At the dorm Scott and Jim were still fast asleep. Quietly he went to bed trying to relax, as Alicia's name and face entered his mind again. Picturing that moment when they made love together holding and caressing, with no words necessary. Finally he fell asleep, waking up he heard a voice calling. "Kevin; you were calling Alicia, Alicia." She isn't here, you must have been dreaming. Did Heather invite you in when you drove her back to her dorm?"

"No, she didn't. You're right I guess I was dreaming. What time is it?"

"It's ten thirty, time for breakfast. Remember it's our last time to be together. Did you forget we're going to the restaurant? Go take a shower, and don't be long."

At the restaurant they ordered eggs, bacon, home fries and coffee. "Yeah, lot's of black coffee" Jim said, suffering from a severe hangover with blood shot eyes. Scott sat on the chair with his head on the table, lifting it only long enough to pick at the food, his head throbbing from mixing his drinks last night.

Separation

The mood was a somber one, each in their thoughts. The respect they had for each other that molded their friendship ever closer together was coming to an end. A few times they would burst into laughter, reminiscing about the fun they had enjoyed. Slowly words came at intervals of the realization they would separate. Now this has become a reality. They knew eventually even E-mails and telephone calls would become almost non-existent.

The meals were half eaten, coffee pots empty, and each one realizing this part of their life was over. What did the future have for them? "I wonder?" Scott, asked, getting up from the table wandering around the almost empty restaurant as he mused about the last four years. "Guys what do you think? Should I go and try out for the Los Angeles Lakers? No, I want to go into politics. Dad would be disappointed if I didn't get involved in the political arena."

He continued walking around a few more times, trying to think of the words to say goodbye. Kevin went to the cashier to pay the bill, but the owner told him it was on him; remembering the many times these three young men came in for a meal. "It's pay back time; good luck, maybe some time you'll come back." It was his time to treat them.

Sitting down Scott looked at Jim and Kevin. "Well guys its over. I better move on, Greensboro is waiting for me to be their next mayor. Dad already has every thing in motion for me to be a candidate in three years. So guys, send me your telephone and E-mail number, remember to stay in touch.

Keep reading the newspapers; I'll be in Congress in the future. Thanks for the memories, see you in twenty years." Scott hugged Jim and Kevin, wiped his misty eyes and headed out, turning for one last look as said, "So long guys, when I run for President, remember to vote for me."

After a last cup of coffee, Jim looked at Kevin, got up and put his large arms around him, giving him a bear hug until Kevin weakly said, "Enough already, I won't miss those hugs Jim, but I'll miss you." There was a deep special admiration for each other. Words weren't necessary or come easy. It was just the look that cemented them together "Take care you overgrown lug. I'll be in touch.." Jim walked out of the restaurant, glanced back, faked a smile, gave a wave, then got into the Corvette, spun the wheels and drove away.

Sitting at the table Kevin realized he was alone. Twirling his fork around he picked up a piece of bacon, toyed with it, and put it back on the plate. Rising up he walked out of the restaurant. Down at the corner he stopped and looked back, remembering how many times they had come into town for breakfast, or go to the nightclub. Thinking for a moment, now it's over. A few tears appeared as he shook his head and blinked his eyes.

Wanting to try once more to find Alicia he returned to the college and walked to her dorm, determined to see her. He was disappointed finding she was gone. He turned to leave when a janitor stopped him. "I'm sorry sir but you'll have to leave."

"My girl friend stayed in this room, and I had lent her a jacket; can I go in?"

"Okay, but you have to go after you get it." Getting the jacket he started to leave when suddenly the janitor asked, "Is your name Kevin? A young woman gave me this envelope to give to a student with that name."

"That's my name." With trembling hands he opened it and read, "Kevin I'm sorry for what happened. I had a wonderful; time and enjoyed being with you. I wasn't ready for what happened. It was my first time, and I was a virgin. At that moment I wanted and desired to have you. Maybe if we had waited things would have been different. Don't try to contact me now; move on with your life. I will always love you. Alicia"

He was devastated. "She tells me she loves me and yet won't see me. I remember when Dad told me when he went into the Army he had received a letter from his girl friend telling him she had met someone else. "If God wants it to be it will happen, my Grandfather said." Kevin paused and then continued. "He married Mom when he got back." Realizing he was talking to the janitor his face flushed, and apologized for talking out loud.

Seeing a phone on the wall he called for a cab. When it arrived he told the driver, "Take me to the airport, I have to catch a plane, I'm going home." Kevin knew these past four years were over. Alicia was gone, and he had no idea how to find her.

"You'll come back sometime, most of them do." The driver said. Looking out the window of the taxi as they drove through the city, Kevin knew this part of his life was over.

He remembered the Bookstore, Movie Theater; and the park where they would take a date and just to walk and enjoy the fresh air. "Just can't let it go, can you? Look son, one of my kids was like that. He came home for a few months and then left one morning. We never knew where he had gone. When we did find him, he was at the college he had graduated from. He thought going to graduate school would bring success. It didn't" It was hard for him to give up what he had for four years.

"That won't happen to me. I'm glad I'm leaving and going home. Driver, wait, turn around, I want take a look for the last time." As the driver turned the car around Kevin said, "Never mind, I know I'll never come back. I made a promise to my Father to return home. Take me to the airport."

"Don't say that son, many of them return, searching for what they had. There'll be reunions every few years. My second son, went back to find what he thought he missed, like my first son. It was four years of college life, sports, nightclubs and good times he was looking for. You see; all his friends and his relationships he had with them were gone. This will happen to you and your friends. You won't come back after the first reunion. Sorry, maybe a few will come back but not many. All of your lives will change. Move on son, commit yourself to what you wanted for your life."

Sitting in the airport, Kevin let all his thoughts move through his mind. "Can we do this?" he wondered. "Twenty years being separated that long. Can I believe we'll be together again?" Hearing the call ready to board, he cleared his thoughts, and walked to the plane.

The college campus is quiet. Another graduation class has completed its responsibility. The members of the class of 1982 have gone their separate ways.

As it has happened many times before, there will many who reap success and some who will fall off life's pathway. Some will pick themselves up; get their life straightened out and continue their journey. Others will become a number and no one will be there or care. What happened to the members of classes past? Were their promises being fulfilled?

Jim, Scott and Kevin coming from different parts of the country have pledged their friendship to last forever by keeping in contact and reuniting in twenty years. Twenty years is a long time. The future of circumstances, people, death, situations and the unexpected can change this.

Some one has said, "I don't know what the future holds, but I know who holds the future." There is sixty seconds to a minute, sixty minutes to an hour. Twenty-four hours to a day and seven days to a week. Fifty weeks to a year ten years to a decade, and twenty years to a score. This is the length of time when the promise will happen.

Why is it at times it has been said, "It's only been a week, yet it seems like a month. Why is time going so slow, I wish it would hurry and go by? I'll be there in a moment, but the moments become many minutes." Which one of these three will be the catalyst keeping the promise on course for the next twenty years? It will be interesting to know. Twenty years is a long time to keep alive a commitment.

Jim 1982 – 2002

In California Jim was greeted by his Father at the airport. "Son, it's good to have you back. I've waited a long time for you to take over the business. It's yours, if you want it. If you want to do something else with your life, we could sell it, but I hope not. Your Grandfather and I have built this construction business, now worth over a billion dollars."

"Don't rush me Dad; I just got back after four years working my tail off in college. These four years of study playing football, has taken a toll on me. Give me two weeks of vacation in Florida, and then I'll be ready to work. You're letting the business kill you. That won't happen to me."

"You be sure when you take over the operation of the company, to never let anyone have this business if not blood related. I'm getting older now. Eventually you'll have complete control. Swear this to me Jim."

"Dad, I could never let that happen, don't worry, I just need some rest time, then I'll be ready to go. This past year has been a real drag. I'm not sorry it's over."

"Okay Son, have a good time. I expect you back in two weeks ready to assume your responsibilities. Here is a credit card for you to use. It has a limit so use it wisely. I do worry about you Jim; I know what it cost me to put you through college, and your escapades while you were there. I don't need any more grief or worries now."

Later on that day in his office Jim picked up the phone. "Hello Denise, we're all set.

I can pick up the flight tickets at the airport. Dad has arranged for a credit card I can use while we're in Florida. We'll be staying at one of the hotels in Disney for two weeks. I promised my Father I'll go to work when I return. I'm packed and ready to go."

Waiting in his office, Joyce the manager of the payroll department over heard his conversation and was tempted to tell him to be careful while he's down there. Then she thought, "I better say nothing. He's like his Father, you don't offer any suggestions."

After one week in Florida Jim had spent over two thousand dollars. In the evenings at the bars he would treat strangers as if they were friends; buying rounds of drinks every night. In the middle of the second week Denise was tired of his excessive drinking. What she thought would become a romantic vacation, and in a few years a wedding. Now became aware it would never materialize. One night feeling helpless and alone she called Jim's Father for help.

"Mr. Walker this is Denise. Jim has been arrested for smashing a mirror behind the bar in a nightclub, and been put in jail. I need your help! I don't know what to do."

"Don't worry; tell Jim I'll pay his bail and I will cancel his credit card. There will be two tickets at American Airlines waiting for the both of you at the airport. You are to fly home after his appearance at the court in the morning."

Looking down into Jim's blood shot eyes, and observing his condition the Judge said, "We've had enough of your kind coming here; thinking you can do what you want.

Between you and me, this is going to stop. You're fortunate to have a Father to bail you out, and pay the cost of the damage. I understand you just graduated from college. Go to work, be a credit to your family. Your name is on record; if any future incidents like his happens should you return here, will result in severe punishment."

His head down and embarrassed, Jim left the courtroom with Denise and drove to the airport to find there were no tickets for them. Purchasing two separate tickets to San Francisco because Denise did not want to sit on the seat next to him. Arriving back in California, she left him at the airport her parting words were, "This is the last time you will ever see me."

Knowing what was coming he tried to avoid his Father when he arrived back home in Stockton. Opening the front door he heard, "Jim, come into the living room, sit down and listen. Don't ask any questions, or make any excuses, I've heard it all before. You're a damn fool. Get your act together or I'll get someone else to run the business, and cut you out of everything."

Realizing his Father meant what he said, Jim settled down learning his responsibilities to become the future president of the company. Working closely with him for two years, he adapted quickly in learning the construction business. He knew any repeat of his past problems meant his Father would not let him be a part of the company.

One morning arriving at work, his secretary told him he had a message on his answering service. He pushed the button to hear his Father's voice. "Jim, I want to see you in my office."

Entering the office he sat down in a chair. "Dad is there something wrong?"

"Well no, on second thought, yes there is. Be careful how you treat Joyce, the manager of the payroll department."

"What do you mean be careful? I haven't done anything to her."

"Son, she does an excellent job. I can't afford to lose her. She has many offers to work in other companies, and can go to other places for more money; but I know she would rather stay here. Let's you and I not bounce this around and get to the point. What's going on between you and Joyce?"

"Dad let her go. Her assistant Adrian can do that job. We can hire someone else. I can put an ad in the paper. All I did is ask her for a date. She needs some action in her life, and I'm available. What's wrong with that?"

"I thought you had changed, but your actions betray you. Slow down your rampaging hormones. You know what I mean. You aren't every woman's shining knight or God's gift to women. You think that money buys your way? You are damn wrong! Your Grandfather and I have worked hard to where we are today, and you will get all of this if you straighten up."

She resents you trying to date her, and claims you're harassing her with your snide remarks and innuendoes. We don't need any thing like this in the business. If you need a woman, go find one and marry her."

"Dad, are you kidding, get married? Who gets married today when there are so many women who would love to go out with me, and have a good time with no strings attached? In fact, many women make the first advance on a date. I remember why Mother left us. Grandpa told me the real story. I guess I'm just like you when you were my age. Goes in the family Dad." Like Father, like Son."

Thinking back of the past, Jim senior's face flushed. "Let's end this conversation now! Either you go and apologize to her, or I'll remove you from your position. I know if you apologize, she will stay. Leave her alone! I need her here. You can forget what your Grandfather told you about the past. It was a long time ago, and none of your business."

"I'm sorry Dad; I wasn't fooling around with her. I just wanted to take her out. She's older then me but man,. She has a body like a twenty year old, even though she must be thirty-five and you'd never know it. Dad she's single and fair game."

"That'll be enough Jim; she is the best of what she does for me. I treat her good, and she's satisfied with her position.

She's a good Mother to her boys and is happy; so leave her alone."

"Dad, am I thinking right? Are you and Joyce a twosome? I don't believe it, you and Joyce? Say it isn't so! Sorry Dad, why didn't you tell me? I would never have tried to date her, and I'm sorry for the wise cracks I made. Why don't you two get married? You're still young enough and she is young enough to have children. I'd love to have a brother even if he would be younger than me." Knowing he reached the limit of his Father's patience, young Jim went over to the payroll department. At Joyce's office he asked her secretary if she would see him." I'll ask her." She replied.

Looking over the glazed glass partition Joyce beckoned Jim to come in. He sat down facing her desk and asked, "Joyce why did you go to my Father complaining about me? You know I was only kidding. I just wanted to show you a good time. I'm sorry, would you go out with me?"

Walking behind Joyce's chair he bent over to kiss her. As she pushed him away, the door opened and Adrian came in, hesitated for a moment and said, "Sorry, I didn't mean to enter without knocking."

"It's okay, I was about to leave what I wanted to discuss can wait until another time. After Adrian left the room Jim asked "Is she single and available?"

"I haven't any idea." Joyce replied. Lying to Jim she knew that Adrian was getting married in a few years."

Leaving Joyce's office he stopped to ask Adrian, "Honey, I hear you'd like to have a date with me. We can arrange that."

"Thank you Jim, I did at one time; but I have a steady boyfriend now, and we're planning to be married in the next year or two. If only you had asked me before I might have but I can't now. Thanks for the invitation, it could have been fun."

After he left, Joyce called Adrian into her office. "Thanks for coming in. We planned it just right. Jim needs to get married and settle down. His Father is concerned because he's spoiled him for years. I told you about his life growing up alone."

"You know Joyce, at one time I wanted to date him, but not now. I could never handle someone like him." He really thinks he's the prize catch for a woman, how wrong he is."

Refused by Joyce and Adrian, Jim started to fall back to his devil may care life style. He had built a beautiful mansion type house in a gated security community, and purchased a new Porsche. Wild parties every other weekend were the conversation of his surrounding neighbors. Police were often called to break up fights that occurred. Jim had been arrested a few times for being intoxicated and driving under the influence. After several more court appearances for drunken driving, the judge told him, one more arrest and his license would be suspended indefinitely. "This is the last time I'll talk to you about your life style."

Jim was warned by his Father to get his act together. He knew there would be no more chances and promised to settle down. It was time to dedicate him self to the business. Things went well for six months, until one Saturday night, he become over intoxicated.

Warned by his guests not to drive, he ignored their concerns, taking one of the young Hollywood starlets Jennifer out for a ride in his Porsche. Speeding excessively he tried to pull her over to the driver's seat to steer the car, as he moved over to the passenger's side. Jennifer grabbed the steering wheel, lost control going around a curve. They plunged down into the ravine with the car over turning into the water. The noise of her screams, and sound of metal smashing against the rocks, alerted near by residents who called 911.

As the police, fire engines, ambulance with their sirens screaming raced to the accident. The highway was soon filled with cars stopping to see what had happened. The traffic was blocking the highway. The police had to call for more assistance. In a few minutes more police arrived to help stop any one from trying to observe what had happened.

Jim and Jennifer were treated first in the ambulance and then rushed to the hospital with multiple injuries. Both of them were unconscious with life threatening injuries and broken bones. The medics and police could not believe they had survived. One medic interviewed by a news reporter said, "I don't think they'll make it."

The car was demolished beyond repair. When they checked Jim's blood level it registered high above the legal limit. The first policeman that arrived commented, "I know him, it was bound to happen, I arrested him a few months ago for drunken driving; another rich kid acting up. One of these days we'll be bringing his body to the morgue rather than the hospital."

"I've never seen a face so beautiful, now all smashed up." One of the other the policeman said, "She had a great career ahead of her. My daughter works in Hollywood at one of the movie studios. She had the potential to become another Marilyn Monroe."

"It will never happen after seeing her face so disfigured. I hope she sues him for every thing he has. His Father is worth millions and been paying his bills for years. Every few months he goes on a rampage. He should go to AA for help." commented one of the firemen. One of the newer policemen remembered him from high school. "He was the same back then. I heard he got a girl pregnant and it cost his old man plenty. He even had a Corvette in his senior year. I think Mr. Walker was re-living his own life of the past. Some parents give their kids what they never had."

When his Father was notified of the accident he rushed to the hospital. Talking to the doctors they told him that young Jim would be lucky if he survives. His sympathy turned to anger; every thing he planned for Jim to take control of the business, seemed to be doomed. To Joyce who accompanied him to the hospital he said, "What's next? I've tried to get him to change and I've failed."

"It's not you Jim, its not you're fault. He has a difficult time when he's rejected. He still thinks that people should do what he wants. When I refused to go out with him and then Adrian my secretary also refused, it was like lighting a bomb underneath him; and in time the bomb exploded. You couldn't have done anything. We have to hope and pray he will survive."

Karen and Tiffany

During Jim's recovery the nurse Karen was assigned to him for his therapy treatments. She was a single parent raising her daughter. Week after week Jim was in excruciating pain creating problems between the hospital staff, Karen and him self. Many refused to be a part of the team to help as he struggled to regain his health.

One day Karen said she would stay and work with him on the condition he would change his attitude. "Listen Jim, I'm here to help you. Work with me and we'll get along. You will walk again, but I have no time to waste. If you don't stop giving everyone here a bad time you'll be sent to another hospital. Jim's flagrant attitude demanding service, berating the nurses, and the cleaning help continued; until one morning after one of his tirades, Karen had a long talk with him. "Quiet down and listen for a change. You went to Ohio State University didn't you?" I've heard all about your escapades, and what a great football star you were."

"You must be anxious wanting to go out with me. When I get better I'll show you a real good time."

"No Jim, your life style is not what I want for mine. I had a friend who graduated with your class. In fact, she dated you a few times. She told me about your last date with her, and how one of your friends had to pull you away from her when you tried to rape her."

"Not true, it was consensual. I had all the dates I wanted at college. If she were truthful she would tell you that it was consensual. She just wouldn't admit it to you."

"Mr. Walker, I heard what she said; grow up. I know you're wealthy and have many things we all would like to have. Having them doesn't make you any better than any one else. My friend did say that you could be a really great guy if you stopped drinking."

Jim was not used to this type of attitude toward him. Only his Father and a few employees visited him on occasions. The months passed slowly until he realized he was the one who had to change. With her caring patience in dealing with Jim, Karen had good results in the progress of his recovery.

During the following year Jim fell in love with her. She would sit by his bed talking about her life, and asking him about his. He told her about his best friends and the plans to have a reunion in twenty years. She would make sure he would get special meals. In time they became friends. Having met Karen's daughter Tiffany, he was impressed with what a good Mother Karen was in raising such a well-mannered polite child.

When the day came for Jim to be released instead of saying goodbye; he said, "Karen, will you go out with me?"

He was surprised when he heard, "Yes, I'll go out on one condition; you know what that is. I don't want you to get too serious. I can't settle down at the present time. I have to raise my daughter first."

"What's the condition? I only asked for a date. Maybe in time we can talk about the future, you have the patience I need."

"Jim one step at a time, you don't know me; my likes, dislikes, or anything about my life past and present."

"I know one thing, you've done more for me then I can ever repay. I have to settle down and have a wife and family, or I'll lose everything I want and need in my life. That's what my Father keeps telling me. I'm ready and want you to be a part of my world."

Jim returned to work on a limited basis until regaining his full strength. They dated for a year, with Jim staying sober. They took a trip to the Bahamas taking Tiffany with them. Karen's insisted on having joining rooms. "Show Tiffany how much of a gentleman you are. Let her see us as good friends, having respect for each other. "There'll be no trying to become involved sexually. I mean it. Holding hands, kissing is the limit."

On the last day of the cruise while sitting on the deck chairs, Karen turned Jim, "Yes, I will."

"You will what?' Jim asked.

"You wanted to ask me to marry you, didn't you?"

"Yes, I did, but you said we have to wait until later." Jim was overjoyed. This is what he was looking for, a stable relationship. "Are we going to live together or get married?"

Her answer was short and to the point. "We'll get married. There is no way we're going to live together."

Mr. Walker insisted they have a big wedding; to have a simple wedding was out of the question. Karen and Joyce along with some of the secretaries planned the event. Jim's Father escorted Karen down the aisle and one of Jim's friends being the best man. The flowers, colorful balloons, horse drawn carriages, and music from a popular rock band made for a gala event. There was dancing, numerous wine toasts and much laughter. Before the celebration was over, the bride and groom slipped away quietly, leaving on their honeymoon to Hawaii.

While Jim and Karen were away, Tiffany found it very difficult to stay with Jim's Dad. He was over-bearing in protecting her. At times he would be waiting at the high school to give her a ride home. This brought tension between them. One day after school when Tiffany saw him waiting, she refused to get in the car.

"Tiffany, your Mother and Father told me to watch over you while they were gone, so get in." Without answering, she turned and walked away joining her friend Julie to walk home. She didn't go to her Grandfather's home that afternoon; and called telling him she was staying at her girlfriend's house.

The following day when she didn't see his car in front of the school she went to his house. The housekeeper told Tiffany her Mother and Father called and would be coming home the next day. When her parents arrived Tiffany was happy. Telling her Mother she would never stay with her Grandfather again. When Karen questioned her she became nervous until Tiffany said, "He's too strict." Relieved that was all, Karen still wondered.

"Mother, he came to the school every day to give me a ride home. My friends would tease me about not being able ride on the school bus." After Jim heard the story, he hired a housekeeper. Tiffany now knew she could stay in their home if Karen and Jim went away.

In the course of time she accepted Jim as her Father. At fourteen years of age she was curious and some times wondered who her real Father was. One day she asked her Mother, "Where is my real Father now?"

Terrified, Karen answered, "Some day I'll be able to tell you all about him, but not now. Just be patient with me honey, okay?"

The curiosity of wanting to know about her real Father became an obsession. One day she asked her friend Julie, "Do you know who your Father is, and do you ever see him?" Not wanting to talk about it, Julie changed the subject and asked, "Isn't Jim your real Father?"

"No, my Mother married my Father Jim. She has never told me who my real Father is. Is your Dad your real Father?"

"No, but I know about my real Father. He and my Mom were drug addicts. She died of an over dose. My real Father raped me. I told the school nurse, so I had to go to court, and they sent me to different homes, until my new parents adopted me. They're so good; treat me like I was really their kid. I couldn't have any better parents."

The rest of the day Tiffany had trouble concentrating in class. She couldn't get the conversation with Julie out of her mind. "I'll ask Mom again who my real Dad is." She thought. Arriving home she opened the door and called, "Mom are you home? I want to ask you something. Did Jim adopt me? Who's my real Dad, and where is he?"

Catching her breath, Tiffany continued, "Did you marry him? Why haven't you told me? Julie knows who her Dad was, but they were drug addicts and she was taken away and placed in a foster home until she was adopted. Mom I want to know about my Father. Why won't you tell me?"

Karen knew the day was coming, and was not ready to discuss this at the present time. Ignoring the questions Karen said, "I'm in the kitchen. Would you like some brownies and a glass of milk?" Karen realized she had to tell Tiffany some day; but she was still not ready to deal with it. "Sweetheart, go sit in the living room I'll be right in." Waiting alone for a moment trying to put everything in order in her mind, hoping what she will say will satisfy Tiffany.

Entering the room she asked Tiffany to sit on the divan beside her. Taking her hands she started, "Tiffany, some day I promise to tell you, now is not the time. We need time to adjust as a family."

Tiffany continued the questions, "Like I said Mother, are you listening? Julie's Mother and Father were both drug addicts. She had to get new parents. Mom, was my Father a drug addict and you had to divorce him?

I hope not; they say sometimes children inherit the desire for drugs if their parents were drug addicts. You never took drugs did you? I want to know."

"No your Dad was not a drug addict. It wasn't the time to get married. I wasn't ready to settle down. I wanted my career first. We never married, but you are not illegitimate. Jim is adopting you and you are legitimate. Sometimes you fall in love with someone, but you aren't ready for marriage when you're young.

Whom have you been talking to? Is someone telling you that you should ask me these questions? Is it your friend Julie, or is it Dad or his Father?"

"No, nobody is telling me to ask. I would like to know."

Jim spoiled Tiffany, which made some of her school friends jealous. Coming home early one day Tiffany came in the house slamming the door behind her. Jim got up from his chair and saw Tiffany throwing her books down on the floor, "Tiffany, what are you doing?"

"Some of my friends hate me. They say I am a spoiled rich kid. I want to go to a different school. The only friend I have there is Julie."

"What's this? You're friends won't talk to you? When did this start?" In the kitchen Karen could hear the anger in his voice. "He spoils her giving her so many expensive gifts that sometimes brought tension between us." Karen thought as she entered the room.

"I know the principal at the school. I'll speak to him and he'll solve the situation." Jim had been good in controlling himself in situations lately, but Karen lived in fear some day he might explode, with the violent temper he once had.

The next day after dinner, Jim called Karen and Tiffany into the living room. "I want to talk to you Tiff." Standing nervously in front of him, she felt the tears escaping from her eyes. Trying as hard, she couldn't stop them.

"Tiff, I did see the principal today, and he knew about the problem between you and your friends. The problem is you're showing off all the things you have, and telling them all the places you've gone to on vacations. You shouldn't do that, be grateful for what you have. Many of their parents work for me; we pay them well, but you have to remember they don't have the things we have."

"I'm sorry Dad; I just want to share with them. I promise it won't happen again. I like my friends, and want them to like me."

When Karen left Jim whispered to Tiffany, "If you need help ask me, but don't tell your Mother. If Mom's have secrets, why can't we?"

"Right Dad it's our secret." Tiffany felt relieved knowing her Dad could get very angry at times.

"Remember you two, no secrets in this house," as Karen tried to listen, seeing both Tiffany and Jim raise their thumbs up. Walking over to she asked, "What did Dad say to you?"

"It's a secret Mom, I can't tell you." Tiffany was changing, maturing and had a boyfriend. They had discussed about dating together but up until the present time her dates were movies, school dances, and Jim bringing her back and forth from any late school activities, including the football team practices. Tiffany was very popular being a cheerleader and the boys were constantly calling, and hanging around the house, sometimes staying too long Jim would say.

One evening at midnight when Tiffany hadn't come home, Jim called the police department to find out if there were any accidents involving teenagers. He was very suspicious of her boyfriend who was older and had a bad reputation in the school. Suddenly a call came from the hospital his daughter was there, but was not badly hurt.

"Karen." He called. "We have to go to the hospital. Tiffany's been hurt." Driving at reckless speed they arrived and saw her sitting on a bench in the emergency room and asked, "Tiffany are you alright?"

"I'm okay Dad. Mother I'm not hurt. Justin's friend had been drinking and driving too fast when we hit a tree." Karen put her arms around her; relieved she was okay. Taking her home she was told no more dates in a car until she was older. Karen for a few moments was reliving her thoughts of what Jim had gone through after his accident.

One day Jim was looking over some of the blue prints for the new shopping center in his office when his Father called. "Jim when you have a moment, come and see me. There are some important questions I have before we wrap up the plans."

Responsibility

"I'll be right over." Hanging up the phone he wondered, "What now? I never seem to satisfy him. I've settled down and have a family. What's next? I suppose he's found something about my past. Just when things are going right; someone slips a monkey wrench into the works."

Walking over to see his Father, he entered the office and closed the door. "Sit down Jim. Do you know a young woman named Jennifer? Have you received a notice from her attorney wanting to meet with you?"

Jim started to speak, but was stopped when his Dad raised his hand; a sign of silence Jim knew all to well. "What now?" he thought. "Everything was settled with Jennifer." Patiently he waited for what he knew would be another conversation of what he did wrong.

"Hear me out, listen, and don't interrupt me until I finish. She wants to sue you for what? What's this all about? Up until the present time, you have been doing excellent work since you've settled down and married Karen. It certainly has made you the man you are now. Our business couldn't be better. We've become the fastest growing business in the country, thanks to your work. Is this something from your past I don't know about?"

The black clouds of his past were rearing up its ugly head to haunt him." Yes to the first question, no to the other two. She was the girl in the car the night of the bad accident I had a few years ago. I settled with her before; now what? You call our lawyers and take care of it."

"I told you from now on, fix your own problems. I'm not getting involved. Your past wild swinging life caught up with you again. I warned you before it would haunt you.

Talk to Karen she has a level head on her shoulders. I know she'll help you to get this settled. Hopefully nothing else is hidden in your past and will show up again some day, but I'm sure it will."

Back at his desk, his hands holding his head Jim wondered, "What can I do now? I did everything that was possible to help her out." On his way home he stopped at one of the local bars and had a drink. Finishing one he ordered another. After the fifth double shot of scotch the bartender told him he was shut off.

"Come on, one more, and I'll go." Looking at his watch his eyes couldn't focus to read the time." What time is it?"

"You've been here three hours, sorry buddy, no more, Give me a telephone number and I'll call your wife to drive you home." Lifting up his glass once more Jim started to drink, then put it down on the bar thinking, "If I do this, I won't stop." Turning the glass around in his hand, he started to lift it up to drink it. He paused; put the drink down and walked out the door to his car and drove home.

Turning into the driveway he left the motor running thinking of what he almost had done. Hearing the motor idling Karen wondered, "Why hasn't Jim come into the house?"

Opening the door she saw Jim sitting in the car, this was unusual for him. He always puts it in the garage. Walking over she could see Jim in the driver's side his head resting on the steering wheel. "Jim are you coming in? Where have you been? I was so concerned I called your Dad and he said you had been with the company lawyers all day."

When no response came, Karen went over to the driver's side and opened the door. With the odor of liquor she knew something was wrong. This is the first time she has seen him like this. Shaking him she raised his head but he couldn't focus on who was there. "Jim what's wrong? Let me help you. What happened?"

Pulling him out of the car, he stood holding on to the door shaking his head to clear it. In the house Karen led him to the living room and sat him on a chair.

"Please Karen, I'm exhausted. Pour me a drink and make it a double. That broad should be thankful I paid all her medical bills, and gave her fifty thousand dollars in cash. Everything was settled a few years ago. Some people never give up. They're like blood suckers, they bleed you dry."

"No Jim you don't need a drink. Who are you talking about? Why did you give all that money? I don't understand? Honey, I'll have Mrs. McKane get you something to eat.

Take a shower, then we can talk." Putting her arms around Jim as he stood and kissed him, patted him on the rear, and said, "Go."

After taking a shower and having a light snack, Jim and Karen sat on the couch and he said, "Remember, when you took care of me in the hospital after my accident. A young Hollywood star Jennifer, hoping to make it in the movies was with me. I told you she was released from the hospital, and her Father called and asked me what I was going to do for her. "

"Jim if you don't want to talk about it that's okay."

"She and her lawyers signed an agreement they wouldn't come back looking for more money after I paid her thousands of dollars. She should be thankful I paid her medical bills too. The courts won't allow this agreement to be introduced as evidence this time. Our attorneys said they want three million dollars. I'm to think it over and make a decision."

"Honey, don't worry, we'll do whatever has to be done. I know you will do what's right, Come on, let's go to bed."

When Karen returned to the bedroom after her shower, she found him awake. She snuggled down eventually drifting off to sleep. The question in Jim's mind kept him awake. "What will she do? I thought my life was straightened out. My Father is disgusted and I could lose Karen and Tiffany."

A week later Jim asked the company attorneys, "Have you heard from Jennifer's lawyers? Can they come back now looking for more?"

"Yes we have Jim. Please, sit down! Their case is that you caused the accident. She has been permanently scarred and has lost her career.

No one will hire her; she will have no income to live on. Talking to some of the court attorneys we work with, their advice is you better settle. Judges have a way of looking at a pretty face some times, and sympathy takes precedence."

"Find out how much they want and then I can deal with it. Wait a minute, what do you think I'm paying you for? You're the attorneys, and it is up to you to reach a settlement. You guys are the experts; just try to keep the cost to a minimum, so my Father won't blow his top. I don't need this now."

With this problem hanging over his head, he slipped into his old style of living; drinking and missing days at work became his every day routine. The strain between Karen and Jim was stretched to the limit. The marriage was perfect, as it seemed on the surface; the respect and love for each other seemed destined for success. Some of their social friends still wondered what was wrong. The real truth of the marriage was revealed to no one.

After a heated argument one day Karen threatened to leave, telling Jim she had enough. He moved out of their bedroom into one of the guest rooms and for the next two months conversation became non existent. Mrs. McKane would leave a dinner for Jim, but Jim would go to a restaurant for his meals. Tiffany was torn between the two of them. Every evening the three of them were together silence reigned in the living room. Karen would find things to do in the den. Jim buried his head in the newspaper, glancing up once in awhile if there was something he wanted to see on television. Not wanting to listen to Jim and Karen argue Tiffany would go to her room where she could be alone.

One evening Karen reached the boiling point. "Why don't you leave Jim, if you're so unhappy, or maybe Tiffany and I should go?"

"Do what you want Karen, just don't bother me. If you're unhappy you have the freedom to go anytime. It's up to you."

"Don't threaten me Jim; I will leave, if you want it that way."

After a month had passed, Jim was reading the paper when Tiffany couldn't stand the silence any longer; she walked over to Jim and sat on his lap. "Dad why can't you and Mom love each other like you used to."

With mist in his eyes, Jim took his hands placing them around her face, "Tiffany darling, I love you too." Rising from his chair, he took Tiffany's hand and together they walked into the den. The two of them went over to Karen, put their arms around her, he hugged her tightly begging forgiveness.

"We're a family again, Mom, Dad; please don't fight anymore. It makes me feel so sad when you do. Promise me we will always love each other even when we get angry."

The next day at the office he called the attorneys, "Let's go to court and settle. Do the best you can." The trial was held in Los Angeles and in two weeks the court was ready to try the case. Jennifer's attorney wanted three million dollars and when threatened with a long drawn out waiting period, she settled for two million over the objection of her attorney.

At the conclusion of the trial, Jim walked over to Jennifer, "I'm sorry; it was my fault. I wish you the best. I was thoughtless and irresponsible."

"I settled with you, because I needed the money. You've ruined my career, and now I can't get any parts in the movies. Look at my face. My agent left me; the lawyers will get half of what I'll get in the settlement. I appreciate what you did for me before."

"Jennifer, I'll get the best specialists there are who will be able to fix your face, and you'll be as beautiful as you were. I have many contacts; and my wife is the head nurse in our local hospital." Karen stood a little away from them listening, until Jim called her. "Karen please come here, I want you to meet Jennifer. I can see by the look on her face she doesn't believe me"

"Hello Jennifer, Jim's really a changed man. If you wish, I'll help Jim find the best plastic surgeon and be the nurse that will help during the operation. I have quite a few contacts in the medical field"

"All my friends have deserted me. Hollywood is so false. They're your friends, until they steal your husband or wife. Some are okay; many of them are just fair weather friends."

Tears started flowing down Jennifer's cheeks as Karen lifted up her face. Jennifer looked at Karen saying quietly, "Thank you. I will never forget you for helping me. I have no family and I've been all alone since I was a kid with a dream that Hollywood would make me a star. I was like so many young pretty faces wanting to be a star, now that has been taken away from me. Only a very few make it there. Don't let this happen to your beautiful daughter."

Wanting a Child

Leaving the courtroom, aware of Jim's past, a reporter asked Jim for a statement to why he settled. Smiling, full of confidence he spoke. "We're moving on, leaving the past and moving to a new horizon of hope. I have a new goal in life, to build the best shopping centers in the country. This is a new beginning and you will see us expanding in many states in the next few years."

One evening Karen approached Jim," We have to talk, we're like two ships passing in the night, you're working late, taking trips because of the business; I rarely see you anymore. We're ending up with nothing in common. We have to start spending more time together. You can't keep telling me over and over saying you want a son. I think I'm ready. We can't wait too much longer because I don't want to be at my son's high school graduation in my late fifties."

Jim was ecstatic, "Karen, I've waited so long to hear this, when do we start? I want a son to take over the business when I retire. With a son the business will stay in the family. Tiffany can be a partner too."

"Slow down Jim, it will take time. Who knows if I can get pregnant? First I have to stop taking the pill; I'm in my middle thirties you know." Excitingly, Jim picked her up carrying her into the bedroom.

He was so anxious he slipped dropping her on the floor.. She started to laugh as she raised herself up. "Slow down Jim." Placing her on the bed his sexual desire running high he started to take her clothes off. Trying to slow Jim down was impossible. She gave up, relaxed, and ready for him. "Be quiet, Tiffany is in her room and she'll hear us."

"I don't care it has been two months since we made love." Pushing her back down he kissed her deeply with a long lost passion that was rising by the moment. With the hunger that had eluded them for so long, satisfaction came quick. "Honey that is the way it used to be."

"Look tiger, there are other responsibilities. I suppose you will be showing up in the middle of the day now."

"You never know, surprises are the most exciting."

As time slipped by Karen had two false pregnancies. Wanting to get pregnant seemed unlikely. One night as Karen turned to Jim, "Why don't we adopt a baby boy? There are many children needing a home. Tiffany said one of the girls in school is pregnant, and giving her baby up."

"Are you kidding? My Father would never let any one that didn't have his blood run this company. I wouldn't mention that possibility. Let's try artificial insemination."

"Okay if that's what you want, I'll see my doctor tomorrow and make an appointment. But if it doesn't work, what then?" Jim was silent, his mind not focusing on the situation. "Why didn't she say yes before?"

He remembered two students at the college. They got pregnant on the first date and he paid for their abortions. Jim wanted to tell Karen but refrained, not sure how she would react?

Mustering up his courage one day, Jim went to his Father's office to talk about adopting a child. As he stood at the door he lost his nerve, and turned away to forget it. Yet he knew he had to face it now or later. He heard his Father's voice. "Come in, sit down Jim. Something's wrong in the business, or at home? We can talk about anything you want. I understand from our attorneys you settled the problem you had. You have to relax. Remember I warned you many times the past will come back and haunt you."

"Yes I did, but I came to talk about something else Dad." Jim stopped speaking for a moment, trying in the best way to present the idea on adopting a child. Hopefully a son if Karen can't get pregnant. Getting his courage up Jim continued, "Our last try of insemination failed, we've been thinking about adoption."

This was met with cold silence. Jim could see his Father's body coil as a snake does before attacking at the word adoption. "Son if you for one minute think somebody else's kid is going to have my company, the answer is no. Over my dead body this will become a reality. Go ahead adopt a kid if you want. Just remember what I'm saying."

Stopping for a moment his Father continued, "Why do you keep bringing this up? Do whatever you have to do to have a child. Remember; if it isn't blood related, forget it.

Never, will I allow a person that doesn't have our bloodline be in the top executive management of our company! Go out, find some good clean girl, get her pregnant, pay her off, and take the child. At least I'll know it will have some of our blood line."

Furious at his Father, Jim's anger was reaching the boiling point. Struggling within him to burst out and tell his Father off, but the better part of judgment prevailed, knowing it would only stir him up to more sarcasm. Jim remained seated, wondering what to say. "Dad we tried and nothing happens. We want to have children, the doctors say that it could be Karen, or it could be me, because of my past life style."

With no response, Jim sat in silence, still feeling the heat of his Father's words. All his pleas had fallen on deaf ears. He was dejected because he knew what the answer would be. But he didn't give up. "Dad you tell me to get some other woman, I can't do that to Karen. It would wreck my marriage. I'll never lose her, no matter the cost. Why don't you go and get a woman and do it yourself. You always had someone else do your dirty work." Realizing what he had said, Jim apologized. "Sorry Dad."

"Jim, that's okay, I know how you feel. If I had been wise when your Mother was here, I would have had more children, maybe another son. I can't change, that's the way I am. I would even have a granddaughter run the business as long as she's a blood relative. Rising from his chair Jim senior looked at his Son and asked him, "What letter in the word 'NO' don't you understand?"

"Dad many family businesses still make money, in some cases even more successful when they turned over the reins to someone else. Times have changed. What would be the difference if Tiffany got married and had a son? She is my daughter, a part of our family."

"I say this for the last time, case closed. This is the end of conversation. Now live with it."

"Dad, Tiffany is my daughter; you know how much you love her. She would make an excellent President for the company when it comes time for you to retire. I will become the chairman of the company, and we could train her together. She is intelligent at such a young age. She can get involved in the business after college."

"Son, leave my office, this is like the last chapter of a book. You know the outcome; there is 'NO' more conversation. Don't bring up this situation ever again. Do I make myself clear?"

With one parting shot young Jim said, "I suppose you would have one of Joyce's sons take over instead?"

Turning to his Son his Father said, "Be careful Son; don't challenge me. I still have control of the business and you will be the loser if you continue to keep this up. So leave now, I warn you." His Father sat back in his chair thinking of the past, remembering when Joyce came to work for the company. She was divorced and needed a job. He hired her and in time he gave her the position of assistant payroll department manager. Her work was excellent and when the head of the department retired he gave the position to Joyce.

Joyce

It had been many years since his wife left him, citing verbal and physical abuse. One day at the closing of the office, he asked Joyce out to dinner. Afraid to refuse, she accepted. "Don't worry about what people say; I know that you're lonely as I am. You need a male relationship and I need a woman relationship. Let's give it a try."

This was a beginning that led to weekends up in the mountains at the cabin he had bought years ago. On one of those weekends she told Jim she was pregnant. He became very angry. "We had an understanding, no kids."

"Jim, when I got pregnant, I had told you before to use condoms. You insisted we wouldn't have any problem; well, we have a problem and what do we do now?"

"Have an abortion, that's all"

Feeling alone and frightened, Joyce went to an abortion clinic. After talking to one of the protester outside of the clinic who handed her all types of material to read, she was still determined to have the abortion. She had two boys and didn't need another child, but she felt guilty.

A year later in the winter, Jim and Joyce were snowed in for a week. It was a difficult time with no electricity, and little to do but listen to the radio or read books. Jim became irritable and angry. Trying to reason with him was impossible, so Joyce walked out of the cabin and refused to come in, until he promised he would leave her alone.

After much pleading and promises Joyce went back into the cabin and told him, "If you want to stop our relationship that's fine. We never should have got involved. I did what you asked. I destroyed a life. I still feel guilty to what I did."

A few months later Joyce feeling sick went to her doctor and learned she was pregnant again. At that time Jim's Father was on a business trip for two weeks on the East coast. She became nervous not knowing, how she could tell him. If Jim finds out, it'll be just like the same thing again.

Going back to the office she called his son. "Jim I hate to do this to you, my Mother and Dad need me at home. Dad is very sick and has only a year to live. I have to be with them, I'll call you when I come back."

With his business trip to the East completed, Jim's Father returned to California. When he realized that Joyce was not in work he called young Jim at his office. "Jim, where is Joyce, do you know what happened to her? Have you tried to contact her parents? I'm sure her parents address is in the files."

"Dad, she called and told me her Mother and Father needed her right away. She looked sick, and when I asked, she said it was nothing. She insisted it was her parents who needed her now."

"I don't know Son, remember the last time Joyce left, she said that she might stay with her parents because they were getting older, and they didn't want to go into a senior place to live."

"I guess she took her boys with her or left them with someone. I don't know what state her parents live in. We'll have to wait until she calls. I know that you and Joyce have a thing going. Stop worrying. She'll be back when she's able to. Adrian is very capable of handling Joyce's position."

"I'll go to the personnel department and look up her application when she first came to work. There has to be something about who was to be notified in case of emergency. I hope it isn't serious that would cause her to leave us."

"Son, you know Adrian is getting married soon. If she leaves we will have no one capable of running that department. My advice is you get involved and have some one trained in a hurry to replace her. Put your effort into helping Adrian with her new responsibility."

"Dad, I've never seen you so concerned over any employee before that took a leave of absence. What gives with you?"

"Just do what I ask. If you find out any address or telephone number, let me know. I don't need any advice now."

The relationship of Jim and Karen grew cold again. Absence from one another seemed to be the only way to sustain their marriage. Mrs. McKane was hired to take care of the house and prepare their meals as Jim and Karen immersed themselves in their jobs; rarely eating at home. It was such a waste preparing meals and having to throw everything out.

Trying Again

Tiffany and Mrs. McKane were the only ones eating in the house when Mrs. McKane asked Tiffany to tell her parents about the waste.

On a rare occasion Karen and Jim would eat their meals separately until one day Tiffany said "Mum, Dad, you are acting like children, each wanting their own way. Please stop, I hate what you are doing. You promised you two would never act like this again. I thought you said you loved each other." Realizing the hostility between them was affecting Tiffany and their marriage would evaporate. Jim and Karen called a truce. Their changed attitudes brought harmony into the household.

Jim's Father knew the differences that his Son and Karen were having and suggested to Jim, "Take Karen on a cruise for your vacation, that's how your Mother got pregnant with you. Maybe it will happen to Karen."

"Great idea, we need something new in our lives. She needs to get away from the hospital. They've put her in charge of the complete emergency department, also the nurses in the hospital.

Back at his office he dialed the hospital. "May I speak to Karen? Hi honey, I called the travel agency to book a cruise for us to the Caribbean. We can take our vacation when Tiffany is in camp this year and we'll be able to travel for at least a month. Why don't you plan for the clothes you'll need. Buy some new ones, especially flimsy sexy ones. This was Dad's suggestion, telling me you could get pregnant.

I know he's hoping with less stress, more relaxation you'll get pregnant, and I won't bug him about adoption."

"Yes Jim, we do need a spark in our lives. We need more then a flicker we need a roaring fire."

When the evening meal was finished Karen broached Tiffany with the news. In the years before she went with them on vacations. This would be the first time they would be alone since their honeymoon. "Tiff, Dad and I will be going on a cruise this year while you're at camp. Mrs. McKane will take care of the house while we're gone. Remember how we talked about you having a baby brother. Maybe on this trip I'll get pregnant."

"That would be great, but when can we have a vacation together? You and Dad will have a good time but I'm left here all alone. I can't even have my friends over. You know that Justin and I often study together."

Later in the week Jim told Karen, "I have an opportunity to go on a two week business trip to Europe and many other executives are bringing their wives. You know even in the winter it gets cold here the northern part of California. It will be a relief to get away and have a mini vacation. We still can have the cruise to look forward to. The wives will be free to go sight seeing every day. Would you like to go along?"

"I'd love to go; maybe I can get pregnant." Touching her stomach she could feel excitement and the thought to have a baby thrilled her. She knew the time was getting short and her desire to have another child had to be soon or it would be too late.

Mrs. McKane – Justin – Tiffany

Tiffany's parents had been gone a week, when one day walking home from school her boy friend asked, "Can I come over to your house tonight? We need to study for the science test we have tomorrow."

Tiffany stopped and thought for a moment it would be okay, but then remembered her parents were away, and the rules were no one over until they return. This was not an unusual request as they had studied together many times. "I'm sorry Justin, I can't have anyone over. My parents were insistent that no one comes to the house while they're gone. It's only for one more week and then you can come."

"You're kidding, you can't be serious! Your housekeeper will be there. We've always studied together before a big test. Come on Tiff, be a sport. I thought we were a twosome. You and me have been together since the first grade, and talked about going to college together, starting our own law firm, then getting married."

"Justin, you know I love you and I know we've talked about our plans for the future. It's just this one time. Please understand. Don't be upset, I hate it when you act like this."

"You've always been my girl friend, and the only girl I've ever loved and wanted. Have you ever been afraid of me? What's wrong with me coming over for a short time?" Why are you shutting me out now? I just want to come over for a few minutes that's all."

"Don't talk so fast. I promised my parents I wouldn't invite any of my friends over to the house while they were gone. Besides, Mrs. McKane will be here, and I know she had explicit orders that no one can come into the house. If you have any questions you don't have the answers, I'll call you." Looking at Justin's face she could see he was disappointed. She had never refused him before. "Please, don't get mad, I can't take the risk. If my parents knew I did, they would never let me see you again."

"Well, if that is the way you feel, call me about nine tonight. I have to go to the school and meet with the coach and some of the football players. I'll see you in school tomorrow. Maybe I can go to one of the cheerleader's house to study if that's possible." Justin replied, hoping that Tiffany would be jealous and let him come over.

After the evening meal Mrs. McKane told Tiffany. "I forgot I had an errand to do. It will take a few hours okay? I'll be back by nine, maybe earlier. You know your parents said no one could come here. I tried to get your Grandfather to come, but he wasn't home."

"I'll be okay. Mrs. McKane. I'll keep the doors locked. Call me when you start back. Don't be too long, I want to take a shower and go to bed early."

"Now Tiffany, I trust you, and I know if your boy friend finds out I'm not here, he'll want to come and see you. Your Mother was insistent that none of your friends were to come over while she was gone."

Mrs. McKane had just left when the doorbell rang. Looking into the small security peephole and seeing Justin, she opened the door. Quickly she remembered, "Justin I told you not to come here. You better leave and go home. Please, before Mrs. McKane comes back."

"Come on Tiffany, I'm pleading. I only need a couple of answers to some questions, no one will know." Pushing the door open, Justin stepped inside and closed the door. He put his arms around Tiffany holding her and started to kiss her.

"Stop, Justin! Let me go, you can't stay here." Struggling to get free from his grasp, and trying to catch her breath,

Tiffany went behind a chair holding on to the back of it wondering, "What should I do, he's never acted like this before?"

"I'll leave. Just give me fifteen minutes and I promise I'll go."

"Okay, fifteen minutes, no longer, then you must leave." Thinking it over in her mind quickly she knew he couldn't stay. "No Justin, you have to go!" Getting her courage up, Tiffany continued, "I'm scared, Mrs. McKane will be back at any time. Call me from your home with any questions you have. I'll look up the answers for you."

"Come on Tiffany? You never objected before!" He said as he approached her again. Nothing will happen to you. You won't get pregnant, I promise."

Realizing what he said she screamed, "Stop it! Don't touch me. Go before Mrs. McKane gets back."

Justin continued to ignore Tiffany as he placed his arms around her and started kissing her in a sexual way like they had done before. Tiffany could feel her body become relaxing, warm and excited. She lifted up to him with her lips pursuing his. They had fooled around touching and kissing before, but never like this. She had to stop, remembering one night when they were in the back seat of his car. She had felt then as she does now; knowing if she didn't stop, they would go all the way.

"No, Justin!" Pushing him she walked over to the door. "You better go home; Mrs. McKane will be back soon, and we'll be in trouble." Justin continued to ignore her. "Please go Justin. I'll tell my parents when they get home. McKane Stop or I'll scream!"

Ignoring Tiffany's pleas, Justin was determined not to leave. He went to the door picked her up and carried her over to the couch, and laid her down. Justin was a football player at school, very muscular and strong from lifting weights.

Tiffany was much smaller and slim. Though very active in sports, she was no match for him.

Struggling, as Justin bent down kissing her over and over, she felt his passion was not to be denied as his hands searched her body. Ceasing to fight, she relaxed and was caught up in her emotions suddenly wanting him to continue. Sliding down her slacks, he started using his hands in places she always denied him.

In the past she had wondered, how it would feel and how she would react. Now she knew, and it was exciting. Fear soon became a reality, when she thought of getting pregnant like some of the girls did last year. Everybody talked about them, and they had to leave school. "No, we better not."

Try as she could to stop him was impossible. Justin was determined as he continue running his hands over her body. "It's okay, we're just fooling around. You never stopped me before." Justin continued touching her in places he was told were off limits.

"Justin what are you doing, stop it." She pushed his hands away. Rising up Tiffany said, "You better go home. Mrs. McKane will be back, and I'll be in trouble if she finds you here." Getting up from the couch she ran to the stairway starting to climb the stairs. Quickly he caught up with her and carried her back to the couch.

"Come on Tiffany, you know you want it. I could tell before you wanted to have sex. You'll like it. You won't get pregnant. I brought protection. I know what to do. Stop worrying, it won't hurt and you'll feel good. This will be between you and me. Once you do it, you'll want more, I know you can't get pregnant the first time you have sex."

"If I do, my Mother and Dad will kill me, and they'll take you to court for raping me." He ignored her and she could feel the hardness of his body as they moved together. She was caught up in the feeling and relaxed having her first experience with sex. When they finished, their bodies satisfied, they lay side by side, falling asleep.

Hearing the doorbell ring they jumped up from the couch. Tiffany took Justin by the hand pulling him up the stairs. "Hide in my closet. It's Mrs. McKane. When she goes to bed, I'll let you out of the house. Just stay quiet until Mrs. McKane comes into my room to check to see if I'm asleep."

Running back down the stairs she opened the door. "Tiffany, I forgot my keys. I didn't mean to be so late.

Is something wrong? What took you so long to open the door? Where are your slacks? Your face is flushed, are you alright?"

Thinking quickly Tiffany responded, "I'm okay. I was going to take a shower when I heard the doorbell ring.

I knew it was you so I didn't bother to put my slacks back on. I guess I'm flushed because I was rushing. Don't worry, I'm not sick just tired from studying for the science test." Tiffany went into the bathroom, took her shower and went to her bedroom, climbed into bed, lying awake listening for any sound.

"Are you sure you're all right Tiffany? Mrs. McKane asked as she entered Tiffany's bedroom. Get some sleep. I'll check on you later."

After a time of silence, Justin quietly came out of the closet, creeping slowly over to the bed and laid down beside her. Reaching over he tried to kiss her and placed his hands on her body. Frightened, she pushed him off the bed. "Are you crazy Justin? Get back in the closet and be quiet. I'll let you know when to come out."

Satisfied that Tiffany was in bed Mrs. McKane sat down to watch her favorite program on T.V. When the grandfather's clock struck eleven Mrs. McKane started putting off the lights in the living room when she noticed one pillow from the couch was on the floor. As she started to put it back she saw a small item lying there. Picking it up she read the label, 'Hercules, as safe as they come.'

Pushing the couch back, under the end table she saw Tiffany's slacks. Her face flushed, when she realized what happened while she was out. "Justin was here! That's why Tiffany was so nervous. They had sex." Sitting down on a chair she became very nervous wondering, "What should I do? Her parents will be upset if I tell them what I found. Tiffany will hate me and I'll lose my job."

She wanted to go to Tiffany and question her but refrained. "It might create a problem and I could lose. Mr. Walker has a bad temper and might fire me because of this. I don't know what to do. I know most of the kids are doing it, some as young as eleven. Mrs. McKane felt her body shake and her mind drew a blank. "Should I tell her parents, or just be quiet and hope she won't get pregnant."

Going up the stairs she stopped by Tiffany's room; opening the door she saw that Tiffany was sleeping. Returning to her room she tried to settle down, but kept tossing and turning over and over thinking, "What can I do? If she gets pregnant, her parents will be angry with me for leaving her alone, when I promised I'd always be here."

Getting up from her bed she walked around the room thinking, "It's not my fault. If Tiffany is pregnant, she must have been doing this before." The fear of losing her job was upsetting. She tried to convince herself every thing would be okay. Hoping to relax, she went to the bathroom to get a glass of water and take an aspirin. Lying quietly for a few minutes, she thought she heard a door open. She waited for a few moments and not hearing any sound she laid back down trying to relax.

Silently rising up from the bed Tiffany slowly opened her bedroom door. Believing the coast was clear; she walked over to the closet and in a whisper called to Justin. "Be quiet." Taking him by the hand, she led him downstairs to the front door and opened it. Reaching over Justin pushed it closed.

"Don't Justin." Tiffany said in a whisper. "If Mrs. McKane hears us she'll know someone is here. Go home before we get in trouble." Tiffany opened the door again and when he tried to kiss her; She angrily shoved him out on to the porch, and slammed the door. The loud sound of the door closing woke up the neighbor's dog, which started him barking. She waited for a moment to be sure everything was quiet. In the darkness she turned to walk slowly to the stairs and on the way hit the end table in the hall, knocking the lamp to the floor. Frightened, Tiffany stood ridged, not knowing whether to run up the stairs or flee to another room.

Looking down from the top of the stairs Mrs. McKane called, "Tiffany, is that you down there? What are you doing? I locked the door before I went to bed. Is there anything wrong?"

"I wasn't sure you had locked it after you came home?" I'm coming right up."

Trying to get Tiffany to talk Mrs. McKane asked, "Was Justin here? What did he do to you?"

Tiffany didn't answer right away, and went up to her room, lay down on her bed and started to cry. Mrs. McKane came into her room to find her down on the floor holding her pillow. "You know, don't you?" She stuttered between the tears. "I didn't mean to let him in. He promised he would go after we studied for an hour."

"We couldn't stop once we started. It was my first time. I'll never do it again. Please don't tell my Mom, he promised I wouldn't get pregnant. I wish you had stayed home. How could he know you were going out tonight?"

Turning over on the floor, Tiffany continued to cry. Mrs. McKane reached down picked her up placing her on the bed.

In time she stopped crying with only a sob coming once in awhile. Mrs. McKane held her close to her body. Nestling closer, Tiffany was seeking the warmth and protection like a lioness does to a newborn cub. Soon she fell asleep as she was slowly rocked back and forth. Mrs. McKane moved under the blanket to lie down beside her, until she fell asleep.

In the morning Mrs. McKane wanted to take her to the Emergency room at the hospital but Tiffany said, "I'm okay, Justin told me he had taken caution and I wouldn't get pregnant."

"All is well and good, but let me take you to be sure."

"No, I just want to forget last night; they will want my name and will notify my parents. You know my Mother works at the hospital, and someone will tell her I was there."

The next day at school Tiffany tried to talk to Justin, he ignored her and walked away. She stopped him in the classroom as the teachers and students were leaving. He tried to avoid her, as she stood in front of him blocking his way so he couldn't leave the room. Suddenly a teacher to their surprise walked into the room and asked, "What's going on here, the class is over." Justin backed away. "Get back here Justin and tell me what's going on between you two?"

After the teacher left Tiffany said, "Stand still Justin, I have to talk to you. Who told you that Mrs. McKane was going out last night; that's why you weren't afraid she would return early. You might as well know, Mrs. McKane knows we had sex. She found the package of condoms on the couch. If you were so careful, how come the package was sealed?"

"Did you tell her Tiffany? You must be crazy. I used a condom, so stop worrying." I had an extra one and a full package. I figured that if you liked it we could do it again."

"She found my slacks under the end table, and heard you going out the door. She promised she wouldn't tell my Mom. Do you know you could be arrested for rape, but I told her it was my fault! We can't let that happen again."

"Come on Tiffany, you enjoyed it as well as I did. You won't get pregnant. Girls don't get pregnant the first time they do it."

"Justin, it's over! You aren't my friend. You promised when we fooled around that's all we would do, I made a mistake and trusted you. You took advantage of me. I hate you."

"Who needs you? I know there are others that would want me for a boyfriend. You liked it, you know you did; I didn't hear you object. You could have stopped me but you didn't, because you wanted to."

"You're just like the rest, you only want me for sex. If that's the reason you love me it will never happen again." Justin kept trying to convince her that he loved her but Tiffany ignored him continuing to talk. "No Justin that was the first and last time. You don't love me, only what you can get, it's over, I don't want to see you anymore."

During the winter months, Tiffany busied herself in basketball and studies, trying to forget what happened. She would see Justin at times with another cheerleader, who had been a good friend in the past, but now ignored her. Occasionally he would taunt her. "I'm ready to be your boyfriend any time. We had a good time, didn't we?"

"Get lost! I told you, I never want to see you again. Maybe I might tell Cynthia what you're like; using her like you did me." Missing her period the first month concerned Tiffany, but her closest friend Julie, told her sometimes it stops, and then it starts again. In her innocence, she accepted that. She was afraid to ask her Mother or the school nurse, feeling confident everything was all right, and that the next month everything would be okay. She wanted to talk to Mrs. McKane but hesitated.

A Child is Lost & Born

Julie kept telling Tiffany to go to the school nurse she would help her, and tell her Mother that Justin raped her. "I told the school nurse when my Dad did it to me," Tiffany was still afraid to tell.

Her parents returned home bringing presents and pictures to show Tiffany. One evening after dinner Karen sat down in the living and called Tiffany. "Sit down honey; I have a secret to tell you. You can't tell Dad."

"Mom, you're pregnant, aren't you?" Tiffany said with excitement. "I hope it will be a boy. That's what you and Dad want, isn't it?"

"I'm not sure, it's really too early to tell. I was having morning sickness before we went on our trip. I'm going to the doctor to confirm it." The following morning Karen became very ill. "Jim, you better take me to the emergency room." I felt very sick on the flight and I thought it was just something I ate. I think I'm having a miscarriage."

"What's wrong Karen? Are you pregnant? Mrs. McKane please help my wife get dressed, I'll get the car."

With Karen in the car, Jim sped off to the hospital. After the doctor finished the examination, it was confirmed she had a miscarriage. Jim took her home putting her to bed.

"Honey I'm so sorry. What can I do to make it easier for you? Just get well, baby or no baby, I love you; there's always another time."

"I'm sorry, I wanted to have our child while Tiffany is still young enough to enjoy the baby, and for the three of us to be a family together."

"Honey, we can still adopt. Dad can't stop us. When our child grows up, he will still be a part of the company; I'll be the chairman and own the business. The decisions will be my responsibility. Let's live for the present time, enjoy life now. We'll go to an adoption agency and put our name on the list."

The winter was drawing to a close; Tiffany could feel her stomach, sensing something was wrong. Her innocence and the heavy schedule of studies and sports kept her busy as she put any thoughts of having a baby out of her mind. She tried to convince herself it wasn't anything to be concerned about. A couple of times in the middle of the game she felt sick and ask the coach to take her out to rest. The coach wondered what was wrong. She always had boundless energy. She convinced herself, it was Tiffany's time of the month.

There was very little morning sickness for Tiffany, and her activities kept her from showing. The winter and spring passed, school was out for the summer. It was time to go to camp. She pleaded with her Mother to let her stay home this year. "Please Mother I don't want to go any more." Pleading to no avail, she resigned herself to go. It became a one way street trying to get her Mother to let her stay home.

Three weeks through the camping season, Tiffany complained one day of severe pains. Thinking it might be her period, she was given Midol tablets, told to rest for the day, also abstain from any activities.

The next morning as the pains continued she was taken to one of the local doctors. After an examination by Doctor Pierce, a friend of Mrs. Johnson he told her; "Tiffany is more than sick."

"What do you mean Doctor? Tiffany is more than sick? What could possibly be wrong with her?"

"Mrs. Johnson you've known me for years, the truth is Tiffany is seven months pregnant, I should do a C section immediately. If I don't, she'll lose the baby. I've given her a sedative to ease the pain. You better come here immediately and discuss the best thing to do for her. I know a small exclusive private hospital that deals with such situations. They're sworn to secrecy; we can't stall on Tiffany's condition much longer. We have to act now."

"She can't be! Oh my dear Lord, how can this be? She is so sweet and innocent. Her parents will be devastated if this is true "I'll be over there as quick as possible."

When she arrived with John, a camp councilor, Doctor Pierce explained in detail why he had to take the baby, and the reason for the urgency of the situation. Mrs. Johnson went into the room where Tiffany was laying down. With eyes filled with tears Mrs. Johnson started to talk. "Tiffany, Doctor Pierce told me that you're pregnant. Did you know? Do your parents know?"

Bursting into tears Tiffany cried, out, "No, I didn't know I was pregnant."

A Baby is Born

"Yes my dear you are going to have a baby."

Tiffany tried to get off the couch crying out in anguish, "No, no, I can't be! Justin promised I wouldn't get pregnant. Please, don't let my parents know, they will kill me. What will they do to Justin? I can't have a baby, I have to finish high school and go to college."

"Sweetheart, don't cry, I'll protect you, no one will find out. I'll take care of the baby until you are older, then you can make your own decision. You're not the first girl to have this happen. I'll talk to your Mother if you wish."

"Please Mrs. Johnson, you can't tell my parents, my Dad will go to the police and have Justin arrested for rape. They'll suspend me from school; all my friends will know. I'll lose their friendship." Sobbing so hard, she shook over and over losing control.

Holding her Mrs. Johnson kept saying, "Its alright honey, everything will be okay. We'll work something out. Just try to relax and we will be sure with the doctor's help everything will turn out for the best."

"No! It isn't okay, please; my Mother will never forgive me. She won't understand that I let Justin do it. It's my fault;. I've betrayed her, and my Dad too. I promised I wouldn't have sex while in high school "

Meeting the doctor and John in another room Mrs. Johnson nervously tried to control her emotions.

"Doctor Pierce, will you help John and me make the decision what is right for Tiffany and the baby?"

Mrs. Johnson rose up and then sat down raising again to ask.

Pacing back and forth, sitting down; soon to rise again. Mrs. Johnson asked, "What can we do doctor? Will you join with John and me and what the decision should be for Tiffany

"I'm not sure that I should have to make a decision for Tiffany. That should be her parent's decision. I really can't get involved. Just understand my position."

"We can save a girl's life and keep a family together, or destroy a family who loves each other, I have known them for ten years. If we don't do this I believe they will fall apart. I know how powerful Mr. Walker is and how angry he can get."

A long period of silence followed until John took his handkerchief from his pocket and dried his eyes, apologizing that this has been a hard time when situations such as Tiffany's enter his life. "Please be patient and hear me out. If we all agree, I will go along with whatever we decide to do."

Stopping, he got up from his chair and walked around the room. "In high school many of the parents have tried to tell us we should be teaching about unwanted pregnancies; this is not our responsibility. It seems many parents today are too busy with their own lives; they don't spend the time in their kid's lives. We have had five girls in the high school this year that were pregnant. Some of them had abortions and some parents take the baby into their home."

Doctor Pierce and Mrs. Johnson sat quietly, as they looked up at the ceiling. Sitting down John continued, "I really don't want to get involved. I have love for this youngster and realize sometimes we have to do what is best." We owe Tiffany our support."

"Thank you John, you've been with me for six years. I value your support and experience in working with these kids. We've never had this happen to my knowledge before that I know of. The owner before me said when I bought this place; all of the children attending this camp were very close to their families."

"She is under age Dorothy, if I become a part of this and it becomes known, I will lose my license to practice medicine; my career will be over. Can you understand that? Most likely I could end up in prison. God forbid the newspapers find out about this. They would exploit it all over the country. Really is it fair to ask me to do this? I'm well known through out the state and respected in the medical field. I have written a book about abortions, and I would rather see a woman go full term unless a life situation is in the balance. If I agree to do this as I have done a few others; how this will affect Tiffany?"

"Tiffany and her boyfriend made a mistake, we have to make a decision, and can't hide under a rock and ignore the situation I understand Doctor, the oath you took is to save lives. Tiffany's life could be in danger, and lose the baby if it isn't taken now."

"We understand your situation Doctor but we have no one else to turn to at the present time," John offered.

"I know the oath and the responsibility that goes with my commitment. I wrestle with the thought, if I don't do a C Section, Tiffany's life will be in danger. Yet, will I destroy her life by bringing this baby into the world?

It's better to tell her parents. This is really their responsibility. In reality we're making their decision, either right or wrong. You have known them for a long time, you tell them."

Mrs. Johnson kept pacing back and forth, mentally hoping Doctor Pierce would join with John and herself in the best interest for Tiffany and the baby. After many hours of discussion they agreed that Doctor Pierce and they would be breaking the law.

Doctor Pierce delivered the baby at the hospital and kept Tiffany there for four days. Returning to camp she recovered quickly. Some of her friends asked what had happened to her. Mrs. Johnson replied by telling everyone it was only some type of a bug Tiffany had contacted, while they had been hiking through a thick grassy area on a field trip.

One day one of the girls who were a friend of Tiffany asked her, "You've lost a lot of weight, and you look so thin. What kind of a bug was it that made you so sick?"

"I just couldn't eat when I was in the hospital, I lost my appetite," was Tiffany's only response. When the camp was closing for the season, Mrs. Johnson asked Tiffany if she would like to see her baby before she returned home.

Tiffany declined, wanting only to see her parents. "Please Mrs. Johnson; I just want to forget what happened. Thank you for what you did for me. I beg you, don't tell my parents, I feel so ashamed. How can I tell them and Justin? If I tell him, he'll be bragging about it all over the school."

"Tiffany you must tell your Mother. She will know the right thing to do. Have faith in your parents. They won't hate you. I've known them for a long time and they love you."

"He promised me nothing would happen. It was my fault too because I let him do it." My Mother would be so ashamed of me, and my Dad would be so angry."

Going back to high school, Tiffany renewed her relationship with her best friend Julie. After a few months Tiffany started having trouble with her studies.

Karen and Jim decided that something was wrong because her grades had dropped from high honors, and missed being on the honor roll. When questioned, her excuse was that the subjects were harder this year. "Tiffany, it must be something more than the subjects this year that are difficult. Every day after school Mrs. McKane said you've been staying in your room all afternoon. What happened? Did you and Justin break up? What's wrong?"

"No Mom it's not that. We did break up. He started to get fresh and I told him to stop. I wouldn't have sex with him. He was really good for a long time until one night we parked and he started putting his hands all over me. I told him to stop, but he wouldn't until I threatened to tell you."

"He tried to get fresh with you? He never seemed to be a young man that would try something like that."

"Mother, get real, that's what most of the boys think of how far they can go. I'm not like that. Maybe I am having a harder time studying this year.

I promise I'll do better the next term." Thinking her secret might be discovered if her marks didn't show an improvement, Tiffany studied harder and improved in all her subjects. One day Tiffany knew she had to tell some one, and called her best friend. Living with her secret became unbearable. She had to share it with Julie. "I have to talk to you Julie. I don't know anyone else I can tell this to."

"I'll meet you tomorrow after my last class, okay?" Julie said. "I might be late so wait for me."

Meeting the next day Tiffany found it very difficult how to begin. "I have to know for certain you will never repeat what I will tell you. If my parents ever found out they would hate me. Mother would be so disappointed in me."

"Finally Julie said, "Remember when I told you that my Father made me have sex with him. I know you never told any one, because I trusted you. We're friends, and friends wouldn't ever tell."

"One night Justin came to my house when my parents had gone on a trip and Mrs.McKane went out on an errand I was left alone." Tiffany stopped talking; putting her two hands together. She found it difficult to continue.

One of the teachers walking by looked at Julie holding Tiffany. "Is there something wrong? I'll be glad to give either of you a ride home or to the hospital."

"No, its okay Miss Donahue, Tiffany slipped and twisted her ankle; she'll be fine thank you. If Tiffany can't walk I can call the hospital to tell her Mother."

"It's okay Tiff, I know how you feel. When I had to tell the nurse about my Dad and me having sex, I cried too, it's okay to cry; it releases the tension."

Julie waited patiently until Tiffany was ready to speak. "Justin raped me last January; I had a baby while in camp this summer. Only the doctor, Mrs. Johnson, and John one of the councilors knows. Mrs. Johnson is keeping the baby boy for now. I can have him when I get older. Justin hates me because I won't have sex with him. He doesn't know about the baby. I'm so frightened Julie, my life is ruined, and I don't know what to do."

They sat silent until Julie spoke. "He doesn't know about the baby? Maybe you should tell him. I don't know if it's rape because you let him do it. Why didn't you stop him?"

"I'm frightened to tell him. Was it rape if I let him do it?" Tiffany asked "I said no but it felt good while we were doing it."

The two of them sat silent for a long time, until Julie spoke, "I don't know Tiffany, because when my Father did it to me it hurt. If you didn't want to do it I guess that would be rape. You should talk to the nurse at school."

A few minutes passed until Tiffany answered Julie's question about telling Justin. "Oh no Julie, I can't do that. He would brag how we had sex. His friends will want to take me out hoping they could have sex with me too if they find out. One of them did get a girl pregnant, and she had an abortion; Justin told me about it. I just had to tell someone."

It was time for the girl's basketball season, and all players were required to take physical examinations each year. Frightened to be examined because of the scar from the birth of her baby, Tiffany worried that the doctor would tell her Mother. Many times while taking a shower Tiffany would look down at the scar and it made her feel sad, because she allowed Justin to take advantage of her.

One day she decided to call Mrs. Johnson and explain the situation. "Mrs. Johnson, I need to have an examination and a paper allowing me to play basketball this year. Can you have Doctor Pierce fill out the paper and would you please send it to the school, not to my home."

"Send me the address where you want it to go and I'll take care of it. How are your parents? They help us each year in the gifts they give for the camp. I'll look forward to seeing you again next year. Your baby boy is doing great, and has blonde hair, brown eyes and looks like you. You can come any time to see him if you would like. Would you like to name him?"

"I really haven't thought about that. Why don't you name him? I'm glad he's doing well, but I don't want to see him. "I can't tell my Mom and Dad. I've broken their faith in me by being so stupid. When I am older, I'll be able to face it. Goodbye and thank you for your help."

"Don't hang up, you're a beautiful young girl. This has been a very traumatic experience for you. I hope some day you will come and take this God given child to love and nurture. Don't have him hate you by not letting him know that you are his real Mother."

Discussions

"Thank you Mrs. Johnson for doing this for me. Just send it to the address I gave you." As she hung up the phone Tiffany wondered, "If only I could tell my Mother. Would she be disappointed for what I'm doing now?"

The following week Karen spoke to Tiffany about playing basketball for the season. "I talked to our Doctor today; he asked if you're playing sports this year? If you do, you'll have to see him and have a physical examination."

"Yes Mother, I know. I've made arrangements and I asked Mrs. Johnson if she would send a copy of my exam for camp. The school said that was okay. I called our doctor last week, he said that as long as I had one exam this spring, it wouldn't be necessary to have another one."

"The principal of the school said they're having an accelerated class for all those students that need more of a challenge. Since you have been chosen as one of the students, skipping the junior class it might be difficult. Remember last spring you had problems with your marks.

"Mother, don't worry, the past is gone. You will be proud of me."

That evening Jim asked Tiffany, "Honey before you start your homework, I'd like to talk to you."

Karen excused herself telling them she was going to play Bingo at the local club. "Jim, come with me; talk to her another time. Some wives have their husbands with them.

We don't seem to have much time for ourselves. I don't want to have the same situation that's happened in the past."

"Karen; next week. I'm going to bed early tonight."

Turning to Tiffany he said, "I was talking with Justin's Father today at my office. He represents a company I do business with. He asked me why you don't go over to his house anymore. Is there a problem between you and Justin?"

"Dad, I thought Mother told you the reason why I stopped going out with him. It's too embarrassing for me to talk about it. It's the things that women share together."

"No, your Mother never told me. Did he get fresh?"

"Let's put it this way Dad, I found out he changed, and didn't have the respect for me that I wanted. I have to study and if you ask Mother she'll tell you. Tiffany started up the stairs to her room.

"Wait Tiffany, I haven't finished what I had to say. Come back here right now! "I'm your Father; give me the respect I deserve."

"Please Dad, leave me alone. I have to study for tomorrow." She hoped this would shut off the conversation on this painful subject. Tiffany ran up the stairs, down the hallway and entered her room, slamming the door behind her. "Why can't he leave it alone? Mom should have told him. She knew this wasn't going to be the end of it. He'll keep it up until he's satisfied."

For a moment Jim was stunned. He had never seen her act this way before. Running up the stairs and down the hallway he started to knock on her bedroom door; then realizing to pursue this would mean that he and Karen would get into a stand off. He didn't want that. "Forgive me. It won't happen again." He called.

"Dad, I'm tired. I'm sorry the way I answered you."

The following months Tiffany kept to herself, spending time at her friend Julie's home. One evening at the dinner table, Karen asked, "Why don't you have conversation with us? You're so quiet; you always give us excuses when we ask you something. What's the problem?"

"No reason Mom, I like Julie as a true friend, we enjoy each others company. We like hanging out together and talk girl things that only we can discuss. You must have done the same thing, talk about about boys when you were my age?"

Changing the subject Karen offered, "By the way, are you planning to go to camp? I guess it'll be the last year you'll want to go."

"I don't want to go this year. I'm fifteen and the kids seem so young; it isn't fun anymore. Most of my friends are going on trips with their parents. Some of them aren't going to camp. Don't make me go."

"Okay sweetheart, if that's what you want. Mrs. Johnson will wonder why you stopped. She has told me many times, how you helped the younger children."

Ending that conversation Karen tried again. "By the way, we received information from some of the colleges and wondered; would you like to visit them?"

"I'd love to go and see what the campuses are like. I know I'm skipping my junior class and going to be a senior next year. When will we go, and can we bring Julie with us? She wants to go to college, but her parents don't have a lot of money. We can help her can't we?"

"Slow down Tiffany,' Jim said. "I'll call some of the ones you're interested in, and make arrangements to have a tour of their campus. You tell Julie she can come if her parents will let her. I'll check around with my business contacts and see if there are scholarships that might be available for her. If we find any she could go to the same college as you. Maybe Scott can find some government money to help her."

"That would be great if we could both go to the same college. Thanks Mum and Dad. I love you both. It's exciting to even think about it. I can't wait to tell Julie."

"Want to take a trip out East this summer? We could go and see Ohio University? It's a great school where I met two of my best friends. Did I tell you we're going to get together in twenty years, and have a great party?"

"Yes you did Dad, you told me ten times already, but that's still a few years away."

Over hearing the conversation Karen asked, "Jim, have you ever contacted them since you've graduated. I think you better start making plans, and call your friends, don't you?"

"No, we really haven't talked to each other in quite awhile. I'll give them a call now." Jim went into the study and looked in his telephone listing, found Scott's number and picked up the phone.

"Hello Scott, how are you? Have you heard from Kevin lately? Karen reminded me the time is drawing close for our reunion; only a few more years. Tell me, how are things going in Washington? Are you dating those young interns?

Were you the Senator who got involved with a young woman, and then she disappeared? Was she ever found?"

"I'm not sure what happened in that situation. I don't know if they ever found her. I can tell you for sure it wasn't me."

Did you get married? Come on Scott, with all those women in Washington and you never got involved. You're kidding."

"I'm too busy in my plans to run for the Presidency, and don't have time to party around. I've had a few close encounters. Why marry when there are so many single. They don't marry; they just enjoy a good time in Washington. The last time I heard from Kevin was a year ago. He's a cowboy at heart, wants to stay in Wyoming. I've never been there in the wild blue yonder and don't know much about some of those states like Idaho, Montana, Wyoming and Dakota's."

"It should be interesting there in the Wild West; but you haven't seen beauty until you see that part of the country I've been told. We should go there for our first reunion."

"Jim, you have to come south and see all the beautiful belles we have there. Our girls have won more Miss American contests then any other place in the country."

"You haven't seen beauty until you see my daughter Tiffany," Jim said. "She's the most beautiful girl in the world. She's only fifteen; and entering her senior class in high school this year. Since she and her boyfriend broke up the boys call every night wanting to date her?"

"If she's beautiful as you say; you better lock her up until she's thirty." I think we better go to Kevin's first. And maybe either your place or mine in North Carolina. Now there is where the most beautiful women come from."

"Don't worry Scott, all the boys around here know what will happen to them if they try anything. I have to run now. Give me a call when you and Kevin decide when we'll get together. Maybe you two could think of coming out here to California."

Scott – 1982 – 2002

Scott arrived at the airport and checked his suitcases. Looking up at the board of departure time and knowing he had an hour before take off, he purchased the Washington Post newspaper to read. The hour passed quickly when he heard the call to board the plane. Finding his seat by the window he settled down for the flight to North Carolina. Quickly he sat up when he heard, "Excuse me sir, I think you're in my seat."

Still having a slight headache from the hangover, he didn't look up but responded, "No, I have the window seat."

"I don't think so." Looking up he opened his eyes. "I don't believe it! Carolyn, what a surprise?"

"Don't move, I'll take this seat. I thought you had already gone home. I live in Greensboro for the summer. My Mother is retiring this fall as a dean at the college. We have a family home in Charlotte but she goes to Florida for the winters. I'm going to Washington and work for the Democratic Party. What are you going to do?"

"My Dad wants me to get into local politics, run for the mayor's seat, and then hopefully in time, become a Representative in Congress. He has been a Senator for twenty-four years, and he knows your Mother. They both have been involved in the Democratic Party for years. He has a program lined up for me to give speeches at local charities, churches and schools. You know the rest of what it takes to be successful. Oh yes, I want to apologize the way Jim treated you the other night."

"Scott, I've been out with him before. He's okay when he's sober, but when he drinks too much he's like a frustrated animal let loose. He thinks every girl should satisfy his desires. I'm no angel, but I do demand respect. It was a good time until he acted up."

"My Father is in good favor with the heads of the party, I know I'll need all the help I can get. Put a good word for me with your Mother. I can use her influence too."

"I will Scott; you do the same to your Dad. Mother speaks well of him. After my Dad passed away, your Father was very kind to her. I hinted one time that since your Dad was alone maybe he would be available. "Sometimes older people get too settled in their ways, and forget there is a need of a friend or companion to share their life with."

"Dad will be glad to know everything is okay with her, and just think; maybe we could have been sister and brother by marriage. That would be a surprise!" Landing at Charlotte airport they parted, wishing each other success.

After four years of working tirelessly and promoting himself as the best candidate for Mayor, he was elected for two consecutive terms in the City of Greensboro. Scott decides to by-pass the run for the House of Representatives and instead to campaign for the Senate. Many of his political friends cautioned him to be patient, but he didn't heed their advice. Some older and respected members thought Scott was too brazen; his attitude was not conducive to what they hoped he would present himself to the public.

The fact he ignored their advice caused friction with party members, and many distanced themselves from him.

His Father warned him not to be so arrogant and self-reliant.

Before Scott became a Senator, Carolyn had been elected to the Congress on her second try. Working for two years in local charitable agencies, had given her the experience and a following. This made Scott jealous, and all the more determined to become a Senator from North Carolina. With his Dad's contacts, he over came the opposition, and was elected to the Senate on his first try. There was a sentiment in the country, that it was time for the youth to assert themselves by getting into politics.

"Scott, why don't you slow down and live; you're being consumed by politics. His Dad said one night "You need to meet a nice woman and find the other side of life. All work and no play makes for a dull existence. I know a real nice woman for you to date. I met her the other night at a meeting."

"I just happen to know her Dad. Her name is Carolyn; her Mother is a Dean at the college. She graduated with my class and knows everybody who is somebody in the party. Maybe you are right; I'll give her a call tomorrow."

"Son, I told her you would call. Like you said, her Mother is very influential in the party. It wouldn't hurt to have her on your side. She also told me a night out is what she needs. She's a Representative in Congress and comes from here in Greensboro. You're missing out if you don't date this very attractive woman."

"Dad, I'm too busy to get involved with a woman now. That will come later. Right now I don't have the time. I have to prepare for my next election to the Senate."

"No, do it now! I could see her face light up when I told her you are my son. I know she would be pleased to receive a call from you."

"Dad, enough; you sound like my friend Jim. He thought he knew everything about a woman, then he met Carolyn, but that's another story." Tired of listening to his Father, Scott picked up the phone and dialed the number.

"This is the Jefferson residence; may I ask who's calling?"

"This is Scott Anderson I'm a friend of Carolyn."

"One moment I'll get her for you."

"Hello, this is Carolyn."

"Carolyn, this is Scott, my Dad gave me your telephone number. Would you like to go out for dinner some evening?"

"Good idea, let me check my calendar and I'll call you back. I need a night out for a change. I'm discouraged with all that's going on in Congress. Why can't we come to agreements without everything being played out in the news media? It's revolting to me. Many of our voters have no idea what's going on with the in fighting, and need to know more about the country. They should vote to replace those in office now."

Carolyn and Grace

On Scott and Carolyn's first date, they had many laughs about his Dad. He didn't realize they had dated a few times at college. Carolyn remembered the disaster times with Jim and other bad dates. Now she was looking for a long time commitment, hoping with Scott this might become permanent.

Scott wasn't ready for a commitment. His desire and ambition was to be the President of the country. He felt a little intimidated by Carolyn. She was a positive person, not willing to change her mind in some discussions they had about the political situation in the country. Living together in Washington wasn't easy for the two of them. Both of them busy in their own political lives left little time for bonding. Their relationship was quickly failing to become a long lasting commitment like she wanted.

The intimacy of making love was more of a convenience at times. It lacked the spark that would build an exciting life together. In time the relationship slowed to a casual, "Hello it's nice to see you again. How are you doing?" Time and effort was consuming their energy as they both readied themselves for a higher goal in the political atmosphere.

The Republican Party was making gains in replacing some of the elected Democrats in certain states elections. This caused quite a concern in the Democratic Party for Scott to become their Presidential candidate. Carolyn was not very happy as a Representative and resigned to become an advisor to one of the new Senators who had been elected.

Her resignation was a concern when a Republican won her seat in Congress. Confiding in Scott, "I want to become an advisory member of the Presidents staff some day."

While on the campaign tour for the Presidency, visiting many states, Scott met a divorced woman at a fund raising event. She had contributed huge amounts of money to the Democratic Party. She was near sixty, very attractive and influential. Scott was impressed not with her, but what she could give to his campaign. She became generous giving a few million dollars to help him in the years ahead. The story around Washington was that her Grandparents had left her millions of dollars, which bought her way into the highest places in the government.

"Don't get involved with her." The Senior Senator from North Carolina warned him. Other Representatives and Senators said the same thing warning him she was the wrong person for him to be seen with. He again ignored good advice, and in time they became very friendly. Scott needed a woman in his life and started dating her.

After six months of living together Grace turned to Scott. "We've been living together for awhile; it's time we thought about getting married. There are many voters that won't vote for the President living with a woman without marriage. Many people would never support you just living with me. If we love each other and I think we do, let's make it legal. I've enough money to put you in the President's chair. My grandparents left me very wealthy. I suppose you already know that."

Not wanting Grace to have the wrong idea about their relationship he said, "Honey, money is not why I'm with you. It's the support you give me." Scott relaxed and leaned back in his chair putting his arms over his head. "When the party nominates me it will be a tough battle. I have to be seen as the person who can win this election. We better wait Grace. There's time, the election is still a few years away."

Scott rose from his chair, circled the room looking at Grace wondering, "How will the voters look at her? She has the money, well versed in the life style of the political ways here in the Capital. If we marry will she try to buy my influence with the way she thinks with her money? Now she is becoming more demanding of my time, telling me how to dress and just about how to do everything. I don't need a Mother. The youth of the country are ready for a young First Lady, like Mrs. Kennedy was. How can I break this off and still get more of her money?"

"Scott, I have to go to a meeting now. The Democratic Woman's club is ready to come out for you as the Party's candidate. Think about us getting married real soon, will you? Remember you have to meet me later, please be on time. I promised you would come and speak to the members after we close the business part of our meeting."

"I will dear." As soon as she closed the door, Scott picked up the phone. When the answering service came on he left a message. "Hello Carolyn, this is Scott. I've missed seeing you. It's been a long time. How about lunch tomorrow? I have some important decisions to make in the next few days and would appreciate your advice."

"How can I tell Carolyn about Grace?" Scott mulled over in his mind. "She's been divorced three times, not a very good track record with the Evangelical Christians. Their getting stronger every year, and their vote is very important to me. I'm in my thirties; and will be in my forties when I become President. Grace is in her fifties now, looks great, but she will look like my Mother by then. I need her, yet I'm trapped with no way out. I want to stop our relationship but I don't want to alienate her. I need her money in my run for the Presidency."

Later that afternoon the phone rang in his office. "I'm sorry Scott; I got your message and I've just returned from the West Coast. Give me the day. I've missed seeing you too. Instead of having lunch, come over tonight and have dinner with me. We can talk about the situation then.

Make it at eight. I'm meeting some people, and really need the time to get settled."

Forgetting about the meeting he had promised Grace, he responded, "Great! I'll see you later and bring the wine."

Many thoughts revolved over and over again, admitting to him self, "Carolyn is great in many things; maybe it was me, who wasn't. I was stupid to have got myself involved with Grace. How can I get rid of her? I should have listened to the others here in the Senate who warned me. I'm guessing there at least three and even more who have slept with her. I'm like the others before me; they took advantage of her for their future. I might as well use her to my advantage too."

Pushing the thoughts of using Grace for her money and support from his mind, he showered and dressed in anticipation of how he could use both Grace and Carolyn in different ways to gain their support for the Presidency.

Arriving at Carolyn's condo with a bouquet of gardenias and two bottles of wine, he pressed the doorbell, and when no one came he pressed it again The door opened and Scott stepped back in awe. Carolyn had on a beautiful gown with her dark black hair down over her shoulders. "Carolyn, you are stunning and more beautiful than ever. I look at you and realize what I've been missing. Don't move; let me stare at this glamorous beauty."

"Scott stop staring, give me a kiss. I won't break."

Handing her the bouquet he took her into his arms. The aroma of her favorite perfume awakened the sexual desire within him. She returned the kiss with a fervent desire that she too had been missing in her life since their breakup, and it was his decision. Carolyn hid her true feelings hoping the relationship they once had, would not disappear forever. The evening started with a glass of wine, which helped the mood of intimacy.

When the meal was finished with strawberries shortcake topped with real cream for desert, they went into the living room and had another glass of wine, sharing what had transpired in their lives recently. "I need your help Carolyn, and I don't know how to tell you why." Carolyn started to say something but was stopped by Scott.

"Please, wait until I finish, then ask me anything you wish. I stupidly got involved with Grace. You know her; and now she wants to get married." For a few minutes there was silence.

Carolyn said nothing for a moment and then responded. "Didn't the Senior Senator from home warn you about her? How can you a man who wants to be President and have to make momentous decisions that affect our country, even the world, seem to be so helpless? You were always so strong and positive. I thought you were as strong as your Father when he was a Senator. Scott be like your Father, show your strength. He could have been President of the country, but he was happy in the Senate and on the many different committees."

"But Carolyn you don't understand I need her money. As foolish as she seems to be, she really knows what she's doing. There are some in Congress who will side with her because she has something on them, and could expose them to the public."

"Break up with Grace Porter, others have done it, you're not the first, nor will you be the last. She'll always help the party as long as she's the center of attraction, and has a man beside her. People have joked about her for years here in

Washington, just like they did to her Mother. Tell you what Scott, how about the two of us give it a try again. My Mother would be thrilled; she likes you so much. She has a lot of influence and can raise the necessary funds for the campaign. I can see the two of us together in the future; You as President; myself as First Lady."

"I'm glad you said that. I'll talk to the Chairman of the Party and discuss this with him. I need his support first and then we can make plans."

"Let's make this a night to remember." Carolyn replied, as she walked over to the entertainment center, turned on a CD and beckoned Scott to come and dance with her.

Holding her tight, while dancing, their emotional desires became more than a thought "I'd liked it the way it was before. Maybe we're having a second chance. Let's not let this one slip by." Carolyn hugged Scott giving him a warm lingering kiss. "I don't want you to go. You can stay Scott. I'd like it if you would. Tomorrow you can tell Grace the relationship isn't working."

Her hopes were dashed when Scott said. "It's late, I better go. Carolyn let me finish with her and then we can make our plans.".

Arriving back at Grace's, he opened the door trying to slip quietly to the bedroom and was greeted with, "Where have you been? Did you forget I had very important people I wanted you to meet? I felt like a fool when you didn't come. It was so embarrassing."

"Grace, get off my case, I just want to take a shower and get to bed. We can discuss it in the morning. Anything you have to complain will have to wait. Goodnight!"

"Get off your case! How dare you talk to me like that? I could ruin you. Remember you said we'd get married. Are you reneging, and backing off on your promise? Running out of breath she paused, and before Scott could reply she continued, "You've found someone else, it's that woman called Carolyn, isn't it?"

As he left the room, Scott turned back to Grace and replied, "As of tomorrow I'll be gone, you can count on that!" With that blistering response he went to one of the guest rooms to spend the night. Scott was restless and couldn't sleep; finally dozing off he was awakened suddenly feeling Grace slipping into the bed beside him.

"Honey, its okay, I'm sorry I got mad, forgive me. Make love to me." Moving her hands over his body, Scott felt cold. He felt no desire, only contempt for her. Turning over, he sat at the side of the bed. "It's over between us. I'll move my things out tomorrow."

"I'll get you Scott; you'll never be President. That's a promise, you wait and see." As Scott got off the bed, she picked up the lamp on the nightstand and threw it at him. He ducked down as the lamp flew over his head hitting the wall.

"You're crazy Grace, really crazy." Going over to the closet he put on his clothes, dressed and left the house. At an all night restaurant, Scott ordered coffee, sat down to think about what had happened. When daybreak came, he went to his office and called Carolyn. With no response he left a message, "Carolyn, Grace told me to get out last night. I need a place for a few days, can you help me?"

Later in the day Carolyn called Scott back. "That's no problem you can stay here, I'm leaving for a month. Come over in the evening for dinner." Twirling around with excitement, Carolyn started to have the warm feeling she had last night. "Why not give it a chance." Looking out the window watching the morning brilliance of the sun push the dark clouds into obscurity, she said to herself. "I'm in love."

That evening when Scott arrived; Carolyn greeted him with a kiss. He responded reaching ever more into his soul for the warmth and security he wanted. After what seemed an eternity, they went inside and closed the door.

After dinner they sat down with a glass of wine, making plans for Scott to move in. Scott thinking of a temporary one, Carolyn in her thoughts, a permanent one. It was late when he said, "Thanks for a wonderful evening, I'm tired and need some sleep, see you in the morning." Leaving the room, Scott went to the other bedroom.

Knowing Scott was still emotional over the incident with Grace she said, "Good night Scott." Reaching into the refrigerator she took out the bottle of wine and filled a glass. Finishing it she sat down on the couch and heard the clock on the mantle strike eleven. Falling asleep she woke again to hear the clock strike one. Quietly she went to the guest room slipping into the bed beside Scott. He woke feeling the warmth of her body and turned to embrace her. It was time to come together and make this a permanent relationship.

In the morning it was time to say goodbye. "Scott, you know I promised to go to a few states to recruit, and help the poor people register and vote. I'll be gone a month, we talked about this last night."

"I'll be waiting for you; please don't be too long. I need to formulate my plans now and get a staff set to start the money raising activities now that I have alienated Grace."

"When I get back I'll resign my job and come to work for you. Move in now if you want. I'll call you every night."

During the day Scott kept questioning himself. "Is now the time to make a commitment for the future?" Going to his office he was not sure Carolyn was the right one for him. She was strong and had ways of taking charge of situations. I wonder he thought, "Is she using me, wanting to become the President herself in the future? I think I better hold back on committing myself to her. This might be her way of getting her own plans started."

Each summer many college students came as interns to Washington, working in different places of the government. Scott had been chosen to explain to them what their functions would be. The meeting had already started when the door opened and a young attractive woman came in.

Jasmine

Looking up from the desk Scott started to speak and found himself at a loss of words. Here is the most beautiful young woman he has ever seen. She reminded him of a ripen peach on a tree, waiting to be picked. Caressing it consuming it, knowing if he did, it would be gone. Her golden blonde hair was falling over her shoulders, just as the waves in the ocean, gently touching the sand on the seashore.

The burning sensation he felt, were as sparks turning into flames, quickly becoming a roaring fire. Gaining his composure he asked her. "Why are you late?" There was a murmuring through the room quickly turning into subdued laughter. He realized he had never given her the time to answer his question. What startled him were her beauty, figure, and the confidence she showed as she walked.

"I'm sorry, I'm late. You didn't ask me my name. Would you like to hear my excuse because I'm late? It's Jasmine Martin. What is your name, may I ask?"

"That's right Senator, you haven't told us your name. "A voice came from one of the students. The class erupted into laughter, as Scott tried to quiet them down.

Caught off balance, he stood up and banged his paperweight down on the desk, until he was able to get control of the class. "My name is Senator Drew. Don't let this kind of disturbance happen again. The purpose for this class is to give you the knowledge about the workings of your government." Still nervous and upset, Scott drank the glass of water that was on the desk before he sat down.

Regaining his poise, he started the meeting explaining his responsibilities as a Senator to his constituents, his country and even the world. When he finished, he opened the meeting for questions. There were different questions as independence from the oil cartel of foreign countries; the neglect in saving of our environment; and the neglect of the wealthy countries to aid the poorer nations. These were just a few of many questions asked.

Scott's answers were not always satisfying, bringing spirited debates. Jasmine pressed Scott for direct yes and no's, letting him try to circumvent around the questions asked. He was pleased when he could end the meeting, because it wasn't going the way he planned; and was glad when noontime arrived, so he could end the discussions.

"Thank you for choosing politics as a career. It will be tough at times, but life has never promised an easy road to walk on. When you get back home at the end of the summer; get involved in your local government. Your experiences here will aid you in your studies when you return to college this fall. You're assignments as to what and where you will be this summer will be mailed to you."

Watching Jasmine as she was leaving the room, Scott called to her, "Miss Jasmine, would you stay for a moment please. I'd like to discuss something with you."

"Did I do something else wrong, Senator?"

"No, but there are rules we have to abide with, and if you're going to be late you must give me a reason why."

Slowly the rest of the students started to leave, but paused long enough to hear her answer. The murmuring started again. Some of them turned to look at Scott and Jasmine as she walked to his desk. "I bet I know what's on his mind." One student said to a few of the others. "I've heard all about the life style that some of our Representatives and Senators have here in Washington."

"I wish it was me interviewing her. She sure is beautiful; I'd like meeting her and teaching her about life here in the

Capital. I think I'll stick around, maybe ask her for a date if he ever let's her go." "I'm an optimist but you gotta be smart. Some say some corny *#%@ about lov'n 'n loss. I say sometimes it's better to have wished you had than to have wished you hadn't."

I'll make a wager with you that I take her out first." commented another. My Dad's a representative here and I know if I ask him he'll set me up with her."

"You guys are all the same," a chorus from a few of the female students sang as they left the room.

When all the students were gone Scott walked over to where Jasmine was and asked, "Why did you come here?"

"Senator, I'm here because I want to learn everything I can about the working of our government. I'm hoping to become an attorney, and perhaps a Senator. I really don't know yet. I have much to learn. If I'm fortunate maybe you can have me assigned to your office."

"That's a great plan for your future?" In his mind he was formulating plans to spend time with this young woman. "I think I can assist you. We can talk about it over lunch."

"I really shouldn't. I have to get back to my apartment and get settled. Thinking for a moment she replied. "Why not, you know Washington inside out. If I can work in your office, not be a secretary or runner for the summer, I can get more information and knowledge at a faster pace. Okay, I'll go, but you'll have to bring me back for my car." Scott was jubilant at her answer.

Walking down the corridor some of the students were still there. "Okay everyone, you can leave now. Why don't you walk around Washington and see the many interesting buildings. The Vietnam Memorial, the World War Two Memorial and there's the Holocaust one."

On the way to the restaurant Scott asked about the college she attends and where her family lives. The odor from her perfume drifting over the inside of the car caused Scott to look over at Jasmine as she applied lipstick to her sensuous lips. Continuing to glance at her while he was driving, trying not to let her see him doing it. His face flushed when he realized she had caught him staring.

At the restaurant stepping out of the car she slipped. Scott caught her before she hit the ground, holding her up. Instinctively Jasmine put her arms around him to steady herself. Impulsively he kissed her. Startled for a moment, she just stood there. As the kiss continued she could feel the warmth, and it excited her. It had been a long time, since anyone had kissed her like that. It was one of gentleness and seeking. In a few moments she pulled away.

"I'm sorry Jasmine, forgive me. That was something that shouldn't have happened. The perfume you're wearing is intoxicating. Do you mind if I call you Jasmine?" Thinking to him self, "That's a lie. If the opportunity comes, I'd do the same thing again."

"That's okay Scott, but I think I'll call you Senator. I wasn't really prepared for what happened. We don't know each other yet. Anyway, I'm hungry." Taking him by the hand, which was warm and shaking, they entered the restaurant. During the lunch they talked about the future, and what they hoped would be a reality for them. "Thank you for the lunch Senator. It's been a pleasant experience. I'll be watching the mail for my assignment. Maybe with luck, I'll work in your office."

"You're entirely welcome, it's been my pleasure. Your assignment won't arrive until next week, so go and enjoy Washington, it's a fabulous city, there is much to see and do. Here's my card, call if I can be of any help." She gave him a light kiss on his cheek and thanked him for a delightful time, got into her car and waved goodbye.

Scott went to his office to study the papers for his next meeting. Picking up the phone he made a call to Senator Burke's office that was assigning the interns.

"Hello, this is Senator Drew, there's a new intern named Jasmine Martin and she asked one of my secretaries if she could be assigned to my office for the summer. Is it possible to make that arrangement for her? I'd be delighted to have her trained here."

"I'm sorry; she was just assigned to the office of Senator Wilson. If you have anyone else in mind and know her name, I'll be glad to help you in any way possible." Disappointed, but after a short pause he heard, "Wait a moment Senator." There was silence for a moment until the secretary spoke again, "I see his office hasn't been called, and the papers are still here."

"What was that you just said? Did I hear right, she hasn't been assigned? Can you assign her to my office? Are you sure you can do this? I would rather not let Senator Burke know I called. Senator Wilson is a personal friend of mine. I wouldn't want to infringe on your responsibilities to do what's right."

"That will not be a problem Senator Drew. I'm glad to be of any assistance. My name is Susan, and I'm sure I can do this. If you like I can bring the assignment paper over to you, and you can deliver it personally. Miss. Martin would be pleased. I know I was when the Senator personally delivered mine to me five years ago. I never thought when as a young woman he would take such an interest in me and help me get settled here in Washington."

"No Susan, that won't be necessary, you can mail it. Just be sure she's assigned to my office. Remember not a word to anyone; I really don't know how to thank you. If you can accomplish this for the summer, I would be most grateful, and perhaps be able return the favor sometime."

After hanging up the phone, Scott dialed another number. "Hello this is Senator Drew.

Please deliver four tickets for the play at the Ford Theater to Susan in Senator Burke's office. Oh yes, purchase a dozen roses also and write on the card 'Thanks for your help.' No signature, I'll be down to pay the bill tomorrow."

When the flowers and tickets came, Susan checked to be sure there was only a card with a 'Thank you for your help.' While placing the flowers in a vase, she was startled when she heard, "Well Susan, who is the admirer sending you roses? I thought I was the only one who sent you flowers." Feeling his jealousy rising within him, "Has she found someone else?"

He and Susan had an intimate relationship for five years since she came as an intern, and the only one who knew of their relationship was Senator Drew. At his age of sixty, he didn't need or want any competition. He was satisfied with the way things were between him and Susan for the last five years "Senator I have no idea who sent me the flowers. There was a card saying, 'Thanks for your help' and beside the flowers there were four tickets to the Ford Theater. Many times I have done small favors for people who wanted to know how to contact people here in Congress. Let's enjoy the flowers and the tickets."

Standing up she put her arms around the Senator giving him a kiss. "Honey, it's you I love. Why do you worry? I don't have or want anyone else. You've taken care of me since I came here five years ago. I want you to stay in Washington for a long time."

"Thanks sweetheart, I just thought that some of these new Congressmen would have their eyes on you Susan. I can't say it won't happen because I'm a lot older than you. You go back to the condo; I have something to do first. I'll lock up the office. Let's have one of those loving times like we used to. You know what to wear, and later if you like, we can go out for dinner and the theater."

When Susan closed the door the Senator picked up the phone. "Scott, how are you? I have a question; knowing you play around a lot; did you send flowers and tickets to a show and dinner to my secretary? You're the only one that knows about our relationship for these past years."

"Come on Ben, You know I wouldn't do that to you."

"Scott, I have a feeling I won't be back to Washington after the next election. My family wants me to return home, retire and enjoy the rest of my life. It's time a younger man takes my place. I'm too old for this fast pace here. Anyway, I'm sure Susan will want to stay in Washington. She's much younger then me, and she'll have different interests as time go by."

"Ben, I never knew your secretary's name, until you just said it. No, I never sent her flowers. I would never infringe on your territory. I knew you had a relationship, but didn't know her. For heaven's sake take her out to dinner and the show. Whoever sent them was just grateful. She's been faithful to you. I don't think you have to worry."

Congress was not in session and many of the members went back to their respective homes. Scott found it very boring with the long days and nights in Washington. Leaving his office one Friday, he was surprised to hear his name called. "Senator Drew; how nice to see you. I was looking for a phone to call a taxi. I'm having a problem; my car won't start. The garage will have it ready Monday."

"Jasmine, let me give you a ride to your apartment.

Are you; enjoying the sights of Washington?" Scott could hardly contain himself. This was an opportunity to share some time with her. Unknown to them someone was around the corner of the aisle listening to their conversation

"Thank you so much; a ride home will be great. Arriving at Jasmine's apartment she invited Scott in. "Would you like to come up and have a glass of wine or a cold drink? If you like I can give you a light meal, a sandwich or something else. It's extremely warm and we can cool off from the oppressive heat of the day. If you want, we can sit on the porch relax and enjoy the evening"

"That's fine, I could enjoy a glass of wine." Scott answered as he got out of the car removing his jacket. She came close to him; the aroma of her perfume excited him. He reached to her with his arms, hoping she would come to him.

Quickly moving away, she started up the stairs to enter her apartment as he placed his jacket on the back of a chair. Walking away from him with an impish grin she said, "Sit down Senator, relax, I'll get two glasses and the wine."

"Call me Scott; we aren't in the office. Let's be friends?" Jasmine kissed him lightly on the lips, and left him standing there, as she went to the refrigerator. Scott was unprepared for this, wondering, "What's this, is she just a tease? Gets you excited and then stops? Can I believe this is happening, or is this a dream, and I'll wake up soon?"

"Come out and sit down, let's enjoy the moment. The city lights will be coming on soon." Sipping the wine slowly, enjoying the cool refreshing taste Jasmine turned to Scott. "I'm sorry for the way I acted at the meeting. I have a lot of desires and dreams. I've learned to be strong and handle anything that might come my way. There isn't anyone or anything will stop me in the goal I've set for my life."

Jasmine stopped and changed the conversation. "That's enough about me. How about a sandwich, chips and a few pickles. Have another glass of wine and relax, because we have the night ahead of us. If you like, we can go out to a show or whatever. I'll leave the decision up to you"

When Scott finished eating he walked back inside the apartment. "What does she want from me? Is it the power and influence I have here? The kisses seemed to say more than that. I better be cautious, things are moving to quickly. What about Carolyn, she'll be back. How deep do I dare go, and will I get burned if I continue this relationship?"

"Scott, what's wrong? You seem to be day dreaming. Is something wrong? Did I say something, causing you to wonder about me? I'm a real person, trying to live life to its fullness. Is that surprising to you?"

"No Jasmine I'm sorry; I have so much on my mind about the next election." Shaking his head and trying to put his thoughts in focus wasn't working. His thoughts were still running rampant in his head. He knew Carolyn was going to ask him to move in with her. His mind was challenging him to make a decision. Pursue Jasmine or put his emphasis on his relationship with Carolyn?

"Scott where are you? For some reason, I think you're somewhere else. Are you sorry you came here? You can leave if you want to."

"How can I tell Carolyn? It would be better if I get an apartment of my own for the present, and just let time flow by? How will my associates in the Senate react, if this turns into something? She's only about twenty and I'm forty." All these thoughts and questions came into his mind and then were lost until he heard Jasmine ask him a question.

"Are you sorry you came here?"

Not answering he looked out over the park below when his thoughts and questions stopped. "No I'm happy and pleased you invited me to be with you." He was still confused, never had such a beautiful young woman enjoyed being with him. "Is this real, or am I losing my mind. It seems Jasmine wants to spend time with me; this can't be real. Carolyn as beautiful as she is; cannot compare to her."

Jasmine and Scott watched as the sun left to bring its warmth to another place. Myriads of colors fiery red, orange and yellow blended together, quickly disappearing into obscurity.

The lights of Washington came to life to give brightness to the night. The heat of the day had cooled and the wine had relaxed the both of them. The noise of the city subdued and the conversation lessened.

"Thank you so much, it's been a long time since I've been so relaxed." She walked Scott to the door and kissed him with a feeling he sensed she really wanted him to stay. "I enjoyed having you here, we can do it again if you'd like."

Having nowhere to go Scott returned to Carolyn's condo. He was getting more confused not knowing what to do. He knew Carolyn would be back soon, and he'd have to get his own place. "I can tell her we have to give each other time. Jasmine is so beautiful, full of ambition and intelligence. She would draw the vote of the younger generation in the next election." On Monday he left a message on Carolyn's phone and did a double check that Jasmine will be assigned to his office.

Two weeks later, much to Scott's delight Jasmine came to work for him. When his office manager started to show her around Scott interrupted him. "Philip thank you for your help."

"Good morning Jasmine, I hope you're ready for work. Everyone, I want you to meet Jasmine, our intern for the summer. Give her the assistance just as you did to the others who were here before."

Philip returned to his desk knowing Senator Drew would not let anyone get too close to this one. "Here we go again," thought Philip.

"Now it's same scenario as last year, another conquest for the Senator. Maybe this one will surprise him. I'll watch like a hawk to see how he'll handle this one. She seems quite different from the others. I don't think he can tie her down." After Senator Drew led Jasmine into his office and closed the door, the murmuring started quietly so as not to let the Senator hear.

Philip couldn't keep his thoughts to himself and started, "Well everyone, the Senator has a new one. I found out he left the rich one. You know Grace, the one who has all the money; and donates much of it to the Democratic Party. She wanted to marry him but there's a difference of twenty years. He's in his early forties and she's almost sixty. He wouldn't marry her, so she threw him out. I wonder who he'll live with now."

"You're a snake." Commented Lisa, one of the secretaries who Philip tried to have an affair with. "You'll never change. You don't walk, you crawl."

Ignoring her Philip continued, "I heard the Senator was involved with Carolyn at the same time; she's the former Representative who resigned. Now she goes around the country getting people to register to vote. Jasmine looks like the next one to get romanced, and dumped after he finishes with Carolyn."

"I don't know about that Candace. She looks so sweet and innocent, but I think she just acts that way. She knows what she wants and will do anything to get it."

"You're just jealous Lisa." chimed in another one of the secretary's. You tried to seduce him, and he wouldn't have anything to do with you. He likes them young, you're over forty, not the age he likes. Like I said, he wants them innocent and when I came here he took me everywhere."

"I've heard about those quickie affairs every summer with the young college interns. I was one of them too. It lasted two weeks but at least he gave me this job. Don't ask and don't tell that's his motto. He's handsome and very rich. The few girls infatuated with him were disappointed when he says he will keep in contact with them. When they leave that's the last they hear from him. He never goes home for the summer like some of the Senators."

"You better be quiet or you'll lose your plush job here." replied Philip. "I tried to date one of girls he had an affair with last summer. Remember Ginger, the cute red head. I dated her once and she told the Senator. He was furious with me, flatly told me to keep my hands off her or else. She was pregnant when she left and later had an abortion." Suzy one of the latest secretaries wanted to say something but thought it would be better just to listen and draw her own conclusions as to what the Senator was really like. He never had bothered her.

Philip hated Scott, and was trying to get something on him that would force him to leave the Senate. "I tried to talk Ginger into having the baby and I would marry her, then I would have something on him. She wouldn't buy it. She wasn't sure it was his baby. I know he paid her off, so stop the jealousy. He was too clever to get involved with you."

"You're a scum Philip; I could say plenty about you. Many of our former interns never had an affair with the Senator. Some of the students in college come here and want immediate success. They told me plenty, so keep your mouth shut. I could make it difficult for you." Lisa replied.

Helen, the longest employee in the office was getting irritated with all the talk. "Let's stop this now. Whatever the Senator does is his business. He's single and can do what he wants. We have good pay, excellent benefits, and our responsibilities aren't difficult. Let's stop this."

The first weeks of work for Jasmine, was getting to know the others who worked for the Senator. She could feel jealousy, and dislike from some of the girls. Helen and Suzy became her best friends in the office. "Listen Jasmine, I've seen it all." Helen told her. "Don't get involved, Senator Drew is a nice person. He had some affairs and will let you down after he's finished with you. For your own sake, be careful, don't get pregnant."

"Thank you Helen, you and Suzy are good friends. I'm afraid of Philip. When he looks at me I feel uncomfortable."

"Philip tried to get involved with me." Janet said. "It was a very trying time. I made a mistake of going to his apartment one night with him. He'd been drinking heavily; I was lucky to escape from him. I'll tell you sometime what happened. Josie can tell you stories, can't you?"

"Yes I can Janet, but the Senator has been good to me, and he isn't always the guilty one in some of his affairs. Many of the interns lied and told stories that weren't true.

Be careful. The same thing happened to me. Foolishly and innocently I went out with him. Not thinking I went to his condo after we had dinner and I had to fight him off to get away. I threatened to tell the Senator."

One Friday night as she was leaving for the day, Jasmine went into Scott's office. "Hi, would you like to come over this evening for dinner? I have an Hibachi grille; we can cook steaks and enjoy the evening."

Momentarily he was surprised when he saw Jasmine standing there. Composing himself he smiled and said, "Remember it's my treat this time. We still have to go out on a date; you promised. Sometime I want you to think about a long quiet weekend at Malibu Beach in California."

"Let's just have a quiet weekend. We can do that another time." Suddenly she realized what she had said. A quiet weekend; why not, let's go for it."

"Jasmine, you go ahead, I'll pick up the wine, and meet you at your apartment. I know where you live." As Scott was locking his office door he thought he heard someone walking down the hallway. Rushing down to the front door of the building he heard a car speeding away from the parking lot.

At her apartment he started to climb the stairs and stumbled, causing one of the bottles of wine to slipped out of his hand and break. His hand was cut as he tried to pick up the broken glass. Hearing the noise Tiffany opened her door and said, "Come inside and let me bandage your hand."

Sitting on the couch, Scott removed his jacket and tie, embarrassed by his clumsiness. "It's only a bottle, no harm done." Jasmine burst out laughing as she poured two glasses. "It's okay, I'll call for more wine."

"I feel like a jackass. It was stupid of me to be so anxious. Jasmine being near you gets my adrenaline going. I feel like a young teenager, thinking what it would be like on my first date. I'm twice as old as you, and don't feel it, forgive me, it won't happen again."

"That's okay; why don't we get our meal ready, then we'll have plenty of time to talk." Jasmine put the steaks on the grille, adding Idaho potatoes and fresh corn for the meal. They finished the meal with chocolate cake purchased at the local bakery.

When they finished cleaning up the dishes, she suggested they take a walk. It was a beautiful evening in Washington. A few night clouds appeared on the horizon bringing the darkness of the night. In the park they walked down the paths, watching children chase each other. Some of the older kids flying kites; young couples lying on the grass, not caring who is observing them. They were lost in a world of their own.

The cheers of the fans as one of the players hit a home run. Senior couples sitting on a bench looking at their watches wanting to make this moment last forever. Some holding hands; walking slowly; not letting time slip away too fast. "I often come down here in the evening to enjoy some time alone. It's filled with activity of people, it's alive, and in those moments I wonder how sad it must be to be alone."

"I'd like to walk with you any time Jasmine." Scott said squeezing her hand, as she brushed up to him. "Careful, I get tempted easily."

"Am I teasing and tempting you Scott?" She asked.

Taken back for a moment he answered, "I'm not sure Jasmine. Maybe you are teasing and tempting me?"

Returning to her apartment they watched the sky darken until Jasmine asked, "Would you like to watch television? Any special program you'd like to see? Maybe a baseball game, or we could go out to see a movie."

"Anything is good for me. Just having you near me is the best it can be. You are one of the most beautiful woman God ever created. I don't understand why you aren't seeking a career as a model. With your face and figure, you could make millions. I'll bet Hollywood and the Modeling studios would snap you up, if they knew you were here, but I'll never tell them"

"No Scott, I've made up my mind to become an attorney first, work for the government for a few years and eventually to have a career in politics. I come from a family that has worked hard and have benefited by what they have accomplished."

The evening passed quickly, as they glanced at the television between kisses and sips of wine. Hearing a church bell ring he looked at his watch realizing it was midnight; and remembered what Jasmine had said. "Let's have a quiet weekend."

He hoped it would materialize. "Do I stay, or come back tomorrow?" Scott mulled in his mind. Picking up his jacket he started towards the door when Jasmine called him.

"Scott; don't go. I meant it when I said, "Let's have a quiet weekend together. I've never stayed with a man before. I've had lots of dates, but never got serious, or wanted a steady boyfriend. My career is the only thing important to me. My goal is to prove to my Father that a woman can run a business as good as any man."

Laying his jacket down, Scott looked at her and said, "You're not a passing desire. I want you more than I have ever wanted anyone. I've never felt this way before."

The effects of the wine made them ready to let their emotions become a reality. Jasmine lay back on the couch pulling Scott down to her, smothering him with kisses that over whelmed him. "I love you Jasmine, from the minute you walked into my class. I knew my life would change. My problem is you're so young and vibrant, so beautiful and full of life. Why would you want me?"

"Scott I've longed for love; to be filled and satisfied as all normal young women want. I'll love you so completely you'll never want someone else. I know we've only known each other for a few weeks. Our love will take time to grow."

He waited until Jasmine had gone to bed, and then joined her. Lying down next to her stimulated him. He reached over caressing her body. Jasmine enjoyed the tingling sensation; an experience she had never known.

Quietly they lay beside each other, listening to the ticking of the clock, relaxing, touching each other's body, and holding hands, completely at ease. Lying quietly for a while until Jasmine said, "I love you Scott." Taking her hands she placed them around Scott's face kissing and searching. With the hunger demanding to be heard, they touched until they were satisfied. Completely filled, they fell asleep until waking in each other's arms.

"Wake up Scott, breakfast is ready." Rising up Scott went and showered before joining her on the balcony. She looked so beautiful with her golden hair falling over her shoulders, "Jasmine is this real? How could I be so lucky? You know what I'm thinking. Let's take a flight out to Malibu Beach. Call the office and say you have had an urgent call to go home; or call in and say you're sick"

"That would be great, but wouldn't people start to wonder why I'm not in the office? I'm afraid Philip will be suspicious."

"Don't worry about him. He's very much aware that I'd fire him if he starts trouble, and he knows he could never get another job here in Washington if I do. He's tried to intimidate some of the other young women that have worked in my office."

"I can't help it. The way he looks at me I feel very uncomfortable and frightened."

California

Jasmine went into the bedroom to dress as Scott cleared the table. Through the open door he could see her and felt his desire once again. He took her into his arms kissing her in a way that she knew he wanted her. She pulled away saying, "Not now Scott."

Scott left a message at his office telling Philip he had an emergency trip and had to leave town. Jasmine called in to say she wasn't feeling well, and hopefully she would be in on Tuesday. Then he called a cab to take them to the airport.

Arriving at one of the Malibu Beach hotels they registered for a few nights. The desk clerk told them of a small nightclub they would find enjoyable. A rental car was arranged and they headed for the beach, with a blanket and towels the maid from the hotel had given them. They rented a large umbrella to shade them from the sun. "Jasmine, I think I'll a take a walk."

"Just be careful, keep your eyes open so you won't trip over some of the cute chicks in the bikinis." After Scott left, Jasmine decided to lie down to enjoy the warmth of the sun; when suddenly a volley ball coming from a group of young men playing close by hit her.

"Well look who's here; aren't you beautiful. Come on play with us, we've plenty of room. If that's your Father who brought you, I'm sure he won't mind if you join us. He can join too." Jasmine was startled as she looked up shading her eyes from the sun's glare.

She was surprised to see a young man staring down at her. Before she realized, he kissed her on the lips. Knowing it wasn't Scott she pushed him away.

"Don't be so bashful, come and join us. That old guy I saw you with can't be much fun. He's too old. What does he have; a lot of money? You should be hanging with your own age; someone like me."

A crowd started to form as Scott came running up to her and grabbed the young man from behind throwing him down on the sand. Standing over him with his foot on his neck he said, "What are you thinking? I could have you arrested for assaulting my wife."

Looking up at Scott the young man replied, "I'm sorry sir. I didn't know she was married? I thought at first she was a high school student and you were her Father. She's so beautiful, then I realized she must be was one of the college girls that come here every day. I'm really sorry."

"Please Scott, let him up. He's just a teenager who thinks he can do anything he wants. He's just having a good time, playing the field."

Scott lifted his foot from his neck. "Young man, the first thing in life you learn, is respect for all people. You don't enter another person's space with out permission."

"I'm sorry sir." The young man said again, turning back to Jasmine he apologized, as all who were standing around laughed, clapping their hands when he headed back to his friends.

Later in the day they returned to the hotel, showered and laid down on the bed. The hot burning sun and the swimming had tired them. After an hour of sleep Scott woke up. Quietly he lay still, looking at Jasmine. How beautiful and innocent she looked, so peaceful. Waking up she turned over on her back to look at Scott through half open eyes. With out stretched arms she invited him to come to her.

Scott moved close kissing her, not a kiss of searching, but one of assurance, knowing he had found the love he had been searching for. Two lips bonded together, lasting like the sweetness of the first taste of a ripe strawberry. "Scott hold me tight, never let me go."

"I'll never let you go. You're so special to me. God has given me you as a wonderful gift. I love you."

Later that evening they met another couple in the lobby of the hotel. Scott invited them to have dinner with them at one of the local restaurants; and then go to a nightclub for drinks and dancing. The club photographer snapped their picture as they were sitting around the table, saying they could see them before they left for the night.

Time passed quickly when Scott checked his watch realizing it was midnight. His head was not focusing clearly from dancing, conversation, and too many drinks. He knew he had to drive and it was time to leave. On the way back to the hotel he ran a red light. In the rear view mirror he saw the flashing lights of a police car. Pulling over to the side of the road, he waited. Motioning with his hands, the officer told Scott to roll down the window all the way. "Sir, let me see your license and another piece of identification."

After looking at the cards he asked, "Have you been drinking? Second, who are your other passengers?" Not hearing the question clearly, the police officer repeated the questions. "Sir, do you hear me? Are you Senator Drew?"

"Yes I am; is there anything wrong? I'm sorry officer. We met them at the hotel and invited them to dinner. This is my wife, and my two friends Mr. and Mrs. Blaine."

"On vacation I assume. Be careful while you're here, and obey the traffic signals. I'll let you go this time with a warning." Smiling at Jasmine in the front passenger seat, and noting the difference in age, with a smirk he said, "Good night Mrs. Drew, have a good time while you're here."

At the hotel the Blaine's thanked Scott for the evening. "Are you really Senator Drew from North Carolina?"

"No, not really, I'm a very good friend. He left his wallet in my car and until now I had forgotten I had it. I put it in my pocket intending to mail it to him."

"You sure look like Senator Drew, doesn't he honey."

"Yes dear he does. My Dad is a reporter in Washington. I'll have to tell him we had an evening out with a Senator Drew look-a-like in California. He could use you as his double after he becomes the President." Hoping the Blaine's had too much to drink and would forget this night, Scott felt comfortable they wouldn't remember what happened by morning.

Quickly he thought of the young woman who was taking pictures at the different tables. He couldn't remember if they bought a picture? After the Blaine's left, Jasmine burst into laughter. "You told the policeman I was your wife and he called me Mrs. Drew. Remember at the beach you told the young man I was your wife. Should we make it legal?" Moving closer Jasmine asked, "Can we get married now?"

"Let's talk about it tomorrow; I'm very tired and a little woozy. I guess I had too much to drink." They undressed neither having much to say. Scott gently picked up Jasmine and placed her on the bed. Within a few moments she had fallen asleep.

Scott lay down next to her thinking, "Is this for real? What would Jim and Kevin think if they knew? Wait until I take her to our reunion." The day had exhausted him; with the hot sun at the beach, the drinking at night, he too fell asleep.

"Good morning sweetheart." Jasmine greeted Scott as she pulled the blanket off his face. "Let's get married today. There must be a Justice of the Peace near here. This is our honeymoon. Scott will you marry me?"

"Honey I want to marry you, more than anything else in the world, but let's talk about it first. What will your parents say? They will want you to have a large wedding, and we haven't talked about marriage before this. You have to complete college first. Why not wait until you graduate. We'll have to keep it secret if we do marry now. Are you sure you can keep it quiet?"

"Scott I'll be finished with college and graduating next spring. I'm going back to Indiana University for my last year. We can see each other on weekends, and that's not too far from Washington. I know some people will say we're stupid, but I know what I want for my life. You're the only one I want to marry. I promise I won't tell."

"Slow down Jasmine, catch your breath. There'll be times of separation; you know that. My position takes me out of the country at times, and I have no control of those situations. Are you are certain realizing what a stress this will be? It will not be easy for you. Believe me, you have no idea how the news media will be relentless in pursuing anything they can find about our personal lives if I'm selected to be the candidate. Are you positive you want this? Do you know the consequences getting married?"

"Scott, I know I can do it. Let's get married today. Why do we wait? I was raised in a family where my Dad had many meetings with news reporters. They would pester him with question after question about his business and union problems. He was strong in his dealings with them." Giving Scott a hug she said, "Let's do it! At least announce our engagement; trust me. I'll never let you down."

"Honey, we've known each other for such a short time. I want you to be sure and not regret later when difficult times come during the campaign." Scott opened the telephone book found the number of a Justice of the Peace and made arrangements to be married. In the afternoon, they said their vows to honor, cherish and love until death do they part.

Commitment

Now they were married; yet inside were thoughts and questions they had in coming face to face in what marriage will give and demand from them. They wandered along Main Street stopping to admire diamond rings. She was excited. "Can we buy our wedding rings?"

"Not yet sweetheart, the temptation to wear them is too great and many questions will be asked. Wait awhile."

"Please Scott; let me pick out my diamond. I'll tell the people it's from an old boyfriend, and when we broke up he said I could keep it."

Stopping at a local jewelry store to examine the different diamonds, the decision was finally made. He slipped the ring of her choice on her finger; and the lingering kiss made the reality of what they had just done slip away. Excitement continued as they strolled past furniture stores stopping to share their thoughts with each other. With the hot sun and the walking, they decided to go back to the hotel and rest.

After the evening meal and having much conversation, Scott was tired and went to bed early. Encouraging him to get some sleep she said, "I'll be there in a minute." Standing by the window looking out at the waves crashing on to the beach, followed quickly by new waves repeating the same process; she wondered if they have done the right thing.

The stars blinking like Christmas lights on the tree. The pale glow of the moon shimmering on the ocean encouraged her, as she thought of the future. "Should I have waited until I finish college?" Going to the bed she knew her husband was waiting for her. All questions and thoughts left her mind. In bed she snuggled close to Scott. Their love making this time was one of deep caring. A time of complete love, sharing each other completely.

It was like climbing a mountain one step at a time, until you reach the top. Never looking to what is on the other side; resting in the present moment, knowing time will take care of itself. For just a fleeting moment Jasmine thought, "What will my parents say? Why did I want to marry now? I'm young and haven't even finished college."

It was Wednesday in the late afternoon when they arrived back in Washington. He picked up his car and drove to her apartment. "I'm going to the office to see if I have any calls I'll call you in the morning. I need to get a place for myself, and make arrangements for furniture. I still have to go to Carolyn's to get my clothes. Temporarily sweetheart I'll stay in a hotel."

"Can't we have weekends together Scott?" Jasmine asked with hesitation. "Remember I'll be going back to college the last week of August; and weekends are the only time we'll have to be together. When you're traveling around the country we'll have less time. Maybe I can go with you on some of those trips."

"Of course we'll have time together. I didn't marry you to be apart. I want to be with you as much as possible."

Back at Carolyn's condo, he heard the phone ringing. He was stunned to hear her voice. "Scott, where have you been? I've good news; I'll be home in a week. Have you given any more thought to moving in with me?"

"Carolyn I appreciate what you have offered, and have done for me. Things have changed lately. You've listened to me when I needed a sounding board, but right now I think it would be better for me to have my own place. I need time to dissimulate these things that have entered my life at the present time. We can talk about it later."

Hanging up the phone the feeling of guilt was evident. He knew he had used Carolyn for his own selfishness. Now he had to face her and it became clear the more he thought about it. He couldn't rid himself of the feeling that he had wronged her once again. "What will she say, when she finds out about Jasmine and myself? She's very popular in the party, and has some influence with the party chairman. My career could be ruined. Stop worrying Scott." he pondered. "She isn't a trouble maker, I can count on her." Scott satisfied himself with this conversation with himself.

Leaving a message on the table he wrote, "Carolyn we have to give it some time. It's better we wait awhile before making a decision to live together. I've contacted a real estate broker, who had one condominium available. I'm meeting with him later today." That afternoon he signed for the condo and had his furniture moved in. Scott then called Jasmine to tell her the news.

Office Conversation

"Scott that's wonderful, we could set up the place tonight. I'll go shopping today and get all the necessary things like curtains, drapes, linens dishes and what ever." Jasmine was aware that the rest of the office personnel knew she was talking to Scott. The bright glow on her face and the smile was a give away, even though they could not hear the conversation.

"Be patient, we'll be together as soon as we get everything settled. I have some business to take care of."

Walking over to Philips desk, Jasmine asked, "Can I have the rest of the day off? I need to get some personal business finished."

"It's okay by me, there isn't much going on today." Unable to contain him self, "Are you meeting the Senator? Did you have a nice time in California over the weekend?" Refraining from answering, Jasmine ignored him, knowing she would tell Scott; and there would be trouble.

As Jasmine was leaving she reached over his desk placed her hands on his cheeks, patting them firmly until they turned red, then whispered loud enough to be heard. "You weasel, crawl back in your hole or you'll be sorry you ever came out."

After she left, the office became a buzz of conversation, each one trying to get a word in. "I know where she's living"

Philip said. "The Senator's car was parked outside her apartment.

I thought he was staying with Carolyn, he isn't. I was hoping to have a date with Jasmine. Her neighbors said they were in California."

"Philip, mind your own business, you're lower then a snake. Why don't you find yourself a good woman, get married? On second thought she said, "No decent woman could love you," said Lisa.

"What do you do with your spare time? Follow Jasmine around like you're a detective? Certainly you must have other interests then just sneaking around spying on her. If the Senator ever finds out what you're doing, you'll be long gone from here." Suzy said

"Good luck to her. She should take all she can get, and look over her shoulder for more. That's what my grandmother used to say," replied Candace.

"You're right." said Donna. "I hope she doesn't get hurt like the others. She'll be leaving at the end of summer. I think she's an innocent young woman, beautiful and what a figure. I wish I had body like hers."

"That's enough; get back to work and stop the gossip," replied Helen. "We shouldn't be so spiteful and jealous. Jasmine is confident and self assured. Let's try to be kind for a change. We have good positions here and if the Senator becomes President, he said he would take us with him."

"I'm not sure; he has had three women in the past three weeks. After my Mother's third divorce she said, men are all the same, they look different so you can tell them apart."

Suzy was getting angrier by the moment. "Stop this! You sound like a group of jealous cats. Jasmine is a wonderful person, just as Helen said. Some of you are so jealous that's the reason the Senator ignored you and your advances to try and ensnare him in your clutches. He was too smart for you."

Leaving the office Jasmine called Scott on her cell phone. "Where are you? Philip gave me the rest of the day off. I told him I had private business I had to do. Give me the directions where you are and I'll come and help you."

"Jasmine, I really can't today. I have to go to Chicago right now to speak to a group of business and union executives. I had forgotten all about it, and I'll need their support later. I should have been there now. Just enjoy the day, I'll be back tomorrow, and we'll go out for dinner."

Jasmine was disappointed, and remembered what he had said. It wouldn't be easy and I had to learn to accept times like this. At the office she told Philip she wasn't able to contact the people she wanted, and decided to return to work.

Carolyn felt bitter and resentful of Scott, deciding one day to go to see him at his office to confront him, and ask why he couldn't come to live with her. Twice she had given herself to him. Now she wanted an answer one way or the other so she can move on with her life. Storming into his office, the office staff was stunned to see her. Walking up to Jasmine she said, "I would like to see the Senator."

"I'm sorry, he's in Chicago, and won't be back until tomorrow. If you give me your name I'll tell him you were here. Can I do anything for you? Do you need some help? I can try to get him on the phone if it's an emergency."

Jasmine and Philip

Looking at this beautiful young woman, Carolyn thought, "This is the reason Scott needs time." Devastated, with tears in her eyes, Carolyn rushed out of the office slamming the door. Bitterness welled up inside of her as she walked down the corridor. "Who do you think you are?" Carolyn said out loud, as she wiped the tears from her face. "I had everything planned; now you enter the picture and spoil it. Some how Scott, I'll get even for what you have done to me."

That evening knowing Scott was in Chicago, Philip decided to go to Jasmine's apartment to ask her out for dinner. As she looked through the small safety glass she saw him standing there. She hesitated for a moment then opened the door. "Philip! What a surprise! Why are you here? Did I do something wrong at the office today?"

"No, everything is okay. I was driving by and thought I'd drop in to see you. I know the Senator is in Chicago and you'd be alone. Maybe we could go out to dinner, share the evening together. Go to a nightclub, dance, and even have a drink or two. I don't think the Senator would be angry, but glad I was being sure you were safe."

"Philip, what makes you think I'm lonesome because the Senator is in Chicago? I told you before I'm not dating; and if you think the Senator is living here, you're mistaken. Don't get the wrong idea of any relationship between the Senator and myself. I'm letting you know there is nothing going on between us. Thanks for the invitation, but I'm really not interested in going out with you. Good night."

Not giving up Philip pushed her inside the room then closed the door. "You're just like the rest. You come here to get what you want, and get surprised when men don't cooperate with you. It's not what you expected, is it? You have no idea what the life in Washington is. You're just one of many young women who are surprised when they learn they have to give to get what they want."

Backing away, Tiffany felt uneasy and frightened. "What are you saying? You better leave now. If I tell Senator Drew he'll fire you. We're only friends, and he's helping me to learn about the workings of the Senate. I'll be graduating next year from college, then come back to Washington and work for the FBI. Where do you get your weird ideas?"

"Come on Jasmine, I know that you and the Senator are having an affair. He has one every year with a new young intern. You think you're the first and only? Don't kid yourself; there will be others after you. I'm telling you the truth. I've picked up the young interns after he discards them. It happens every year."

"That's not true! Helen told me they're only false rumors, and Suzy confirmed it. Philip you better leave. I don't want to have this type of a conversation with you. The Senator has been very good to me, and he's only a friend."

Ignoring Jasmine, Philip continued, "They were hurt so bad even after I offered to help them recover from their senseless affairs. I tried to tell them like I'm telling you. You'll be sorry, you're only one of many that believed his lies. I admit I took advantage when they were vulnerable, and even had an affair with a couple of them

There are some of the members in Congress who take advantage of the young interns every year, but there are some that are faithful to their wives most of the time; though sometimes even they have a quick one night stand."

Philip caught Jasmine by surprise when he lurched toward her, trying to push her down on the couch. With all her strength she pushed him away. "Damn you, Philip! Get out of here, and I'll forget this happened" Going to the door, she tried to open it but he stopped her.

Again, Philip pulled her away from the door getting her down as he tried to kiss her. Now Jasmine knew fear. The odor of his breath from liquor was sickening, almost causing Jasmine to pass out. He was too strong for her, as she tried to get out from underneath him. "Help me! Help me!" she screamed. Philip continued to fondle and kiss her, his hands on her breasts as he kept her down on couch.

Josh the neighbor across the hall hearing a muffled scream coming from Jasmine's apartment, opened his door and called out, "Are you all right, can I help you?"

Jasmine was finally able to push Philip on to the floor, and as he lay there she kicked him twice. Screaming in agony he got up and staggered out of the room. Josh was standing at the doorway and tried to grab him as he ran by. Jasmine staggered over to Josh holding on to his arm for support. "He's just a guy I know having a little too much to drink. Thanks for coming out to help me."

Outside of the building Philip doubled up in pain, his hands holding on to his body where Jasmine had kicked him.

He got into his car, vowing that some day the opportunity will arrive when he would get even with Senator Drew and Jasmine. "I'll get you into bed Jasmine before you leave for college, you can bet on that." Philip promised himself.

When Jasmine arrived at work the following morning, Suzy noticing the scratches on her face and asked her what happened. "It was nothing. I don't want to talk about it. I'll tell you during lunch hour." This answer didn't satisfy Suzy, but knowing when Jasmine was ready she would tell her.

The following day Philip returned to work, walking slowly, not wanting to look at Suzy. She surmised something had happened between Jasmine and him. With a smirk on her face she raised her thumb at him mouthing, "You got what you deserved. I hope you live in pain for weeks, you're sick."

At lunchtime, Suzy walked out of the office with Jasmine and sat on a bench in the foyer. "He tried to kiss me and pull off my blouse to touch my breasts. I pleaded with him to go, and told him I would forget it, if he would just leave. He persisted and knocked me down. As he tried to lie on me, I pushed him away and was able to kick him. He screamed in pain, as he ran out of my apartment. Thank God, my neighbor Josh heard me yell and came to help me."

"Jas I know the young girl that Philip is living with. We went to the movies last night and when she got home, Philip told her that you had assaulted him. He claimed he went over to your apartment last night just to visit you.

She also said you had a few drinks, got drunk and started to fight with him. Then she continued to tell me you scratched his face, kicked him in you know where."

"That's not true Suzy. It happened just as I said! You can ask my neighbor Josh. He heard the whole thing." At that moment the scene of last night of her lying on the floor trying to get away from Philip came into her mind. "What I'm telling you Suzy is true. My neighbor across the hall heard the noise and came out of his apartment. Philip pushed him aside as he ran down the hall to the stairs. He deserved it. I hope the Scott doesn't find out about this."

"Jas, you'll have to tell Scott or Philip will continue to harass you. Look you'll be going back to college soon, and he'll show up there and be a real pain. If Scott isn't told, it will never end. We can handle him here because Helen is a favorite of the Senator. I wouldn't be surprised if she'll take Philip's place some day. You have to tell him."

"Honestly Suzy, I don't want any trouble with him. All I want is to finish college, and come back here next fall to start working in Washington."

"Philip knows quite a bit about the affairs that some of the Senators and Representatives have and had; they will do most any favor he wants. What they're doing is buying his silence. In the short time I've been here, I know of good people who have lost their jobs because they crossed Philip."

"Thanks Suzy, I'll be careful. I just wish Scott were here. Every night now I'll be frightened that he might come to my door. I'm no match for him if he is determined to get me.

"Do you think I should call the police and put in a restraining order against him?"

"That's up to you. Let Scott handle it. I'll stay here with you if you want."

It wasn't too long before the rest of the office staff became aware that something happened concerning Jasmine, Suzy and Philip. They were anxious to know, realizing they will never get any information from them. They had to be patient until someone would break their silence. At lunchtime Philip left the office and Suzy started to parade around the office, bending over holding on to her crotch. The staff burst into laughter; knowing what happened.

When Philip came back someone started to snicker. That started a time of some the office personnel to laugh, finding it impossible to hold back. This infuriated Philip because he knew they were laughing at him. Suzy not wanting to keep this going on walked over to Philip and stared into his eyes. "Let me assure you Philip, if you try to harm Jasmine, I'll tell the Senator how you tried to rape me a year ago. I'll press charges against you, even if it cost me my job. Your girlfriend knows the truth. She's leaving you."

He snarled back, with a look of hatred on his face. "I don't believe you. I've been here a long time, and have a lot of power over some people who will protect me."

During the day Suzy watched as Philip repeatedly picked up his phone, held it for a long time; then put it back down; not getting through to whomever he was calling. This was repeated time and again.

When he left for the day Suzy started dancing around the office. "I did it! I've waited for a long time to get even with him and it finally happened."

"What did you do Suzy?" Jasmine asked.

Going over to Jasmine's desk she whispered softly, "I convinced Philip's girlfriend that he attacked you, and now she's leaving him. At first she didn't believe me, but after a long talk she was convinced. She told me she's going back home to start a new life."

"Suzy, you shouldn't have done that. He will hate us even more, and do anything to get us fired."

"Don't worry Jas; Scott will take care of him."

Kevin

Arriving back in Wyoming, Kevin was greeted at the airport by his Father and some of the cowboys who helped in the operation of the ranch. Looking at his Dad he could see how much the cancer had aged him. He started thinking, "He's only fifty five years old but looks older." Kevin knew he had to get involved quickly in the operation of the ranch. The raising of cattle, horses, growing grain, and many hard winters had taking a toll on his Father's physical being.

His Dad never took time for social activities. Kevin's Mother had left the ranch after he left for college four years ago. She told Jon she hated this part of the country. One day she took the two girls and returned to Florida. The hot, dry summers and the lack of rain caused a few lean years. This made increased demands on all that shared the workload. Still in spite of all the hard times the ranch was profitable.

"Dad, it's so good to be back in God's country. I plan to be here for the rest of my life. I've missed these wide open spaces. Living in a large city for the past four year's I know now this is the place for me."

Kevin loved being raised in this part of the country. The flat rolling plains and mountain with snow capped peaks rising majestically into the heavens. The sunsets, with colors no man could paint he knew this is the perfect place to live. At times the blazing red-hot sun, burning so bright would be replaced in the evening with the soft radiance of the moon. Then as the sky turned into darkness, millions of blinking stars would come, calling you to make a wish.

Several months after returning home, Kevin and his Father rode their horses over the plains and stopped to watch the wild horses as they raced to find a place to mate. Turning to Kevin his Dad said,, "I miss your Mother. I don't blame her for going back East. She just couldn't handle the winters anymore. Remember she didn't grow up here. Now I can understand why she left. It's a hard life. I'm getting tired Son, let's turn back."

As they turned their horses around and headed toward the ranch, Kevin could see the deepening lines on his Dad's face, that were made from the many years of hard labor as he built the ranch to its current success. Back at the barn they removed the saddles, bits and reins from their horses, leading them into the corral. "Lunch is ready, and it'll get cold if you don't hurry." Angela the housekeeper called.

Walking to the ranch house Jonathon turned to his Father wanting to say something, but his Father spoke first. "I hope you don't mind Son, I've invited Katy and her parents over for the evening. You need a social time in you life. She hasn't married, and I think she would make an excellent wife for you." Forgetting Jon repeated again what he said out on the range. "Kevin I miss your Mother"

"Dad you said that, and I understand. Are you feeling okay? When's the last time you've seen a doctor?" Jon ignored the question, so Kevin changed the subject and continued, "I still have a lot to learn about the operation of the ranch, and I know Jason will help me. He's the best foreman on any spread in this state."

Later in the day Katy and her parents came to the ranch as the sun was slipping over the earth to a new horizon.

Kevin and Katy

Finishing dinner they went out on the porch, enjoying each other's company, sharing cocktails and reminiscing of what had happened these past twenty years. "Katy would you like to take a ride out to the river?"

Just the opportunity to be alone with Kevin pleased her. Quickly she replied, "I'd love to, just like old times." After a long ride they stopped at the river to let the horses drink. "Kevin it's good to see you again."

"I know Katy, the ranch work kept me busy when I came home every summer. There's always so much to do, and learn about the operation here. I had no time for fun."

Getting down from their horses, Katy took Kevin's hand looking up to him. "If you'd like we could spend more time together. I use to dream as a kid that you'd be my boyfriend, and when we grew up we'd get married, have a lot of kids."

For a little while Kevin was quiet as he looked over the horizon, watching the wind blowing over the water and the open plains. It brought back memories of many times he would come to this special place. "I'm concerned about my Father's health. Look what it has done to him. How can I think about marriage when my Dad is so ill?"

"Kevin, I'm not thinking of marriage and being Mrs. Kevin Curtis right now. I want to renew our relationship for the time being; that will make me happy. Did you think I was proposing to you? No way! When the time comes. You'll have to do the proposing to me."

"Sorry Katy, I didn't think that you were suggesting getting married now. I remembered how we had talked about it happening after I finished college." Sitting on the bank of the river, Katy reached over held both of his hands pushing him down on the ground as Kevin landed on his back.

"The truth is Kevin, I have dreamed many times, wondering how you would react and respond in this situation. You were always so bashful when we were young. Your return back here, raised my expectations and excitement. I've waited so long for this day."

For a moment he was taken by surprise, and responded gently pushing Katy over on her back, smothering her lips with kisses. For a fleeting moment, Alicia's face became an image in his mind, re-living that time on the beach. Kevin relaxed, looking down at her face, continually moving his lips back and forth with a burning desire.

Laying still, the only sound they heard, were their breathing, and the sound of the river as it tumbled over the rocks, heading for a new destination. He held Katy as she snuggled into his arms. Looking up at the sky, trying to count the stars to stay awake they soon fell asleep. The neighing of the horses woke Kevin. Looking at his watch he reached down to touch Katy. "It's one o'clock, we really should start back."

Slowly opening her eyes she pulled Kevin back over her, kissing him gently on the lips. "Umm that tastes so good. Kevin this was more than I ever dreamed it would be." Lying there for a moment she stretched as Kevin lifted her up.

"I used to dream of the day you would make love to me. I know it was only a wishful dream. Now it was worth waiting to give all of me to you."

In silence they rode slowly back to the ranch to find the place in darkness with only the porch light burning. Going inside on the table there was a note for Katy, "We'll be back in the morning to get you."

After bedding down the horses in the stable they went into the house. "It's too late to take you home now. You can sleep in the guest room." Taking her once again into his arms he held her tightly, kissing her with a revived feeling that had been lacking in his life. Katy responded with a newfound passion, now ready for a new beginning, realizing it would take time to develop.

Quietly they parted. She was ready to commit herself to Kevin. He went to bed as his thoughts went back to the image of Alicia. "What am I getting into? I like Katy, but do I really love her? We've been apart for four years. I'm not ready to commit myself to marriage and kids when Dad needs me to manage the ranch."

Katy was reliving her first experience in making love to the one man she wanted. "It was so much more then a dream, it was real. "I could touch his body so alive, and when he touched me, it brought my passion full circle," she thought.

It was late in the morning when a knock on the door of his room woke Kevin as he heard his Father's voice, "Kevin, wake up, breakfast is ready. Where's Katy? Her parents were concerned when you gone so long."

"Dad, she's in the guest room. It was too late to drive her home. We rode way out to the river; by the time we returned it was too late."

At the breakfast table Jon looked at his son Kevin with a twinkle in his eyes, "Then you had a good ride? I guess you made up for lost time. That's good for you; take some time to enjoy your life." He knew what his Dad was thinking and remained silent. Words were not necessary. He was right, we did enjoy ourselves. Katy joined them looking at Kevin's Father she knew what they were talking about. Jon excused himself saying he had to get to the barn for he had work to do.

"Katy put her hand over Kevin's mouth. "Kevin I know my coming on to you like I did was a surprise. Believe me, it was the dream I've had for a long time.

Hopefully you have no regrets what happened. I've been planning to leave my parents home and buy one of my own. It's time to get on with my life."

"Katy, I'm not sorry. Leaving here for four years in college then coming back proved this is where I want to spend the rest of my life. I met a beautiful girl at college and fell in love with her. My dreams were to spend the rest of my life with her. In a note she left me, she told me to get on with my life, but if we were to meet again, she would be ready for a commitment. She instigated our love affair, said she love me and then walked away. I'm trying to get over her, but it isn't easy, so this will take some time, okay?"

"Okay Kevin, what happened, happened. You're here with me, and the one I waited for. I want you as my husband and the Father of our children. I thought about this last night while I was lying in bed."

"Katy, be patient with me, I love you and want to marry you. What happened last night was not a one nightstand. First let's share more time, move slowly finding more about each other. We can talk about our future, and what we want for the rest of our lives together. I know you have to get to work so I'll take you home now."

Months went by; Katy a computer expert, refused promotions when her employer asked her to move out of Wyoming, waiting for the day Kevin would ask her to get married. She purchased her own home, often having Kevin over for meals and to spend an evening together. Some times they would go out to dances at the local clubs. A few times Kevin would stay for the night, but as time went by, the over night stays became less frequent.

"Kevin." Katy asked him one evening, "Why don't you want to stay over night any more? Is there something wrong? At first when we were together our lovemaking was great. Now you are always tired or you can't stay. If you want to break it off, say so."

"It's not that Katy, I just need more time. I can't get Alicia out of my mind. I've tried to forget her but it isn't working; can't you understand? Please Katy, I love you and want to marry you. I'll never harbor Alicia in my thoughts again. I never want to do anything to hurt you."

"Kevin, I told you I love you, and want to marry you. If you don't want to get married say so. Just don't keep me dangling on a string. I feel like you're using me for your own sexual satisfaction."

Weakly and stumbling over his words he responded, "I promise Katy, I'll forget all about her."

"That night out by the river, it was love as its best. We came together with a passion I felt would last a long time. You touched me in places only I knew would satisfy me. Now when we make love I wish it would be over." With this out burst Katy broke down crying. Kevin took her into his arms and could feel her body trembling, uncontrollable.

"Katy, don't cry, I love you, and I want to marry you."

"Alicia told you to get on with your life. Well do it. I want to be sure your love is genuine and mine alone. If we marry, where will we live? I know that your Dad is not well, and you will be taking over the ranch. I'm willing to rent my house and live with you at the ranch. When we have children, it'll be the best place to raise them." The next six months, were times of dating only. Katy told Kevin, "There'll be no staying over until you're sure we are getting married."

"I agree Katy; we have to be sure that we want our life to be one of love not just a physical encounter." In six months they announced their date for their wedding. Waiting for that day Katy kept herself busy making plans for their honeymoon.

The wedding was held at the ranch. Sharing their vows as they sat on their favorite horses. Katy and Kevin had decided to take a camping trip for their honeymoon. They rode over the plains, climbed the mountains, cooked their meals on an open fire each day and slept under starlit skies at night. Daily they would ride into a small town for supplies, and then head back to the plains and the mountains. They explored the rivers, looking for gold, not knowing what they might find; but having the pleasure of laughter and sharing each moment together. Each night they would camp by the river discovering the lovemaking they had before.

At the end of two weeks they made reservations to spend the rest of their honeymoon in Hawaii. It was exciting making plans knowing on their return, the ranch would demand most of their full attention. One evening after they had been married six months Kevin sat reading the newspaper in the living room when Katy came behind his chair, reached over pulling his face up from the paper and said. "I've wonderful news for you. I'm pregnant; we're going to have a baby, Dad."

"Really, you're kidding! We've only been married six months." Jumping up from his chair realizing what Katy had just said, he picked her up tenderly. "When did you find out?"

"The doctor confirmed it today. I don't want to know if it's a boy or girl, only to know the baby will be healthy."

"Is it true what I heard." A voice came from the porch? Walking inside, Jon hugged both of them. With tears streaming down his weathered face. He felt he wouldn't be around in a period of time, as the cancer spread in his body.

Children

Slowly going to the bar in the next room Jon took down a bottle of wine and filled three glasses. "Dad, Katy can't have any alcoholic drinks while she's pregnant. One drink is enough for you. You can't have Katy's drink, I will."

Words of the coming birth spread quickly around the local area. Baby gifts came from the owners and families of other ranches. Later the wives of the ranch hands gave Katy a baby shower. The last time there was a birth at the ranch was when one of Kevin's sisters was born. Three months later, Katy gave birth to a baby boy. Kevin's Dad was exuberant; knowing his life in developing this land would be passed down to another generation.

Gazing over the vastness of his land one day with Katy standing beside him, Jon turned to her; "You've made me so happy; I have a grandson. The ranch and our land will never be turned into a town of shopping centers, high-rise apartments or condos, and who knows what else. This is God's country of open plains, snow white capped mountains and clean fresh crystal waters, finding its way in the valleys. Will Kevin always feel as I do Katy, or eventually tire of the demands to keep it up and sell?"

"Dad, you don't have to worry, Kevin loves this place more then he loves me. No, I'm kidding. He grew up here and now with his son, we know that will never happen. Your grandson and I promise this. The land is our heritage. We'll have more children and we'll teach them. They will learn to love the ranch and land as you do."

"I hope you're right Katy, but in time he might get tired of the work it takes to maintain it. You say that now, but we don't know the future. The doctor told me my cancer is growing quickly, my time is short." With that, Kevin's

Father turned away so she wouldn't see his tears. Changing the conversation, "Katy having grown up here, have you ever seen a place so beautiful, untouched by man and so free? Many people in our country have never seen what a great state we have."

"Yes Dad, I understand. We who have been born here cherish this land. Don't worry, Kevin will never sell this land he loves so much."

"We own one hundred thousand acres. With the growth of population here, we need protection from the poachers that will mutilate the land, and pollute the water. With their guns they will kill the animals that have so much freedom, including the wild horses. They're taking away their natural habitats."

It took five years for Katy to get pregnant again. This time it was twin girls. Kevin was kept busy with the management of the ranch, while Katy was kept busy with the new twins and their brother Jonathon, a little over six years old. Kevin wanted more children but Katy had told him three was sufficient. She told him it was all she could handle for the present time.

The ever increasing demands from the three children at times, the absence of Kevin as he brought his cattle, and grain to market; also the training of horses played heavy on her emotions.

Caring for Jon, as his cancer was taking complete control of his body, would leave Katy in tears. She longed for a change in her life. She missed the excitement of the former job she had in the computer industry

One evening after the children had gone to bed, she asked Kevin if they could go somewhere for a vacation, just to break up her daily un-interesting routine, as she called it. "I ask for very little, but I too get tired and need a change of scenery. Can't we go away for a long weekend?"

"We can't go any where right now. Dad is sick and dying. I have to be here with him. Can't you understand this? He has only a short time to live! We can't discuss it now. Sometime later we'll sit down and talk about a vacation, but right now is not the time."

"I didn't say right now, just make some definite plans! All I want to do is to get away, a commitment that we can have a vacation. I need a change, and so do you."

Each day Katy and Kevin found their nerves becoming more frayed with each other. Months passed with no mention of any plans to go on a trip that Katy wanted so much. She kept asking Kevin to get someone to help his Father, but it fell on deaf ears. "Kevin, I need to get away for awhile. The doctor said he would live for a long time. You have no idea what I'm going through with three young children! Taking care of your Dad is exhausting. I'm not a nurse."

As the weeks passed, her disappointment turned to anger. Leaving Kevin now, seemed to Katy an option in her mind, as each day passed.

Conversation between Katy and Kevin evaporated, until very few words passed between them, as his Father struggled to stay alive. The many hours and days in caring for Jon continued and increased.

One morning Katy as usual was bringing his breakfast to him and found him in a comma. With Jon placed in a nursing home, it became necessary to have the ownership and control of the ranch be transferred into Kevin's name. This was an agreement in the trust should his Father's health continued to decline.

The following month Kevin opened the mail and received an invitation to attend a reunion at the college. "Katy how would you like to go with me to my class reunion at Ohio University? We can get a way for a while, like you wanted. You want a change, here's your opportunity."

"Kevin, that's not going away, I want our trip to be just for us. Going there will end up with the wives left alone, while the husbands celebrate their memories getting drunk every night. Forget it; maybe your lost love will be there.

I'll bet you're hoping to see the ex girl friend." In anger and disappointment she started to leave the room.

"Katy, stop it! I told you before; I've forgotten everything about her." Frustrated he said, "Maybe she will. Come on; be reasonable! I told you she's out of my mind. Why do you bring this up now? Okay you stay, I'm going." Thinking, "It would be nice to see Alicia again."

Reunion in Ohio

Katy with great patience tried to convince him once more, "Kevin, I think our life has turned into a relationship and not the true friendship we had wanted. We need a vacation from here. We can have Carlos's wife Angela take care of the house. She takes care of the children now when I go out."

The image of Alicia's face started to surface in his mind again. He could see his marriage was starting to fall apart. They had lost communication between them, as when they first married. Katy continued to refuse to go to the reunion at Ohio University. Each day the conversation would become bitterer between them. In anger and frustration Kevin left the ranch one morning for Ohio.

At the college some old friends greeted him. Jim and Scott didn't come, and he was disappointed. Asking around for Alicia no one seemed to know where she was. Meeting her former roommate Allison, he asked her, "Have you heard from Alicia?"

"No Kevin, we kept contact for a few years, then she stopped writing and her phone was disconnected. She didn't leave any following address, and the last time I heard from her she was married."

"You said she was married? Did she say to whom? Why didn't she invite you to the wedding? Allison you were her best friend, and roommate for four years. By the way did you get married and how many children do you have?"

"No I haven't married. Alicia's Father died and she felt free. Some guy she was dating asked her to marry him and she said yes. That was the last word I've heard from her. You shouldn't have had sex with her. She wasn't ready. She was just an innocent girl, and you should have restrained yourself. I told you back when we graduated you guys are all the same."

"Slow down Allison, you weren't there. I remember her Father and he wouldn't even listen to what I had to say. For some reason she became frightened. I didn't attack her; we had a good time having a cookout and swimming. You didn't help the situation either Allison. You could have been a better friend to her and explain everything to her; but you the know it all. You don't like men."

"Come on Kevin when she came back into our room she was nervous and afraid, fearing she had done something wrong. The problem is you don't know the difference between relationship and friendship. You missed out on marrying a wonderful woman. But no, you're just like most of the guys, wanting what you want with no respect for women. I thought at one time you were different, you weren't."

"Knock it off Allison that's all in the past. What did she do, tell you everything about our date? What happened between us was none of your concern. In fact if you want to know, she started it. Does that satisfy your curiosity?"

"Kevin, do you have children, why are you trying to find Alicia? Forget her, and get back to your family like any decent man would do. Stop living in the past."

Walking away, Kevin knew no further explanation would make any difference in Allison's mind. She was sure he was at fault. He visited the old familiar haunts; the nightclub, it wasn't the same. Having a few drinks with some of his former classmates, they remarked how old he looked. It was the last time he vowed he would return.

After two days Kevin felt alone and decided to call for a taxi to take him to the airport. When the cab arrived the driver greeted him. "Was it what you expected? I knew you'd come back. Like my son, he returned to his college after graduating. Both of you thinking there was something that you had left, and you came back to find it."

"Do I know you?" was Kevin's reply.

"I was the taxi driver who took you to the airport after you graduated a few years ago. Like I said then, some come back and find out that it isn't the same as when they spent four years here."

"We have time; drive me down to the river. Walking along the shore, he scaled a few stones trying to make them skip on top of the water. In his mind he tried to bring back the memory of Alicia and himself of their last time together. Time had taken its toll; he couldn't turn the clock back. It had become a faded memory.

"Sir, I have another call. Are you ready to leave? Listen young man. Let me give you some advice Go back to where you came from.

"Okay, I guess you're right. It's time to go home."

Katy leaves Home

"There are two things you can do now for your life. Don't repeat the same mistakes, and build on your successes for the future. You see I'm driving a cab because I didn't do what I said; now I'm learning the hard way. It's too late for me but you still have time."

Disappointed, Kevin returned home to the ranch and was greeted by Angela. "Mrs. Walker left a note for you. She said she was going away. I asked her when she would return, she didn't know." Opening the note it said, "Kevin I can't stay here with the relationship we have at the present time. Hopefully this will be a shock to you. I'll let you know when I'm settled. I need something else in my life beside horses, cattle and grain twenty-four hours of the day. Katy"

"Angela," Kevin yelled. "Where did she say she was going? What did she tell you? When did she go?"

Question after question he continued to ask, with Angela repeating over and over, "I don't know, I don't know!" Please sir, I don't know. She did not tell me, only to take care of the children so you could work here on the ranch. She said your Father can't do the work anymore because he is very sick."

Taking the note Katy had left he opened it to read it once more. Scanning the page and re-reading it, he noticed there was more on the other side. "My parents know where I am; but they will not tell you. Please don't try to intimidate them; when the time comes and you're ready to include me in your life, I'll come back.

Shallow Love

I miss you and love you, but sometimes I wonder why. Tell the children I miss and love them too. Have Angela take care of them so you can continue to run the ranch, which I think is your real love. Maybe in your mind that ex girl friend is your true love." signed Katy.

After finishing the letter he sat stunned trying to figure out what went wrong with their marriage. "What did I do? She has everything, a home and three children." Trying to convince himself it wasn't his fault. It didn't work. As time went by, Kevin started to renew friendships with some old high school buddies. Nights at the local tavern became many visits for Kevin, trying to erase the reality that Katy had left.

One evening at the local tavern, Shelly one of the waitresses came to the table where Kevin was sitting and invited him to dance. When the song, 'Are You Lonesome Tonight' was playing, she held him tightly to her body, moving in a motion that suggested an invitation. His body answered, willing to accept her request, slowly their bodies moved in harmony together.

Katy had been gone three months. His sexual wants were escalating, until now, he had refused some of the women who were regular patrons at the tavern.

Now with a few too many drinks and his head heavy, Shelly was giving him the opportunity for a night of pleasure. He was weakening, wanting to go to her place.

After the tavern closed that night Kevin was walking toward his truck, when Shelly approached him. Coming close she kissed him with a searching desire to have an answer, yes or no. With no words he kissed her back, letting her know he was ready. For a few minutes they clung to each other trying to be satisfied. Something was missing and needed completion. "Kevin can I have a ride home?"

"Why not; let's go. Where do you live?"

After she told him the directions Shelly asked, "Why the change of heart this time? Every time I asked you to come to my place you always refused."

Not really hearing her, Kevin was tormented, realizing what he wanted was alien to what he had promised. He remembered what the minister said, "Will you honor, obey and be faithful to Katy as long as you both shall live?" Putting these words out of his mind he let his emotions rule.

"Come in Kevin and sit down; give me a few minute. I'll get you a drink. I'll have one after I shower and change my clothes. You know I can't drink at work." Kevin's sexual desire was increasing as his drinks started to wear off. Sitting there he waited for Shelly to get out of her uniform. He was becoming extremely impatient.

Looking into the bedroom he saw her standing naked. He started to go into the room, but Shelly pushed him away. "No Kevin, sit down. I have to take my shower. Don't be in a hurry."

"Come on Shelly I can't wait forever. You've wanted me for a long time, and now's the time. You can have the drink later."

"Relax, I'm not going anywhere, and you don't have to hurry home. I heard Katy has left you. Let me enjoy my drink first."

Coming out of her bedroom in a flimsy nightgown after taking her shower it left nothing to the imagination. Kevin rose from the chair and approached her. "Wait honey don't, let me have my drink first." When she finished he picked Shelly up in his arms, taking her back into the bedroom. She unbuttoned his shirt. Laying her on the bed he quickly removed her gown. Then he removed his clothes, and started to lie down beside her.

She laughed saying, "Honey, take off your boots. We have a long night ahead of us to make love." Impatiently, Kevin moved over on her as she was running her hands all over his body. "Please Kev, easy, go slow, and enjoy the moment." Kevin wanted her immediately he couldn't wait. It took but a minute to be satisfied. Finishing, he got up from the bed, dressed; bent down kissed her and left. Feeling guilty of what he had just done, he closed the door behind him; got into his truck and sat for a moment He could hear Shelly call to him.

"Please stay Kevin. Spend the night with me. There'll be more, don't leave now." Lying on the bed she waited and when he didn't answer, she called out again. "Kevin you're rotten, treating me as if I was a whore, thinking only of yourself. This is the last time for you."

Katy Makes Contact

Ignoring her call he started towards his home, his eyes not focusing, he ran his truck into a shallow ditch beside the road. Shaking his head to clear it, he said to him self, "What have I done? What's wrong with me? I'm married with a wife and three kids; I've betrayed them."

Racing the motor and spinning the wheels, he was able to extract the truck from the ditch, and drove back to the ranch. Getting out he looked over the horizon, realizing how much he needed Katy back. Thinking, "This isn't the same place without her. I need her and the kids need her too. I have to get her back home."

He went to bed, but couldn't sleep. The guilt he laid on himself for the betrayal of his promise to Katy wouldn't disappear. There was no sleep that night. In the morning he called Katy's parents and they told Kevin they had a letter for him. Driving over to their home he thanked them.

When he opened the letter he read, "Dear Kevin, I have returned to work for the company I was with before. They have given me my old position; financially this is good because I can support myself. How are the twins, and Jonathon? I miss them. We have to be separated for now."

Two weeks later, her parents called again and said that they had received another letter. Quickly he got into his truck and sped over to their ranch. He thanked them, wanting to ask where she was, but refrained; knowing what the answer would be. Her Father contemplating what Kevin wanted to ask remained silent.

Opening the letter he read, "I have signed a contract to work for a year, with an option to renew. I'm working in another state so don't try to contact me. I'll keep in touch."

Turning the page over he read more. "I'll see how things are progressing this year. Tell the kids I miss them, and hopefully I'll be able to come home soon. Katy."

The days turned into months and Kevin felt lonely, disappointed and sad that Katy still wouldn't come back home. He worked tirelessly at the ranch and stopped going to the clubs at night; knowing that he didn't feel strong enough to resist the temptation. The nights were long and the children constantly asking, "Where is Mommy?"

The year passed and Katy had to make a decision, to return home, or sign the contract for another year. It was a difficult decision to make because she loved the freedom, the challenge in the computer industry. Her supervisor, Mr. Jenson was getting too familiar, taking her to dinner, and buying her small gifts. One night after he brought her to her place he became aggressive after she kissed him on the cheek. He became persistent wanting to stay for the night.

Closing the door she stopped to look at the pictures of the children she had taken with her. Tears started and she felt sad and alone; realizing the kids were growing up and she was missing that part of their lives. Something was wrong, it was time to return home and be with her family.

One day, her supervisor came to Katy and told her that her work was slipping, and she had to improve in her performance.

She knew it was time to leave because what she thought was a friendship with her supervisor was becoming trouble. With a feeling of uncertainly Kate called Kevin. "I'm coming home to Wyoming. I know what I need; I need you and the children. Tell Dad I was asking for him?"

Kevin remained silent on the phone until he realized what Katy said. "You're coming home? I'll fly out now."

"Kevin I asked how is your Dad?"

"He's better now. I'll come and get you? Angela can care for the kids."

"Kevin, I'm in California. I'll take a plane home in a few days. I have to give up my apartment, resign from the company, and tell my supervisor I'm leaving. It's my family I need, and they need me too."

"Please Katy, we'll fly out there. I can call Jim and visit him. we can have that vacation you've wanted. He told me the last time we talked to come out anytime. We've never been to California, there's plenty to see."

"That'll have to be another time. I have to finish here, and give them a two weeks notice. I'll see if I can leave in a day or two instead of staying two weeks. I'll call you when I'm coming back. Tell the children I'm coming home."

The following day Katy went to work and had a meeting with her supervisor. "Mr. Jenson, I'm giving you my resignation as of now. I'm very grateful for how you have treated me, and for the attention you've shown me.

I'm a married woman with children, and it's time for me to return home. I admit that your attention to me was very flattering. There were times I could have weakened and become involved. If I had a relationship with you, and sex became a part of it, as it usually does in these relationships, I could never have forgiven myself."

Mr. Jenson felt disappointed thinking Katy would relent, giving him the opportunity of a relationship. "I'm sorry Katy; I made a mistake thinking you were happy here, and in time we could be together."

"Recently you became too aggressive with me. Your help and kindness I'll always remember. I thought until then we were getting along fine. You were a good and true friend. The trouble with most men is they don't know how to be just a friend with a woman. They have the wrong ideas about the difference of a friendship or a relationship."

"I'm sorry Katy, and I apologize for my bad behavior the other night. You've filled a void in my life since my wife died. It's been three years, and I have fallen in love with you. I can give you anything you desire. You mentioned one night that you and your husband were having problems, and I thought maybe in time we would get married."

"Mr. Jenson you knew I had a husband and three children. I told you before we started going out it would be only a friendship we would have. You've been more than kind to me. I thank you for all you've done to make my life easier while I worked here."

Two weeks went by and Katy called. "Honey, I'm at the airport. Come and get me, and bring the kids." When the children saw Katy they raced down the aisle and were swept up into her arms. Kevin walked up to Katy, stopped and waited. Putting her son down and with the twins hugging her knees Katy fell into the waiting arms of Kevin. The tears flowed as water rushes over a dam. In between sobs and squeals of happiness from the children, the family had come together again. Arm in arm Kevin and Katy walked out of the airport, both speaking at the same time. "It's good to be back home."

"I'm so glad you're back. Katy, since you've been gone, my Dad has recovered and is able to do some things by himself. You won't have to worry about taking care of him. He's so happy that you are home."

On the way back to the ranch, they stopped at Mc Donald's for lunch having hamburgers, coke and ice cream. Traveling back to the ranch she knew that she and Kevin had to have a long discussion where their future was going. It had to do a ninety-degree turn around.

The children were growing up; Jonathon in high school and the twins in middle school. There were studies, sports, and school activities occupying the children's time. Dating was limited to weekends, as well as sleepover and dances. Weekends also became a begging time to go to the mall in the city, to spend their allowance if the chores were completed at home.

Making Plans

Growing up on the ranch, most of the days were spent learning about the land the children would own. They enjoyed horseback riding over the plains and climbing the mountains, swimming in the river. It was the out doors that they learned to enjoy the most. During the summer they would camp out by the river that flowed gently near the mountains. Life for the moment was good. It became a sad time when Kevin's Father suddenly passed away. Hundreds of people came to the funeral, as he was well known. He had given thousands of dollars to many small farmers to help them develop their land in the past when times were difficult. He had graduated from the local high school. In his memory they renamed the school the Jonathon Curtis.

One evening Katy asked Kevin "Isn't it almost time you started making plans for your reunion date with your friends Jim and Scott. You know this is the year 2000. You graduated in 1982 from Ohio University. That means if they are coming out here, you better get on with the preparations." Thinking back of those years, he was reminded how communication had diminished over the years with Jim and Scott.

Instead of monthly reminders it became a yearly one, if they remembered. Kevin wondered had their friendship fallen back to just a relationship?

He was sitting on the porch one evening enjoying the sunset when he heard Katy call. "Honey, didn't you hear the phone ringing? It's for you."

Going inside the ranch Katy handed him the phone. "Hello this is Kevin."

"Well you old dog, how are you? This is Scott; I just heard the news broadcast. There's a large fire out of control in Wyoming. Is it near you?"

"No, thank God! We're very fortunate, and thanks for thinking about us. By the way Scott, it's been eighteen years since we made a commitment we would meet in twenty years after graduation, remember?"

"I sure do. Now tell me Kevin, how is the family? Correct me if I am wrong. Do I remember a boy and twin girls, and of course there is Katy? I talked to Jim and he bragged about this daughter of his. I'm waiting to meet her and see if everything he says is true."

"I don't know about Jim. I haven't heard from him. How about you? Did you ever get married?

"No! I've had a few women in my life but no children. I'm planning to marry a wonderful girl. She's still in college and graduates next year

By the way Kevin, whatever happened to that girl from college you were smitten with? Wasn't her name Alice or something like that? What ever happened to her?"

"No." Quietly he mentioned her name with a choke in his voice. "Her name was Alicia, I never saw her after we left college." I went to the fifth reunion of our class but no one had heard from her. Allison said she had married someone."

"Kevin, are you still thinking about her after all these years? I can't believe you! She has to be married and have kids by this time."

"I contacted organizations that look for lost persons to no avail. Even her girlfriends I saw at a reunion had lost contact too." Thinking Kevin asked, "Scott maybe with your influence we can get some information that would help me locate her. That's on the Q.T."

"Kevin I don't believe it, you're still thinking of her? Silence is the word; no one will ever hear it from me. We're friends you know, bound to secrecy forever. What about Katy your wife? Does she know you're still trying to get in touch with her? I'll call Jim and Carolyn, Heather and Chante and let then know when the date is set. Any date is fine; The Senate is out of session now."

"Tell them to bring their family. I'll be in touch Scott."

"Was that your friend on the phone Kevin? Is he coming? Your other friend Jim is he coming too?"

"I hope they have some kids near the same age as the twins. Is he the Senator who is thinking about running for the Presidency in the next election?"

"Yes Katy that was Scott. He's the Senator from North Carolina. They're all bringing their wives or girl friends and any children they have. Also the girls that were at our last graduation party are coming."

With tongue in cheek Katy took a chance to ask, "Does that mean the girl you were in love with is coming? I know you said you were over her. It would be nice to meet this woman who impressed you so much. Maybe she's still single and you would be able to show off your beautiful teenage twin girls, your son and gorgeous wife too."

"She doesn't let it go" Kevin muttered under his breath. "No, she wasn't at the graduation party. No one has ever heard from her since." Wanting to change the subject, Kevin continued, "I'm hoping Scott can have some influence in stopping the poachers that are drilling for gas in our state; and prevent them taking away the rancher's farms that their grandparents homesteaded on. There is talk the government is going to allow the drilling here in Wyoming. We certainly don't need that. Let them get their oil from Alaska."

"I'll do what ever you wish to make it a good time. I know you have some great ideas sweetheart."

"It'll be a lot of work Katy, if everyone comes. Would you believe Jim wants to bring his plane here? This means we'll have to clear a runway for him.

Listen to this. Scott intends to marry a woman twenty years younger then himself. I thought for sure he would marry Chante, a student he was dating at college."

On impulse Kevin dialed Jim's number. "Hello Jim, this is Kevin. How are you? I just got a call from Scott and I'm starting to make the arrangements for our reunion in two years. Does it seem possible that eighteen years have gone by? Time sure does fly."

"Kevin, I haven't heard from you for a long time, wondering what happened to you. Is everything is okay?" "I'm fine and my family is too."

"Jim listen to this, Scott wants the plans all set this year. I hope you can stay at least three weeks. He said he has enough time to stay a month. I'll call you with a confirmed date. Would you believe he's engaged to marry some young college graduate? By the way we have plenty of room for you to land your plane. There are many things to do and see, so plan to stay as long as you want."

"I've talked to Scott occasionally and I can't believe he never married. I'm busy right now; I'm on my way to an appointment. Call me when you have the plans set."

After hanging up from Kevin, Jim dialed Scott's number. Scott you old dog, you're divorced?" I thought you and Carolyn were still married. Now, you're marrying some young college graduate? Are you nuts? She's just a kid; and she'll take you for everything. You can't tell me you're in love?"

"Jim I never married; had a couple of live in companions. Now I've found the most beautiful young woman I've ever seen. She's an intern in my office and we fell in love. Wait until you meet her!"

"Are you out of your mind? You'll be over forty, and she's half your age. They call it robbing the cradle; leave the young to the young. I'll bet you haven't met her parents yet. Well, good luck, I had my fun before I settled down. I now have a lovely wife and a beautiful daughter."

"Wait a minute. Did Kevin ever find out what happened to his girlfriend back in college? Wasn't her name Melissa?"

"No her name was Alicia. He married his high school sweetheart and they have three kids. He says he's happy and settled down just like you. I doubt that, because he asked me to help him locate her on the QT. I guess he doesn't want his wife to know."

"Jim, I have to make a call, I'll see you out there." Scott called Jasmine to tell her the news. "Jas, how would you like to go to Wyoming for a vacation with me? I told you how my friends and I agreed to meet in twenty years after our college graduation. The time is coming and it will be good to see the guys again. It will be interesting to see how much we have changed. It'll be a surprise when I tell them I am getting married. They'll say I'm robbing the cradle to marry you."

"I remember you telling me; it'll be great, then we can announce our engagement and make our wedding plans."

"Let's wait until after the vacation; you still have one year in college and your parents will need time to prepare for our wedding. You can still be my intern next year. I love you so much but patience dear, we'll be together. I promise you."

Communication increased between Jim, Scott and Kevin in the ensuing months as they discussed their plans for the year 2002. Jim continuing to move his business into the neighboring states, building more shopping malls, as he was able to convince the local political leaders of the benefit it will be in bringing more business into their communities.

Time Moves On

Karen had given up the thought of having a child of her own, and kept herself busy at the hospital, wishing Jim's Dad would relent on the adoption of a child. Her relationship with his Father had dulled, and they would only see each other on rare occasions.

Joyce returned to her job as the payroll manager in the company, telling Mr. Walker her sister had been in a horrible accident that left her crippled and not able to care for her young son. The sister's husband had left her right after the birth of the child, so Joyce brought the little boy with her as knowing young Jim's situation in wanting a child.

Maybe, she thought, Jim and Karen could adopt this little boy, but being afraid to suggest this, she decided to raise Eric herself. Her two sons were now seniors in high school, independent, and they both welcomed their cousin Eric as a brother.

Kevin was busy with the demands of the ranch as he continued to train horses, grow grain and fight the oil drillers from being able to get the government to let them start drilling. He spent many days with fellow ranchers in Washington, lobbying their Senators and Representatives to fight the establishment that was entrenched deeply in Congress. Katy and Kevin's love and devotion for each other became what it was when they first married. "Let's have another child Katy."

"Kevin, we've been down that road before. We have three healthy children and that's enough."

Seeing the doubt in her face, and ignoring her answer, he continued, "Why not Katy, we love kids, why not have more."

"Easy for you Kevin, you have one night of pleasure and I have one night of pleasure, plus nine months of getting fat."

Kevin persisted, "Come on Katy, just one more child." Katy told him she was moving into one of the guest rooms if he didn't stop pestering her. He realized that to pursue the subject would cause a deep rift in an already frail relationship; and accepted it when Katy said, "This is the end of any conversation about having more children."

The summer of 2001 had ended. Jasmine closed out her apartment, telling the owners she would not need it the next summer. She returned to college, and continued to see Scott as often as their schedules permitted.

Scott continued to travel the country, building relationships with the Mayors and Governors in their respective states. He needed their commitments if he was to be the next President.

The fall of 2000, and the spring of 2001 have disappeared. Having completed the necessary requirements for her junior year, Jasmine returned to Washington. This year Philip kept his distance from her, knowing he still had time to get his revenge for what had happened the year before. Each family kept busy. Kevin, Katy and the children in the operation of the ranch. Jim and Karen continued in their work. Scott traveling and laying ground work hoping he would be elected President.

One morning Suzy asked Jasmine if she would go to the cafeteria for a cup of coffee. As they sat at a table Suzy approached Jasmine with a question. "Jaz how about staying in Washington next summer and share my apartment? It's so slow at the office. We could have a great time traveling on weekends there is so much to see in this area."

"Suzy, I'd love it. I could fly home for a weekend once in awhile to visit my parents. I could see Scott when he's in town."

The summer of 2001 passed quickly. Philip still kept his distance from Jasmine. All the plea's, and begging for Scott to relent and announce their engagement fell on deaf ears. Jasmine had to be satisfied with a few weekends spent with him. Her intentions for this summer had to be put on the shelf.

She kept pressure on him, wanting him to change his mind about waiting to announce their engagement. Scott finally warned Jasmine to stop talking about it. Now was not the right time due to the pressure he was under.

In the fall Jasmine, went back to Indiana University for her senior year, renewing her friendship with classmates. At times she would put on her wedding ring, until she had a hard time explaining when someone saw her wearing it. Two of her close girlfriends at the college chided her "Stop kidding Jas, the ring is brand new. Who's the lucky guy? Did you get married this past summer?" Her different answers did not wash with them.

Jasmine longed for the times Scott would come and rent a motel in a small town. They would make love with a passion she hungered for. The weeks were long when he didn't come. A few times there were disagreements with Jasmine wanting to tell her parents. On one of his visits Scott became upset when he saw she had the wedding ring on. "What are you doing? Take the ring off and give it to me. I told you this has to be our secret for now."

She had never seen Scott so demanding. Pleading with tears in her eyes, "I won't do it again, just let me keep it."

"Okay, remember, not until the time is ready. I thought I made it clear. We can't let anyone know about us now. We'll have time to announce it after our engagement and marriage dates are set."

The fall of 2001 and the winter of 2002 passed quickly. Spring came early, with the flowers coming into bloom. Trees, except in the high elevations, brought forth leaves in different shades of green. The mountains still held tightly to the snow, giving skiers one last time to fly down the slopes, before the sun turned the snow into water. Baseball was returning to their respective cities to start their seasons.

The children were growing up fast; the twins now into the teenage experiences and Jonathon's graduation from high school in 2002. He turned nineteen, looking forward to college in the fall. He saw it as freedom away from the heavy workload of the ranch. Spending so much time there left no opportunity for a social life. The twin girls Kaylee and Kabee enjoyed school, and being members of the 4 H club.

As identical twins; at times they fooled the kids at school; also the teachers wondered if they were talking to the right one. Boys became an interesting challenge to them. Dates, and what transpired on them, became times of laughter as they shared them with each other. Katy talked with the twins, warning them of what could happen at times on dates. This was met with, "We know about that."

"Be careful, we worry about you when you're on dates." Kevin said one day after the girls asked permission to attend a local teenage dance.

When they disappeared Katy asked, "Kevin have you ever talked to Jonathon about life away from home? What it means to be on your own. Have you ever talked to him about the facts of life?"

"Of course I have, a long time ago. I had a conversation about sex with Jonathon. We discussed the three D's. I told him about the danger of dating, drinking and drugs as well as sex. He sure was innocent about the facts of life. Soon he'll be going on his own. I told him we have to learn to trust him, and hope he'll stick to his studies and stay out of trouble.

Did you talk to the twins about this?"

"Sometimes Kevin I have to wonder about you. Of course I told the girls about life. They know more about life than I ever knew at their age. I just hope they'll fit in with the people that are coming. You know they will be the youngest here. I don't want them to become bored."

Jasmine's Graduation

Mean while back in Washington. "Scott, I want you to come to my graduation. It's important to me."

"Honey I can't. They're sending me to China with the Secretary of State to help with the negotiations between Taiwan and the Mainland of China. I don't know if I can get back in time. I know it's an important day in both of our lives. I don't want to meet your parents until we can tell them our plans. The shock will be enough when they realize the difference in age. They'll try to persuade you not to marry me."

"Here's a ticket to come if you get back in time. I gave Suzy a ticket too. It would mean so much to me. Please come and share this with me."

The Conference with the Chinese government went along with no accomplishments in easing the tension between them and Taiwan. Scott flew back hoping to be on time and asked Suzy if she would fly with him to Jasmine's graduation?

It was the month of May 2002, graduation time and it would start at one in the afternoon. A young news reporter from the Washington Post noticed Senator Drew standing behind the stands in the field.

"Hello Senator, I thought you were in Taiwan. Do you have someone graduating here? I could take a picture of the two of you and put it in the paper. Good publicity never hurts. With you running for the Presidency no exposure is too much. By the way, I saw Philip from your office today."

"No I'm sorry, no photos today. Maybe if circumstances were different I would. I have someone else to meet while I'm here. You'll have to excuse me."

"Wait a minute Senator, there's Philip? Look he's over there." Noting the surprised look on the Senators face, he waited for an answer.

Glancing to where the reporter was pointing, he answered, "Yes it is." Forgetting for a moment Scott said, "What the devil is he doing here? This guy is a leech, always around when you don't want him. Showing up like some of the news media."

Scott realizing what he had said apologized for the outburst. "Sorry young man I didn't mean to say that." He was upset at seeing Philip, wanting to ask him why he wasn't back in Washington. Holding back his anger he thought, "How could he know that Jasmine was graduating at the University of Indiana today?"

"Hello Philip, I'm surprised to see you. I thought you would be in Washington minding the store. Do you know someone graduating from here?"

Philip countered with a question, "When did you arrive back from China? "I thought you were still over there."

Ignoring the Senators questions, Philip answered with a grin like the cat that had just swallowed the canary. Sarcastically he continued, "I'm sure she'll be happy to see you. Have you seen her yet?"

Before Philip could say any more, Scott turned to the reporter and said, "Excuse us young man, we have something to discuss in private."

Knowing you don't refuse one of the most powerful men in the Senate, he sensed there is a story here. The reporter walked away in frustration, staying close enough to see that Senator Drew was disturbed to see Philip here. "Something is going on between the two of them," he thought. "I can hear the anger in the Senator's voce. I think I'll stick around for awhile."

"Senator Drew, you came to see Jasmine graduate. You're one of the lucky ones to have a ticket for the celebration tonight. I over heard the women talking in the office. Jasmine said when she was leaving, and sorry not having enough tickets for everyone to attend the graduation. I thought I might be able to get a ticket here at the college."

"Philip," Scott replied, faking surprise and with as much sarcasm he could muster, "I'm not staying, I have to go back to Washington. Just so you know, I had a few hours to come and to wish her success and happiness today."

"Seeing you aren't staying, could I have your ticket for the celebration tonight?" Philip replied with hope and a plea. "I'll tell her that you called and were still in China. I'm sure she would be happy to see a few of us here from the office."

"Philip you know Suzy doesn't like you, so why should she be happy to see you? She and Jasmine became very good friends last summer while working together.

Suzy will have a good time with Jasmine and her friends here at the college." Pausing for a moment enjoying the look of disappointment on Philip's face, and then sarcastically continued, "You know they're near the same age. I'm sure Jasmine will introduce her to some of her male friends she has here."

Satisfaction welled within Scott, as he knew he'd put another one over on Philip. Jasmine had told him how Philip attempted to take her out, after being warned to have hands off from trying to date her. Still upset, "I'll have to fire him; he's been a thorn in my side." He thought. "Every time I tried to have a relationship with different interns, he would make it difficult. He can't prove anything, so why worry."

The young reporter listened intently hoping that one of them would slip and say something that would erupt into a full scale argument, giving him a great story, but his hopes were dashed when Scott said, "Goodbye Philip, see you in

Washington tomorrow. Remember we have a lot of work to cover, as I start to make my run for the Presidency. If you want to be with me when I'm elected you'll have to buckle down. No play time, only work, right?" Not waiting for an answer, Scott turned and walked away.

After Scott was gone the young reporter turned to Philip and asked, "What did you do to aggravate him?"

His face flushed, Philip started to think, "How can I get this guy? If only I could get one of the former interns to admit he had an affair with them.

Thinking of Ginger, the one who had an abortion, "I could tell how he gave her fifty thousand dollars to have it. That will smear his reputation, he'll be unable to run for the Presidency; and be forced to resign. Then I'll be able to develop my relationships with some of the new interns that will be coming. How I hate him."

Scott knew that to out maneuver Philip was impossible. To see Jasmine for a moment before the graduation exercise began would be futile. He was trying to think how he could fool Philip. "He won't leave. He'll hang around waiting to tell her I was here." Finding a phone in the field house, he called hoping she would be in her room. "Hello is Jasmine there?"

"One minute, I'll get her. Jasmine you have a call."

"Hello, who is this?" Thinking it sounds like Scott but it can't be, he's in China."

"Hi sweetheart, I thought I could wait and see you before I have to leave, but that damn Philip is here, and a reporter is hanging around asking questions. "I'm in the field house by the basketball court using a phone in the hallway.

Don't let Philip see you. I kept him busy with the reporter. He loves the limelight boasting about his knowledge of Washington and the scandals in it. You'll have to hurry.

The reporter is aware of something going on, and he'll stick around I'm sure."

Slipping into jeans and a light sweater, Jasmine ran over to the field house, opened the door and called, "Scott where are you?"

Running down the corridor and turning a corner, she threw herself into his arms almost knocking him over.

"Sweetheart, I had to come and see you today on your graduation. I was surprised to see Philip here. He tried to get me to give him my ticket for the graduation ceremonies. Suzy will be here to see you graduate."

"Thank you Scott, I gave one to Helen, I hope she can make it. I would like them to come and meet my parents. Why can't you stay and meet them?"

"I should be in Boston now for a rally tonight. There will be other times when I'll be able to."

"Can't you stay just long enough to see me graduate?"

"I really can't stay sweetheart. I told you before, I have commitments."

They sat on one of the benches with Jasmine's sitting on Scotts lap, holding each other tightly and kissing until they heard the door open from the far end of the court. Hiding their faces they heard a strange voice. "Excuse me; there will some guys coming to play basketball. You can stay."

Relieved it wasn't Philip, but embarrassed, they got up quickly and left. Going outside the field house Scott turned to Jasmine, "I have to go now. I wish I could stay. Call me at my office, maybe we can get together the next day."

With tears in her eyes, Jasmine held Scott tightly. "I do love you darling." He gave her a kiss, then left.

She stood still, her eyes brimming with tears; wanting to run after him, but felt riveted to the floor. "Why does he always have to run. He said it wouldn't be easy."

Opening the door, he looked out, and seeing no one there, he headed to his car in the parking lot. Suddenly he heard a voice calling him. Looking around he saw Philip and the young reporter waving. "Wait a minute." Philip called, as the two of them started to run toward him. "Senator, wait!"

He knew this would delay him in getting back and not wanting to get involved he answered. "Sorry men, I just don't have the time to talk now. Some other time you can meet me and discuss whatever you'd like." With a wave of the hand Scott drove quickly from the parking lot.

They realized they couldn't catch him, so Philip and the reporter stopped running. "Okay, you've told me about what goes on in Washington, but no names. Are you making all this stuff up? By the way, who's graduating that you came to see; a relative, or someone the Senator knows?"

Grinning, Phillip responded, "Everything I've told you is true, but I can't betray the people involved."

"Who's paying you off? You've worked for Senator Drew for a long time; what have you got on him?"

"You'll find out some day, but not now." Philip walked away, continuing to try to see Jasmine and some how get a ticket. Going to the Presidents office he told them he was representing Senator Drew.

"The Senator had forgotten to give me his ticket. When I called him he suggested I go to the Presidents office and was sure you would give me one."

"I'm sorry there are no more available," Trying to influence the secretary with different names well know in the country was fruitless. Tiring of his insistence to get a ticket, she called the security, and he was told to leave. Out side of the building he saw Suzy and tried to talk her into giving him her ticket. The reporter was surprised when he saw her suddenly push Philip, knocking him down.

Watching him trying to get up was embarrassing. She was holding him down, her foot on his body glaring at him in disgust. After a few moments she removed her foot and walked away; slapping her hands together with a look of satisfaction on her face.

The reporter summarized there is more to this, as he ran over to Philip, assisting him in getting up from the ground. "Who is she, do you know her? Philip, come on! She pushed you down; it was obvious. Was she one of the Senators secretaries that work in his office? I've heard stories about what goes on in Washington. You must have tried to make out with her."

"I never tried to make out with any intern, like I told you, it was just a misunderstanding we had. She accused me of saying something about the Senator and it wasn't true."

Reunion Time

It was the end of May 2002; Kevin called Jim to tell him the date was set. "Don't forget to tell your daughter and her boyfriend they're welcome to come, and your Dad too.

I remember the stories you told me about him. I'm looking forward to meeting him and your wife Karen. Tell me Jim, how did she ever get you to settle down? You don't have to bring anything except yourself and the family." Saying goodbye, he called Scott.

"Scott, Our date is June 30th and everything is set. Like I told Jim, it's our treat, don't bring a thing, only you and the girlfriend. Remember to notify Carolyn. She gave me a kiss twenty years ago and said I could return it when she gets here. Maybe I'll kid Katy, tell her she's the one I had told her about, my long lost college sweetheart. No, on second thought, I better not. Let sleeping dogs lie. Time will tell."

"I hope Chante and Heather will come. Those two were the hottest things on the campus. You lost out when Heather wanted to make it with you. I think they were more of a tease, not really wanting to get involved. You were so much in love with Alicia that was her name wasn't it?"

With as much bravado as he could, Kevin replied, "That was a long time ago. I've forgotten her now. I've too many years invested here. I have a beautiful wife Katy, a son Jonathon and twin daughters Kaylee and Kay bee."

"Not by the sound of your voice. You still think of her at times, don't you?" There was no reply. "I still remember you and Jim almost got into a fight when he teased you."

"Okay Scott, enough of this. I hope everyone will be able to come and share this time together. I'm looking forward to seeing you."

Hanging up the phone, Scott called Carolyn. "Hello Carolyn, I just had a call from Kevin our reunion date is set for June 30th. I hope you will come and bring a boyfriend."

"Scott, can I bring a small boy I've been taking care of? His grandmother could not keep him any longer, and he's been like a son to me. My sister took him for a while, and then when she decided to get married and move away from North Carolina I volunteered to raise him until he could be adopted; or until they find his Father. I heard that he was an incest child, but who knows if that's true or not. He's a beautiful boy and I love him."

"Of course you can. Kevin said bring whomever you want. By the way, how are you? You're the type of woman who wants to have children. I'm glad we never had any kids when we were living together."

"Scott you know I wanted to marry you. I tried twice with you, the third time you totally rejected me. It took me awhile before I realized you were using me for your selfish needs. I failed, so now I've moved on, never to fall in that trap again."

"Come on, we had a good time together. It didn't work out"I fell in love with a wonderful angel, and we'll be married in the near future."

"I hope the beautiful girl I met in your office, will still love you when you're sixty and settled down. Looking at her she will still look great at forty, and you at sixty will look like an old man. She'll still have the eyes of the young men following her, and seeing you as her father."

Carolyn I'm sorry it didn't work out with us. I feel bad you think I used you. That's not true. I loved you then, and I still love you, but not the way you wanted that would make a good lasting marriage. It was our sex life that held us together"

"Thanks for the compliment; what makes you think you were so great? Your new girlfriend will be disappointed with you. I should have made a move on Kevin twenty years ago when I had the chance. The night he took me back to my Mother's apartment, we kissed with a passion we both wanted. That night I made a mistake, not taking advantage of the opportunity. Next time I meet someone special, he'll make the first move. Now that's enough of the past mistakes. I'd like you to send me the information when we are going."

Jasmine called her Mother to tell her she wouldn't be home this year. "I have a job at the Smithsonian Institute for the summer months. My friend's Dad is the Curator, and my boyfriend is taking me to Wyoming for a vacation in June."

"Sometime I hope to meet him. I hope he is everything you say."

"Mother, he's handsome, has a great job, makes lots of money and he loves me so much. We have a surprise for you and Dad."

I want to ask, but I won't. I'm sure we'll be surprised."

"Please don't pressure me to tell you. You'll meet him, just be patient. Bye for now, I love you. Oh yes, before I say goodbye. I'm not pregnant if that was your question."

Out in California Karen approached Jim; she was nervous with what she had to tell him. "I'm sorry, I can't leave with you tomorrow, the hospital wants me to stay for another week; there is a shortage of nurses during the summer. I've made arrangement to fly on July 9th. Take my suitcases with you and pick me up at the airport. Remember to have your flight schedule called in before you leave."

"Karen, I'm disappointed, we've planned this for years. I've been flying for years now; I've never missed one flight schedule. I just wish you were going out with me. You know honey; it seems that we are drifting apart again. We can't have a child of our own, and you don't want to try anymore. Let's adopt one anyway, ignore my Father. Tiffany wants her own life, and deserves it. She has a boyfriend and it seems like she wants to get married, settle down and raise a family from what she says. I guess he must be thirty years old, I was really hoping she would have a career first."

Back in Wyoming Kevin turned to his son, "Jonathan, my friend's daughter is bringing her boyfriend and a girlfriend out for the reunion. I hope you'll be available to share some time with them. Take them riding and show them how great this place is with the wide open range, mountains, and hopefully see some wild horses."

"Dad, maybe the three of you men could go camping for a few days. It's something they've never done. Seeing as they are big city people, you could show them what country living is like. Can I go along with you because it'll be all women here?"

"Son, did you hear what I said? There'll be my friend's daughter, and she's bringing one of her girlfriends. Her boyfriend will be coming later. These next weeks are yours to enjoy. I have enough hands to cover for you. I'll miss you as you leave for college in the fall. Kaylee, Kaybee you must be available to help. Our cowboys and their wives are doing the cooking, serving and cleaning up for all the meals. You'll continue to feed and handle your own horse; check with your Mother if she needs help."

Waiting patiently, knowing that Jim would arrive today, everyone at the corral stopped what they were doing, when they heard the sound of a plane coming over the horizon from the west. "Look Dad," the twins yelled. "There's the plane now." Everyone started to wave as Jim waggled the wings and came in for a perfect landing. Kevin out distanced them all as they ran toward the plane. When Jim exited, he saw Kevin and waved to him. Jumping down, he ran to Kevin giving him a bear hug.

"Let go man, you're crushing me to death!" Releasing his grip, he placed him back down on the ground as Kevin tried to pry himself loose.

Standing with his arm around Kevin's shoulder Jim asked, "Well, are you going to introduce me to all these people here?"

Struggling to catch his breath said, "Jim, this is Katy my wife, our son Jonathon and the twins, Kaylee and Kaybee. The rest are those who help me operate the ranch.

You'll get to know them as the weeks go by. Family, this is my best friend Jim."

"Karen will be here in a couple of days. Every time we plan to go some place, something screws it up. My daughter Tiffany will be here in a few days."

Walking back to the ranch Kevin's cell phone rang "Hello Kevin, Scott here. I'll be there tomorrow and should arrive about eleven in the morning. Has my girlfriend Jasmine and her friend arrived yet? Should I rent a car?"

"No and no. Jim just arrived and we'll pick you up at the airport. I'm sure Jasmine will be here any day now. What flight number are you coming in on?

"Yes, she's coming. I hope nothing's wrong. She told me she and her friend would get there before me. I'm coming on American Airlines flight 1922. Arrival time is 11:00 am."

The next morning Jim let Jonathon take all the children into the plane with strict orders not to touch any instruments on the panel in the pilot's cabin." Just be careful, I'd hate to see my plane flying off with the kids inside."

Kevin called the airport to check if Scott's plane was on schedule. Hearing it was they left early, stopping at a local coffee shop for breakfast. Kevin introduced Jim to some of his ranch neighbors who were there.

At the airport they saw Scott waiting for his luggage. Quietly coming up from behind him they picked him up swinging him around as he fought to get free. "Enough you guys, I'm a Senator of the United States you're fooling with. I can have you arrested for assault." With a firm handshake and a wrap around from Jim and Kevin, they let him go. "Twenty years! A lot of water has gone over the dam since we have seen each other. You two guys sure have changed, what happened to those young studs I once knew?"

"You don't look so hot either Scott. Take you out of that business suit, and you'll look forty-three too, or do you still lie to the young teenage girls that work as interns in Washington. Where's your girl friend?" Jim replied.

"She'll be here soon. You wonder what Mother had the privilege to bring such a beautiful young woman into this world. "Wait until she arrives, you'll be dazzled by her beauty; she is truly one of a kind that God makes in a century. I haven't met her Mother, but I'll tell you this young woman is the one who keeps me young."

"What is she, a statue?" Jim asked. "Her Mother must be as beautiful."

"Come on Jim, we can see Scott's in love. Wake him up; the family is waiting for us."

Back at the ranch Scott asked Kevin, "Where are you going to put everybody?"

Laughing Jim responded, "Kevin has tents all set up to sleep in, and we're going to cook all our meals outside."

"He's kidding you Scott. Look over at that large building to the right. Dad built it many years ago when he took over the operation of the land. He built it to accommodate the men and women he needed in operating the business. Let's walk over and I'll show you the small cottages he built for those who were married and had children. He paid them well, never had a problem with the men he hired."

"In the big bunk house, there are eight single rooms with some double beds, some others have twin beds. There are about four bathrooms and showers, a large kitchen and a large living room with a big TV. Some of the men were married but had no children. Their wives shared the kitchen responsibilities and the cleaning of the place."

"Sounds like a motel. Your Dad must have been a genius. He left you with no problems in taking over the ranch. I wish I had men working for me like him. I'd say he passed his work ethics to his son."

"In reality they aren't employees but a part of our family. That's the way he treated them. Yes, you're right Jim; he was one of a kind. He sometimes had the solution before he had the problem. We lost him a few years ago. I miss him. He suffered with cancer, but never complained. He worked too hard, and never had a real social life. My Mother left with my two younger sisters as soon as I went to college. She came from the East and never cared for this place. It took my Dad a long time to get over losing her."

"I know the feeling," said Scott. My Father was never home. When he was a Representative in Congress I would never see him.

When he became a Senator he rarely came home." He was traveling all the time. My Mother died when I was in high school. When I heard of all the places he went to, the famous people he met, and the places he visited; I decided politics was what I wanted for my life."

"Well my life's story is construction, Jim said. "I love it. My Dad and I have learned to share our good fortune, by giving much of what we have to charity. I knew as a little kid, I would end up in the construction business. The reason, that's where the money is, and I was right. I'm fortunate to have been so successful. I thank my Grandfather and Dad for my good success. I see many of my business friends living in mansions, and expensive cars that sit in their garages. They forget it is the people that work for them that have given them the success they enjoy today."

"Look guys, why don't we go to town for the evening. This is the one time we can celebrate, just us three. Kevin, you ask Katy if that's okay. We want to keep peace at the ranch. It's just for the evening. I vote that you do the driving Kev, because you know the territory out here."

"I'll try." With some apprehension, Kevin approached Katy in the kitchen. "Honey, the guys thought it would be a good idea if we went out tonight. A private party just us three. A mini celebration like we did the night before we left. College. Any objections?"

"No, that's okay, but only this one time, and be sure you come back at a decent hour. The other women will be coming, and you'll have to be ready to welcome them. Please don't over do it. Have fun, sweetheart, I love you."

Jim and Scott were waiting on the porch when Kevin told them, "Katy gave us her blessing, but don't over do it, were her exact words."

After the evening meal they took off for the city. At one of the nightclubs they sat at a table ordering their first drink, and watched the different people dancing. Looking around Jim saw a table of three young women and no men, inspiring him to asked one of them for a dance. When they finished he invited the other two women to join them at their table. With only four chairs the waitress moved them to a table that seated six. "Just like twenty years ago; and three beautiful women to help us celebrate." Scott said as he ordered for the six of them.

Enjoying their drinks Kevin was surprised when he heard a strange voice, "Well guess who's here! Kevin, what are you doing here? Remember me; Don Sheridan. I played baseball with you back in high school. I'm the one who hated you because Katy was your girl. I heard you married her and have three kids. I see you met my girls; how's everything?"

"Just great Mr. Sheridan; we just met these three fine gentlemen, and we're going to show them the best time of their lives tonight."

"I told Katy we wouldn't stay too late; we have other guests coming tomorrow and I have to be there."

"Look Kevin by the time you leave here it'll be too late to drive back to your place. I own a motel in the city and have some empty rooms; you can stay here for the night."

A Repeat

"Have breakfast with me in the morning before you head back. Call the wife and let me talk to her."

After pressure from Don, Jim and Scott, Kevin called Katy. "Hi honey, the guys out voted me and decided to stay at Don's for the night. I'll do my best to convince them not to stay, is that okay? Just a minute honey, someone here wants to say hello."

"Tell me Kevin, who is it? I understand but I'd rather you come home tonight. If it's who I think it is, be careful, I heard he also has call girls available."

"You remember Don Sheridan? He owns a motel here in town and he said we could stay there for the night. Don't worry sweetheart, we'll be okay. Here's Don."

By the time the club closed, Scott and Jim were in no condition to go back that night. Kevin called Katy again.

"I tried to convince Jim and Scott to come back to the ranch, but they really had too much to drink, and I'm dead tired honey. I promise we'll be home early tomorrow."

At the motel Don greeted them at the door, and gave them a quick tour of his place. Finishing, he gave each of them a key to their rooms. Walking down the corridor Kevin opened his door and snapped on the light. "Well, look who's here!" There in the bed was one of the girls that had shared the evening with them. "What gives? You must be in the wrong room. Are you a prostitute?"

"No, Don has a dating service. We pay our way through college by working here. If a gentleman wants to have more then a date, we decide whether to stay or not. If you don't want to that's okay. I live here and work for Don. It's too late to get another room because the motel is closed now and all the rooms are locked. I'll sleep on the couch, you can have the bed."

"That son of a, sorry; I didn't mean that. This is a poor excuse for you to earn a living; Don is hoping to get something on us. How can a nice young woman like you do this? Are you sure you can't get another room?"

Because of the heavy drinking, being tired and with a heavy head, Kevin undressed and laid down, not realizing she was still there. His head hurting and aching he fell off to sleep. Reaching down to touch him as he slept, she looked at his tanned handsome face. With heavy breathing sounds coming from Kevin, she pulled away.

Her impulse became one of thinking. "He wouldn't be like others. He would be one that would have sex and loving you at the same time. Not doing it for selfish gratification."

Deciding to try to kiss him she leaned over Kevin placing her lips on his chest lightly kissing and touching him. Moving ever so slowly feeling his body reacting to hers'. He put his arms around her responding quickly. "Katy, I love you."

As she moved away he opened his eyes, to see her face looking at him as she bent to kiss him again.

Pushing her away he leaped up from the bed. "Who are you? You're not Katy, Where am I?" Waking up slowly, and the feeling in his body he realized what happened. "I swore I would never betray Katy again. God, I've failed! If you tell Don my marriage is finished."

"Don't worry; I shouldn't have taken advantage of you. I won't tell. Your Katy is lucky to have you. If you were single I would have you in a minute." Kevin offered her one hundred dollars, but she refused, so he left it on the table.

"I'm leaving this life style after I finish college. Take your money, please. I'm sure there are nice guys still out there like you. Go home to your wife and children; tell them how much you love them."

"If Katy finds out I'll lose my kids, and it'll be the end of every thing I've worked for. How could I ever forget that Don Sheridan is nothing but a scum? Katy warned me when I called her. He would do anything to get her away from me. Why am I telling you this?"

"You'll feel guilty for awhile; just think of this as a learning experience, never to be repeated. My name is Margie. I promise, Don will never know."

Leaving the room he knocked on the next door. "Wait a minute." The door opened and Scott unshaven, with bloodshot eyes greeted him. "Your friend Don really sucked us in. I paid this girl two hundred bucks for a little sex. After we finished she took off. By the time I got dressed she had disappeared. The guy at the desk told me he didn't see anyone leaving. This is nothing but a glorified whore house."

Have you seen Jim?"

"No, he's most likely still sleeping. Let's go down to his room to see if he's still there. You know he had a lot to drink last night, and who knows what's happened to him"

Going to Jim's room Kevin knocked on the door. With no answer he opened it and there was a girl holding Jim's pants, taking his wallet and removing money from it. "What are you doing?"

"I'm taking the money he owes me for spending the night with him. He got what he wanted. I had a hard time dealing with him. He was just like an animal"

Inside the shower they saw Jim slumped on the floor. Turning the water off Kevin said, "Come on Jim, the party's over." Together they put him in a chair trying to wake him.

The girl was gone and Jim's pants and wallet were on the bed. Scott looked into it and found the money was missing. Looking down the hallway it was empty. Back in Jim's room

Scott had finally revived him. "Jim, she took all your money. I went down to the front office and the clerk said no one had left the motel. I think this is a scam. The girls and Don are in it together."

Slowly coming to Jim asked, "Where is that little bitch? After we had sex she gave me something to drink, I guess I passed out. My wallet's empty? I still had a thousand dollars in hundreds after I paid the bill at the nightclub."

Just as Jim said that, Don came into the room. "How was your night guy? They're quite the girls. They know how to satisfy, and you don't have to worry about anything."

"Don, this place is nothing but a whore house. We got taken. Two hundred dollars from Scott, and Jim had one thousand dollars stolen from his wallet. The girl and I did nothing. I wanted to give her some money but she refused. Now you either pay my friends back, or I'll get you closed down. Don't try me."

Jim now in focus but his eyes not clear, grabbed Don by the throat. At six feet six inches tall he picked Don right off the floor. "Listen buddy, either you return our money or I'll wreck this joint, then tell the police what kind of a place you're running. When everything is settled, this will be just between you and me. Do you hear me?"

"Okay, big guy, I don't want any trouble. I'll give you your money. Don't mess up the place."

Kevin called Katy as they were leaving the motel, telling her they would have their breakfast and then head straight back to the ranch. Driving to the nearest town they stopped at a local restaurant. The conversation was nil, each of them felt guilty for what had happened and betraying of the women they loved.

"Guys, I feel sick about what we did last night. Now after twenty years, falling into the same situation we did twenty years ago. How do we tell our wives? "It's easier for you Scott; you aren't married and have kids."

"Look! It was wrong what we did. Let's just try to forget this happened. "We'll just keep this episode between us. "Come on Kevin, I'm next to being married. Jasmine means everything to me. She told me as long as I am faithful to her, she didn't want to hear about the past. Let's just put last night out of our minds, promising we'll never do it again."

"Easy for you Jim, you'll go back to California, Scott you to Washington. I'll still live here and sweat it out that Don will keep his mouth shout."

"Remind him once in awhile what I said, and what I would do to him and his business. He won't open his mouth you can bet on that." Jim replied.

When they arrived home Katy said, "Whatever you three did last night, I don't want to hear any excuses. Let's see it as a learning experience and let it go, okay? By the way Kevin, you had a call from Carolyn, she'll be at the airport at three this afternoon. She would like to have Scott come alone. She has somebody and wants to surprise him."

"I'll tell him Katy. I'll make him sweat it for awhile, and wonder; a husband, boyfriend, maybe a baby."

Wanting to kid Scott, Kevin called him off to the side. "You have to pick up Carolyn at the airport, alone. She has a surprise for you. Could it be a husband or a baby?"

"No, she never got pregnant to my knowledge. We were careful about that. We haven't been together for a year. So if she brings a kid, you can be sure it isn't mine."

Jim joining in the conversation, "Scott if a woman wants a baby and you lived with her, it will happen. It's people like Karen and me.

Guests Arrive

We want a baby, but Karen can't conceive. We have tried and tried. Her daughter Tiffany is my child. I adopted her legally. We could adopt a little boy, but my Father says, no child not of his blood will ever manage our company. He might condescend in time to let my daughter."

"I have no concern; I know Carolyn has no child by me. Be assured it didn't happen. We have been on swords end lately, and our communication isn't the best. We tried to make a go of it but we failed in time. We just didn't meld."

It was three fifteen when Scott arrived at the airport; he was late, knowing Carolyn would be upset. After parking the car and getting to the arrival area, he saw a small boy holding her hand. "Oh no," he muttered. "She has a kid."

As Scott approached the youngster looked at him, trying to hide. "Hello Carolyn, sorry I'm late. The traffic was heavy, and I had a hard time finding a parking space."

Trying to make conversation he looked at the little boy with a smile; "Hi son, what's your name?"

With no response from the boy, Carolyn said, "Tell him your name son."

"My name is Robbie. Are you my Daddy?"

With a broad grin she answered, "Scott, you called him son. Would you like him to call you Daddy?"

Carolyn and Robbie

"Only a figure of speech, don't be wise. Who is he?"

"Could be your son, you never know."

"Look, I warned you to be careful; we talked about not having any children that would interfere with our careers when we lived together. Now look what's happened."

"Oh, look what's happened. You're concerned that maybe he's yours. You remember all those times we had together Scott. I told you who he was when I adopted him. Well guess, was I lying? Is he yours? Figure it out for yourself. He has the same color eyes and hair as yours. One night while you were making a speech on TV He asked, "Is that man my Daddy, Mummy? Maybe I told him yes."

"You're trying to get even with me, because I changed my mind about living with you. I'll get a DNA test taken to prove he isn't mine."

"Go ahead; your new girlfriend will be surprised if she finds out he's yours." Tiring of the banter Carolyn finally said, "Okay enough. I'd like to go to the ranch now, Robby's tired. Let's not spoil this vacation. Knowing you, maybe somewhere there is a child who can call you Daddy."

"Okay a truce while we're here. If we continue to argue it will spoil all the plans that Kevin and Katy have made. Let's enjoy the time out here. There is a lot to see. Kevin has told me there are many things to do in the area."

At the ranch Kaylee and Kaybee immediately took charge of Carolyn's boy by taking him to see the horses. With hugs and kisses between Carolyn, Jim and Kevin and the introduction of Carolyn to Katy; for a moment things were quite hectic. "Wait a minute, those were welcoming kisses. Now I want to collect back from Kevin the kiss I gave him when we said good bye twenty years ago." Wrapping his arms around Carolyn, he kissed her.

Laughing, Katy said, "Kevin, I'm going to tell your friends to take you out more often. Last night you were out all night and didn't come home until this morning. Did he have some strippers there?" Kevin remained very quiet, embarrassed as he thought back to last night's episode. Kaylee nudged her sister, "Kaybee did you see Dad kissing Robbie's Mother. I didn't know old people still kissed like that. Wow! If Dad kissed Mum like that, we would have another brother or sister."

When they're alone in their bed, I'll bet that's the way they kiss."

"I wouldn't let any boy kiss me like that."

"I saw you kissing Aaron behind the barn when Mom and Dad had the Robbins come to visit us."

"I did not. I never let Aaron kiss me ever."

"Yes you did." After he kissed you behind the barn you went inside up to the loft and I heard you saying, "Stop it Aaron, don't do that."

"I tried it. It was lousy. I'll never kiss a boy ever again! I wonder why they kiss so long Kaybee. I didn't like it the way Aaron kissed me."

"Yes you will, I kiss Jamie and we kind of make out a little bit."

"You mean you had sex with him? You better never let Mum and Dad know."

"No we didn't. He tried to and I told him I would scream if he didn't stop; so he climbed down the ladder and went home. He's never come back."

"You know what Mother told us, if we got pregnant we have to take care of the baby, and the kids at school would tease me. I don't want to have a baby now. I'd be stuck in the house and lose all my friends."

"The only problems all the people here will have a good time and we'll have to take care of Robbie. We should ask Dad if we can have some of our friends over too."

Later Kevin suggested to Jim and Scott the three of them go on a camping trip. Looking at Jonathon's face of frustration he said, "Sorry Jon, we'll have another over night camping trip sometime, then you can come." Jonathon was disappointed hoping he would still be able to go. "No Son; not this time! We want to spend some time alone."

Disappointed, Jon took Robby and gave him rides, allowing him to handle the reins on his favorite horse.

Sharing Time

Talking to his Mother Jonathon said, "He still treats me like a kid. I can do anything he does here on the ranch, in fact I do some thing's better."

"Son your day will come. This is a once in a lifetime for your Dad. Be patient. It's only for a month or so and then everyone will be gone. Remember there are younger people coming."

Before the over night trip, Jim and Scott took a few days getting used to riding a horse. The cowboys and Kevin had many laughs, as they would provoke the horses resulting in the riders being thrown off. Jim and Scott were good-natured, and finally mastered the reins in directing the horses.

"Be careful guys, enjoy your camping trip. Please Kevin, no longer than four days." They started off riding leisurely for a while, marveling at the vastness of the lands and the mountains. Jim and Scott kept asking Kevin questions about why he enjoys such a quiet life style.

Kevin would try to explain what it meant to him, about the beauty, and virginity of his place, the friendliness of his neighbors. It seemed to fall on deaf ears. "You have to live here to understand the changes that occur in the weather, and any other obstacle that comes your way. You have to fight and work hard to overcome the adversities and enjoy the many peaceful days. It's a constant challenge, but what a satisfaction when you succeed."

"Look There's a herd of wild horses, stallions and mares. Isn't that a beautiful sight?" Scott called.

"No wonder, they're nervous. The two horses you are riding we captured last year."

As they started to turn to go in another direction they were met with opposition. The horses sensed that something was amiss. Pulling with all their strength the horses bucked and ceased to obey. "Stop for a minute and let the horses relax. They'll be okay once this herd is out of sight."

"Come on Kevin, what's wrong with them?"

"Jim it takes time to have them forget where they came from. These are a part of their family and we separated them from the herd. In time they'll be okay."

"Look at the mountains instead. You can see for miles out here on the prairie, untouched by man." After riding for a long time, Kevin said, "It'll be getting dark soon. I suggest we go to the group of trees where the river runs right by them. We can stay for the night and have a fire to cook our steaks. Later we can sleep under the stars."

Taking the horses down to the river for a drink of water, gave Scott and Jim a chance to stretch their tired aching legs. Finishing their steaks and baked potatoes, they sat down to have a few beers, which they had put in the river to cool, and shared a time of reminiscing. Over to the west the sky darkened and started to disappear over the horizon.

"It's been a long day guys, we better start to think of sleep. The horses are quiet and settled down for the night."

Standing and looking over the vast prairie, remembering the wild horses, Scott remarked, "You could make a fortune turning them into race horses. If I back you up with money, you could train them. We could make a fortune and be rich."

"I don't think so. They're better off where they are, and free to roam the range without interference; protected as much as possible and in what we ranchers can do for them."

"I know what we can do." Jim said, joining the conversation. "I could come out here and build shopping centers and get someone to build houses. The retail people would flock to bring their business out here. It would reduce some of the over crowded population in our larger cities, and help the poor and immigrants to have steady work. Get them off welfare, and have our Congress help pay for this with the money they spend foolishly on their special projects in their own states."

"Not a bad idea Jim. I could never live out here; but I can help pass the bills necessary to help fund such a project."

"Sorry guys, you're plans aren't for me. Watching those wild horses and knowing your plan Scott is to capture and take away their freedom is devastating to me!

"Kevin you grew up and made your life here. You think differently. Jim, your plan wanting to dig up this land which was made for farming, to help feed the population is very sad. We have our friendship because we are different; we respect each others ideas of what is best for ourselves."

Silent for awhile Kevin paced back and forth then said, "Jim, Scott, I know now you would never locate out here. Your life is established as is mine. Certainly Katy would not move. I promised Dad I would never lose the ranch and the land. Time has really changed us. Jim you have your business and have done extremely well. Scott, your dreams for your life are coming true. I'm happy, and will die here. We'll have to plan another get together in twenty years. Imagine, we'll be over sixty years old."

"Next one will be in California. Then when we're eighty we'll go to North Carolina that settles it. All in favor raise your hand." Three right hands raised in unison. It was unanimous. Time had slipped by and they were tired from the ride. Going under the trees, Jim and Scott laid out their sleeping bags, crawled into them and within minutes fell asleep.

Kevin thought of the people who live here, who love this land. He must do all in his power to preserve it. To protect it from those who would destroy it. He was tired but couldn't sleep. He stood up and stopped for a moment, listening to the wind as it rustled through the trees. He couldn't see the wind wending its way, gently touching each leaf.

Kevin remembered when he would take his kids out here, telling them they were so blessed to be growing up in this area. Walking down by the river listening to the water slipping by making loud sounds over the rocks.

Thinking back to the days when he was young, and walked along the bank. He would ply his Father with questions. "Why is the river so quiet, in the daytime and at night so loud?"

"Because Son, during the day there are the sounds of birds, wild horses and the wind when it is strong. At night when it's quiet and the river has no competition, it is then with no interference it can be heard." Kevin stood quietly, listening to the sound of the water gently touching the sides of the riverbank; looking up at the vastness of the sky, with the mountains ever so high.

He remembered when his children were sick and he would hear a moan from their bedrooms. He'd rise and walk quietly into their rooms to touch them lightly; it was then they would turn over, falling into a peaceful sleep. So too, the river is restless until the quietness of the darkness takes over. It had no competition as it tumbled down over the rocks. "Thank you God for this country."

The next morning the three of them went for a quick swim. "There's a town close by. We can have breakfast and head back to the ranch." They nodded their heads in agreement. Jim was anxious to see Karen and Tiffany, as Scott was to see Jasmine, but Kevin was disappointed.

On the ride back Jim asked a question. "Scott, what will you're girlfriend think about you having a son" A young college graduate sure wouldn't want to start a marriage with a built in kid."

"He isn't my child, I know that! Come on Jim enough, lay off. Change the conversation about me being a Father.

The kid is not mine." Scott just wanted to see Jasmine and to get Carolyn to admit she was only kidding; this little boy was not his son. This would wreck his whole vacation and destroy his marriage.

Kevin was disappointed and concerned this camping trip wasn't as good as he hoped it would be. He was glad when he suggested they return to the ranch, to which Jim and Scott agreed. Arriving back Katy met the three men with a message from Jim's wife. "Karen called and said the plane is on time, and she'll meet you at the airport."

"Do you guys want to come with me?" Jim asked.

"No thanks." Scott replied. "I want to talk to Carolyn for awhile about my coming campaign. I'll meet your wife when you get back. Carolyn is upset with me for the present, but she'll get over it. She's a loyal person."

"I'll go with you. I'm anxious to meet this woman who was able to hog tie you down to a normal life. She must be an exceptional person. Tell me her name again."

"Karen; she's a beautiful woman; and coming into my life changed me for the good. She showed me what life is all about. My Father had spoiled me, giving me everything I wanted when I was young."

Karen – Alicia

At the airport, Jim and Kevin went to American Airlines arrival station. Watching Karen, as she came from the plane to where they were standing; Jim ran and picked her up to kiss her. Kevin waited in the crowd, as arm in arm Jim and Karen walked towards him. "Kevin, meet my wife Karen." Staring at Karen one thought came into his mind and Kevin's face flushed. "She is older, but she's the spitting image of Alicia. The shock that Jim's wife could be Alicia stunned him. "It can't be! Jim never met her at college."

He could feel his body shaking, almost losing control as he steadied himself. "I'm glad to meet you," pausing he added, "Karen? You remind me of some one I met a long time ago." Catching himself from blurting out, "Alicia! You are Alicia." With the sweat running down his face, he reached for a handkerchief to wipe it away.

Not believing her eyes she answered, "Yes that's been my name for a long time." Is he Kevin? She wondered. "Jim has told me a lot about you. I know we'll have a great time while we visiting you and your family." Turning to Jim she asked, "Has Tiffany arrived yet?"

"No, she should be coming in the first of the week. Let's get back to the ranch and meet the rest of the people. Kevin I don't think I told you Karen went to Ohio University and graduated with our class. Don't be bashful give her a welcoming kiss. Come on; enjoy one of the best kisses you'll ever get. It's the only one I'll let you have."

Standing close to Karen he gave her a light kiss on the cheek. She reached over to Kevin and responded with a kiss on his lips that was playing with his memory. They were both shaking as they broke away. Rushing across his mind were the words, "The next time we meet I'll be ready. I know she's Alicia! How could I ever forget her." Leaving the airport Kevin kept glancing in his rear view mirror watching Jim kiss her as jealousy rose up inside him. His mind was torn apart. "Alicia, she married Jim! How could this happen?"

"Watch it Kevin! You almost hit that car!" Jim yelled, as Kevin swerved to avoid the on coming car. "Let me enjoy our vacation before we die." Shaking his head, Kevin tipped the rear view mirror up and used the side mirrors to watch the traffic behind him. Thinking to himself, "That should be me, not Jim."

Jim catching Kevin's eye in the mirror said, "Isn't she the most beautiful woman you have ever seen? Admit it Kevin, right?"

Mumbling with an affirmative weak "yes," was Kevin response. By the time they reached the ranch, Kevin was sweating profusely; He excused himself and walked into the ranch telling Katy, "I'm going to take a shower, I'm wringing wet. If any one wonders where I am, tell them I'll be out soon."

Rushing up the stairs he stripped off his clothes and started the shower with cold water, trying to cool himself down. His thoughts were running wild, confusion of what might happen, wondering what to do.

What had happened in the past could ruin their reunion. Should he tell Katy who Karen really is? Even more, how can he tell Jim that Karen is Alicia, his girlfriend back in college? He stood there in the shower with the water continuing to run, until Katy called. "What's taking so long? Come on down, our guests are waiting."

Jim took Karen up to the room they would be staying in, and after unpacking her clothes and hanging them in the closet she laid back on the bed and nervously wondered "Has Jim any idea of our past together?"

"Kevin seemed strange when he first saw you? When he looked at you and kissed you, he acted as if he had seen a ghost. Did you ever date him back at college?"

"I don't remember. I could have been out with him. I can't remember a date with all the guys I went out with years ago." Karen knew the next few days here would be difficult every time she would see Kevin. It seemed so unreal; after twenty years they would meet. Flashing through her mind she remembered the last date they had on the beach.

Jim came over to Karen with one thought in his mind, "Jim not now, its too hot and stuffy. I'd like to take a shower and just relax." It was no time for making love, not with this on her mind. She hoped he wouldn't insist. Disappointed, he left the room and went to the porch on the ranch wondering, "Does Karen know him from somewhere in the past, and she doesn't want me to know. No we never met each other at college."

"Where's Kevin?" Jim asked Katy

"He'll be out in a minute; he took a shower to cool off."

"Is he okay? "He seemed nervous when he met Karen at the airport and acted like he had known her before. I asked her and she said not to her knowledge had they ever met."

"I don't know. He never mentions anyone, except you two guys. There was a girl he was in love with, named Alicia. When we first married he would mention her name. It's been years, since he has talked about her."

"You're right. I remember, that was the girl's name he was so much in love with." The conversation stopped as Karen came towards them.

Hearing voices Kevin came out of the ranch. "What are you guys talking about? I heard your voices and when I came out you stopped."

"We were talking about nothing important. I was telling Jim what a wonderful husband and Father you are."

Changing the subject Jim asked, "Does any one want to go for a ride in the plane? Katy excused herself and went into the kitchen. Karen begged off, she was too tired. Jim took the twins, Jonathon, Carolyn, Robby and Scott for a short ride over the mountains.

Leaving Karen and Kevin alone on the porch, Kevin lifted his chair and moved closer to Karen. "Alicia it is you! I know it's you. When I saw you at the airport, I knew. Why did you walk away from me back at the college? I loved you then, and have always been in love with you."

Confession

Reaching over to take her hands she quickly pulled away. "Kevin, my name is Karen now. What we had twenty years ago is gone by. Time and circumstances have changed our lives."

"You promised in your note. You said if we ever meet again, you'd be ready. I still have the note and cherish it."

"Kevin it's twenty years, our lives have changed. We can't go back. You're different, and I am too. Jim loves me and we've been married for eight years. He would be devastated if he knew about us. It would end your friendship with him. We have to keep our secret between you and me! You can't leave your wife and three children."

"You don't really love him, I can tell. In the car I saw you pulling away when he kissed you. When you saw me it brought back that day on the beach didn't it?" Your letter told me, you loved me. There's still time for us."

"We're in our forties, and we can't build a life together. Kevin, don't be foolish. It's been over for a long time. Let's not talk about it. Throw that letter away. Don't punish yourself." When Katy came out to the porch, he quickly moved his chair away.

"You don't have to move away from Karen honey. You two seem to be getting along real well. Would you both like a drink?" I can bring out a pitcher of cool lemonade and join you. Tell me Karen about yourself and family?"

"My parents are gone. I'm a supervisor of the nurses in a hospital. I have one daughter who's coming. She has graduated from college and is bringing her boyfriend with her. We have never met him. Jim adores her, spoils her with everything she desires. Officially he adopted her when she was thirteen. Her real Dad has never been in her life, so he considers her his daughter."

Darkness was settling over the ranch, when Jim brought the plane down. He joined the rest of the family and guests, enjoying the cool refreshing lemonade that Katy had made for them. The evening was a time of laughter, trading jokes, reminiscing and enjoying the moment. "Did you call my Dad Karen, reminding him not to forget to come?"

"I did Jim. Your Father is bringing Joyce and her sister's son with him. Carolyn's boy and Joyce's youngest boy are near the same age. It'll be good for them to be together. I think Joyce would make a good wife for your Dad. Their age shouldn't be a factor."

"You know; it never dawned on me that they had a thing going for a long time. He always kept his life a secret from me while I was at college. I tried to date Joyce one time. My Father was upset telling me he had her work for him because she was excellent at her job, and had two sons to support. All the time he was dating her."

Karen said, "She's quite a bit younger than he is. Maybe Jim, dating her settled your Father down from hitting the nightclubs. Joyce is still young enough to have children. Hopefully your Father would have a child, a boy and he would be happy having someone take over the business."

"Before he met Joyce Dad was lonesome and had everything that money could buy. He would stay at the office late in the evening trying to use up his time. He never could accept the fact my Mother had the nerve to leave. I think Joyce would like to have a child with him, but he says he's to old."

The evening went by quickly. "How about turning in? We've all had a busy day." Jim said as rose up from his chair and turned to Karen, "I'm tired honey." After showering, Karen slipped into bed beside him, knowing he was ready and anxious for what was to be. Reaching over to Karen he kept running his hands over her. His excitement increased as he felt her body respond to him. Moving slowly, increasing the movement of their bodies as he held her tight; until their passions exploded in a moment of joy.

Lying quietly side by side, with no words necessary; Jim fell asleep as Karen looked out the window seeing the brightness of the moon, lying awake wondering and questioning herself. "What will I do? Why now? I'm happy with my life, or am I? God, what's next?"

In the morning, Jim looked at Karen with concern. "Sweetheart are you okay? There are circles under your eyes. It looks like you didn't sleep at all. I asked Katy if Kevin was okay. I hope he's financially set because we can help him if he needs help. Ever since you arrived he seem so quiet. Are you sure you never met him before?"

"I never knew him before today."

Karen was feeling guilty. She pondered, "Why did our love making last night be different? We were satisfied, but it wasn't the same for me. I shouldn't have come here. Kevin, I thought you were over in my life. If Jim ever finds out, perish the thought." Looking down at her body she felt good. It still excited Jim. Shutting off the water she toweled down, trying to erase the thoughts of Kevin and twenty years ago.

Jim placed his arms around Karen, kissed her and said, "Honey, it was great last night. We can still make love, like we did the first time. I love you."

"I know Jim." Karen replied, feeling guilty in lying. "No," she thought, "It wasn't the same. I remember my room mate Allison telling me, you'll always remember when you had your first time. Now I know what she meant. The memory of twenty years ago on the beach has come back." Tormented she tried to erase it, by hugging Jim, trying with a desperate kiss to prove she was satisfied with her life.

Standing by the window Kevin looked out over his land thinking of Jim and Alicia, "I have to remember, her name is

Karen. If she will only come back to me, her name will be Alicia again."

A feeling of jealousy came over him when he'd see Jim kiss her and touch her. "How could she ever marry him, when she promised me? Maybe it's his money, and she feels secure." Kevin realized he had to stop this trend of thought. "I've made enough mistakes; I can't repeat it, why did she come back now? I have Katy and the kids. What do I do?"

Jim Sr. – Joyce – Eric

The next few days Karen and Kevin kept apart from each other as much as possible, they didn't want to have questions that might lead into a situation they could not control; always making sure Jim or Katy was present with them. It was difficult knowing that sometime, somewhere, the truth would be revealed that they knew each other in college.

There were times Karen regretted coming out here, but how could she know that Kevin would suddenly appear in her life again. "He'll want to know all about my past life. Did I marry anyone before Jim, and if I did, who was he."

The phone rang and when he answered it he heard a strange voice. "Hello is Jim there? This is Jim's Father; we need a ride out to your ranch." I have my friend and her nephew with me."

"Just a minute please I'll call him, "Jim your Dad is on the phone. He's at the airport."

"Hello Dad, you came, great! We'll be right out there to get you. I'm bringing Kevin with me; hang tight. I'm so happy you decided to come."

As they drove back from the airport, Jim was stunned when his Father said, "Jim I want you to meet my wife and her nephew Eric. Joyce and I were married the other night, and thought we would make this a honeymoon trip, thinking you would be shocked by the news."

"You're wife? Are you kidding, at your age! Come on Dad, you can't be serious. I'm stunned but glad, hear that Kevin? My Father got married. I can't really believe it! Come on Dad tell the truth are you for real?"

"Yes Jim, we did get married" Joyce laughingly said, "I'm your mother now."

Turning to his Father and Joyce, Jim repeated, "I don't believe it! You have a new wife? She's only a few years older than me. Wait until the people back at work hear about this. Now I can kiss her and you can't object. Remember when I asked her to go out on a date, and you were upset?"

"Kiss on the cheek." Joyce replied with a laugh, and then continued, "Son, I could end up being the chairwoman of the board in the company, if your Dad retires." Waiting for an answer and when young Jim didn't respond; finally she said, "Only kidding Jim."

In the evening the ranch help set up a dance floor outside. A live local band was hired for entertainment and dancing. There were plenty of party platters with all kinds crackers, cheese, cold cuts, including Buffalo wings and drinks of soda, water or alcohol. Some times Kevin would have a dance with Karen, and hold her close to his body. Occasionally, she would forget, relax, and respond, then quickly pull away, so he would not misunderstand any intentions on her part that she was trying to excite him. She was glad when someone would break in and sweep her away from him; twirling her across the dance floor.

Heather – Chante

Jim and Joyce joined the festivities while Angela took care of the little boys. At times they would do a dance where everyone could join together. Some times a rock and roll, then a swing, once in awhile a waltz. Not to be left out the men took turns dancing with the twins, and the women with Jonathon. The heat of the evening, the dancing and drinks, by midnight everyone was exhausted, with good nights coming quickly, as in most cases the wives literally dragged their husbands off to bed.

The twins thought maybe Kevin would let their boyfriends come over. Jonathon kept hoping that maybe Jim's daughter and friend would spend time with him.

Heather and Chante arrived the next day in a silver Corvette. After they were settled, Jonathon asked Heather if he could drive her car. With Jonathon at the wheel they headed out for a ride. Driving for a while they pulled off by a lake where there was an ice cream stand. "Let me treat you."

"I'll have a strawberry sundae." They parked where they could look over the water. Heather was still a slim curvaceous blonde. She had changed very little in appearance over the past years. Sitting in the car having finished their ice creams sundaes, Jonathon reached over to Heather, putting his arms around her to give her a kiss. Surprised, Heather responded to Jonathon for a few moments. Realizing what was happening, she pulled away. "No Jonathon." as she got free from his grasp.

"I'm sorry, I shouldn't have done that."

"Forget it." To herself she thought, "If only you weren't so young. This could be an exciting vacation here." Speaking out loud she said, "This is a beautiful place but I think we should join the rest of the group don't you? Why don't you drive back?"

Back at the ranch, Jonathon thanked Heather as she whispered to him. "We wouldn't want anyone to know about this. We'll keep our little romance between you and me, okay? We have to wait and see. Maybe we can go and have another ice cream or do something else. Be patient, I'll be here for a long time."

Looking at her, Jonathon could feel the heat in his face and knew it had become red like those who stay in the sun too long. He felt embarrassed. Heather looked around and with no one looking kissed him moving her lips over his. When Jon tried to hold her tight and return the kiss she pulled away. "No Jonathon, don't get excited. We can talk about this later."

Jim and Karen were concerned when they hadn't heard from their daughter. "He called her cell phone number again, thinking something must be wrong." He was relieved when he heard her voice. "Tiffany, where are you?"

"I'm sorry Dad, my cell phone was dead. We were sight seeing and stopped a few nights at a motel. We're at Mount Rushmore and we'll be there tomorrow. Dad my friend is waiting for me. See you later."

"Honey wait, we're going on a short trip with Kevin and Katy. We'll see you when we get back."

It was late in the afternoon when Jasmine and Suzy arrived at the ranch. Seeing Jasmine, Scott ran to the car flung open the door and helped her out. "Where have you been? I have been anxious hoping every thing was okay."

That evening after dinner, having shared a lot of conversation with each other, it was time to retire. Scott wanted to sleep with Jasmine, as it had been some time since they had been together. "We can't. I'll tell my parents when they get back. They'll have to know, and then we can share our own bed." She kissed him with her lips parting his, wishing for the time when it was right for them to be alone.

The following morning they all gathered together for breakfast on the porch. "Jasmine, Suzy I'd like you to meet Carolyn, Heather and Chante. We all graduated in the same class at the University."

Exchanging handshakes and pleasantries, Carolyn looked at Jasmine with envy and said, "Jasmine what a pretty name. Didn't we meet at Scott's office?" Having heard all about Scott and their relationship from Helen back at the office: Jasmine smiled with a look like the cat that swallowed the canary.

"Yes we did. You seemed so distraught at the time. I hope everything is okay now. I wanted to help you and let Scott know that you were there in the office but you walked out before I had a chance to."

Scott interrupted them, sensing it was time to end the conversation He didn't like the direction in which it was headed if it continued. "Why don't we take a walk, and I'll introduce you to Kevin and Katy's family." He called to Jonathon and the twins, who were busy in the corral to come and meet Jasmine and Suzy." With their ages not too far apart, it didn't take long for the conversation to be one of openness.

"Want to take a ride on the horses?" Kaylee asked.

"Sure, I'd love to, if you go slowly until I get used to it." "Are you coming Jonathon?"

"Sorry, not this time. I have to get my chores finished that are a requirement from Dad. I can go later today."

Scott begged off, "You four go. I have many phone calls to make."

Saddling the horses they started off. Suzy had riding experience, so she and Kaybee rode ahead. Kaylee stayed behind with Jasmine until she felt comfortable to move faster. Riding together ahead of Jasmine, Suzy asked Kaybee. "How old is your brother? He looks twenty four?"

"No he's only nineteen. When he goes into the city with some of his friends from the college they make dates for him. Some girls go for him, because he is tall and handsome like our Dad. He comes home and brags about it."

"Kaybee, I'd like to have a date with him."

"Okay, I'll tell Jonathon you'd like to take a ride with him. He has no steady girlfriend. We wonder if he has even kissed a girl, probably kisses the horses." I think kissing boys is ugly. Suzy burst out laughing. Hearing Kaybee say that about her brother. "I know he's always getting calls from the high school girls he knew. They call him all the times to come to parties and everything."

Catching up with Kaybee and Suzy, "Kaybee, what are you talking about that's so funny?"

"Nothing Kaylee, we were just laughing."

"We saw you laughing about something. Why can't you tell us?"

"Come on Suzy, we don't have any secrets, tell us. We won't tell anyone what you were talking about."

"Honestly Jasmine, I can't tell you now, some other time after we leave, okay?"

"Okay with me. I don't care." Kaylee said, as Kaybee and Suzy burst into laughter again.

After watching the wild horses racing over the plain, the sun became so hot making the ride uncomfortable; it was decided to head back. Arriving back at the ranch Kaybee and Suzy tethered the horses while Jasmine and Kaylee went to the ranch to cool off. Suzy waited as Kaybee went over to see Jonathon. When she finished talking to him Suzy turned, walking toward the porch. Jonathon looked at her, raised his thumb in an acknowledgment.

Because the rest of the day was hot and humid, Angela had made a chicken salad for lunch. The humidity so high, everyone just sat on the porch trying to cool off with fans. The twins, and Eric went inside the ranch to watch television. Carolyn went to her room taking Robbie with her so he could nap.

Later in the day a cool breeze came up and Jasmine decided to take a walk. Heather and Chante chose to drive into the city. Scott wanted to walk with Jasmine, but knowing what he wanted to talk about she replied, "No, honey, it's too hot. Later Suzy can have our room and we can be together real soon. I just want to be alone for a little while and think about our future. I want you to be with me, but we have to wait until we tell my parents. We still can't share the same room. They don't know we're already married. If they find out, I know my Father and Mother will say, forget it, no sense in having a big wedding; and they'll be heart broken. We have to announce our engagement first, and then make plans for the wedding."

It was late and there was no news from Kevin and Katy. Jonathon worried that something was wrong and was just about to call the Sheriff's office asking if there had been any accidents. As he reached for the phone to call, it rang. "Hello is this you Dad? Where are you?"

"Everything is fine Son. We're in Iowa; we went to see the Corn Palace. It's too late to drive all the way back tonight. We decided to stay at a motel and will be back tomorrow. How is everybody doing?"

"We're having a good time Dad, but Carolyn, Scott, and his girlfriend Jasmine, seem bored. I think they wish you were here. Heather and Chante went into the city to do some sight seeing. Suzy is very nice. We're doing okay."

Every one was sitting on the porch when Kevin's car entered the driveway the next morning. Jasmine ran to the car to greet her parents as Scott waited. "Mother, Dad, I want you to meet my friend Scott. He's the one I told you about."

Jim looked up to see his long time friend "This is your boy friend? Scott is your boy friend? You must be kidding!" Jim stepped back in amazement, his head spinning. "No, I can't believe this! You're kidding? Scott is your boy friend? He's twice as old as you." Jim was stunned, and it hit him what his daughter said. Turning to Scott, "Is this true? You're the one Tiffany's in love with?"

"It's true, you're right Jim, she's the one I'm going to marry. Why are you calling her Tiffany?"

Jim's voice became loud with anger as he looked at Karen in disbelief. Kevin motioned to the rest of his guests and his family to leave. Karen in a state of shock, but with presence of mind, pulled him to the side. "Keep your cool, let's hear them tell us what this is all about. All your raving will only harm the situation. She's over eighteen; don't let her say to us, she can make her own decisions."

"Jim," said Kevin. "Why don't you use the family room, then you will be alone. I've told everyone to stay clear." Squeezing Jim's hand, he put a finger to his lips, giving him a sign to be still.

"Thank you Kevin." Jim responded

Going into the room Jim and Karen pulled up two chairs. Scott and Jasmine sat together on the couch holding hands. Jim trying to speak was stopped by Karen. "Please let them talk. Let's hear what they have to say."

"Mother, I changed my name. I didn't want any one to know about my family. I didn't want to be that little rich girl. It was a stigma when I was in high school and college. "I work in Scott's office. He was very good to me. Please don't blame him. I was the one who initiated the first move. I fell in love with him and Scott with me. We made a promise to marry next year. I hoped we could announce our engagement here at the ranch with my parents blessing."

Looking in amazement Scott was stunned as he spoke. "Why did you call her Tiffany? Your name is Jasmine, isn't that right? What's this all about?"

"Jasmine turned to Scott. "Sweetheart, I really am Tiffany, not Jasmine. Please forgive me. Our age difference doesn't matter, we talked about that."

"I love you, not your name. It doesn't matter what your name is. I can start calling you Tiffany with no difficulty, knowing there will be times I'll slip. Karen, Jim, we were drawn to each other, it just happened. Most likely you had something in your lives you didn't want to talk about."

Upset, because Karen had restrained him, Jim finally spoke. "Scott, now I remember you telling me you had a young girlfriend you were going to marry. I told you then you were robbing the cradle, and to leave the young ones to the young and you should try to date the Mother. For heaven's sake you're twice her age. Tiffany you've just graduated from college. Your have your whole life before you, think what you're doing. Scott, be my friend, not my son in law."

"Jim, I have told Jas, sorry, Tiffany, everything about my past, and what can be expected in the future when I'm elected President. She understands all the ramifications that might happen; and knows she will be the target of the press. Tiffany could become the youngest First Lady the country has ever had. We're friends Jim, I don't ever want that to change, but it will, if you oppose our marriage."

Jim was getting increasingly angry. Rising from his chair he walked over to Scott, looking at him, Scott's face paled, not knowing what to expect. With his body tense, and his face heating with anger, Jim burst out. "Scott, don't try to threaten me. I have many friends in Congress and in the business world, which will not support you."

"Dad, don't fight with Scott. We're going to get married next year. This is what I want, and for you to give me away.

I've thought so often about you taking me down the aisle since we started to think about getting married."

"Mother, I'd like you to help me plan the wedding. Please, talk to Dad? I don't know who my real Father is, and I don't care to know. You're my Father and that's all that matters to me. I love both of you, can't you understand?"

"Why didn't you tell us before, instead of surprising us like this? I think now is not the time to discuss this any further. We're all upset. Let's sleep on it, do some thinking, and talk another time. Jim, let's go to our room." Karen took him by the hand and left.

As soon as they were gone Tiffany burst into tears. "It's okay sweetheart, he'll come around. He loves you so much and seeing you disappear from his life. He's imagining everything he wanted for you pouring down the drain. Your Mother is a very sensible woman; she'll make everything okay, try to relax."

"Scott come and stay with me tonight. I can't stop shaking. Please ask Suzy if she will take your room."

When Suzy saw that Jim and Karen had left, she came back in. "Would you sleep in my room, so I can be with Jasmine tonight?" Scott asked.

"It's okay with me, but you better be quiet. The way Jim is acting he is really upset. He seems like a man who could lose control of him self; and then who knows what he might do. Don't let him catch you with her tonight."

"I know Suzy, thank you. I'll always remember what you are doing for us right now. I will certainly remember you after I'm elected as the President of the country."

Alone, Karen and Jim had some heated words. "Please be quiet Jim, other people have gone to sleep. You have to accept the fact no matter what we say Scott and Tiffany will get married. Nothing you say or do will deter them."

"Say what you want, I'll do everything I can to prevent him from marrying my daughter. He's too old for her. Robbie is probably his child but he won't admit it. Karen how can you side in with Scott? I knew what he was like in college. I'm sure he's still the same."

"Jim please, you took me for who I am. We all might have secrets from the past that we don't want others to know. Let the past be gone, let's look to the future with the love and commitment we made to each other."

"I'm sorry Karen I just don't feel right about it. She's at least twenty years younger than Scott."

Quietly Scott went to Tiffany's room. Once inside the room the two of them stood looking at each other; their desire escalating; Quickly Jasmine pulled off Scott's shirt, and pulled him to her. They joined their bodies together until their love desires were satisfied. Turning on his side he faced her, and gently kissed her.

In the morning Karen looked for Jim, because he wasn't in the room. Going out into the hall she saw him pacing back and forth. "Jim" she called softly. "Come back to our room, what are you doing? For the last time, let things be. Time will tell what will happen between Tiffany and Scott.

Let's not spoil everyone's vacation. You'll ruin your friendship with Scott and Kevin. "Jim, are you mad? What they do is their business. You'll destroy our relationship with Scott and Tiffany if you pursue this. Come back in the room, now!"

"I just want to be sure they're not sleeping together. Karen, where is his room?"

After breakfast Joyce and Jim's Dad were walking around the ranch, stopping to see the horses. Leaning on the rail, he looked at Joyce and he could see a strained look on her face. "What's the matter? Are you worried about Jim? Don't! He's angry now, but he'll over come the situation when he realizes he can do nothing about it. His daughter is going to marry his friend. So what! She isn't his biological child. Look at the age difference between us Joyce we love each other. Age doesn't matter when you learn to enjoy the same things together."

"Honey, I have something to tell you. I've waited a long time but I keep secrets at times because like your son, you also have a temper that can explode at any time. Will you promise not to say anything until I finish?"

"What is it Joyce? What ever it is, this is the time to tell me.

"Just listen, please." These words were met with dead silence. "I know how you've felt about accepting anyone that is not a blood relative owning the company. Remember when you told me to get an abortion? Well I didn't, I had a boy, and you could have had a son. I wanted so badly to have a child by you, but you only wanted sex. When have you ever told me you love me? A woman wants her man to tell her that he loves her, at least once in a while."

Eric

"I do love you Joyce; I'm sixty two years old. Older people know they love each other. You don't have to say it."

Laughing, Joyce asked, "Say it louder. Jim, it's just that a woman wants to hear her man say it." A few tears started to run down Joyce's face. Not knowing what to say, Jim put his arms around her, whispering in her ear, "I love you."

"Say it louder Jim."

With a loud voice Jim replied, "I love you." his loud voice startled the horses in the pen and they stared racing around frightened by the sudden outburst.

"I didn't mean you had to tell the world, but that's okay."

With confidence Joyce turned to Jim. "Remember how your Son wanted so much to adopt a boy." Joyce paused to control herself. "You insisted you wanted a blood relation only to manage the company when Jim became too old. "Well! You have another Son. Eric is your Son."

"He's my Son? You're kidding! Come on, there's no way he can be mine! I'm too old to be a father."

"For once in your life Jim, listen. Remember the time we were snowed in for a week at the cabin, we did nothing but read and have sex. I got pregnant for the second time and the truth is Eric is not my nephew. He's your Son. I made up an excuse that my parents needed me.

Truthfully, I needed them to help me through the pregnancy, hoping the day would come, you would accept Eric. Yes, I lied to you, and hope you will forgive me. I made up my mind I was going to have this child with you or without you, no matter the circumstances."

"You're kidding me! I can't believe it. You know Joyce, one time when Karen couldn't conceive, Jim told me to go and have my own child. He'll have the last laugh on me now. How can I tell him this? You tell him Joyce."

"No Jim, he's your son and you have to tell him. "

Finding Jim down by the corral, he could hardly contain himself. "Sit down! I have something exciting to tell you. I'm a Father again! Did you hear what I just said? I just found out Eric is my Son. I have two Sons. Can you believe it? Joyce you tell this Son of mine. He won't believe me."

"Slow down Dad, you're over sixty. Slow down or you'll have a heart attack. What do you mean? Eric is your son?"

"It's true, your Dad and I have had a relationship for years, it was casual for a time. After some dates and spending time up in the cabin on weekends we discovered we loved each other. Eric is his son, and your brother."

Remembering his Father who was always so strict now seems changed; which had never been his character. What he had thought before, he now knew was right. His Father and Joyce had been in a relationship for a number of years.

That evening as they were talking about how happy his Dad and Joyce were, telling all of them about Eric. Jim asked Karen. "Maybe the stress in trying to have a baby is the reason we couldn't. Before we adopt, let's try to have our own once more. Please honey; let's give it a try this year, if you can't conceive, then we'll adopt. I promise sweetheart, if we are unable, I will never ask again."

"Okay, but this is the last try Jim, this is it. I mean it; I don't want to go through another miscarriage." I'm over forty and I don't know if I can. I don't want to be disappointed again. You have no idea what it's like to want to have a child, and not be able to."

Meanwhile on the other side of the corral Kevin said to Scott, "Maybe the news of his Father having another son will take the edge of Jim's bitterness. Talk to Karen about Tiffany and you getting married. She's very intelligent. You know it won't be easy if you become the President. I think you should remember how the media and the other party treated the previous President. Keep Tiffany out of the limelight. Some of the Presidents wives kept a low key when their husbands were in office, that way the press couldn't misconstrue everything they said or did."

It was getting late and the sun had disappeared. Jonathon was alone on the porch listening to the radio when he heard a voice asking him, "Can I call you Jon?"

Looking around he saw Suzy dancing on the grass by herself. "Will you dance with me?" The music was slow as Jonathon took Suzy in his arms.

Jon & Suzy

The opportunity was there. Suzy moved against his body slowly but deliberate, exciting him, letting him know when he is ready, she will be there for him.

It was a difficult situation for Jonathon being asked to go to parties, he was nervous, not knowing how to get involved. He always declined with some excuse. The guys would tease him about his lack of confidence and he wasn't sure how to talk to his Father. Kevin was against premarital sex and had warned him the results of pregnancy and disease.

Inside the ranch Kevin told the twins it was time for bed. "Kaylee, where's Jon?"

"He's with Suzy; they were taking a walk toward the corral."

"Kevin, he isn't a little boy anymore. She has an eye for him. Let them alone. He never dates, and spends all his time here. He needs a girlfriend even if only for the present time.

Why not, I had my eyes on you. It's about time he had a girl friend, if just for a couple of weeks."

"That's right Dad, Suzy asked me to talk to Jon and tell him she'd like to go out with him, he said okay."

After the twins left Katy looked at Kevin, "We were young just like they are. Let them go. He knows the score of what's the right thing to do."

When the music stopped Suzy walked over to the barn and went inside. Looking up she saw bundles of hay, stacked on the loft. Noticing the ladder, she climbed up and sat by the side of the bundles. Jonathon followed and heard Suzy call, "Come on up and join me." Jon hesitated, remembering the time his Dad caught Kaylee and her boyfriend up there. Waiting quietly Suzy called again, "Are you afraid to climb?"

"No, I'm not." With a new determination, Jon climbed up and sat down beside her. Stretching her body she lay back on the hay, and reached over to Jon, pulling him on her. Kissing his lips as his body shook with excitement.

"Murmuring softly, "Easy Jon" placing his hands on her breast. Unbuttoning his shirt, she touched his chest, moving her lips slowly back and forth gently teasing him. In a moment what he had thought of doing many times, now became a reality.

With her passion satisfied, Suzy relaxed and with her arms around his waist she rested beneath him. Jon embarrassed, started to apologize, and was silenced when Suzy told him, "Jon, it was great, maybe we can be together again. I know it was your first time. Next time move slowly, and you'll enjoy it even more. Don't worry I won't tell anyone. Remember, this will be our secret."

Jon remembered those words from Heather, between you and me. Climbing down the ladder they parted when they heard Jon's Father calling, "Son, where are you?" Quickly Suzy went out the rear door of the barn, waiting quietly, patiently, to see what would happen.

Trying to act surprised Jon said, "Hi Dad, Suzy and I were just taking a walk around the place. She's gone to her room. We were looking out at the horizon, enjoying the night, that's all."

"Well son it's late; we have to work tomorrow; it's time to turn in."

Suzy remained hidden behind the barn until they went into the ranch. She remembered Jasmine had told Scott they would have to be separate for a time. Thinking Jasmine was asleep, Suzy got into bed reliving her love making with Jon, and surprised when Tiffany quietly asked "Were you with Jonathon?"

Startled for a moment she replied "Yes, and while we were in the barn we heard his Father calling for him. He's so innocent. I'll be sorry to leave this place when it's over."

"You devil Suzy, you're kidding? Are you saying he never had sex before?"

"That's right, and I know he'll be looking for me again. My concern is that I see Heather has her eyes on him. She's constantly talking and laughing with him when he's around. She's at least forty years old, much too old for him. It was a good evening but now I'm tired, and I want to go to sleep."

"Good night baby snatcher."

"Good night Jasmine, you old man's lover."

The following day Jim had to fly to California on business. He wanted Karen to go with him, but she begged off. "Jim, I want to relax and enjoy this place and our hosts. It wouldn't be fair to them and leave for a few days."

"You know Karen; I might have to stay over night, so talk to Tiffany and Scott. He's had a fast life. I received a letter from his assistant Philip telling all about Scott's life style. He's had young interns every year, wines and dines them, uses them for sex, promises they are the one and only, then dumps them each fall."

"I don't believe it Jim, and how would this Philip know. I don't want to talk about his past. If Tiffany doesn't care, there's nothing we can do about it, even if it's true."

"Just do me a favor, talk to them. You're Tiffany's Mother. She'll listen to you. Honey, he's never been married and in time she will tire of the fast life in Washington. I've talked to many politicians and they say Washington is a party town Young women are used for whatever, and then discarded like a piece of paper."

"Jim if these stories are true, maybe he's ready to settle down. If we disagree with Tiffany she will marry him anyway. The only thing we can do is go along with her wishes. We made choices about us. Talk to Kevin I'm sure he can help."

"Karen I know what he was like back in college, and I think he's the same. He was chasing women all the time night after night. He was lucky he wasn't thrown out of the college for some of the things he did."

The Past is Gone

Karen was alone on the porch with her eyes closed as Kevin approached her. "How about taking a ride today? Katy can't go, because she has an appointment at the dentist office. I'm expecting about twenty calves this year, and I have to take a ride to check on them. It's only a few hours out and back. Angela will make a picnic lunch for us. There's a cool place with beautiful trees right by the river where we can stop eat and rest for a while. I'm sure you would love it. Are you game?"

Forgetting she had promised herself not to be alone with Kevin "Sure, I haven't been on a horse for a long time." They rode leisurely, stopping to watch the wild horses as they were grazing, also enjoying the view of the mountains in the distance. The herd had scattered, so it took time to find the ones who would be giving birth. Satisfied everything was good, they stopped by the river for lunch. He spread out a blanket under the trees and brought out their food to eat. When they finished they took off their boots and walked in the water feeling the coolness and refreshing sensation of it.

"Alicia we have to talk. What has happened in your life the last twenty years? Is your Father still alive? Remember he stopped me from seeing you when we were in college and I wanted to apologize to you. Why didn't you see me?"

"Kevin, the past is gone, why rehearse it all over. It won't change anything. You're married and I'm married. Jim and I are looking forward to Tiffany's marriage next year."

"No Alicia; we have to talk now. I meant the past twenty years of your life. "How did you ever meet Jim? Did you know him back in college? How long have you been married?"

To stop Kevin from talking, she put her hand over his mouth. "Let it go, please. Remember my name is Karen now." Hesitating should she tell Kevin or not. Torn within she realized there would be no better time then now. He would continue with these questions and more. If Jim ever finds out before I tell Kevin what he should know, my marriage will be ruined.

"Kevin, Jim had an accident, and was almost killed. Being a nurse I was given responsibility to nurture him back to health. At first he was horrible, conceited, had plenty of money, and thought that bought him a free ticket to life. The accident changed his life. He's not the same person he was before."

"Were you were married before you married Jim? Is he Tiffany's father?"

"No Kevin, I had Tiffany when we got married."

"Did you tell Jim? Does he know the Father of your daughter?"

"No, I had a short affair with some one. I never told him. He said he doesn't want to know. He's adopted Tiffany legally and spoils her." With that last answer her tears started to flow down her cheeks. "Why do you ask me all these questions? We can't change what has happened."

Moving closer to Karen, he put his arms around her as she leaned her head on his shoulder. Trying to get words out was impossible. Taking his handkerchief he wiped her tears as they increased.

"Kevin I was frightened when you came to my room back at college. I was very innocent, and I know it sounds foolish for a twenty two year old woman. My Mother died when I was young and my Dad was my world. He warned me never to get involved with a man, because they only wanted sex. I had the feelings and inner desire to want a relationship but was scared. After we had sex I called my Dad to bring me home. He adored me, protected me. I really didn't want to come out here, fearing that this would happen, hoping you were happily married and would forget about me, now I know, you haven't."

"I've never forgotten you Alicia I went back to a reunion and looked everywhere for you. I met Allison; you remember her. She said I didn't treat you right so I deserved to lose you. I've been haunted by the memory of when we swimming that day. I still love you."

I've lived for a long time with a guilt feeling I had betrayed you. I buried myself in my work forgetting what happened. Now I have to tell you. With tears and her body shaking she blurted out. "You're Tiffany's Father!"

Stopping long enough to get control of his emotions, he looked at her in anguish. "Why didn't you tell me? You could have called the college and got my address. All these years I've felt so guilty.

I've kept the fire burning inside of me, hoping we would be together some day." Pausing for a minute he continued, "You left me a note saying you would always love me; and would be ready if we met. I tried and tried to make contact with you, but your Father stopped me. I have waited twenty years to marry you. I love you with all my heart."

"I'm sorry Kevin; we'll destroy the lives of all the members of our families if we tell them. Why can't you let the past stay in the past?"

Kevin stood up, silent for a moment and then continued. "Will Katy ever understand if she finds this out? Alicia, I promised my life to you. I'm angry and confused, what can we do? Jim will be furious to find out I'm Tiffany's Dad. My kids, what about them? Yes we could wreck our marriages!"

"Kevin, please, my name is now Karen."

"Katy left me one time because I kept mentioning your name. It became so ugly she left us for more than a year. You think you have a problem? This never would have happened if you had told me you were pregnant." All his pent up emotions over the years, nothing else mattered at the moment. Pulling her to him, he smothered her with kisses on her lips and neck. "All I know is that I have found you and I'll never let you go again." Karen relaxed for a moment, and then quickly realized what he wanted.

Gaining control of her emotions she pushed him away. "Stop it Kevin, stop! We had an affair it's over. It was one sex encounter, it wasn't love we had, it was a physical desire. A few dates don't build a foundation for the future. Jim and I are in love, we've built a future, and some how I have to tell Tiffany about you. Yes I thought I was in love but I wasn't. At that time of my life I was searching not knowing what love meant."

"Wait a minute!" What do you mean just a quick sex affair? I've loved you since we first met. Because of you, I've lost years of having my daughter with me. Now you come into my life and expect me to forget you? Let me tell you it isn't that easy."

Karen started to shake again not knowing how to stem the tide of his anger. "Please Kevin; don't spoil our time out here. When I feel comfortable and the time is right, I'll tell her. The rest is up to you. If she wants a relationship with you, that will be her decision. We must keep this between you and me."

"That's so easy for you to say." Kevin responded sarcastically. "You can go back to California and hide from this. It isn't that easy for me."

"No it isn't easy. To have a baby out of marriage broke my Father's heart. I disappointed him; he had great plans for me. He was a doctor and while operating on a child he made a mistake during surgery. The baby died and he brooded over that and committed suicide two weeks after the operation. Do you think this had been easy for me? Please let it go."

On the way back to the ranch Kevin and Karen were quiet. There was no conversation. In his mind he tried to come to the conclusion the past was over. This is what they had, a brief relationship that ended twenty years ago

In the cool of the evening, Kevin asked Katy to go up to the loft. He knew he had to clear away the doubt she had about him still being in love with Alicia. When they had their differences, they would often go to there to be alone.

"Kevin, I don't think I want to go now. Remember one time we went up there and we ended up with twins. That's a frightening place for me, you still wanting a larger family."

"Honey believe me, it's the last thing on my mind now." I have things I have to tell you, and it won't be easy for me."

In side the barn they climbed the ladder and sat on the hay. "I have something to tell you. Listen as you always do. Karen is really Alicia, the girl I loved."

With a questioning look she responded. "Kevin, do you know what you're saying? I've had a few surprises in being married to you, but this sounds impossible to believe. When did you find this out?"

By passing an answer to Katy's question Kevin responded back, "I thought if Karen and I took a ride to be alone today, she might still feel the same way about me as I did for her. We had a long talk. I told you about our relationship at college."

"Wait a minute, can I be hearing right?"

"Please Katy, What I didn't know until today. She said because of me she got pregnant and Tiffany is my daughter.

Being pregnant, and frightened, her Father told her she could never see me again. Loving and respecting him, she obeyed"

"Kevin, I can't believe what you're saying."

"I want you to wait until I finish. Don't say anything. Jim doesn't know her real name is Alicia, and that I'm Tiffany's Father." Quietly he searched Katy's face for some reaction to what he had said, it brought no response.

After a time of quietness, Katy placed her hands on Kevin's face, looking him in the eyes asking him, "Tell me again what you just said, because I'm confused."

Kevin repeated what he had said until she stopped him. "Why didn't she get in contact and tell you? What are you going to do? You know if Jim finds out his marriage can break up. Tiffany will be torn apart; most likely she'll never forgive her Mother for not telling her the truth. Question Kevin, will Tiffany or Jasmine still want to marry Scott? I think you'll have to let Karen make the decision whether to tell her, or to keep it a secret?"

With no answers to Katy's questions he sat silent as the dream he wanted for his life; and the woman he wanted to share it with, was dissimulating at a rapid pace. She waited until he had digested her questions. "I think it might be better not to tell any one. My Mother said to my Dad, after an argument. Sometimes it's best to let things left unspoken."

Only time it seemed could heal a broken heart. There was no easy answer for the present.

Looking For Love

Time was moving on and Carolyn wondered why she had come out here. It seemed each woman had a man; even Suzy had put a clamp on Jonathon, keeping him busy, disappearing either for long late afternoon horseback riding, or coming out from the barn. Everyone else had someone except her. Angela loved to take care of Robbie but Carolyn felt guilty asking her. She knew that to be part of this reunion she needed someone. Thinking for a moment, she remembered that Jason the ranch foreman had been very attentive to her at the dance. It was a few days later he asked Carolyn if she would like to go out for the evening.

"I'd love to go out with you Jason."

"I'll pick you up at seven, dress casual, everybody does." When they arrived at the nightclub, heads turned when they saw the two of them enter. Carolyn walked past a group of cowboys who gave her a few stares and whistles. Sitting at a table with some friends of Jason the introductions were made. "Bill, Bette, John, Samantha this is Carolyn. She works for the government."

"No Jason; I work for the Democratic Party! I travel around the country trying to get people to register and vote. Telling them they are privileged to have that right."

"Doesn't matter, let's have a good time."

The evening went well, sharing drinks and Jason teaching Carolyn some of the western dances. It was a great time for her.

On the way home, Jason pulled over by the lake and parked the car. The moon was bright with it's light shimmering over the water; a soft breeze removing the oppressive heat of the evening.

"I often stop here, it's so peaceful and restful; like you're in a different world. I reminisce what it would be like if I could have raised my daughter and son here. I met my wife when I was in the Army. She came from the East, and hated it out here. Took the kids one day and disappeared. I could never locate her. That's enough of my sad story, how about you? Maybe some day I'll have time with your help to try and find them. It would be good to let them know who their Father is. They at least deserve that. "Now you tell me about your life Carolyn."

"I've been a Representative in Congress from my home state North Carolina. Served one term and decided it wasn't for me. Scott and I had a relationship but it didn't last. He's very ambitious and wants to be the President; that's not for me. I want to settle down and raise a family."

Leaving the car they walked to the water, removed their shoes kicking the water as they went along the shore. Jason picked up some smooth stones making them skip. "Show me how you do that." Carolyn tried with little success.

"We'll have to do this again." On then way back to the ranch she rested her head on his shoulder. When they arrived Jason stopped the car at the bunkhouse. There was silence for a moment until he leaned over and kissed her gently. "I'd like to take you out again, if that's okay with you?"

"All you have to do is ask."

As the days went by Carolyn and Jason began seeing more of each other. It was a good start toward a future relationship. He hadn't been interested in anyone until he met her, and was content with his responsibility at the ranch.

"Jason, let's take a trip to Mount Rushmore? I've never been there. Ask Kevin if you can get the time off."

"Well I do have some vacation time coming. I'll ask him for a few days off. There isn't much to do here at the present time. He's been good to me and helped me when my wife took the kids and left. She took all of our savings with her. Now you and Kevin are the only ones I have shared this with."

Jason went to Kevin the next day and asked him for a few days off. "Carolyn would like to see Mount Rushmore." At the same time, she asked Angela to take care of Robbie while they were gone.

"Of course you can have the time off." Kevin answered, knowing that he rarely asked for any thing. He was pleased to see him with Carolyn." Go my friend, have a good time."

It was early in the morning when Jason picked Carolyn up. They drove away from the ranch heading to Mount Rushmore. It was a perfect day; the blue sky with white puffy clouds seemed to surround them. Carolyn enjoyed the breath taking scenery as they drove to South Dakota. He had made a registration for two rooms at one of the motels in the area. "Is that okay?"

"We can get one with twin beds if you'd rather. We're adults with no attachments. Have you any reason why we need two rooms?" Carolyn questioned

After getting settled they walked around the town. It was a busy time as they joined the other tourists who were doing the same thing as they were; visiting many of the gift shops; sometimes buying souvenirs. In one of the stores they saw a photographer taking pictures of tourists dressed in early American clothing. Looking over their choices, it was difficult to choose. Finally Jason gave up and told Carolyn to make the decision. It would be a half hour before they could pick up their picture.

When the time was up, they returned to the photo shop and were shown their picture. Happy with the results, Jason ordered two copies. "Why two copies Jason?"

"So we each have one for our memory book when you go back to Washington. I won't be able to see you in person; at least I can have your picture and say if only."

"What do you mean by if only, Jason?"

"If only we could have this time continue, hopefully becoming permanent. You've lightened up my life. Maybe in time we can get married. I love you Carolyn."

In the motel room Jason turned on the television and started to read the newspaper he had picked up in the lobby while Carolyn went in to take a shower. When she finished she came out and sat down beside him.

"Did you save some hot water for me?" He asked. Finishing his shower he came out and sat down beside her. He picked up the paper to finish reading. Gently she it took away and laid it down on the end table, looking him straight in the eyes. Taking her finger she traced it back and forth over his strong muscular face. With a nervous apprehension he turned toward Carolyn not being sure what to do.

She kissed him with a fervor that told him to continue the kiss. It had been a long time since he had made love and had a relationship with a woman. Slowly he relaxed as they continued to discover each other. Opening her robe he moved off the couch as she stretched out. Kneeling by Carolyn he took both hands touching her as she reacted to his every movement. Gently he lifted her up and laid her on the bed. He knew she wanted him to continue; yet he hesitated. Feeling she might reject him he moved away.

She pulled Jason back to her; he leaned over caressing her as she held him.

Joining together Jason's desire came to completion quickly, followed with Carolyn reaching her fulfillment. It had been a long time since they each had made love. Looking at each other they kissed again, as they lay completely relaxed beside each other.

In the morning they took a drive around the mountains watching the buffalo from a distance. Many donkeys were walking in the middle of the road, thrusting their face inside the cars wanting and demanding food to eat. You could hear the squeals of the children from other cars as they ducked away from the windows as the donkeys tried to take their food.

They saw charred land, devastated from some of the roaring fires in the past. It was slow driving along the narrow winding road, crossing over bridges; other times under them.

The weather was extremely hot the next day, and the temperature was in excess of ninety degrees, making it very uncomfortable with the heat. They stopped to have a sandwich and cold drink for lunch before continuing their tour. That evening they went to a local restaurant to enjoy a full course meal before going back to the motel. They were tired it was time to rest. Closing the door Carolyn peeled off her blouse and shorts hastening to be first in the shower. Hearing her singing he thought," Why not." Stripping down he went quietly into the bathroom, slid open the shower door to join Carolyn. Startled for a moment she covered herself.

Standing there with the water pouring over them they took turns bathing each other. It was like being kids, taking a hose and spraying water over their friends when they were young. After awhile Carolyn stepped out of the shower, toweled down and went to lie down on the bed. Before she could, Jason had already dried himself and with his arms out stretched, the radio playing a slow romantic song they started to dance.

Their bodies were heating with desire. Swinging around to the bed Carolyn landed on top of him. She could feel his body anxiously wanting her. Within a few moments, last night's love making was repeated. Lying on the bed, they exchanged light kisses, enjoying the quietness. Carolyn softly asked, "Jason, is this our honeymoon, or am I just wishing?"

Holding her hands he said, "I want this to be our special time. I know this is sudden, but why should we wait if we feel like we do towards each other. You said you wanted to be a teacher. There are plenty of opportunities here in Wyoming. It's been ages since I've met someone I wanted to be serious with. I know you are looking for stability and I am too. I would love to be a Father to Robbie, and be your husband. It will happen if you take a chance. I'm willing to give it a start. Will you marry me?"

"Jason you're the first person I've ever met that's been honest with me. I've had relationships before and they turned into a disaster. This time I must be sure with no doubts, or condemn myself to being an old maid. I have to return and fill my commitment and responsibilities to the Democratic Party for six months. Then there are no more obligations to them. Yes I will marry you. First, let's see if absence makes the heart grow stronger, or maybe it will be out of presence, out of mind. I'm willing to wait. Can we give it six months?"

"It's a promise, if we can at least call each other on the phone." All the way back Carolyn was filled with happiness and excitement with thoughts of a new dream that would end in marriage. At forty years of age it was time to settle down. With Jason and Robbie it would be a beginning of a stable marriage."

"Welcome back Jason, Did you have a good time?" Kevin asked Jason when they returned.

"I sure did Kevin; I believe there will be a second chance of marriage for Carolyn and me. We're going to wait at least six months until she finish's her obligations."

"Hey Scott, did you hear that? It looks like Carolyn and Jason will be a twosome. Isn't that great!"

"Congratulations." Said Scott. Thinking, "Now that should put the nail in the coffin about Robbie being my child." Carolyn looked happy as she was telling Katy what a great time she had, until Scott broke into their conversation. "You look like you had a good time." He said with a smirk.

Noting the hostility between the two of them, Katy excused herself. "Why does Scott act the way he does toward Carolyn? She seems so nice and loves Robbie so much. Is he jealous because she found someone that treats her so well?'

"Carolyn, did his performance make you happy?"

"You're disgusting. Excuse me, I'm sorry. You better think about Robbie being your son. I'll let you sweat it out. Maybe just when you say, I do, when you are marrying Tiffany, I'll come down the aisle at your wedding and say, "Scott, I want you to meet your son!"

"You'll do what Carolyn? You wouldn't dare!"

"Just try me Scott. In the mean time you'll have to wait and see. You have forgotten the way you've treated me over the past few years, well I haven't. Now you have something to think about."

Jim had returned from his business trip to California. Karen could feel his anxiety, as he held her at arms length asking, "Did you talk to Tiffany about what I asked you to do?" He was upset when Karen confessed she hadn't.

Discussions

"No, I haven't Jim. We can't spoil everyone's vacation. Kevin understands, and doesn't want to spoil what he and Katy have worked so hard for."

"Look Karen this can't happen, I had such great plans for her wedding, having all my business associates come and see how beautiful she is. I want her wedding day to be the happiest day of her life, and ours too."

That evening Tiffany and Karen went for a walk, distancing themselves from everyone. Going over to the barn, a place Kevin had suggested, they climbed up to the loft. "Tiffany what can we do for you? What do you want?"

"Mother I want to announce our engagement here and tell everyone we will be married next year. Don't tell me I'm too young. Look how happy and content you and Dad are. I want the same; to have children while Scott and I can."

Watching Karen and Tiffany go inside the barn, Jim walked over calling, "Where are you two?"

"We're up in the loft." Climbing up he sat down with them. "Dad, I want to get married next year. I want you to walk me down the aisle." Jim started to speak but was silenced by Karen. "Dad, listen until I finish what I want to say. You have given me everything; what I need most now is your love and understanding. If you don't want to I'll ask Kevin, he's one of your best friends, beside Scott." I love his family, and want to maintain a close relationship with them."

"Tiff, more than anything I want to give you away and walk you down the aisle at your wedding, but not with Scott. Don't take that away from me."

"Jim, we're a small family. We have your Father, Joyce and Eric. My Dad died fifteen years ago, and you know I'm an only child. I know of no other relatives except my uncle, aunt and their family who live in Alaska. Now we can have Scott, Kevin, Katy, and their children. We can call them family. Please be reasonable and understanding."

"Karen, that's great, but I want to have children of our own, even if we have to adopt. The house is empty without kids. Tiffany will be gone soon."

The air was heavy and still, the only sound was the hum of the bats as they darted back and forth. Jim was deeply troubled. What he thought he wanted for Tiffany seemed to be fading away. "I'll have to think about this. He's twice as old as you. I thought you would marry some one near your age. How can you have the same things in common?"

"Dad, you aren't marrying him, I am! We like the same things. I want the challenge of a political campaign. It will be a great learning experience for me as a new young lawyer. You still see me as a young high school teenager. I've grown up a lot since then."

"Tiffany, listen to me for a change. Scott is twice your age. How do you think your children will feel when they graduate from high school, and your friends look at Scott and say, is that your grandfather? He might be elected President of the country.

Do you realize the pressure on your family; it will be devastating. The news media will haunt you day and night. They'll seek out your past lives and expose you if you have any dark secrets. Can you handle that?" These words were familiar as she remembered hearing them from Scott.

Watching Karen and Tiffany go into the barn, Scott went to the far end and stood silently by the door. He was startled when Jim entered and called for them. Edging along the sidewall, he was within hearing distance of their conversation. Everything was quiet in the loft until he heard Karen speak. "Its getting late we can talk about this another time." With no more conversation they went down the ladder. When Tiffany didn't come Karen called, "Are you coming?"

"No Mother, I want to stay for just a minute, you go, and I'll be along soon." Tiffany sat quietly crying, not wanting her parents to see her break down. She felt alone. What she had planned for didn't materialize. Instead of joy and happiness there was only sadness and despair. She controlled her emotions before descending. Waiting what seemed a long time she finally decided to go down.

At the bottom of the ladder Scott silently approached putting his arms around her. Jasmine started to scream but was silent when Scott placed one of his hands over her mouth and whispered, "Honey it's me. I'm sorry, I was anxious to see what would happen. I wish Jim would listen. If he insists, we'll have to tell him we're already married. I know it will be a shock to them."

Suzy's Plan

"Please don't ever do that again. I've had enough for the night. My Father is against our getting married, and it seems as if my Mother can't change his mind either. Quietly they managed to get to his room with no one seeing them. Scott knew only holding her is what Tiffany needed. Caressing her gently would be the only way he could calm her fears. The next few days Tiffany spent time with her parents. Scott kept trying to come to an agreement with Jim.

One morning Heather and Chante decided to go into the local town. With Heather gone for the day, Suzy saw her chance. Going over to the training pen, she saw Jon sitting on one of the rails of the fence. Thinking quickly she saw a chance to be alone with him. "Want to take a ride?"

She felt alone now that Carolyn had made a connection with Jason, Heather was always showing up, when she tried to be alone with Jonathon, it became frustrating "Sure, give me a few minutes to saddle the horses." Getting an extra blanket he decided to take Suzy out where his Dad and friends camped when they first arrived.

Running back into the ranch he asked Angela to make up sandwiches and put soda and cookies in the small cooler. When she finished she gave the cooler to Jon who took a bottle of white zinfandel wine, and placed it inside the container. Going outside he gave the cooler to Suzy.

"What's this for Jon?" As she held up the bottle of wine wanting to hear what his answer would be.

"Just a little surprise. I'm going to take you where the men camped a few weeks ago. It's beautiful with tall trees in full leaf for shade. We can go swimming. It's our land and no one ever goes out that far except us. At times our whole family would go out and camp for a week. In the winter we would go skiing. This part of the country is the most beautiful place in the world."

Trying to test him to find out if he would ever leave here she asked, "Jon, just think for a moment. What would happen if you fell in love with a girl, and she didn't want to live here? Hypothetical, suppose if we married. Then one day I said I don't want to live here. Would you leave?"

"I can't answer that yet. I still have college in front of me, and a decision to make for the future. Dad is hoping I'll take over the ranch when he's too old. His sisters went to college in the East. They never liked it here in Wyoming. They were exposed to a different life style in the big cities and married men who wanted no part of this life."

When they reached the river they let the horses graze and drink from the water. "Suppose the horses wander away, what would we do? How can we ever get back? I didn't bring my cell phone. They might not find us for days."

"Don't worry they are well trained, if they do, all I have to do is whistle."

"Oh, just like the old movie when Lauren Bacall whistled for Humphrey Bogart?"

"Keep watching." Jonathon said as he climbed on one of the horses, rode him about two hundred yards and stopped, telling the horse to stay. Walking back he whistled. Instantly, the horse looked up and returned to him..

Jon took the cooler over to the trees as Suzy stripped off her clothes and dashed into the water. Seeing Suzy's clothes lying on the side off the river He stripped off his clothes except his shorts and dove into the water. Together they swam until they reached the other side. Coming back, Jon started to leave the water when Suzy pushed him under, playfully pulling at his shorts "Come and get them if you want them."

"Suzy bring them back." He called, as he tried to cover himself. After moments of pleading he ducked into the water.

"No, you'll have to come and get them." She was anxious to gaze at that strong, tanned muscular body; knowing soon it would be hers.

Standing in the water up to his waist, Jon realized he had to come out. Suddenly Suzy started to run. Within a few moments, he caught her. She turned around to face him, kissing him as the urge to make love increased. "What are you doing?" Not listening to her he took the blanket and spread it out on the ground. When he let go, Suzy lay down and wrapped it around herself.

Standing over her Jon looked down wondering, what should he do. She lifted her arms up, her hands beckoning him to come, hoping to keep the fire in their bodies alive. "Jon, it's more exciting when you can't see what you want.

She was teasing him. Pulling the blanket off, they lay side by side unashamed, as the sun peeked through trees shining on them. Their bodies spent, they fell asleep in complete satisfaction. Feeling the coolness of the late afternoon breeze settling in, he woke up. "Suzy, it's getting late. We have to start back. Dad will be worried."

Stretching, she kissed him. "Jon, can't we stay a little longer? It's not only our making love; you're the one I would like to get seriously involved with. Why can't you go to Maryland University? It's a great school and not far away from Washington. We could see each other on weekends."

"I'll have to talk to my parents. They counted on me going to Ohio University, where my Dad did. They'll be disappointed if I don't. How can I tell them I've fallen in love with you? Most likely they'll say I'm too young to know what love is. It would shock them if they knew we had sex, then they would insist that I go to Ohio."

"Jonathon we made love, not sex. Calling sexual love just sex, loses its meaning. Just consider going to college somewhere around the Washington area. If you go to Maryland University we could see each other more often."

When they returned to the ranch Kevin and Katy greeted them. "Son, we were getting concerned. You were gone so long, and it was getting dark."

"Sorry Dad, we were both tired from the hot sun and fell asleep. We never realized it was so late." Knowing this was not the time for any discussion Katy said, "You two come with me and I'll get you both dinner. Kevin, why don't you take the horses and put them in the corral. After Jonathon was gone he checked and found a blanket with dirt particles clinging to it; this was not like Jonathon. He was so meticulous about everything he had. "I can't tell Katy." He thought. "I hope he isn't getting too deep in this relationship with Suzy. If she finds out she'll be upset."

When their dinner was over Suzy went to her room. "Can we talk?" Jon asked. "I've changed my mind about going to Ohio. I decided I'd rather go to Maryland University instead. If you ask Scott, I'll bet he can help me get in there. People in Congress have ways to accomplish what ever they want."

"It's too late to change, you're committed. We've sent in all the necessary papers to enroll you in Ohio. Can I ask you what's between you and Suzy? You've only known her for a few weeks. Is Suzy the reason because she lives in Washington and Maryland University is near by?"

"Truthfully yes, I've fallen in love with her. I can get my degree at any college." Kevin thought for a moment. "The blanket! Jonathon having sex with Suzy, is this what it's all about? Bad enough he doesn't want to go to Ohio; now sex is the only thing on his mind."

"Son, are you having sex with her?" This stunned Jonathon, not knowing what to say.

Katy looked at Kevin with a look of surprise. Why did he ask a question like that? "Wait, we have to hear his reason."

"Dad, why do you question me? You told me what could happen if I have sex before marriage." Changing the subject he continued, "Suzy is only three years older than me. Look at the difference between Scott and Jasmine or Tiffany whatever her name is. It's about twenty years between them. Suzy is in love with me."

"You've known her for a month. It takes time to build a relationship. You said you'd never leave this place. She's a city person, who knows if she'll ever consent to live here. Please give it time, before you commit yourself."

"Try to be reasonable Dad. You were in love when you were my age, weren't you? I've done everything you have wanted me to do here at the ranch. It's time for me to start my own life. You two were only twenty four when you got married. We aren't going to be living together. I could even help Scott on his campaign."

"Jonathon you're still too young to have a serious relationship with Suzy. We like her but she is established with her life and you are just beginning to start yours."

"Mother, I remember when you and Dad had a disagreement, and you left us. I've learned from your experience it will never happen to me. I'm very mature for my age, and you know that. Look what I do here at the ranch. Suzy won't interfere with my goal to have my education and degree. I love you both and my sisters too."

"Son all we are asking is that you and Suzy think seriously about your relationship. Take time to let it develop."

Later that evening Kevin found Scott sitting on the porch. "I have to ask you some questions about Suzy. I'm concerned about the two of them."

"If you're worried about Suzy, don't! She's a good woman, and would never do anything she would regret later. Don't under estimate your son Jonathan."

"Tell me about Suzy, and the type of person she is. Jonathon wants to change and not start his freshman year at Ohio University, but go to the University of Maryland.

As you know it's close to Washington where she works for you. They have been seeing a lot of each other and I have a feeling it could only be a sexual relationship."

"Come on Kevin, you know today there are very few couples who don't have sex before marriage. He's young, vibrant and testing the waters. You did, didn't you?"

Scott started to laugh, but seeing the serious look on Kevin's face he stopped. "I hired her three years ago. She's bright, comes from a wealthy family. She and Tiffany were talking about having a law office together. We must stop thinking our young people only believe in having a good time. They will be the leaders of the future. They are more advanced in the technology of science and medical world today then we are."

"Hold it a minute Scott. I hate to ask you this. We both know the reputation you have around Washington. I'm sure it's only gossip that you had a few affairs. How about Suzy and you?"

"I never tried to have an affair with her. She has a good reputation. I'm not the lover they portray me to be. My swinging days are over, you can count on that. I've settled down with Jasmine, I mean Tiffany. I really have to get used to her name. She's going to marry me, whether Jim likes it or not. The girls have become close friends. I'm sure we would be watchful over Jonathon, and spend time with them."

"I trust you as a sincere friend. When he graduates I'll need him back here to help fight those who are trying to take away the land from the tenant farmers. They want to start drilling for gas and oil. This will destroy the natural beauty of our state. All that I ask is that you keep your eye on him. Washington is taking away our freedom piece by piece, catering to the big companies, caring nothing for we who live here."

Seated inside the ranch, Jonathon heard what his Father had said. Looking out he could see Suzy standing near the corral; he raced to tell her he was going to Maryland University. "That's terrific!" she exclaimed with excitement. "If you live on campus it won't be the same as having your own place."

"I can't as a freshman, but the next year I can depending on my grades. Mom and Dad are expecting me to return to the ranch after graduation. Thanks to you this has been the best summer of my life."

Confession

It was a few nights later, Carolyn asked Scott to take a walk with her. "Scott I have to confess to you; Robbie is not your child, and not mine. My aunt has an adoption agency, and a friend brought Robbie to her. I understand her granddaughter got pregnant and the girl's Mother would not let her keep the baby. My aunt tried to raise him, but when my uncle passed away, it was too much for her."

"What has this to do with me? Now tell the truth."

"Let me finish. You know there's one trouble you have; you never listen. I came in a nice way to tell you I was sorry, but you didn't listen to what I said. My Mother said she would take care of him; and so far he's an excellent child. If I get married I'll raise him as my own. Jason's children are with their Mother. He has missed the opportunity to watch his children grow up. They're out in the East and their Mother has poisoned their minds about him. I'll have to find where Robbie really came from and legally adopt him. I might need your help."

"Well thanks for telling me the truth. We haven't been together for over a year, and Robbie couldn't be mine. It didn't work out with us. No one got hurt. I have Jasmine, you have Jason." Sarcastically Scott continued, "I thought we were real friends. If the public found that out I had fathered an illegitimate child, I'd never be able to be the candidate for the party. I'll forgive you, if you promise to actively work on my campaign."

Vacation is Over

"Okay, it will be only for six months. Jason won't have to leave here; he'll continue to be the foreman of the ranch. We can build our own home on the property Kevin gave him. I'm ready to live here and become a teacher. It's crossed my mind on occasions to be involved in the educational system. My suggestion to you Scott is to be careful. Jasmine will have a difficult time adjusting to the Washington life style, it won't be easy for her."

"Carolyn, I hope we can remain friends. If there's anything I can do for you, please don't hesitate to call. When we get back to Washington give me a ring and we can set up a plan for you to start working."

Vacation time was nearing the end, some of those who had come were now anxious to get back to their own home. "Heather, I really have to start back. It's been fun but there nothing left for me to do. I talked to my boyfriend; he's getting impatient for me to return. He wants to get married and told me before we left. I won't have another chance if I refuse him again. His two children need a Mother. If you want to stay I can catch a plane."

"You're right Chante, we'll start back tomorrow. One more day and that's it. I was only fooling around with Jonathon, trying to make Suzy jealous. He's so innocent, there is no way I was serious with him. When he gets to college, Suzy will have her hands full trying to keep him reigned in. Jim is talking about planning another reunion in twenty years. I think this is enough for me. I'm going to settle down and get married. Times have changed."

"Who are you kidding Heather? Give it up; Jonathon is in love with Suzy, don't spoil it for them. We had a good time. We've only been here six weeks and it's been fun."

"Come on Chante, you probably thought Scott would be good catch, and were disappointed when you found out he had someone else. Jasmine is a beautiful woman; I hope he can keep her. It won't be easy."

"Grow up Heather; you're not getting any younger. You might have the body of a college student but that won't last. Suzy works at Senator Scott's office, she's a smart cookie who'll get what she wants; so forget Jonathon, he's just a kid."

"Joyce, we have to leave. Our son is having a good time but somebody has to run the business. I need to be back at the office, and Eric has to go to school. We have to make arrangements for him unless you pick him up every day."

"I know Jim; our life style will change now that we have Eric. It's hard to believe after all these years we'll have the excitement and challenge of raising a child in our home."

"I've seen everything I wanted; it's been nice to have enjoyed the rest and relaxation, getting to know Eric. This trip has opened my eyes to different places in the country. I know with the migration of our citizens, also for the immigrants that are flooding our nation we'll have to start going into these smaller states and making jobs available."

"You're right Jim, I'm ready to go home too. I miss my co-workers and Adrian is getting married. She'll need my help. Her parents are gone, and if you will help me, we can give her a nice wedding."

"Of course Joyce I'll be glad to help. I miss the business and the challenge to get started on Jim's plan for a new shopping center he wants to build in Stockton. This is a great part of our country here, but not one I would like to live in every day."

The next morning Heather and Chante said their good-byes to everyone. "Thank you Kevin and Katy. We had a wonderful time." As Heather got into the drivers seat, and everyone started to wave, she called Jonathon over to the car.

Pulling him down to her she kissed him long and firm. Jonathon's face turned red. Finally he got loose and looked over to Suzy, hoping she would understand

"Jon a reminder of what you missed. You have to try a little harder, and not give up so easy to get what you desire. Remember when we were parked together and had ice cream? You know what we did." Saying it loud enough for Suzy to hear. "Remember it's our secret between you and me. I hear you are going to Maryland University maybe I'll see you there. I work in Baltimore, that's not too far away."

Driving away, Chante turned to Heather, "Embarrassing Jon in front of everyone. How could you do it? You're such a flirt, no wonder you can't keep a guy. Some day you'll meet up with someone who won't take 'No' for an answer."

"Just kidding; I was just trying to be funny." Putting the gas pedal to the floor, She sped off to go back East.

After the dust has settled Suzy asked, "What did Heather mean by and 'you know what we did'?"

"When you weren't around she would come up to me, run her hand through my hair and tell me how handsome I am. She was trying to get me excited. I'd just walk away."

"What did she mean about a secret?"

"When they first arrived Heather and I took a ride in her Corvette. We stopped at an ice cream stand and parked by the water. On an impulse I reached over and kissed her. She took her hands and held tightly to my face, kissed me and wouldn't let me go. After awhile she pulled away and said she was sorry."

"She's a fool; what happened after she kissed you?"

"Nothing Suzy, she shouldn't have let me kiss her when she arrived. I think she just decided to tease us. Dad told me at a party in college she wanted him to spend time alone with her in his room. He said she had too much to drink that night and refused to be alone with her."

"I doubt that Jonathon, older women like younger men. Just like some of the men in Congress go for the young interns. Look at me going for you, I'm older than you."

The suitcases were filled with clothes, souvenirs and presents for friends and family. Jim's Father, Joyce and Eric were ready to leave. Jim senior wanted to talk to Kevin, asking him to think of building a shopping center on his land in the future. Kevin told him he would never sell his ranch because it's for his children."

"Kevin, think of the many jobs a shopping center would create. I wouldn't need all of it and this would bring industry into this area and create many jobs. Real estate is no longer available to expand business on the coasts of our country. Your state and the others around you would profit by selling part of your land and theirs to us who are builders."

"Sorry Mr. Walker not for sale. Thanks for coming to visit us. Please feel free to come back again."

As they sat on the porch relaxing with a cup of coffee Katy turned to Karen asking," Tell me about the relationship between you and Kevin while you were in college. I know he had deep feelings for a long time. I guess he told you I left him because he wouldn't let you go. I had to leave him so he could make a choice, a past memory or a present reality."

Continuing the conversation Katy said, "What we face is that Tiffany doesn't know about her background, and someone has to tell her. We can't delay it any longer. She'll get curious and want to look for her real Father, and then finds out she's been seeing him for the past six weeks. This will crush her. Then there's Jim, Kevin feels it could ruin their friendship."

Dilemma

Listening quietly, Karen's eyes started to fill with tears. "I know Katy, I'm between a rock and a hard place. Jim is unpredictable when he is hit with something like this. He has adopted Tiffany, and loves her as if she is his own. When he hears that I'm the girl he kidded Kevin about in college, and then finds out that Tiffany is his daughter; who knows what he'll do. How do I tell her?"

"I don't know Karen. Someone has to; you know him better then anyone else. To tell him after you leave would be devastating."

"Tiffany has said she's going to marry Scott, and I'm sure she will. I should have told her before I married Jim.

It would likely have solved a part of this problem." Coming up on the porch, seeing Katy and Karen with their arms around each other, Carolyn asked, "What's wrong, what can I do?"

Breaking apart Katy responded. "We have a problem, and we don't have the answer. Where are Scott and Tiffany?"

"They're out horseback riding with Jason and Robbie." I'm sure they won't be back for awhile."

"You have a great man in Kevin. I tried to get involved in a relationship with him when we were in college, but he had his mind on the one girl he really cared for, whoever she was. Jim and I had a few dates at college; never to the serious part of a relationship. We were just friends."

"What we haven't told you is the rest of the story. Kevin is Tiffany's real Father, and Jim has adopted her legally. Can he accept this, or will in time hate us for not telling him and

Tiffany years ago? Hopefully time will heal this wound, and he can move on in having understanding and peace within him self we hope."

"Just think if I had got involved with Kevin and became pregnant which I would have liked back then. Can you believe this Karen; I would have been in your shoes and having to share this with Katy instead of you. You have to tell him. It will hurt, and no one knows how he will react.

I had Scott worried for a few weeks telling him Robbie is his son. After meeting Jason, I felt guilty and let him off the hook, by admitting he wasn't. I'm planning to adopt him next year. My Mother and I were raising Robbie together when I was living at home."

"I'm Tiffany's Mother," Karen said. "I'll have to tell her. Maybe we should sit down together and tell Jim first. Look how happy he was to find out he has a brother. He spent hours with Eric as if he was his own. Carrying him on his shoulders, giving him rides on the horses, telling him he was his big brother. He's in a great mood, and now would be a good time to tell him. He has to be told some time."

With the evening meal over Kevin poured a glass of wine for all of them. Finishing their drinks, Carolyn and Scott wandered over near the corral leaving the two couples alone. Karen sitting next to Jim slipped her hand into his. "Honey, there is some thing I want to tell you. I should have told you long ago."

"Okay Karen stop! I see you are upset. I get nervous wondering what's coming next. What can you possibly tell me that I don't already know?" Kevin, can't you say something?"

Kevin broke into the conversation. "Karen let me tell him. Jim, think back to when we were in college, and I told you about this girl I had fallen in love with. Remember when I came back from that date, I was upset and the next morning when she wouldn't answer the phone I slammed it down on the floor?"

"No I don't remember! How can you ask me what happened twenty years ago? What's this all about? If you want to tell me something, then say it. You might remember; but for me the past is gone."

Karen, with tears in her eyes said, "I'm sorry, I never told you that I had a short relationship with someone after we graduated. I wanted to tell you so many times."

"I knew you were either married or had an affair, because you had Tiffany when we got married. That didn't bother me. I adopted her and it's legal."

"Jim there is more. The young man I had the affair with was Kevin." Putting her head down she started to cry. "I'm so sorry. I should have told you when we first met."

"The girl Kevin went out with was named Alicia, you're Karen. Wait a minute! Are you telling me you're Alicia, not Karen?" Slumping back in the chair, perspiration running down his face, he was at a loss for words.

Lifting her head up her cheeks stained with tears, Karen struggled to speak but couldn't. The silence was eerie until Jim said. "Then who is the Father of our daughter? Were you married to some one else or just had another affair? I'm having a difficult time trying to separate all of this in my mind."

Kevin looked at both of them. "I'm sorry. I knew nothing about you and Alicia. We never kept close contact for the past twenty years, occasionally you and I called or E-mailed. I can honestly say, I'm glad she married you."

"Jim I never had a so called affair with anyone. If my Father had allowed me to see Kevin when I found out I was pregnant, I would have married him. My Father wouldn't let me see him. I was weak, and couldn't go against his wishes."

Jim sat silent; mulling all of this information. He found this extremely confusing. "What you're really telling me is Kevin is the real Father of my daughter. Have you told her?"

"No, I haven't had the nerve, she's happy you're her Father. She's told you many times over she loves you. She only knows Kevin is one of your best friends. She has to be told. I need your support. Kevin already knows she is his biological daughter."

"I know this hard to understand and accept." Katy said. "Kevin has told me everything, and hopes you will still be able to keep your friendship. We've all voiced our opinion. Now that we've met you, it's like we've known you for a long time."

It was a sobering moment and as much as everyone tried, they all had a heavy heart. Each of them praying that in time everything would work out. Kevin thought back to their last breakfast together. "There were times of laughter and kidding, but knowing it would be twenty years before they would meet again. There were three of us then, now more lives are involved. We promised a friendship that would never end. What will Jim do?"

Suzy was out back of the ranch when she heard Jonathon call her. "Come upstairs, be quiet. Have you seen the twins?"

"I'm not really sure. I think they're out by the corral with Jason."

"I just heard that my Father is Tiffany's Dad. He and Karen had an affair while they were in college, and she got pregnant. Her name is Alicia not Karen."

"Jon they talk about us having sex; they did the same thing when they were young; yet they tell us not to have sex. It happens to some of the interns in Washington. They get involved with one of the legislators. Sometimes a girl gets pregnant and paid off to have an abortion."

"Not only that, I heard Dad tell my Mother that Jim was real wild when he was young. He had an affair with some high school girl and she got pregnant. Later on he took a young starlet for a ride and cracked up his car almost killing her and himself. Karen was a nurse at the hospital and that's how they met."

"You better not let this slip out. If the twins find out they will ask questions and your parents will be upset that you know. I wonder how Tiffany will act when they tell her, and they'll tell Scott too. This could make your parents renege on sending you to Maryland University."

It became very quiet, not hearing any voices they left the window. Going to the bed, Jonathon laid on the top of the cover, pulling Suzy over on him. Kissing her with intent. She enjoyed it for a moment, and then pulled away. Getting up she walked over to the door. "No Jon we can't. If we got caught your parents would send me away and you would never get to Washington."

"I'm sorry Suzy. When we came back from our ride yesterday I could see my parents on the porch. Dad didn't seem happy. They seemed to have been in an intense discussion. When he got up from the chair he looked upset in whatever they were talking about. Now I know."

As they left the room, Kaylee peeked out the bedroom door. "Kaybee, guess what? Suzy came out of Jon's room. Mother said that was a no, no. Do you think they were kissing and?"

"What do you mean and? Suzy wouldn't do that. Don't you dare tell Mom, or I'll tell Jon you saw Suzy and him making out in the hayloft"

"Don't worry, I promise, I won't tell." Kaylee said as she ducked back into their room and slowly closed the door.

When Tiffany and Scott returned from their ride Kevin asked if he could have a word with him. Tiffany excused herself saying she wanted to take a shower. "Scott, I have something you should know, and you can't tell Tiffany.

Karen told us that I'm her real Father, and they're going to tell her later."

"What are you saying? You're her Father? I can't believe it! I hope Jim and Karen can find the right time to tell her. They'll have to do it before we leave. I have to get back to Washington so I can start campaigning in the fall. The party will be making plans for me to speak at many state conventions during next year."

Jasmine came back from her shower and interrupted their conversation. "Scott you promised I could go with you when you tour the country. The voters should see us together; like the former president who took his wife and daughter with him."

"We'll see what can be done. I know everyone will be leaving by the weekend, but I have to go tomorrow. After Jasmine left, Scott said to Kevin, "I hope Jim can work things out with Karen. To be hit with all of this, he must be confused when his world is falling apart."

Scott left Kevin and approached Jim who now was sitting alone on the porch. Placing his hand on Jim's shoulder he said, "I'm leaving tomorrow. We've been friends for twenty years and I hope we'll remain that way. This isn't easy for you and Tiffany. Sounds like a TV soap opera, but isn't this real life? People have disruptions in their lives? It does happen."

"So you know too. What else can happen to bring my world crashing down? Why in hell didn't someone tell me before this? I could lose my beautiful daughter, and my wife, the lights of my life. It would have been better if I had never come; then I would never known about this."

"Karen loves you. You won't lose Tiffany. She'll always be your daughter. We'll see you and Karen many times during the year."

"Remember," Jim said, "Don't ever call me Dad. I'm your friend and we'll leave it there. I know you'll have many things on your mind before the next election. Whatever you need, I'll support you. Nothing would please me more then to say, my daughter is the First Lady of the land. It will take time for me to change. You know I don't accept anything the first time."

With that said he put out his hand and as Scott grasped it Jim gave him one of his bear hugs and held on until Scott yelled, "Okay, Dad." Backing away, he said, "Don't touch me! Thank you for being so understanding."

"Scott in reality, do I have a choice? I don't think so."

That evening Katy had prepared the meal consisting of prime rib, Idaho baked potato, a variety of vegetables; the dessert was a choice of four different home made pies topped off with the ice cream of your choice. The wine flowed freely as the evening passed by. Some of the cowboys brought their musical instruments to play and sing many country songs for them.

Once More

The evening hours passed swiftly; it was time to stop. Carolyn and Jason disappeared. Scott and Tiffany soon followed suit, knowing that this would be the last night they would be together for awhile. It was after midnight, when Katy told Kaybee and Kaylee it was time. But all the pleading and begging was to no avail. "Good night you two." Lastly, Jim and Karen, Katy and Kevin said their good nights, going their separate ways.

The musicians picked up their instruments and. Kevin turned off the lights leaving Jonathon and Suzy alone by themselves. Knowing that she would have to sleep in Scott's room; did she dare ask Jonathon to come with her? She was surprised when Jon asked, "Can I come with you?"

With excitement in her voice Suzy tried to contain herself. Teasing Jonathon she replied, "If you want to."

Quietly they walked over to the bunkhouse, stepping lightly on each of the stairs. They opened the door to her room and stopped when they heard a voice from the bed, "Who's there?" Holding hands they ran to the other end of the hallway. In her excitement of having Jonathon with her she thought, "How could Tiffany forget she was to go to Scott's room for the night instead of theirs?" Still holding his hand she laughed quietly as she tried to explain to him in a whisper the mistake Tiffany made.

"What's going on?" Jonathon asked in amazement. Feeling nervous and upset, he told Suzy he couldn't stay.

She tried to calm him down, but he was too nervous knowing they couldn't be together for the night. "I really shouldn't stay Suzy. If my parents ever find us together, they will cancel my going to Maryland University."

"It's okay, we'll have other times." Walking back to the room Jon hoped his parents wouldn't hear him and was surprised when he heard his Mother say, "Goodnight Son, sleep well."

The next morning Jason asked Kevin if he could take Carolyn to the airport. She had forgotten her flight was for today. "Use my car, and would you mind taking Scott along?" Their plans to meet twenty years ago for a reunion were over.

Now only Tiffany with her parents and Suzy were left. All agreed this was one of the most enjoyable vacation times they ever had. Feeling out of place, Suzy excused herself, walked over to the corral hoping to see Jonathon. Last night had been quite an experience and she was dying to tell Tiffany when the opportunity would arise. They were building a relationship, and hoped it would last.

"Let's go out to the river for a picnic?" Jon asked Suzy. "I'm sure Angela will pack a lunch for us. Get your bathing suit; we can go for a swim too." When Jonathon returned with a cooler it was filled with food and cold drinks. He saddled the horses and put a second blanket on his horse.

Noticing Jon took an extra blanket Kevin thought, "They're having sex, and I can't say anything; it happened to us. Our situation was different; we were getting married.

I lied when I told Katy I had talked to Jon about sex. I'll have to talk to him now, or he'll be in trouble if she gets pregnant. I should have told him long before this. He remembered another sermon the minister once said; be sure your sins will find you out. Why do these things keep popping into my head? I guess I'm as guilty as the rest. Is it a sin when you love someone?"

When Suzy and Jonathan reached the river they tied their horses in the shade of the trees after letting them drink from the water. Suzy took her swimsuit and went behind a tree to slip it on.

Jon undressed, putting on his trunks and spreading out the blanket, placing his clothes on it he ran down to the water and dove in calling Suzy to join him. The trees on the mountains were beginning to shed their leaves, quietly falling. The wind would lift them up; then gently drop them down to the ground.

It was a beautiful sight; one Suzy would not see when she returned to Washington. She was getting hungry. "I'm starving, how about having something to eat?" Jonathon swam over to the shore, removed all of the food and drinks from the cooler.

"Close your eye Suzy; I have a surprise for you." From the cooler he brought out a bottle of wine and poured it into two glasses and said, "You can open your eyes now." He handed Suzy one of the glasses of wine with a toast. "May our love become stronger each day."

She pulled Jonathon down beside her; kissing him gently as her eyes glistened with tears. "Jon, sweetheart, I do love you so much. We can make it."

"I hope so. My Dad is very disappointed I'm not going to Ohio University. I have a feeling he knows we've got involved. I can tell by the way he watches me."

"Suzy said, my Father would say, if you take one step at a time toward the goal you have set for yourself, you will reach it. There isn't a mountain you can't climb over; or an ocean you can't swim across, if you have the desire and effort to prevail over any obstacle."

At the ranch Katy asked, "I made a pot of coffee; anyone interested?" With affirmative answers, she went inside and brought coffee and a coffee cake.

As they relaxed, Kevin said, "I think before you go we need to talk to Tiffany. Tell her who I am, and the relationship Karen and I had in college. She has the right to know."

"I think Karen should tell her alone. She can explain it to her better then we can. She's her Mother, and should do it. When the time comes for her to get married, I'd like to give her away. She's my daughter as well as yours Kevin."

"There's no better time than now. I'd like to share some time with her too. I know my children will love to have her as a sister. If you want to walk her down the aisle alone, I have no objection; let her know now, before she makes plans to get married. By the way, where is she?"

More Truth

"She's gone to the airport with Scott and should be returning soon. Jim, I'd like you to be with me when I tell her. She knows you as her Father and Katy is right. She will make the decision how her wedding will be."

"Kevin I think we should disappear for awhile and let Jim and Karen be alone with her."

After they left Karen said, "I know I shouldn't have waited. When she was fourteen I didn't feel comfortable to tell her. She didn't pressure me and was happy that you were her Father, so what could I do? The only problem I had was when she decided to stop going to camp. I tried to find out if anything was wrong, her reply was always the same, nothing was wrong. I called Mrs. Johnson and she didn't have any answer. I gave up, and changed the subject. Here she comes now."

There was tension in both of them as Tiffany approached. "What a beautiful country out here. I never want to live here, but it's a wonderful place to come on vacation. Where are Katy and Kevin?"

"They've gone for a ride out on the range to the river. Kevin suggested we should come out next year and go hunting. Tiff, your Mother and I have something to talk over with you. Would you like something to drink?"

"Come on Dad, you know we always could talk openly, we never hid anything from each other. So what is it you want to talk about?"

"Karen you tell her, you're the one who should start."

Her hands sweating and her face flushed, she looked over to Tiffany, trying to find the right words to say. "When you asked me at fourteen who your Father was; I would tell you it was not the time, but I would tell you later. You accepted it and never pressured me again. Dad and I agree you should know." Jim could see by the expression on her face she had many questions to ask. Sitting on the edge of the chair Tiffany was anxious for Karen to start. She was crossing and un-crossing her legs, impatiently waiting. Karen had difficulty getting her words out.

Watching Tiffany moving nervously on the chair, her hands clasped together, Jim finally broke the silence "Honey relax, Mother will let you ask any questions you have; don't be so nervous."

"I'm not nervous. Now you have opened up the subject, and you have me anxious. As was said, and now for the rest of the story. "

"Tiffany, when I was in college, I had a relationship with one of the students. It was the first time I had made love. with any one. It was not just having sex. I fell in love. I was the one who lost control, not him. He respected me, and didn't force himself on me."

"Mother, I'm a young woman now, and capable of handling anything you want to tell me. If you're too uncomfortable to talk about it in front of Dad, we can wait for another time. There's nothing that will shock me."

"You're right, now is the time to tell you who you're Father is. You'll be getting married next year, and I don't want to have any secrets as you start your new life." Karen stopped for a moment to compose herself, and then softly said, "Your real Father is Kevin!"

There was dead silence as Jim looked down to the floor. Karen's eyes continued filling with tears, her voice quivering as she tried to continue, but was unable to. Tiffany's face went ashen white, staring at her parents in amazement. After many minutes had gone by, they were still at a loss to speak.

Tiffany finally broke the silence. "What am I suppose to say? My Dad is here! Right here! Jim is my Father. He's the only one I know as Dad." Getting up from the chair she went to him holding him tightly. Releasing herself she stood in front of Karen and said, "Mother, why did you wait until now? What do you want from me?"

"Tiffany, I love you, I'll always be your Dad. Kevin is my best friend and I know he loves you too. When the time is ready, you and Kevin can share time together, get to know each other."

Looking away from her Mother, Tiffany answered with a question. "What will Katy say, and there is her children and Scott? This means that Kevin's children. Jonathon is my half brother and the twins are my half sisters. Do they know?"

"Katy knows and will tell her children. She's very understanding, and is delighted you are a part of her family. Scott and Carolyn know about this and are glad for you. Now you have a brother and sisters."

Stunned at the reality of what her Mother had said, Tiffany walked down the stairs toward the corral. Looking up at the clear blue sky as the sun dispensed her thoughts of the situation, quickly consuming them as more thoughts entered her confused mind.

Turning toward her parents she asked, "What can I say to Kevin? How will he react toward me? Oh God, help me! I don't know what to do or say. Why oh why did you wait until this time?"

"Where are you going?" Karen called. Not answering, Tiffany went into the barn and brought out a saddle. Hanging the saddle on one of the posts she thought, "I need to get away for awhile." Climbing up on the fence she slipped falling from the top rail, landing on her head inside the corral. Jim realizing what had happened leaped off the porch and raced to her.

He started to pick her up and stopped, when Karen yelled, "No Jim, let her stay, she might have broken something. "Call 911." Running down to Tiffany, leaning over her Karen said a silent prayer. When the ambulance arrived, the EMTS checked Tiffany and decided she had no broken bones; but to be sure there were no internal injuries, they took her to the hospital for a complete examination.

Later sitting in the waiting room they received good news, Tiffany had no serious internal injury, but had been badly bruised.

No visitors were allowed to see her until the next day. The doctor decided she had to stay the night as a precaution to be sure she would be okay. Jim and Karen returned to the ranch after hearing the encouraging words to tell Katy and Kevin who had returned from their ride. They sat out on the porch just trying to get adjusted to what the events of the day would mean to each of their lives in the future.

The sound of the siren of the EMT'S ambulance earlier had kept the twins and Jonathon nervous until they were given the good news Tiffany would be okay. Suzy joined them hoping her friend would have nothing serious. It was a sleepless night at the ranch hearing the grandfather's clock chiming every quarter hour. Finally at three in the morning Kevin went down and stopped the clock.

Karen called the hospital at eight o'clock and was told they could see Tiffany at ten, and she would be discharged. Jim asked Kevin and Katy if they would mind staying here when they went to bring Tiffany back. "Jim you know she can stay here as long as she wants. Everything we have is at your disposal."

"I just want her to be okay. That's all that matters. Any thing else we have to do can wait for now. In time, we can get together and hash over what has to be resolved."

When Tiffany was released from the hospital and brought back to the ranch Karen put her in bed to rest and gain strength for the long ride back to Washington. Lifting up her head from the pillow the next morning, Tiffany was startled to see her Mother. "Mother, what are you doing here?"

"Honey, how are you feeling? We were concerned when you slept so long. Don't you remember what happened?"

"No, I remember slipping off the fence and nothing more, until I came to in the hospital and a doctor was asking me if I could hear him. Where is Scott?"

"He left yesterday and told you that he would see you in Washington. He flew back with Carolyn and little Robbie. Just relax; I'll bring breakfast to you. Stay in bed and rest."

"Please don't tell Scott what happened. He'll rush back here. He has to start his campaigning right away. I'll tell him when I get back. My head is still so fuzzy, my eyes are not clear. "I have to get back to the office and start working. It will be at least three days of driving, so we'll have to hurry. I don't want him to worry."

Having breakfast alone with Tiffany, Suzy reminded her they had to leave the next day. "It will take us at least three days to get back. I can call Helen to tell Scott we'll be there as soon as we can. I'll think of some excuse."

"Okay, just give me today to talk to my parents. Something very important has come up; I have to understand what they had told me yesterday. I'll tell you later. It was a terrible shock to me and could change my life forever."

"I hope it isn't serious. You don't have to tell me if you don't want to."

Feeling better Tiffany went out to see her parents and sat down facing them. She had questions to be answered, but didn't know how to begin. Not being sure what to say. Katy came out to the porch asking if there was anything they would like to do for the day. "If you want to be alone I'll keep everyone away." It was a difficult time; words were meaningless. Katy turned and started back inside the ranch to help Angela clean up the morning dishes.

"Tiffany, we told you that Kevin and Katy know about the situation and we're both okay with whatever you choose to do. It won't affect Kevin and Scott's relationship with me. I'm your Dad, and willing to share you with Kevin if you decide to get to know your biological Father." Because of no response, Jim continued. "I'm sorry; your Mother didn't tell you sooner. It's just a twist of fate that this came out. We want to be a part of your future life, and to help you."

"Sweetheart, when you came into my life, I wasn't ready to have a child. I was looking to pursuing my career as a nurse; later on getting married and having children. I didn't plan for this to happen, but it did. I fell in love with Kevin at that time of my life. It was my fault I didn't tell you, when you asked me. I regret it now. Your grandfather was very strict with me. I was innocent then.

Jim walked over to Tiffany, reached down lifted her up holding her close. Karen rose up from her chair, looked at this big, rugged man so strong, showing in words and action how much he loved her. While she continued to watch them, Karen felt a strong feeling within herself. She knew she had done the right thing for Tiffany and herself.

Justin Calls

The day was slipping away and Tiffany decided she couldn't leave until she talked to Kevin alone and to tell Suzy of what had happened. Everyone was sitting on the porch when the phone rang. I'll answer it." Katy said. "Hello, who's calling?"

"Is there someone by the name of Tiffany there?" This is an old friend from her past. I've been trying to find her for the last six months since I've returned to the states."

"Yes, may I ask who is calling?"

"If you don't mind, I want it to be a surprise. She'll recognize my voice as soon as I speak. That's why I would rather not give my name."

"Wait, I'll ask her if she wants to take the call."

"Tiffany, it's for you. Someone out of your past he said. He wouldn't tell me his name, He wants to surprise you."

Tiffany started to think as she went inside to answer the call. "Who would know me out here, how did they find me? Could this be Philip, still haunting me? Maybe it was someone I dated in college."

"Tiffany, it is you! I'd recognize your voice anywhere. You were so beautiful, how could I ever forget you. You were the only one I ever wanted. I've been in England attending Oxford University. Can we get together, share some time, and talk about the old days."

Her hands began to shake, as she thought back to her teenage years. "No, it can't be!" She clasped her hands together, finding it hard to control them. "Justin, is that you?" Her body felt cold, as if someone had dropped an icicle down her back. She tried to keep calm, but dropped the phone. Gaining her composure she picked it up; remembering it was six or seven years ago that he took advantage of her.

"How did you find me? What do you want? We haven't seen each other for six or seven years. The past is over between us. Thinking, "Has he found out about the baby? "What can I do, if he knows?"

"Are you going to college? Tell me Tiffany, has someone else taken my place, or am I still the only one? I'd like to see you again, take you to dinner, and maybe have a date or what ever you'd like to do. Your boyfriend doesn't have to know. It'll be between you and me, for old time's sake."

She remembered the night when they had sex. Why has he come back into my life now, she wondered? Gaining her composure, "Justin, I don't know how you found me. I'm graduating from college, am engaged and will be married next year. I'll be working for the FBI in Washington. A lot of years have passed and I've found a new life, as I'm sure you have. We have nothing in common and what we had was just teenage things. I told you a long time ago it was over." She wanted to tell him about Scott, but thought better of that for now.

"Come on Tiff, let's get together for one more time, and share what has happened since we were teenagers. I remember how frightened you were thinking you would get pregnant. "You didn't, did you?"

"You're right. I don't have a child." Knowing she lied, touching her stomach as her memory of giving birth to the baby came alive. She shuttered to have that situation return in conversation, which was lost in her past; and now revived.

She became nervous and upset as tears started. Gaining her composure she steadied herself again. "Our relationship was over a long time ago. Let the past go and look to the future."

"Wait, Tiffany! Don't hang up!"

"A lot of years have passed and I've found a new life, as I'm sure you have. We have nothing in common and what we had was just teenage things. I told you before it was over. It's been a surprise to hear from you, and I wish you the best in your future. I must hang up now."

"I want to see you. Here's my phone number, call me." Justin was unaware she had hung up the phone, until he heard the dial tone.

Not wanting to face those on the porch, she went into the bathroom dried the tears, washed her face, and put on fresh makeup. When she returned to the porch everyone wanted to ask who was on the phone; but knowing Tiffany had enough surprises, they sat silent. Feeling the mood of all of them wanting to know, she told them. "You would never believe it. It was a former boyfriend of mine from high school. He never did tell me how he found out that I was out here."

"Do I dare ask Tiffany, or can I guess?"

"Mother, you don't have to guess. What boy did I date for a long time?"

Jim jumped into the conversation, "Had to be the star football player. If I remember, his name is Justin."

"You're right Dad, it was him. He's been attending Oxford University in England. We had planned that we would go there together when we graduated."

"Come to think about it, whatever caused you to break up? Looking at each other, cautiously waiting which one would try to answer Jim's question.

"I know Dad; we had what you would call a kid thing. Every girl in high school had to have a boyfriend, or the kids would think you were a nerd or queer, whatever."

Karen remembered she never did tell Jim that Justin had tried to have sex with Tiffany. "It's been our secret, and I'm glad they broke up. Thank God she didn't get pregnant."

After a time of quietness Tiffany responded, "He found another girlfriend. I guess she was more of a party girl; did things I wouldn't do. That's enough of my past. Let's talk about job, and my future wedding plans."

"Justin was the same age as you wasn't he?" In a moment he was sorry he said that when he looked at Karen's face, and saw the anger she had for him, keeping the subject alive.

Katy's Advice

It was getting late and everyone decided to retire early for the night. Suzy and Tiffany went to their room to pack their suitcases for their journey back to Washington. Jim and Karen also went to get ready. They wanted to get an early start to fly back to California.

Finishing packing her suitcase Suzy told Tiffany she was going to say goodbye to Jon. Going over to the ranch she saw Katy by the corral. "Jon is sitting on the porch, I think he would like to see you before you leave."

When he saw her coming to the porch he reached out to hug and hold her, but she quickly pushed him away. "Easy Jon. Your Mother can see us. You'll be living on campus, and we can see each other only on weekends; your studies must come first. I'll be sharing an apartment with Tiffany until I can find my own. Be patient, I love you and just want to spend a little time tonight with you before I get some sleep. We'll have many times to be together."

After Suzy said her goodbyes to Jonathon, she went to the corral where Katy was waiting. "Suzy we've enjoyed your company and getting to know you. We like you very much, and hope you and Jon will move slowly. Please encourage him to get his degree before you get too serious about marriage. You're the first girl, I should say woman he has become attracted to."

"I'm a few years older but I've fallen in love with him. I understand how much you want to see him be successful. You can be sure I'll encourage him to attain the goals for his life. I'll keep in touch with you." Reaching over Katy gave her a hug. She could see her eyes well up with tears that made her aware Suzy had the determination Jon would succeed.

Katy knew she would be losing her son little by little, as time went by.

When Katy went inside the ranch Jonathon came to Suzy and said, "I'm sorry. I shouldn't act like I did. I know my life will change Some times my parents look at me as if I'm still a little boy needing their protection."

"Jon you Mother had a lot to say about you and me. We have to move slowly and your education is the first priority in your life not me. I want your Dad to like me. Men think differently then women. I want him to be like one of his daughters and that will take time."

The time had come for Jim and Karen to say their goodbyes. They thanked Katy and Kevin for their kindness in hosting the first reunion. "Kevin, next time its California. Can you believe we'll be over sixty? I wonder what the next twenty will bring. Let's keep in touch; maybe we should consider making it ten years, I'll contact Scott and ask him."

"I think you're right Jim, probably we'll have grandchildren by then, and more marriages too. Thanks for coming Karen; it's good to see you again." Suddenly Kevin took Karen in his arms and kissed her long and hard. Jim said, "That's enough now. I suppose you want her to return that kiss the next time, like Carolyn did."

Dad and Daughter

"I guess Kevin is still carrying the torch, not accepting it has burned out. I still love him and I know he loves me." Katy thought. "They say absence makes the heart grow fonder or out of presence out of mind."

It was difficult for Karen and Jim to realize their daughter was now a young woman and leaving her home.

Seeing Tiffany Karen said, "Please take the time to come home once in awhile, and Scott too."

"Don't worry Mother, we will." Tiffany replied as she started walking to her car, then suddenly turned and asked Kevin if she could talk to him alone. Going back to the porch she said, "Kevin, I had no Dad or Grandfather as a male figure until Jim came into our lives. A few times I asked my Mother about my real Father and she would say sometime I'll tell you. That time never seemed to come when she was able to tell me what I wanted to hear."

Feeling nervous, Tiffany stopped, drew a breath and continued. "You have three great kids, and Katy who loves you. Jim my Dad, my Mother and myself, are the only family we have. I can't do anything that would destroy our love and friendship; Mom is happy where she is at this stage of her life. You three will always be friends. Dad has spoken so much of your great friendship. I hope you can find it in yourself to accept me not as a daughter, more as a friend."

With those comments Tiffany took out her handkerchief and wiped her eyes. Kevin sat silently looking up toward the sky, finding it difficult what to say.

Shaken by Tiffany's words, he wondered, "What's coming next." Reaching out, Kevin held her close. "I do love you Tiffany and I had hoped we could be Father and Daughter. I see now this will never happen. Yes, we can be friends, if that's all you want."

"I can never be a real daughter to you, but as I said, I want to be a friend to you and Katy, a sister to Jon and the twins. This isn't goodbye. Will you be one of the best friends that I'll ever have? Can you do this for me? I do love you, because you're my birth Father. It was circumstances that we had no control of that has made our lives what they are."

"I'm disappointed that it has turned out this way." Kevin replied. "I was in love with your Mother and tried desperately for years to try and locate her after we graduated from college. I thought you might be happy to find your real Father; but I guess young people feel different today. I didn't abandon you, I never knew about you."

"It's nobody's fault. We're one of many that have had similar things like this happen in their lives. Please, will you be my friend and let me be a part of your family?"

Breaking away she continued, "Don't blame my Mother. She did the best she could have done in that time of her life." With tears coming down her face, she left the porch. Kevin stood there trying to come to grips of what Tiffany had just told him what she wanted. Slowly with a heavy heart, he descended the porch steps to stand by Katy.

With a wave of her hand, not looking back Tiffany drove out of the driveway, heading for Washington. Once out of sight she pulled to the side of the road suggesting Suzy drive. "Are you alright? Suzy asked

"I don't want to drive right now; just sad that it's over. I have so much to think about. I can't talk about it now. In time I need to share with you what has happened this past week. My mind is all mixed up."

"I'll be there for you Tiffany, when ever you decide."

Sitting on the porch it was quiet. "It's all over; what a great time we had. We shouldn't wait for twenty years, maybe just ten years. Now we have to get back to reality. We can see some of them before that, can't we Kevin? Looking over at her husband Katy could see that something was troubling him. Kevin! What's wrong?"

"Yeah Dad." said the twins "Isn't it great. We have a new sister and she said we could go to Washington on a trip sometime and see where Jon is going to college. That'll be neat."

"What's wrong Kevin you seem so sad?"

"Nothing honey, I guess being busy these past weeks is finally catching up with me; and the shock of Jonathon going to Maryland University hurts me. I really wanted him to go to Ohio. Finding out I have a daughter I have now met for the first time! One of my best friends is married to the girl I was in love with in college, and she's the Mother of my first daughter.

Then to top it off, my other best friend is marrying my daughter, the one I never knew until now. To finalize it all, my new daughter has just told me that she couldn't call me Dad, but I could be her best friend. Figure that one out if you can Katy!"

"Kevin, I'm sick at heart for you. It's been one of the hardest times in your life. I'm trying to understand what you have gone through and had to learn these past weeks. We still have each other, a son Jon, our two girls Kaylee and Kaybee. A wonderful home you have worked so hard on. We have each other, what more can we ask?"

"You're right Katy; we have everything that we desired. We're blessed with this ranch Dad gave to us, and enjoying the fruits of his labor. I have our three children, and you my wonderful wife. Thanks Katy for being you. Let's celebrate the good times yet to come. Thanks especially for your patience and understanding."

Kevin went inside brought out a bottle of wine and poured a glass for Katy and him self. "To you Katy, who has loved me through all of our married life. When I fall down, you're always there to pick me up. If I run to fast, you slow me down. Thanks for your love; you're the only one for me."

"I think we better slow down. I don't want to make any mistakes like I've done in the past. Remember we agreed, no more children." Finishing the glass, he poured another. In a moment of time they finished that bottle and consumed another. Katy knew they had better stop before the children see them. Going into the living room he put on a CD.

Growing Up

Kaylee and Kaybee were watching in the window as their parents danced. Soon the wine took control of their actions, and Kevin and Katy started kissing. Moving over to the couch, they laid down on it, their emotions rising. "We better stop the kids will see us."

"Kaybee, we better not look anymore, if we get caught we'll be in trouble, and there'll be restrictions for a month. Dad is very funny when he has too much to drink."

"They aren't doing anything, only kissing. I think they're getting drunk. We can look a little longer to see what they'll do next."

"What are you two doing?" At the sound of Jon's voice they turned to run, but he caught them before they got away.

"We were just watching Mom and Dad dancing."

Looking in the window he quickly turned away. "Is that all you saw them doing? Are you sure? Don't let me ever see you spying on Mom and Dad again!" They were just dancing, and then they started to lie down on the couch."

We promise we'll never do it again." Thinking Jon had left, Kaybee said, "Remember when Mum and Dad were up in the hayloft last summer, we heard them laughing."

"Yeah, and Mom was telling Dad to stop; then it got quiet and you fell off the ladder. Dad saw you as you were running out of the barn. "Did you tell him?"

"No, I never told. They would have been mad. Dad asked me what I was doing on the ladder and I didn't know what to say. I can't tell you what they were doing"

"What did you see?" You can tell me, I won't tell. I bet you they were making love. I tell you everything."

"I don't know. I hope Jonathon doesn't tell Mom and Dad. We'd be grounded for the rest of the summer."

"No, he won't, if he does I'll tell about him and Suzy up in the loft, and what they were doing. I heard them talking and she was saying take it easy Jon. They were probably only kissing and doing what my boyfriend tried to do to me."

Walking away Jon over heard Kaybee and Kaylee arguing. "What did you just say?" He asked. "Who was saying take it easy? Were you listening to what they were saying? If you saw Mom and Dad doing anything, just forget it."

Before Kaylee started to walk away, she turned around to Jon. "If you tell on us, I'll tell Mom what you and Suzy were doing in the hay loft, so there!"

"What did you think you saw?" He took Kaylee by the shoulders. "You never saw anything?" Squeezing her His face turned red as he remembered what Suzy said to him in the hayloft. That goes for you too Kaybee just forget it."

"We know why you want to go to Washington, so you can be with Suzy. We know what you've been doing. Mom told us not to do that until we get married. You'll be sorry if she has a baby."

After driving for two hours Tiffany took over. They both were relaxed; their voices joined together, singing the songs coming from the radio. Turning to Suzy for an instant, then quickly turning back to keep her eyes on the road. "Will you be my maid of honor in my wedding?"

There was no answer. With a second glance Suzy had fallen asleep. Tiffany kept thinking of Scott and the plans she hoped for in the future, to be married next year before the election. Stopping for lunch they found a small interesting restaurant in Iowa. Finishing lunch, and filling the car with gas they continued on with Suzy driving.

The sun had disappeared over the horizon and it was time to stop for the night. They started looking for a place to stay.

Finding a motel they paid for one night, planning an early start in the morning. Two days later they arrived in Washington. Parking the car in the garage, Tiffany hurried ahead, anxious to call Scott. Suzy followed, struggling with some of the suitcases. Finally calling out, "I need help!"

Putting the phone back in place, Tiffany replied, "I'm sorry. I'm anxious to call Scott to let him know we're here."

Turning around she was startled to see her neighbor standing across in the hallway at the open door of his apartment. "Hello Josh, how's everything in Washington since we've been gone?" Not waiting for an answer she continued, "It's beautiful; in Wyoming. You should plan to go out there some time. I'll show you the pictures we had taken. The herds of horses running wild are something else to see."

Washington D.C.

"It's good to see you back Jasmine. There was a young man the other night asking if you lived here. I didn't tell him because he said he was your boyfriend in high school, and wanted to renew the good times he had with you. He didn't seem the type you'd go out with."

"Thanks so much. I know who he is; and he's a part of my life I'd like to forget. Thanks for letting me know." Turning to Suzy she said, "Lets get settled, I'll have the front bedroom and you can have the other."

"I'm glad we can share this place. We can use one car; unless something comes up and we have different hours or have to take a trip somewhere." The drive back had been exhausting; it didn't take long for them to retire early.

The next day they were surprised to find floral arrangements on their desks, with cards to welcome them back. Glancing over to Suzy, Tiffany could see the look on Philip's face. When she saw him rise up from his chair, and walk toward her, Suzy quickly stepped in front of him blocking his way. In a whispered tone she said to Philip,

"Remember five years ago when you tried to rape me; I told you if you ever tried to do that again I would tell the Senator, and bring charges against you in court for rape."

They stood glaring at each other for a moment until Philip backed away and said to Jasmine, "We're glad to have you back." Then turning to Suzy continued speaking just loud enough for her to hear, "I'll get even with you Suzy, no matter how long it takes."

Helen was hoping some day she would replace him as first assistant to the Senator. Seeing the glare of hatred in Philip's face she decided to speak to him. "You better be careful how you treat Jasmine, or it will be the last year you'll work here. She will be his wife in the near future, you can be sure of that. I've been here, almost as long as you. I know everything that goes on in this office." With all the control he could muster, his face turning red, he said nothing.

Helen stopped for a minute to catch her breath. "Don't go yet; I haven't finished what I have to say. I could have you fired, and you know it. This is the last time we'll have a conversation about this. If you want to be with the Senator after he assumes the Presidency you better change your ways. He promised he would take his whole office force with him. My advice to you is, don't press your luck."

Philip wanted to lash back at her but he thought better of it. "Okay everyone, the Senator will be back in a day or two and everything he wanted done must be completed and on his desk. Let's get back to work." The rest of the staff completely ignored Philip, and continued to gather in a group, asking about their vacation.

"Wait a minute! "I have to tell you something. Jasmine is not my real name it's Tiffany. It's a long story. Please call me Tiffany."

The day passed quickly; and when Suzy and Tiffany arrived back at the apartment there were messages from Scott and Jonathon. "They sure do miss us Suzy, don't they? Not as much as we miss them though. Truthfully it'll be good when we each have our own places won't it?"

When Scott occasionally came over for dinner it was very difficult for Suzy. Knowing they wanted to be alone. she would go on long walks or take in a movie. She wanted her own place, knowing Jonathon would be arriving for his first semester at the University. She felt that sharing an apartment would interfere with her relationship with him.

While sitting on a bench one evening in the park, a young man sat down beside her. "I saw you coming out from that apartment complex," pointing to where she was staying. "Do you know some of the people who live there?"

Surmising this seemed like a pickup attempt she answered, "Yes I do. Why do you ask?" Not waiting for a reply she continued, "Well, not really. I'm staying with my sister, she was in a car accident and can't be alone until she is fully recovered."

"I've been trying to find an ex girlfriend, and want to get re-acquainted with her. We had a great thing going when we were in high school. She was beautiful, with golden blonde hair so bright and natural. Her name was Tiffany. Do you know anyone by that name that lives there?

Looking at him, she saw a handsome athletic man, the type many women would love to have a date with. She continued to look into his eyes and had other thoughts; this guy was egotistical, sure of himself, frightening to be near.

Suzy felt uncomfortable when he would stare back at her. and became uneasy in his presence. She wondered, "How did he find her here?" Gathering her composure she replied, "Not that I know of. It's hard to know everybody in the complex."

Justin could sense her uneasiness; she was either not wanting to talk with him, or maybe, just maybe, she knows Tiffany. "Did Tiffany tell her about my telephone call out in Wyoming? I wonder are they friends?"

It was getting dark and they were alone. Suzy became more leery of him by the minute and gave him an excuse. "I have to leave now. I'm sorry; my sister needs me back at the apartment. I can't stay any longer. She's frightened to be alone."

"That's too bad. Let me give you my card, my telephone number is on it. If you meet Tiffany tell her I would like to see her. She came from California and her Father is a multi –

millionaire. He builds large shopping centers all over the country. I think he's very friendly with the Senator from North Carolina. It must be tiresome taking care of your sister. Would you like to go out some time? My name is Justin; and your name is?"

"Ignoring his request Suzy replied, "No thank you. I know my boyfriend wouldn't appreciate it. He's extremely jealous and if he saw you with me, I would be afraid for you." To make sure he had left, she wandered around the park to be sure he was gone. Opening the door of the apartment she heard Tiffany and Scott in the bedroom. Not wanting to embarrass them, she turned on the television.

Hearing the door close Tiffany and Scott were startled and realized they were no longer alone. Quickly they rose and Scott went to take a shower, Tiffany slipped on a robe and came into the room. "Suzy you're back so soon? I know it's warm outside. It's cooler here with the air conditioner."

"Sorry Tiff, I should have stayed out longer, but I have a surprise to tell you after Scott leaves."

"What surprise? Scott can't hear us, the water's running; he's taking a shower. Tell me now."

"Not now! It's a long story. If he hears us talking he'll insist we tell him what we're talking about. I don't want him to know, and neither will you. This will be between both of us. Be patience, I'll tell you later, after he leaves. Trust me; you don't want him to know."

They were surprised when they heard Scott say, "What was that you said Suzy?"

"Nothing that would interest you; just some things between Tiffany and me. You wouldn't want to know." Scott said his good night to the girls and left.

"Okay Suzy tell me. What can it possibly be? Don't stall, is it good news or bad?"

"Tonight when I was sitting in the park, this handsome young man sat down beside me. He told me his name is Justin; and he knew you back in high school days. He claimed you two had a love affair, and wants to get together with you. I have to tell you, he's one hunk of a man, but there's something about him I didn't like."

"Remember the call I got just before we left Wyoming? It was Justin who called me. I can't believe he still wants to see me. He doesn't give up easy, and is very persistent until he breaks you down and you give him his way.

I should have known when I went with him something would happen, and I'd live to regret it, and I have. One night he came over to our house; my parents were away and the housekeeper went out on an errand. I didn't want to have sex with him, but I did. It was the first and the last time."

"Tiff, he even asked me to call him and would take me out on a date. He knew all about your family. I thought he was a real conceited jerk. He has that devilish look in his eyes. You had a feeling you'd like to date him once, but there was something about him I didn't trust."

"Suzy, don't even think about it. I can see that look in your eyes. You would like a challenge, wouldn't you? Believe me he's powerful and persuasive."

"I wouldn't have sex with him. I'd like to let him try, just to see how far he would go, before I shot him down." With that, Tiffany burst out laughing.

"If he's the same as he was when we were young, you would lose. He's so convincing. I told you I gave into him when I was fourteen. I often wanted to try sex but was afraid. We broke up because he would want to do it all the time. I was a virgin. Suzy, you're my best friend and there's more to the story. I want to leave it there."

"Tiffany I'll never ask you about your past. Don't tell me if you'd rather not."

"Thanks, I'm not ready yet. I'll tell you when I feel comfortable about it."

It was a sleepless night for them. Suzy wanted to be a good listener. Tiffany wanting to tell her she had gotten pregnant. Feeling some day she would have to share what happened that night with her Mother. The guilty feeling of betrayal had to be confessed. She needed to have her Mother's forgiveness and how her Father would react?

Tiffany went quietly to the refrigerator remembering what her Mother had told her. Looking up as Suzy entered the kitchen she said, "My Mother told me if you can't sleep, get a glass of milk, it'll calm you down."

Suzy agreed saying, "You know, that's what my Mother used to say." After finishing their drink they stood in silence for a few moments, gave each other a hug and headed back to their own rooms.

It was September, Jonathon entered the University of Maryland; Suzy had found an apartment of her own, and Washington had again become a beehive of activity. Scott was traveling about the country leaving Tiffany alone

To fill up her time and loneliness, she would join Suzy and Jonathon for lunches or dinners. Telephone calls from Scott, telling her how much he missed her was not the same as him being here in Washington. She wanted to hear those words from Scott, "I love you."

Suzy had to be the stronger of the two with Jon wanting to see her every weekend and stay at her apartment. She refused to let that happen. "We're not married. I promised your Mother to be sure you stayed at the college. We have to wait until you graduate."

Justin Calls Again

One evening Tiffany found a note tacked to her door. "I must see you again. I have news you would be very interested in. It's important that we talk about what I learned from my Mother. I found out where you're working, and want to respect your privacy; but I must see you. Here's my telephone number. I've only two more weeks in Washington before I go back to California, please contact me."

Tiffany was stunned, thinking back to the times of camp. "Does he really know I had a baby and signed a paper to give him away? Does he know where the baby is? The little boy must be about six years old by now. I feel no attachment to him, and yet I feel guilty at the same time. Should I tell Scott? My parents will be devastated. I'm so humiliated."

Going into the apartment, she closed the door, staggered over to the couch, bursting into tears. "Please God, what should I do?" Don't let me down now!" She picked up the phone and called Suzy. "Please come over! I have to tell you a secret I've kept silent for six years. Even my parents don't know."

Hearing the anxiety in her voice, she asked, "What's wrong; are you hurt? Is anyone there with you? Please just stay as calm as you can. Before I come, should I call Scott?"

"No! Don't call him, please don't! I need to talk to you now!" Driving as fast as she dared, Suzy arrived at Tiffany's place in a few minutes. Running up the stairs she knocked on the apartment door. "It's me, Tiff, let me in!"

Tiffany opened the door flinging herself into Suzy's arms. Holding her, Suzy kicked the door closed with her foot as she guided Tiffany over to the couch. "Relax Tiff, everything will be all right. Try to calm down, then we can talk about the problem."

It took a long time before Tiffany was able to talk. Still shaking she dried her eyes and started to tell her story. "Remember the telephone call I had back in Wyoming before we left. I told you it was a boy friend from high school days. Then you told me about the jerk you met in the park. That was Justin, and he's found me."

"Let me get you a glass of water. Just be quiet for a minute."

"When I got home from work tonight, there was a note tacked to the door. It was from Justin and it said, "We better talk because I have something very important to tell you. Suzy I need your help. Just be patient with me, this is going to be difficult for me. I have no one else to share this with but you."

"I told you Tiff, we're friends, and I'd never betray you. If it weren't for you I wouldn't have met Jonathon. Let me call Scott. He would want to be here with you."

"I've told you some things, now I need to tell you the whole story. When I was fourteen, Justin came over to my house one night to study for a very important exam. My Mother and Father were on a cruise, and Mrs. McKane the housekeeper and I were there alone. She had to go on an errand, and left me by myself.

When I heard the doorbell ring I was frightened until I saw it was Justin. I now regret letting him in. I knew I was breaking the promise I made to my Mother. Any way, I let him in. I tried to convince him he had to leave but he refused. Excuse me Suzy, this is hard for me to say, just wait a minute and I'll be okay."

"Slow down Tiff, take it slow and easy. We can talk some other time."

"No I have to talk now. He picked me up, laid me on the couch and forced me to have sex. At first I struggled but then I wanted to do it. We almost got caught, when Mrs. McKane came back sooner then I thought, so I hid him in my closet. The rest of the evening she kept opening the door of my room checking to see if I was sleeping. When she finally went to bed I let Justin out of the house."

Catching her breath she continued, "While I was closing the door Mrs. McKane heard a dog bark. Looking up, she was at the top of the stairs and asked me what I was doing? She said she had locked the door and to go to bed. Later she heard me crying, and came into my bedroom. I confessed to her we had sex. I think she knew, because she had found my slacks under a table, and on the couch was a package of condoms that were never opened. She promised she would never tell and to this day she hasn't."

"Many parents are aware that their teenage kids have had sex at fourteen. As long as you didn't get pregnant, what's the problem? You have nothing to worry about. They most likely did the same thing."

"He said he used protection but he didn't" Tiffany hesitated and no words came out as her tears flowed, "I did get pregnant, and had a baby boy."

Suzy was at a loss for words. The room was silent until she spoke, "Where is the boy now? You should have told your Mother. She would have had him arrested and put in jail. I'm sorry Jasmine, I understand at fourteen I likely would have done the same thing."

"I don't know where my child is. I tried to forget what happened. I have my life all set and yet I feel I deserted my son. Will God ever forgive me for giving him away? I was at summer camp; I was very slim and didn't look pregnant. One day I got very sick and they took me to a doctor. After I was examined he told the owner I was pregnant. Mrs. Johnson, her assistant and the doctor had me sign a paper giving up the child for adoption. Mrs. Johnson said she would raise the baby until I was able to care for him. I told her I didn't want him, and I couldn't be a Mother. I don't know where he is."

"Tiffany I feel so bad for you, and I don't know what to do or say. I guess you must be wondering how you'd tell Scott. Does Justin have any knowledge of this?"

"He never knew. When we were in high school he said he heard some girl at the summer camp had a baby. He asked me, if I knew who the girl was. I tried to convince him I didn't know of any girl having a baby at camp; I think he knew I was lying to him. He has that way about him."

"I think you'll have to meet with him. If what you say about him is true, he'll seek out everything about your life. God forbid he finds out about you and Scott. He seems to be someone that will never give up until he gets an answer. If Scott's ambition to be President fails, he would never forgive you."

"I know it, but how can I meet with him? He'll press me for answers about someone who had a baby at the camp. I know he will. He's very intelligent and never forgets anything. You know how lawyers are. They keep trying to get you to say what they want to hear. I could get confused if he starts questioning me."

"Meet with him; see if he really wants information, or if he just wants to have a relationship with you while he's here in Washington. Meet him at a place where people are, like a restaurant or in a park. Don't let him ask all the questions. The time is going to come when you have to tell your parents and Scott before the election. I'll stay with you tonight and go back to my apartment in the morning."

The next morning Tiffany called Justin at his hotel. "Justin I'll meet with you. Can we go for dinner tonight?"

"Tiffany, why don't you come to the hotel? I can order dinner for the two of us in my room? We could be alone without any disturbance of people."

"No, I think its better that we meet in the dinning room. Make the arrangements, and I'll see you at eight tonight."

Waiting in the hotel lobby she was surprised when someone came from behind spun her around and kissed her.

Taken back she pushed him away, wondering who would do this to her. She was stunned to see a very tall handsome young man standing in front of her. "Justin," she exclaimed. "Is it really you?" He had matured so much since their high school days, and seemed quite different from that cocky, self-assured teenager.

"It's me in the flesh." Looking into her eyes he kissed her again. For a moment, Tiffany forgot, and responded to him.

Realizing what she had done, she pulled away." I think we should go into the restaurant, people are watching as if we are honeymooners."

"We could make plans now if you'll marry me. He said with a grin. At the table Justin ordered a bottle of wine and filled their glasses. "To you and me, for our memories especially one. Now, another toast for our future to spend our lives together forever as we had planned."

"No Justin, the past is gone, we have no future together. I'm getting married soon, so let's just be friends. That's all it can be. We made a foolish mistake when we were young. Why can't you let it go? My life is all planned for me. With whom I can't tell you. Let's have a pleasant time tonight. Why don't you tell me about your life and what you have been doing these past years?" Tiffany kept talking hoping to change the subject. "What are your plans?"

Their conversation ended when the waiter asked for their order. Tiffany ordered a Caesar salad; Justin ordered a New York sirloin steak.

When the waiter left, Justin continued the conversation. "I've been attending Oxford University in England, and returning in a few weeks. When I finish I'll get my degree and continue on for my doctorate. I'm going into the Foreign Service and visit countries to help them stabilize their fragile government.

My plans are to teach them democracy and the benefits they would have with such a government. I still think about our plans having our own law office and getting married."

"Justin times have changed; we're two different people now."

"Tiffany what I really want to know; who was the girl that had a baby at the summer camp you attended? One of the girls I went with went to the same camp you did. I was told she had a baby. If you had a baby I'd like to do the right thing, if you did get pregnant."

Shuddering, Tiffany remembered that Mrs. McKane had found the package of condoms. Looking Justin in the eyes she told him, "It wasn't me, so don't worry, and I have no clue whoever had a baby. It wasn't the years I was there. None of the girl I knew had a baby."

"Then you're telling me you didn't? If I had a son or a daughter, I'd like to get to know and support my child."

Wanting to end the conversation Tiffany stood up, "Why after these years would you bring this up. Justin it's nice to see you again. I said on our telephone conversation a few weeks ago, it's over. I wish you good luck in your future."

"Wait a minute Tiffany." Finish your meal. We have so much to talk about. I want to get back with you. We can start all over. I'm sorry that I forced you to have sex."

"No Justin you didn't force me, you raped me!" Losing control Tiffany leaned over to Justin, and said loud enough for the next table to hear. "You raped me, the word is raped. It's over and finished." With that as the final word, she rose from her chair to leave the restaurant. Turning back she saw him starting to follow her.

"Tiffany wait, come back." Following her he continued o call her, "Tiffany, Tiffany, wait!" He was too late. By the time he reached the parking lot she was driving away.

She drove back to her apartment and called her Mother. After the fourth ring the answering service came on. "Mom, I'm coming home for a week, I need to talk to you." Tiffany then called Scott, "Hello honey, I need a week off to see my parents. "

"Okay. Honey I know by the sound of your voice, something is wrong. I can't help you if you don't tell me."

"No Scott, I have to settle something between my parents and myself. I'll be back by the time you return to Washington. I'll tell you all about it when I see you. Don't worry there's nothing serious." She knew she was lying.

Watching from her balcony she could see couples holding hands as they strolled through the park, enjoying the peace and tranquility. Some would stop and kiss, which filled her with loneliness and the wants she needed.

Truth Time

"Why Justin, did you have to reappear in my life? I have everything I need and want, and then you show up. If you find out about the baby, it will ruin my life. When I tell my Mother and Dad, what will they think? Questions will come; how will I handle them?" Tiffany hoped the wine and the warmth of the of the shower would relax her, and she could go to bed and fall asleep.

In California she hired a taxi to take her home, rather then disturb her Mother or Father. Mrs. Mc Kane greeted her at the door. "You've been gone for so long. Are you going to stay for awhile?"

"I'll be here for a week, and then I have to go back to Washington."

"We've missed you. The house is so quiet. You're Mom and Dad are so busy they're seldom home for meals. It's lonely being here by myself."

"I'll stay home for a week, and we'll have our meals together as a family, I promise. I'll make them agree to eat every meal here" This made Mrs. McKane happy and she went to the kitchen singing her favorite Irish songs. Picking up the phone she ordered food for the week.

Exhausted from traveling Tiffany went into the living room, picked up the evening paper, searching to see if Scott's name was in print regarding his campaign. Leaning back on the divan, she dozed off, wakening when she heard the phone ring.

Rubbing her eyes, she answered. "Hello this is Tiffany. Who's calling?"

"Tiff, this is Joyce; your Dad told me you're home for a week. Can we get together and have lunch while you're here? You set the day and time. I'll meet you wherever you wish. I have something to share and I need a shoulder to lean on."

"That would be great; I'll be bored just hanging around. My parents are so busy in their careers. Our housekeeper says they're never home, and when they are, it's just to sleep, and I need to tell you something too."

Karen and Jim left their jobs early now that Tiffany was home. Mrs. Mc Kane was happy as she prepared the evening meal, the first one in a long time. She had flowers on the table, goblets filled with wine, a platter of seafood dinner with lobster tails and shrimp with rice scampi as the main course. The dessert was home made apple pie and vanilla ice cream.

When the meal was finished Jim brought out the family movies and they watched them until Karen said, "Enough, let's just sit and share time together and talk." They reminisced about their vacation in Wyoming until the conversation led to why Tiffany had come home. "Is everything okay between you and Scott?"

"Dad, I wanted to come home for the week. I miss you. I was lonesome for this place, and the many good times I had growing up here. I know I'll have to move on, and I just wanted to turn back the time, if only for a little while."

The next morning Joyce called Tiffany and suggested they meet at the office. "I have the afternoon off and thought we could go to a small out of the way restaurant for lunch. Along the way Joyce turned to Tiffany, "I'm so glad you came back, because I need to share something very personal with you, woman to woman."

"That's very odd Joyce, I came home to share a secret I've been burdened with for years. I feel you would understand my problem."

At the restaurant they looked at the menu deciding what they would have for lunch. In between bites of their sandwiches, they shared generalities of what they had enjoyed in Wyoming. When they finished eating they found a garden of flowers behind the restaurant, also a bench placed by a pool filled with gold fish. Joyce reached down, swirling the water, watching the fish. It was quiet and relaxing, a place to share their intimate thoughts. After a few minutes each one waiting for the other to begin.

Tiffany was wondering what she was going to share with her that was so devastating? Joyce started. "First let me tell you what I have to say; then I'll give you all the attention and time you need. I'll go back to the beginning of my relationship with Jim's Father."

Pausing for a moment her eyes got misty "One winter we went for a weekend to the cabin and got caught in a large snow storm and couldn't get back home. I was frightened, hoping my boys would be okay.

During the day we would hike around the mountain. At night things started to happen that I wasn't prepared for. There was no electricity up there, so we would listen to the battery powered radio and read books. At night we would retire early and make love. It was a wonderful relationship. The only problem we had was I wanted to have his child, and he was absolutely against it. I know he loves me. "

"It's okay if you want to stop, I'll understand."

"In a few months I was pregnant. To tell him was difficult, and when I did he was furious, and told me to have an abortion. I pleaded with him but he wouldn't listen. To have an abortion was against all that I had been taught and believed. I would do anything for him, because he's been so good to me. After a long anxious time, I went and had the abortion. Life is precious and a gift from God my parents said." Joyce became emotional and sat silent for a while.

Tiffany started to talk, but was stopped as Joyce placed her fingers over Tiffany's mouth. "Please just be patient. You're the first one I have ever bared my thoughts to. When we came home I struggled with the ultimatum he had given me; either the baby or my job and him. My heart aches at times when I think of what I have done. I have two boys from my previous marriage that gave me the love I needed. They never let my secret out. Jim believed me until I told him in Wyoming Eric was his child."

Stopping again for a moment, Joyce cleared her throat and continued, "What I'm trying to tell you is, that was a lie. Tiffany be truthful in all that you do, because the lies will catch up with you. I live with this lie.

How can I ever tell Jim that Eric is not his child? Karen and Jim wanted to adopt a son and Jim's Father was against that. "No child, not having his blood, will ever manage the company he said. I thought of giving him to Karen to raise.

Then maybe some day I could tell my husband the truth. I couldn't lie to him again."

They both sat in silence until Tiffany spoke. "I can't say anything that would ease your sadness."

"There is more to this story. My sister had adopted a child about six years ago. She had breast cancer and died in two years. The courts gave Eric to my Mother, which made all of the family happy. In two years my Mother started to have many physical problems and wanted me to take the little boy. I took him and then after a year I had the idea of telling Jim that Eric was his son."

It was getting late, and Tiffany thought it would be better if she shared her problem another day. This was enough for the present time to absorb for both of them what Joyce had just said. "You don't have to worry, I'll never tell anyone; this will be between you and me."

"My real heartache is that I had another child. I could never go through an abortion again. I gave this baby to an adoption agency. Jim kept telling me it's the woman's responsibility to be careful when having sex, not the man's. He's selfish but I love him; I know he loves me in his own way."

Tiffany never did get the opportunity to share her problem with Joyce. Time was passing and it was time to go home. On the drive back Tiffany said, "Why don't you come to my house tomorrow night?"

"How about your parents; will they be home?"

"Come for dinner; they're going out with some of their friends and Mrs. McKane always goes to her room to watch television. We'll have the house to ourselves. Come over about seven." The next evening Joyce and Tiffany enjoyed a light meal of chicken salad, and a slice of meringue pie for desert. After finishing they went into the living room. "Would you like coffee?"

"Yes and thanks. I felt better today knowing that you're my friend. Now I've burdened you with my problems, what can I do for you? Do you need money, or help of any kind?"

"No Joyce! I need the support of some one like you. I too gave up a baby boy for adoption when I was only fourteen. I told Suzy, but she hasn't had this situation happen to her, and it's difficult for her to understand."

"Having the experience of bearing a child and giving him away I understand. You had a child, and gave him away?"

"I haven't told anyone what happened to me when I was fourteen except Suzy and my friend Julie. Mother and Dad will be so upset with me. I feel all their love for me will disappear. I let them down because of what I did. I shouldn't tell you, and yet I have to confide in someone."

"Tiffany if you don't want to, that's okay."

"No, I need a friend and I know you understand my situation. It's been hard keeping this to my self."

"Justin and I were friends in high school and spent a lot of time together. We fooled around, but no sex until one night I became excited when he kept touching me. He promised I wouldn't get pregnant because he said he used a condom. He couldn't have, later on Mrs. McKane found a sealed package on the couch."

"I was at summer camp when I became ill. When the doctor examined me he said I was pregnant. Being slim I didn't look it. He said I had to have a cesarean. I had the baby prior to seven months, and signed a paper giving him up. The owner of the camp kept him and said I could have the baby when I was older; but I didn't want him. He must be about six or seven years old. I feel morally responsible to raise him; but I'm not ready to be a Mother."

Suddenly a thought came into Joyce's head, and she asked, "Do you think Eric could be your child Tiffany?"

"No, I don't believe he is. I know signing the paper is not legal, and Mrs. Johnson, her assistance and the doctor would be in trouble if they gave the child away. My problem is how do I learn to love a little boy? Suzy said I should tell Scott, but in the position he's in, I'm afraid he'll leave me."

"Do you want this child? If you do, why not contact Mrs. Johnson and find out if she has him. Is she alive and still has the boy. You should tell your Mother and Dad."

"Will you help me? I need all the support I can get."

"Yes I will, and I'm sure Jim and Karen will be thrilled to have a grandchild. Then you can tell Scott. He's so much in love with you. I know my husband will support you now that he has Eric. He needs a challenge in his life now that young Jim has taken over most of the operation of the business. Life is strange and has many complications. It's getting late now, and I have to be in work early tomorrow. Call Mrs. Johnson and I'll wait until I hear from you."

After a quick shower Tiffany laid down on the bed wishing she could look over to the other side and see Scott lying there. "Oh Scott, how I wish you could be here to hold me." With these thoughts Tiffany fell asleep.

The next morning at breakfast, Karen asked how her day went with Joyce. "Great Mom, we had a long talk, sharing about our lives and things of the last twenty years. We got personal, sharing some intimate things women do. Don't ask now. I'll tell you later."

This was a blow to Karen. Tiffany had always talked openly about any subject. Now it seemed she was turning to Joyce for advice and counsel. Trying her best not to let her know she was hurt, Karen replied, "Sure sweetheart, don't worry you can tell me when you're ready." Later that morning Tiffany called Mrs. Johnson and asked if she could come and visit her.

Arriving at the camp she was greeted by Mrs. Johnson "It's been a long time. Come in and sit down. Can I get you something to drink?"

"No thank you, I've come to talk about my son."

"I've heard you're going to marry Senator Drew is that true?"

"Yes, we intend to marry next year. My problem is, what to do about my son? You said you'd raise him until I was ready. Right now I'm not sure what's the right thing to do. I have to tell my Mother, Dad and especially Scott. I don't know what to do."

"Well Tiffany dear, you certainly should tell your parents and the Senator. First, there is a problem. I have developed Alzheimer's disease. It's in its early stages, so I have given your son to my daughter Jeannie to find some one to adopt him. Right now it's in the courts. Doctor Pierce knows a judge who is taking care of all the legal papers."

"But I just told you I want him back. I'm getting married and ready to be a Mother. I'm sure I can do it."

"Well if you really want him you'll have to make up your mind quickly. I know I made a promise you would get him when you were ready, but time is of the essence. First, do you really want him? Are you prepared to be a Mother to him? You can't be pretty sure, you must be sure!"

Tiffany started to speak but was silenced by Mrs. Johnson. "There are too many abandoned children in the country. You're fortunate your son has been raised in a good home. You never came once to see him. Nurturing a child takes a lot of your time."

"I don't know if I'm ready to be a Mother. I'll have to talk to my parents and Scott first. I need them to help me make the decision. If they think the best thing to do is for me to raise him as my son, then I want him now. We have many plans for the future, if Scott becomes President."

"No Tiffany, you have to make that decision. You can't expect someone else to make decisions for you. Life doesn't work that way! You've never shown any interest. What makes you think you are ready? To me, it doesn't sound like you are. I'll call Jeanne and ask her to wait two weeks, how much longer is up to you. The Senator might be delighted to have a son. Remember you'll have a difficult time trying to explain this, and how about the young man who is the Father? He might come into this too."

"I don't know where Justin is."

"He has rights as the Father, unless you can have him sign papers, freeing him from any responsibility. He could be married and not want the boy, or maybe he will. My advice is to check everything carefully before you make a decision."

"You said you would keep him until I was ready to take him? Why did you give him to your daughter, and even tell her to find someone to give him to? How could you, when you promised?"

"I'm sorry Tiffany, when you didn't call or come to see him, what could I do? I assumed you had no interest in your son and felt it was necessary that he have a stable, loving home; go to school and make friends his own age.

My daughter is living in North Dakota. I'll call her and tell her there's been a change; and not to make any commitments. I haven't heard from her recently. If papers have been signed there isn't much we can do."

"Thank you Mrs. Johnson. I'll call you within the next week. I have such little time left to make a decision. If you can, would you have your daughter get in touch with me as soon as possible?"

Leaving Mrs. Johnson's her mind was a whirl, thinking what she should do? Arriving home she called her Mother. Unfortunately she was not available. She left a message for her to come home as early as possible, and also tell Dad to do the same. Tiffany had just hung up the phone when it rang. Picking it up, she heard her Mother's voice. "Is that you Tiffany? What's wrong? Are you home?"

"I'm home. It's important I talk with you and Dad." Hearing the anxiety in her voice, Karen left the hospital.

Opening the door, she expected to see Tiffany waiting for her. "Where are you?" With no response, Karen called again, "Tiffany, Mrs. McKane, anyone home?"

Coming out from the kitchen, Mrs. McKane answered, "I'm right here. You're home early. Is there anything wrong?"

"No, is Tiffany here? I had a call from her."

"I don't think so. I haven't seen her."

Going upstairs Karen went to Tiffany's room slowly opened the door and saw her lying on the bed. Quietly she went toward the bed hearing her crying.

"What's wrong sweetheart?" Startled, Tiffany rose up opening her eyes.

"Mother you scared me! I don't know what to do!"

Karen put her arms around Tiffany and held her tightly. In that moment Tiffany burst out sobbing as though her heart would break. "Its okay honey, I'm here, relax, whatever it is we'll work it out."

Gaining her composure Tiffany asked, "Is Dad home?"

"He'll be here in a little while. Nothing can be that bad. Haven't we solved our problems before? Lay back and rest."

Jim arrived home to see Karen holding her fingers up to her lips, a sign to be quiet. "Shh, she's resting. I'll wake her in a little while. Evidently she has something to tell us."

Hearing a door close, they looked up to see Tiffany standing at the top of the stairs. "Dad, I'm glad you're home. I need to freshen up; I'll be down in a minute."

"Tiffany what's wrong?"

"Dad, I'll tell you when I come down."

"Jim, don't impatient; she'll be down in a minute. Let's give her a moment to compose her self."

Tiffany remained at the top of the stairs. "Do I dare tell them they have a grandson? I've kept this secret from them for at least six years?" Turning to go back to her room she stopped, realizing she had to face reality. Hearing Karen say, "Are you coming?"

Holding her head high, Tiffany looked down and said, "Yes Mom, I'm coming." Entering the living room Tiffany sat on one of the chairs facing her parents who were sitting on the couch. The very one where she had sex with Justin. Impregnated, and now the Mother of a son.

"Mom, Dad, I'm having a hard time trying to tell you something I did. You will probably hate me. I hope this won't happen. I do love you two so much and pray you'll forgive me. I have to tell Scott too. I can't blame him if he breaks up with me, that's up to him."

"No matter what you tell us, we'll love you, and accept what you're going to say."

"While in Wyoming Dad, our lives changed after you and I found out who my biological Father is, and that my Mother's real name is Alicia. Now I have more news.

"The time the two of you went on a business trip to Europe. Mrs. McKane and I were alone in the house. You gave me strict orders that no one was to come in while you were gone. One night Mrs.McKane had forgotten she had to go on an errand. While she was gone Justin came over to study for a very important test. I tried to keep him out, but he forced his way in. When we finished our homework I told him to go, but instead he picked me up, laid me down on the couch, and forced me to have sex. I tried to stop him but I couldn't."

Jim jumped up in a rage. "That rotten son of ah,"

Before he could finish, Karen pulled him down on the couch "Stop it! Stop it Jim, this is no time to act like this."

"Honey, why did you let him do that to you?"

"He was too strong and after he started I tried to stop him, but I couldn't. Then I got excited and didn't fight him anymore. Please don't blame Mrs. McKane; it wasn't her fault. I told her I wouldn't let any one in. It was my fault."

"Honey, don't think for a moment we would blame you. We love you no matter whatever happened. So you had your first experience with sex. This happens to many young teenagers. I just wish you had told me. I could have shared and helped you when that happened." Thinking for a moment of her first experience with Kevin, how she too first stopped him, and then became the one who initiated their lovemaking.

Tiffany could see Jim ready to burst in anger." Well you didn't get pregnant and that's a blessing. Tiffany how could you let him in the house when we told you, nobody in the house while we were gone?"

"Dad it wasn't Justin's fault, I let him in. Please don't be angry with him, be angry with me. There's more to this. I won't tell you any more, unless you both promise that you won't look for revenge from any person I'm going to mention. Now will you both make a promise? Jim responded with a nod of his head. "When I went to camp that summer I got very sick.

You had gone on a cruise, and they couldn't contact you. Mrs. Johnson took me to a doctor and he said I was almost seven month pregnant. I couldn't believe it, Justin told me he had taken precaution."

There was dead silence until Karen said, "If only you had told us. Everything would have been okay. We could have helped you. We understand."

"Wait Mother, I haven't finished. The doctor said he had to take the baby, because my life was in danger. It was a baby boy, and I signed a paper giving him to Mrs. Johnson. She said she would keep him until I was older, and then give him to me if I wanted him. Now I don't know what to do."

The revelation of Tiffany having a child now six or seven years old stunned them. Having sex at fourteen seemed irrelevant to the news of Tiffany being a Mother of a child. "We have to go and bring him to our home. This is where he belongs. Tiff, we are his grandparents."

"It's okay. Bring your son home. He belongs here; he's a part of our family. We'll love him. Please don't deprive us of sharing his life with us."

"Mom I want to do what is right. I can understand how you feel. I should have trusted both of you. I guess Motherhood was not in my mind. When Justin showed up it all came back to me and I realized I needed your help."

Jim sat silent. He had nothing to say, remembering in high school, he was like Justin, the football hero.

The cheerleaders wanting him to be their boyfriend, and how close he came to having the same situation when one of them got pregnant. His Father had to pay for the abortion, giving the family of the girl one hundred thousand dollars to keep him from facing a rape charge.

Slumping back in the chair, Tiffany buried her head running out of questions. The room remained silent until Mrs. McKane entered, asking if they wanted dinner tonight.

Karen and Jim were at a loss for words as they looked at each other. And "Maybe later; anything you have would be fine."

Karen walked over to Tiffany, placing her arms around her daughter as the tears flowed freely. It was a tender moment of love that had been missing for a long time between them.

"Mom, how can I tell Scott? I'm concerned and frightened how he'll take the news that I'm a Mother."

On Saturday Jim and Karen took Tiffany to the airport. She called Mrs. Johnson and said she would be contacting her by the end of the week. "I'll be seeing Scott on Monday. I should have told him before we got so involved. This may change how he feels about me. Please say a prayer for us. I have no idea how he'll respond. We've talked about having children after we get married. He loves me, but I wonder if he'll accept there is a seven year old boy involved."

When Tiffany arrived at the airport in Washington she saw Suzy waiting for her. Driving down the freeway Suzy asked, "How was your trip back home?"

"It was good, I told my parents about my son. They were wonderful and accepting, wanting me to bring him back to them. They want to take care of him until Scott and I are married. Maybe we should move up our wedding date; but that'll be up to him."

"Tiff; come over for dinner tonight. I'll pick you up, and later I can take you back to your place. Give me a ring when you're ready. This will give you the afternoon to rest."

Agreeing that would be a good idea Tiffany unpacked her suitcase. After showering she decided to let Scott know she was back. With no answer at his condo she called his office, "Hello, this is Senator Drew who's calling?"

"Hi honey, this is Tiffany."

"Tiffany, you're back. I'll be right over."

"Not right now Scott, I need to rest for a while I'm very tired. Suzy invited me for dinner and I promised to go. Come tomorrow, okay."

"Please Tiffany I've missed not seeing you."

"Be patient, it's only one day, and then we'll have time to talk."

"Okay sweetheart, I'll see you tomorrow about nine."

"Come for breakfast. I've something we should talk about, don't worry." Not waiting for a question she hung up. The phone rang but she didn't answer it.

Suzy picked her up later in the day. Tiffany was surprised seeing Jonathon at the apartment. "I didn't know he was coming, he's been so good staying at the college. We haven't seen each other since Wyoming. Need I say more?"

"I understand Suzy. Scott and I have been separated too. We've planned to spend tomorrow together. I'm so worried. It will be a very trying day for me. I have to tell him about my son."

"Hello Jon, how are things at the college?"

"Great; I'm happy to be here. It sure is different than high school." The evening passed as they shared about their time in Wyoming, and the plans and desires for the future.

The next morning Tiffany was preparing breakfast and heard the lock turn in the door. Seeing Scott she ran to him smothering him with kisses. After some time, they broke apart. "Darling, what have I done to deserve this?"

"Because I love you. I missed you and need you more then ever." Standing together holding each other Tiffany said, "I think we better have breakfast first, and then we can talk. Have a cup of coffee.. Sit down and read the newspaper. I'll be ready in a little while."

With breakfast over, the dishes in the dishwasher, Tiffany and Scott sat down on the divan. "I have something to tell you. What I'm going to say may change our plans for life. If you want to get a divorce, I'll accept that."

"Wait a minute!" Scott said as he jumped up from the divan. "What are you talking about, get a divorce? That's out of the question. What in heaven's name can you tell me would ever make me want to do this? What's wrong?"

"Never mind, let's forget it, I was only kidding."

"No, I can tell by your demeanor something's bothering you." In exasperation Scott shook his head. "How can you say I might want a divorce, when I have no idea what you're going to tell me?"

"Please sit down, we have to talk."

Scott looked at Tiffany, questioning her. "What's coming next? Are you changing your mind and want to end our relationship? I told you it wouldn't be easy, and there would be times we would be away from each other. If you want to tell me about your past, I don't want to hear it. I'm sure it isn't that devastating. You've never asked me about mine. Let's talk about our future, the planning of it, and spending the rest of our lives together."

"Scott I have to tell you. A boyfriend raped me when I was fourteen years old and I had a baby. My parents knew nothing about this until this past week. I was in summer camp when I got very sick.

Mrs. Johnson, the owner of the camp raised the boy until he was four years old." Pausing to catch her breath, Tiffany continued. "When her health started to fail, she gave him to her daughter to bring up. If you want to know all the particulars, I'll try to tell you later. I told my parents last week and they're behind me one hundred percent. They even want me to bring him to them."

"Wait a minute! You're going to fast. One sentence at a time, give me a chance to understand what you're saying."

Tiffany repeated very slowly what she had said. When Scott nodded his head she continued. "Scott, we have a difficult situation, and have to come to a resolution. Do we go on from here, or call it quits? I might sound strong now, truthfully I'm ready to break down at the thought I could lose you forever." Tiffany leaned over to Scott laying her head on his shoulder.

"You've never asked me about my past. Our lives started when we first met. If you have a son, and you have a desire to raise him, he'll be a part of our family. Later your parents can announce our wedding."

"Do you really mean we can have my son? How can you break the news to the public, and the party? They might resent you because you haven't told them before this. It will be a big scandal."

"Don't you understand, I need you in my life? You're going to be the beginning of many younger First Ladies in this country. Our generation will move the country into this new millennium. Times must change, the old ways must go."

"The news media will know I had a child at fourteen and will hunt for the Father. Justin will find out, and want him. He tried to get me to confess I had a child but I denied it. Now he will know the truth. He'll want parental rights. What a mess I've created for you Scott."

"What we have to do is keep what our parents and grandparents have; honesty, faith in God and the desire to succeed. He will be our son Tiffany. We'll work together to bring him to your parent's home. If I become President, he will live in the White House. I'll adopt him. We have to find the Father and have him sign the papers. I'll have a lot of power when I'm elected."

The day and evening passed swiftly as Scott and Tiffany planned their future. It was eleven when they when to bed. Pulling her close Scott realized how much she meant to him. Tired and relaxed, holding each other, quietly they fell asleep.

In the morning they decided to go out for breakfast at a local restaurant. "During the meal Scott suggested she go to work. He would go back to his condo and try to contact Mrs. Johnson and explain who he is, and the possibility of regaining Tiffany's son. "Honey, give me Mrs. Johnson's telephone number."

"No Scott I have to be the one to contact her. I don't want you involved. It's up to me to handle this."

Reprimand

When she arrived at the office Tiffany told Suzy that Scott had been with her. "I told him about the child and he was very understanding."

Philip walked over to Tiffany and asked, "How's the Senator this morning? I happened to drive by your place last night and noticed his car parked in front of the building."

"You're mistaken, you were seeing things; it must have been someone else's car."

Scott entering the office saw Philip standing in front of Tiffany's desk "Come into my office now." When the door closed after them, murmurs started to fly around the office. "He's in trouble now. It's about time."

"Now, what's with you and Tiffany? Is something the matter? "I've heard rumors you're constantly bothering her. If you're wise you'll stick to business at all times?"

"I was just talking to her. Nothing's wrong sir. Any thing you want me to do is okay with me." If I may, is she like the rest of them you were involved with?"

Ignoring him Scott replied, "This is none of your business. One more crack like that and you're gone! I'm warning you for the last time; stay away from her. Stop bothering her! Do I make myself clear?"

"Yes sir, you certainly do. I didn't mean anything by it. I just thought where you've had so many women in the past; she looks like the best of all of them. Remember Ginger, the one who got pregnant? You do remember her don't you?"

Scott's face flushed. "Tiffany and I are getting married; and if you're wise you'll stop what you think you can get a way with. I promise, you will be out looking for job if you continue. Do you understand what I'm saying?

"Yes sir, but I've never bothered her. I was only trying to be helpful; keeping my eyes open to be sure she was safe when you were away. The only thing I did was check on her once in awhile at her place."

"Stop the lying Phillip; this isn't the first time I've been told about you annoying the young women in the office. Some of the interns that worked here have filed complaints against you. Let this be the last time you and I have this type of conversation. I saw your car parked over across the street where Tiffany lives yesterday afternoon." Putting his hands on Philip's shoulders he squeezed deeply into them until Philip cried out in pain. When Philip left the Senator's office he put on his suit jacket and left for the day.

Suzy turned to Tiffany and said, "Maybe Scott has fired him, I hope. It's been coming for a long time. He deserves everything he gets, it was bound to happen."

Late in the afternoon Tiffany made a call. "Mrs. Johnson, this is Tiffany, I'd like to take my son back. Everyone is pleased and willing to help me get settled in my life."

Where is the Boy

"I can't thank you enough for what you've done. I talked to Senator Drew and he will adopt him. I didn't tell anyone who the doctor was or your assistant. I'm sorry to say I don't remember his name."

"I named your son Jim after your Father. He's still young, maybe you can change it if you want to."

"I don't know. I'll wait and see how my Dad reacts."

"This has to be taken care of this week. My attorney said that the judge would wait until this Friday and no later. That's a final answer. Can you come up this weekend? I'd like to get this over with; also my daughter needs to move on with her life."

"Right now I'm in Washington. It's impossible for me to get there today. I'll make arrangements to get a flight back to California as soon as I can." Tiffany walked over to Scott's office while the rest of the staff stopped working, watching to see what is going to happen next.

One by one they gathered around Suzy's desk asking if she knew what was going on. "I have no clue," was her response. It seemed a long time before Tiffany left Scott's office. She stopped by Suzy's desk telling her plans were being made for a flight back to California.

Opening her apartment door she noticed the blinking light on her answering service. Picking up the phone she heard a woman's voice, "Hello"

"Tiffany, this is Mrs. McKane; you just had a call from Mrs. Johnson you must come home immediately. It's important she see you." Tiffany could hear the anxiety in her voice.

When the plane landed in California Tiffany hurried to the taxi stand noticing a man standing there with a sign with her name on it. Broaching her he asked, "Is your name Tiffany?"

"Yes it is. Why do you ask?"

"Senator Drew arranged with the owner of our company to be sure we bring you to your parent's home as soon as you have landed." Arriving at the house, Tiffany looked into her purse but could not find the key. Ringing the bell Mrs. McKane opened the door and stood silent for a moment seeing Tiffany standing there. Shocked, Mrs. McKane hesitated. "Tiffany dear, how did you get here so quickly?"

"Excuse me, I have to make a telephone call." Not bothering to remove her jacket she picked up the phone and dialed Mrs. Johnson's home. "Hello Mrs. Johnson?"

"Tiffany, where are you? I thought you were in Washington? I can't reach my daughter. It's been weeks since she's called me. I don't know what to do."

"I just arrived in California. You called my parents home saying there was an emergency and said I had until Friday to see you. Do you know if my son is okay?"

"My daughter hasn't returned my calls." She goes away on weekends and isn't at her home. I left a message for her to call me as soon as possible. I'll call you the minute I hear from her. Perhaps my attorney can make contact with her." It was over an hour before the phone rang. Picking it up Tiffany answered it. "Tiffany, you have to come here tomorrow. My daughter called, we have to talk."

"What's wrong? There was silence with no answer coming. Tiffany could hear sobbing over the phone. "Mrs. Johnson is everything okay? Don't cry, I'll come right now. Stuttering Mrs. Johnson said, "What I have to tell you is very difficult for me. My daughter has given your son to another couple, because the man she intended to marry said there would be no wedding unless she gave up the boy. She has since moved and married a few months ago."

"What are you saying, she can't do that! Where is he? You promised me I could have him when I was ready. Call your daughter; tell her to bring him back wherever he is. I'll come and get him." Realizing anger would be fruitless in attempting to get her son back she apologized. "I'm sorry; I didn't mean to be so angry. It's just that I want my son. If you give me your daughter's telephone number I'll call her."

"It isn't that easy, the papers are sealed. There is no way anyone can get the name of the couple that has your son."

Minutes went by before she was able to speak again. "After the procedure of adoption in court was started they moved to another state, requesting that no one be told where they were. I've done everything I can do for you Tiffany. I'm sorry."

"Just give me your daughter's telephone number. You must understand; I don't want to put you, your daughter, Doctor Pierce and your assistant John in a precarious position. My Dad will back me one hundred percent, and do whatever it takes to have him. He knows what to do. He has a lot of connections."

Mrs. Johnson's words came slowly, "Don't do that. It will ruin four lives and possibly your son's life too. It was your decision not to notify your parents, that was a mistake."

"I was only fourteen and never thought I'd get pregnant. I believed what my girl friend said; you don't get pregnant the first time. You also kept this a secret. Just give me your daughter's telephone number. Senator Drew has a lot of influence."

Understanding Tiffany would go the limit to get her son back, she gave her the daughter's number. "Please, let me know how you make out. You know I'll have to tell Doctor Pierce, John, also and my daughter of your intentions. This will be devastating when they learn what happened seven years ago, is now raising its ugly head."

Tiffany meditated how to handle the situation. Dialing the number she called Jeannie. "Hello this is Tiffany. I'm little Jim's Mother. I understand you gave him to a couple that couldn't have children. Your Mother had promised me she would care for him until I made a decision to have him."

"I've been expecting your call. When my Mother found out that she couldn't take care of him she asked me for help.

I know the story Tiffany; we don't have to rehash it. I'm sure it wasn't a good experience for you as a teenager. She told you I have married, and my husband wants his own children, not someone else's."

Tiffany started to speak but was silenced as Jeannie continued, "My Mother is not physically strong. I will be losing her, when her mind goes with Alzheimer's. There is a difference between your family and mine. You think money will solve anything. If only you had come to me earlier this year, everything would have been solved."

"All I need is any information you can give me. My family and my future husband are delighted I have a son. Can you tell me what court you went to for the legalization of the adoption, and tell me the couples name?"

"The court is in California. I think their name is Parsons. I understand they moved because of the constant badgering of their families as to when they intended to start a family."

Gratefully Tiffany thanked Jeannie wishing her the best in her new marriage. At the dinner table she told her parents what happened, asking for their help. Jim and Karen were more then willing. The thought of having a grandson delighted them. After a lengthy conversation she called Scott. "Hi honey I've found more information about my son. I mean our son. What do you think I should do"

"Nothing just now. I'll call the Chief Justice of the courts, and call you when I have some new information.

Perhaps your Dad can help; he must know someone in the judicial system out there."

Using up time, Tiffany went to the plant to see the designs of a new shopping center being built in the state of Washington.

The following night Scott called with good news; he had found the court where the adoption was started, the name of the couple and where they had lived in California. "Now all we have to do is find their relatives and see if they know where little Jim is. I'm sure they've kept in contact with family or friends in California. If they don't know maybe the records will tell us where they are now."

Tiffany was ecstatic with the news. "That's wonderful Scott. What's our next step?"

"Be patience Tiff. I'll have some of my friends in the Party start the search. Go to the Headquarters and introduce yourself, so they will know you. I told them you're my future wife. I would like them to meet you."

At Scott's suggestion, Tiffany drove to the party's headquarters to introduce herself to some of the people. The receptionist asked her to wait a few minutes and the chairperson would be out to meet her. It wasn't too long before a tall-distinguished gentleman came out from one of the rooms. "To whom do I owe the credit of having you come to visit us?"

"Good morning, I'm Tiffany, a friend of Senator Drew."

"Scott told me about you. In fact, we have good news for you, and bad news. We have found your son, and know where he is."

"Just give me the good news please."

"We went to the court and tried to get some help, explaining to them the whole situation. They refused us saying it's a closed case. The law says they cannot release any information about the couple that is adopting your son. It seems you refused to take him one time. The woman, who took care of him, had every right to give him to someone; with the stipulation they would find a good home for him."

"But he's my son, and I couldn't take care of him back then."

"Tiffany, we have the best lawyers available and they said you can never win. My suggestion is you move on, get married and have children; my dear let it go! You will make your life miserable; learn from experience. You failed to tell your parents when they could have helped you. You abandoned him."

Heart broken she returned to her parent's home and called Scott. "Hello, is the Senator there?"

Disappointed she heard the words, "No I'm sorry; he has left for the day. Can I take a message?"

"Would you tell him that Tiffany called?"

Not knowing what to do she left the house and walked aimlessly around the neighborhood. On her way home from the hospital, Karen was surprised to see Tiffany standing on a corner. Lowering the window she called, "Tiffany."

Seeing it was her Mother she went to the car. "What are you doing honey? It's getting dark; you shouldn't be alone. I'm glad I spotted you when I did."

Silently they drove home. Karen knew it was not the time to engage in any conversation. She felt something was not going right, but was afraid to ask. During the evening it was quiet in the living room. Jim having been warned previously, not to question Tiffany in regards to what she had learned about her son. Karen looked over the ads, searching for clothes for her hopefully new grandson. Tiffany sat watching television. The only sound was the voice of a news reporter talking about the world affairs. Tired of the silence Tiffany asked," Doesn't anyone want to know what I've found out?"

"Of course we want to know sweetheart." Karen responded. "We didn't want to interfere. What have you found out? Will he be coming soon?"

"No the courts have sealed the papers, and all the lawyers say I can't have him because I haven't tried to make any contact with him until now. The papers are sealed until he is eighteen. If the people that raise him never tell him he is adopted, he'll never know I exist."

When she finished talking the telephone rang. The three of them sat up straight in their chairs hearing Mrs. McKane say, "Yes Senator, she's here. Just a minute and I'll get her."

Leaping up Tiffany went into the hall and grabbed the phone from Mrs. McKane's hand. "Excuse me, I'm sorry. I shouldn't have been so rude. With her trembling hands and quivering voice Tiffany said, "Scott."

By the sound of her voice, he sensed some thing was wrong. "Honey, I have great news! Want to take a trip?"

"I don't understand; why are you asking me that? Where are we going?"

"Would you like to see your son?"

"You're kidding! The lawyers said I have no hope of getting him. Scott, don't get my hopes up! If I had only told my parents about the pregnancy, things would have been different."

"Trust me, I know where he is, and we're going there as soon as we can. If you're able, make arrangements for a return flight back here tomorrow. Let me know your flight number, and I'll pick you up at the airport. We're going to see this thru. I can't talk; I have a dinner meeting in a short time. See you tomorrow. I love you."

Before she told her parents she called Mrs. McKane. "Would you please bring us three glasses of wine. No make that four, I want you to hear the news and celebrate with us.

Scott says that I have to get back to Washington tomorrow, and he is taking me to see my son. Can you believe it?"

Can we come too?" Jim asked.

"No Dad, not just yet. You'll see him soon enough. If everything goes right I will see him in a few days. I can hardly wait!"

Mrs. McKane brought in the wine. Jim raised his glass to make a toast. "Here's to our new grandson, whose wish will be my command."

"Dad, just enjoy and love him. You're not going to spoil him like you have me. Well, maybe spoil him a little."

The next day arriving back in Washington she saw Scott waiting for her. She told him her parents were excited because she was going to see her son. Scott tried to tell her that he had appointments he had to go to, and would be coming back later that evening. Pleading for him to come up to the apartment now and knowing she would not be denied, he parked the car and followed her

"I have my appointments to go to. "I told you I have things to get done. Come on Tiffany, I can't stay now."

"You'll come back tonight? Don't disappoint me."

Silently Scott thought of what he would like to say, but changed his mind. "I'll come back or we'll have troubles won't we?" He didn't wait for her answer. "Okay I'll be back later tonight."

Patiently Tiffany waited until ten p.m. and Scott still hadn't come. Calling his condo and office; all she got was his answering service. She then resigned herself that he wasn't coming. "He must have a good reason, but at least he could have called." She thought. It wasn't a good night for sleep; twice she got up from bed to get a glass of milk.

The following morning Scott called full of apologies. "I'm sorry I didn't come last night. I almost missed a very important meeting if Philip hadn't reminded me. I have good news and two tickets for the weekend. We're going to meet the lady who negotiated this meeting for us. When she found out the child was your son, she didn't want to become involved. It's quite complicated; be patient when we meet her."

"I promise, I'll do whatever you say. All I want is to be able to see my son."

The week seemed as if it would never pass. It was Friday when Scott and Tiffany drove to the airport. All the pleading from Tiffany as to where they were going, fell on deaf ears.

After the plane leveled off at thirty thousand feet, Scott told Tiffany. "Sweetheart we're going to my home town Greensboro, North Carolina."

"Are we going to see your Father?"

"Yes we are, but we have to meet someone else first."

When the plane landed they saw a group of people waiting for their flights. At the baggage claim Scott was surrounded by many of the citizens of the city who recognized him, wanting to shake his hand. Comments came from the crowd saying. "The next President. "It's a sure thing Senator. You'll get my vote!" Waving his hands and stopping to sign autographs, he held Tiffany close to him. "Honey, can you handle this?"

Pressing Scott's hand tightly, "I love it Scott, I love it." The ride seemed like an eternity before the driver turned into a long driveway, which headed up to the entrance of one of the old Southern mansions. At the front door one of the servants came down the stairs to open the car door for them.

Another servant was waiting at the top of the stairs. Taking Tiffany by the arm Scott explained, "This was a home of one of Thomas Jefferson's relatives, a cousin they say. It's steeped in Southern history."

They were led down a long hall to one of the rooms; as they entered they were stunned when an attractive elderly Lady greeted them. Scott stood speechless for moment. "Welcome to our home. I'm Mrs. Jefferson; and pleased you have come. We can help you in the finding of your child."

"Mrs. Jefferson, I can't believe it is you! It's been years since I dated your daughter. This is my future wife Tiffany from California, and a graduate from Indiana University. She is an attorney in my office."

"I'm please to meet you Tiffany. Scott always had an eye for beauty. Certainly you are one of the most beautiful young women I've ever met."

"Thank you so much, it's my pleasure to meet you. We hope to be married this year."

"I wish you the best. Just be strong and be ready when the news media starts to attack you. They will dig up anything they can to sell their papers and magazines. But never forget there are many good people and honest ones in the news media."

"I've seen you on TV Scott. Never forget those who have helped you to attain the position you have now. We will be glad to continue to help you on your way, hopefully to be the next President of the United States. Before we start to talk, come to our library and share a cup of coffee."

"You're home is beautiful, so different than in California."

"We're steeped in history here in the South. We cherish our life style, and will do anything to protect our beliefs." After a tour of the house with their hostess, they went back to the living room. "Please sit down and let's begin our conversation of why you're here. Let me begin with my first surprise. Mrs. Johnson the owner of the camp you went to each summer in California is my sister. In college she met a young man and fell in love. She was a very out going person, full of life, looking for excitement. She married him and settled out in California. She was very independent and would never ask for help."

Tiffany sat back, stunned at this revelation. Scott too, wondering, is this possible what he was thinking? No, it was too far fetched. "Her husband became an alcoholic and died young, leaving her penniless with a young child to support. She started the summer camp, this way she had more children to love. Everything went well until her daughter called to tell us her Mother had Alzheimer's. We have tried to have her come back South, but she won't move or accept help. We are resigned to her wishes, but very sadly."

Breaking into the conversation Tiffany offered, "Mrs. Johnson is a wonderful person. You would never believe she came from the South. She has no Southern accent like Scott has at times."

A hearty laugh came from Mrs. Jefferson "I guess through out the country there are many different accents, for example, the people from the New England. One of my daughters is a teacher, one a doctor and the other is an attorney. They have been successful in their careers. Scott, you're deep in thought. Are you troubled about something?"

"No, Mrs. Jefferson, just thinking."

"At one time in my life I thought Scott would marry one of my daughters, and he would be my son in law. That never materialized, all he ever wanted was politics, and so far very successful in that area of his life."

"Mrs. Jefferson, which daughter did you hope he would marry?"

"Any one of them my dear, you see my husband died early in life. For a while I had hoped Scott's Dad would ask me to marry him. He too was in politics and served the country in Washington for thirty years. Politics was his life."

"That's enough of me. I know where your son is. I must tell you the person who has him will not let him go with out a fight. You will have a difficult time convincing her to give up your son. Tiffany, you don't even know him. You have never seen him according to my sister. How can you say you love him and miss him? Is it because those around you want him, and you want to please them?"

Stunned by this question, Tiffany started to repeat the story. "I was young, frightened and ashamed what my parents would think. Mrs. Jefferson, I want to be a Mother to him, I do love him, and he is a part of me. Being a Mother you can understand that."

For a moment there was silence until Scott entered the conversation. "Mrs. Jefferson, I've always admired you. I often came to you to ask your advice, and you know I still do at times."

Suddenly the door opened, and standing there was Carolyn. Both Scott and Tiffany stared in amazement realizing she is one of Mrs. Jefferson's daughters. "Hello Scott, Tiffany, how are you? You should have let me know you were coming. Mother, why didn't you tell me you had invited them to visit with us?"

"Carolyn, we'll discuss this later. Have you forgotten the conversation we had about Scott and Tiffany, and they're looking for Tiffany's son?"

"Mother, I thought we'd finished that discussion a long time ago."

"Carolyn, please sit down and listen, you knew they were coming."

Finding the Boy

"Are we missing something that's eluded me? I thought we were here to find Tiffany's son and bring him to California. Isn't that right?"

"I'll give them anything, money without limit. I want my son. Scott wants to be a Father to him, my parents want to be his grandparents, and I'm his Mother"

"Carolyn, this is the last time I will say it. Sit down! We will discuss this once more. If you won't tell them I will."

"Do what you want Mother, it won't change anything. I've made up my mind, no one or anything will change it."

"Tiffany, Scott, the little boy that you met in Wyoming named Robbie is Tiffany's son."

"The only audible words coming from Tiffany were, "Robbie is my son?" With those words, Tiffany went limp with shock and slipped off the couch falling to the floor.

Scott quickly bent down and picked her up, gently placing her on the couch. Carolyn rushed out the door to get something to revive her. Within a minute she came too, as Scott took his handkerchief gently wiping her face, bringing her color back

"Carolyn, please sit down and listen. You knew they were coming." Standing beside her Mother, Carolyn stood silent as Mrs. Jefferson looked up at her daughter with a look that could kill.

"Are you up to continuing sweetheart? We can discuss this another time if you aren't up to it now."

"Please Scott, I 'm okay."

Just as her Mother started to speak, Carolyn turned and started to walk towards the door. "I want you to stay and be a part of this conversation. It's important that you hear what I have to say. I'm your Mother, and deserve the respect and courtesy of your presence now. You're a grown woman, not like an adolescent child who sulks because they can't get their own way."

"There is nothing to say that will change my opinion. We've gone over this time after time. You know exactly how I feel." Refusing to say any more she stood silent.

"Carolyn, we have known each other for a long time. We've worked together and dated at times. I thought we were friends. You promised that you would work for me in my bid for the Presidency this year. Are you changing your mind, what brought this change of heart?"

There was still no comment from Carolyn. Ignoring her daughter Mrs. Jefferson continued. "My sister's daughter Jeannie never looked for a couple to adopt Jim your son When my niece decided to get married she called Carolyn and asked her to take the boy and adopt him. Carolyn was interested, and thought maybe she could get Scott to marry her."

"That is not true Mother."

Ignoring Carolyn, Mrs. Jefferson went on. "We changed his name to Robert after my late husband. I often called him Robbie. I have taken care of Robbie when Carolyn was in Washington. I wasn't aware that Carolyn instigated a plan to adopt him. One of the local judges I've known for years called to inform me of her plan. I've always believed that a child belongs with the family he was born into; providing they are an upstanding family of the community they live in. A child belongs with his Mother."

With anger in his voice Scott responded, "How could you do what you did to me in Wyoming? To bring Robbie with you, knowing he is Tiffany's son. What kind of a person are you? I respected and admired you, but this! Jason told me before we left that how he was looking forward to marrying you and raise Robbie together. Maybe you could have children of your own when you get married."

"I want Robbie for my son! Can't you understand that? I'm his Mother. I have the right to raise him. Now I'm older; and I am his Mother."

"Let's stop this conversation now." Mrs. Jefferson said. "You know the right thing to do; he isn't yours. Give him up. You were not raised to act like you are now. Please do the right thing, let Tiffany have her child. There are many children that need a loving home. You and Jason can provide this for some unwanted child."

"Take a moment and think about it. I've found out I have an extended family. I found out who my biological Father is, and all of us have accepted what transpired in the past.

If you want time that's fine. I want my son; I don't want it to be a battle between us that would end up in court." Hesitating Tiffany continued, "Mother and Dad are waiting patiently for the news we're bringing their grandson home. I've cheated them for years; now I have a chance to redeem myself by bringing Robbie back to California."

"Well you had your say. Now listen to me and give me, my time. Scott I would never trust you again. You used me for your pleasure, and at that time I was in love with you. I hung on to the hope we would be married and have our own children. That dream is over, and I'm glad it never materialized, because we wouldn't have lasted a year."

"Carolyn, you're right, it never would have worked out."

Scott started to continue but stopped when Carolyn said. "Tiffany, I won't hang out my dirty laundry for the entire world to see. Robbie is the first one I can say really loves me. He calls me Mother, and when Jason and I get married, we will give him a brother, a sister or maybe one of each.

I'm over forty; you're only in your twenties, you have time for children, I don't"

There was silence until Carolyn softening her voice continued. "Tiffany, I'm twice your age, and have found at times life isn't fair. With Jason, I still have the hope that not money or a position is the only thing that gives success and happiness. It is when someone loves you unconditionally.

Jason and I pledged not to see each other or write for six months. If we can handle that, I'll move to Wyoming and marry him and start a new career as a school teacher."

'There are plenty of young children that need a good home. Having a custody battle in court for Robbie will hurt every one of us. I don't want my Father getting involved. He loves me as if I was his real daughter and not an adopted one. He will fight you all the way through the courts. No matter the cost or the time."

"It's getting late," said Mrs. Jefferson I think it's time to stop. Let everyone relax and be able to think what is the right thing to do. I have room for you to stay the night; we can continue this tomorrow, if you'd like."

"Thank you. We'll take you up on your invitation. It's time to give this a rest."

"Carolyn, tell Jeffrey we'll have guests for dinner. I think it's best you don't have Robbie running around the house. He can eat with the servants tonight. He says he likes their food better. Dinner will be served at seven."

Going ahead of them Carolyn remained silent as they climbed the stairs to their room. Closing the door Scott said to Tiffany, "We'll get Robbie, I promise you."

Standing outside of the door Carolyn said quietly, "Oh no you won't."

"I don't know Scott, we've no idea what name is on the birth certificate, and who was named the Father and Mother? We'll have to ask Mrs. Johnson. She must have a copy."

They lay on the bed trying to rest, which was impossible. Their minds kept racing on what to do if they get Robbie; or Carolyn refuses to give him to them. Getting up Tiffany stood by the open window, watching Carolyn pushing Robbie back and forth on the swing. She could hear his laughter the higher he went. Silently tears drifted slowly down Tiffany's face as she wondered, "Will I ever get a chance to do that with him?"

Robbie jumped off the swing; looked up at the window, and with out stretched arms to Carolyn, Tiffany heard him say, "I love you Mummy."

"I love you too, son," Carolyn's said glancing up.

Going down stairs they were greeted by a servant. "This way please." Following him into the dining room they were directed to their chairs. Carolyn came and sat down at the end of the table facing her Mother. "Were you surprised at the smallness of the table Scott?"

"Yes, I remembered the length of it. You could sit twenty people around it. My Dad often told me about the many times he came here."

"I don't entertain like we used to. I'm not active in the party as I once was. You know Scott many important people in the world including kings, queens, other royalties and leaders of the free world have dined in this room" After the dinner was finished, they retired to the drawing room to share a glass of wine. The evening passed slowly, politics being the subject of the conversation.

When the grandfathers clock struck eleven Mrs. Jefferson decided it was time to retire. As Carolyn was leaving the room she turned to her Mother. "Mother I won't be here tomorrow, I have business to attend to."

Sensing that a situation of unpleasantness was brewing, Scott and Tiffany excused themselves. Her eyes flashing and anger clearly showing on her face Mrs. Jefferson walked over to Carolyn. "Evidently you have forgotten your manners. You will be here tomorrow morning, and I mean it! If you aren't here, I make this promise; you will not keep Robbie." Carolyn turned without a reply and walked out of the room.

Retiring for the night and things not going well. Scott said, "Honey, are you willing to go all the way with this? Remember this is only a taste of what's to come if we have to go to court to get Robbie." Scott was wondering if Tiffany could handle and be willing to go through with the situation not going well.

"I don't know Scott. Carolyn was so much fun in Wyoming when we were there. Is she that spiteful towards you? What did you do to make her hate you so? No, don't tell me. I don't want to hear of your love affair with her. What should I do? Uproot Robbie from his security, and have him learn how to live with a different family and life style?" She lay silent for a few minutes, and with no answer, she continued, "Will he become a malcontent youngster and not be able to adjust if we take him? Can I change my dreams of becoming an attorney working for the government?

Do I really want to be a Mother at the present time? I honestly don't know what is most important; what I want for me or what is best for him?" Turning away from Scott, she said, "Good night honey, I love you."

"Good night Tiff, I love you too."

It was a long restless night for them, trying to reason in their own minds what was best. Their thoughts became like an out of a controlled river as it wended its way between the mountains and over the rocks that rose up from the bottom. The strength of the water turned their boat of questions upside down, as they tried to escape to some quiet place that had the answers. Sleep seemed to elude them.

In the morning, they agreed any further discussion now would be detrimental. "We would be completely frustrated and nothing would be solved. Let's wait until we see what happens today. Maybe Mrs. Jefferson can persuade Carolyn to change her mind" I hope so. Okay Tiffany?"

After breakfast they were invited into the drawing room. There was tension between them. Carolyn felt the three of them had banded together to take Robbie from her anyway they could. She knew the power of Scott's influence in Congress, Tiffany's family with the money and her Mother against her too, would make it difficult to win in any court battle. After being seated Scott looked at Mrs. Jefferson and Carolyn and said, "At the present time I think it's time to end the conversation. It's fruitless when we are at a dead end. We'll go back to Washington for a few days, which will give all of us time to think"

"Mother, I won't be here for a few weeks. I really have business to attend to."

"That's okay. We want to take time and decide how far we want to pursue this. We're not important, only Robbie is. Where and who should he live and be with; that's the issue we should be dealing with.

Carolyn, I hope you will be reasonable and honest with your convictions. Is Wyoming the right place? Only you can make that decision. "Mrs. Jefferson, I have no concrete thought of what is right. I'm his Mother and I don't know what a Mother is supposed to be like. There's no pattern for them. I believe it's a trial and error in making decisions with a child as he grows. Can we come back in two weeks and then agree what is the right thing for Robbie? Thank you so much for letting us come here and share this with you."

"Please call me when you are coming. Talk to your parents and get their input. It does affect them, as they are his real grandparents. I would fight you to the end to keep him if he was really Carolyn's son, but he isn't. Have a safe trip back to California and call me."

Returning to Washington Tiffany and Scott entwined themselves into the fast pace of the political world of Congress. Conversation between Tiffany and her parents were made daily over the phone. Karen and Jim were frustrated they didn't have Robbie back in California with them. Their disappointment was obvious as they waited for a positive answer. "Be patient Mother, I need the time to make the right decision." Turning to look at Scott she hung up the phone and said, "I know what I must do."

"Honey, what ever you decide I'm with you. Don't tell me now. Wait until we're at your parent's home, this is a decision you alone have to make. Regardless what you do, I will agree with you."

Carolyn had also returned to Washington and was thrilled one evening when she picked up her phone to hear "Carolyn, it's been a long time since I've heard your voice."

"I know Jason. I can't wait for you to ask, "Will you marry me?"

"Will you marry me? He answered.

In unison across the wire from North Carolina to Wyoming a unified answer, "I will."

"Kevin suggested we have the wedding down here, is that okay?"

"That's fine with me Jason, but we have to wait for a few weeks. I have two weeks to make a decision and when I have the answers I will call you first."

"Sweetheart I'm so anxious to see you. I'll call you every night until you come down. Katy and Kevin are waiting to hear from you too." The telephone call went on for hours until they realized it was time to say, "Love you, I'll call tomorrow."

Right or Wrong

Tiffany and Scott decided to spend a few days with her parents before they went back to North Carolina. Karen could not contain herself when she picked up Scott and Tiffany at the airport. Starting with questions regarding Robbie. She wanted to know every detail. "Mother, please wait until we're home. There's plenty of time to discuss it later. The rest of the ride was in silence. While waiting for dinner to be served Scott and Tiffany took a long walk, knowing there are questions yet to come.

When the evening meal was over they went into the living room anxiously waiting to hear about the plans for Robbie to come to live with them. Taking a deep breath Tiffany started to explain all that had happened. "We spent two days there and got nowhere, as Carolyn seems determined to keep him. Her Mother is on our side, but I think Carolyn will not give him up without a fight."

"Mrs. Jefferson thinks Robbie should be given to me as I'm his biological Mother, but Scott and I have come to the conclusion that he would be better off with Carolyn and Jason. I know how disappointed this will make you, but the welfare of Robbie comes first. Scott and I can have other children. I'm not ready to be a parent, and neither is Scott. The demands for Scott's campaign will take all of our time."

Karen and Jim were shocked, not believing what their daughter was telling them. "You can't be serious Tiffany. He's our first grandchild. He's a part of me too. Please say you aren't going to do this? I find this difficult you are giving your child to someone else?

You are his Mother and can give him the love he needs. We can give him everything, until you are settled and able to take him."

"Mom I hoped you and Dad would understand. I'm not capable of being the Mother he will need. I know what will happen. He'll have a nanny, or child sitter, most of the time, until I give up my life style that I want now. I just can't do that to him. He needs both parents and children around him. Carolyn and Jason will be living near Kevin and Katy. He'll have a family life."

Jim listened quietly during the conversation, and then spoke out. "Tiffany, I'm disappointed, more for your Mother. I grew up as an only child though I had two sisters. My Mother took them away when we were very young. I never got to know them. Dad gave me everything growing up. Now I realize I was too independent and selfish. It took me a long time to learn how to share my life and my possessions. Even though we know Kevin is your real Father, I love you as if you were my own flesh and blood."

Stopping for a moment he turned to Scott "You are one privileged, lucky man to have a woman like Tiffany. Do what you have to do, I'll support you what ever you need."

"Thank you Mom and Dad. I hope you understand why I'm doing this. It's because of what you two have done for me as a young child. With Jason and Carolyn he too will have the same opportunities. When Scott and I have children you can have the joy and privilege of having grandchildren to spoil just like you spoiled me."

"Honey, I'm disappointed knowing someone else is raising my grandchild. I know the decision is yours. I hope it's the right one for all of us."

Tiffany felt California was not where her future would be. Knowing if Scott was elected President, then Washington would be their home for at least four years, hopefully eight. Using the phone in her room she made a call. "Hello Mrs. Jefferson? This is Tiffany."

"Hello, Tiffany, How nice to hear your voice. When are you coming back? Have you made your decision?"

In a soft voice Tiffany answered. "Scott and I have decided, the best interest for Robbie is for him to stay with Carolyn and Jason."

Stunned Mrs. Jefferson took a moment to compose her self. "Why is that? Are you sure of what you're saying. Remember, this has to be final. I've spent a long time with Carolyn on this, and she is still not convinced to give Robbie up. Wait a minute please."

Not believing what she heard she was stunned. After a few moments she called Carolyn, "The call is for you."

"Who's calling?" Carolyn asked. Her tone was brisk; it was almost possible to see the chip on her shoulder.

"Carolyn, this is Tiffany. I have good news for you."

In a cold icy tone, "What do you want?" What can I do for you?" she answered with a questioning response.

"Just to tell you Scott and I have decided that the best thing for Robbie is to let you have him; and raise him as your own. We feel this is the best decision for all, right or wrong. I've told your Mother this."

"Are you sure of what you're saying. You're willing to let me keep him?"

"Watching you and Robbie in your yard two weeks ago, I knew he would be safe with both of you. I don't know him. When I heard you and Robbie exchange I love you; I knew he should be yours. My heart is heavy about the decision but know it's the best thing to do. I don't even know him."

Almost in a state of shock, tears filled her eyes." Thank you so much Tiffany. I promise I will be the best Mother in the world. Jason and I are planning our wedding so please come and share it with us."

"We will come. Just let me know when, and we'll be there. Scott and I have to wait until next year to get married because of his campaign. We want you to be sure and come to our wedding in California."

Carolyn called Jason. When the answering service came she left a message for him to call her. When no call came during the day, she called Jason again. She dialed Jason's number, but disappointed when the answering machine clicked on. She was about to hang up when a woman's voice answered. "Hello, just a minute, I'll get Jason for you."

Hearing a strange voice with an accent Carolyn wondered, who would be answering Jason's phone? A minute later she heard his voice. "Hello, Carolyn, what's new?"

Who answered the phone, a Mexican beauty?"

"Yes, she is Mexican. She helps her Mother in cleaning the rooms where we single men stay. How soon can you come down so we can get married? Kevin and Katy are ready to have another party. They insisted they want to do this. Beside if you want to teach, you better get an application in with your résumé. I can hardly wait until you get here."

Carolyn's Mother was unaware that the plans had been changed, and was making arrangements for the wedding. Invitations were in the process. Caterers were to be notified and flowers ordered. She was stunned when Carolyn approached her with the shocking news.

"Mother, I'm not getting married here. I'm getting married in Wyoming. Jason's employer insists he'll make all the arrangements for us. I've been away for twenty years. All my friends from here are gone. I can make arrangements for you to get to Wyoming."

Satisfied she had done the right thing for her son, yet realizing that she had hurt her Mother and Father, Tiffany felt torn and empty inside. "Scott, I know we haven't gone to church and all that. Can we go Sunday before we go back to Washington?"

"Of course we can sweetheart; anyone in particular?"

"I just feel I should go to church and pray that I did the right thing. I know I did, but I still need to talk to God. I believe in Him, and I need His assurance."

On Sunday Tiffany asked her parents to join them. Jim had a golf match that morning and it was too late to cancel. Karen was delighted to go with them. The sermon that morning was titled "Choices." The minister told the congregation God has given everyone the right to make choices as to what we should do with our lives. He explained all the different ones we could make. Sometimes it would be difficult, some times easy. We have to live by the choices we make; having faith to believe."

At the closing of his sermon, the Minister looked down on the congregation and left them with a decision. "I repeat again, you are free to make any choice you want; but remember, you have to answer for the choices you make in your life."

Leaving the church Tiffany turned to Scott and said, "I know he was talking to me, and I'm at peace knowing I did the right thing. I guess time will tell. Do you agree?"

"Yes sweetheart. You made the right decision for both of us. Later we'll be able to have a family of our own."

Scott did not want a tearful goodbye, and was firm in taking a taxi to the airport. They all tried to make conversation on the porch; each one was deep in their own thoughts. When the taxi arrived the goodbyes were quickly said, leaving Karen and Jim alone with their heartaches.

Standing on the porch; tears streaming down Karen's face. "I understand what she's saying; it's the right thing to do, but what about us as we're his grandparents. Will we ever see him again? We're the real losers. He's a part of me."

Walking down to the taxi, Scott put his arm around Tiffany's shoulders; she slipped her right arm around Scott's waist. The decision was over; the heavy burden had been lifted off their minds. It's time to move on.

Jim turned toward Karen, cradling her face in his hands. Gently he kissed her. "Honey, sometimes we have to let go, and let our kids walk their own road of life. I'm reminded of what someone had said, for everyone there's a new beginning, but for everything there is an end."

Arriving back in Washington Scott left Tiffany at her apartment and went to his office. Helen told him he had many calls from the Director of the Democratic Party. "He was anxious to have you call him as soon as you can. He has something of great importance he has to discuss with you."

"Thank you Helen." Thinking what could be wrong? He went inside his office to call Paul. "Hello Paul, what's wrong and so important?"

"Scott, We might have to change our plans for you."

"Come on Paul, I don't understand. I have my plans set for the fall and intend to visit the important states we need in the election. Give me a day or two to get ready."

"No I have to see you today." When Scott arrived at the Party headquarters he was surprised to see all of the committee members seated at the conference table. "What gives Paul?"

Presidential Plans

"Sit down and I'll explain what's happened since you were on vacation. We just heard the Black and Hispanic members in Congress are planning to present their own choices for the President and Vice President at the Convention." Starting to object Scott was silenced by some of the members. Paul continued, "Do you realize how many minorities we have in Congress? I can tell you if the majority of women voters give their support and agree to place a Black or Hispanic person as your running mate, it will change our plans."

"But Paul, we've already asked the Senator from Alabama to be on the ticket. If he refuses, there are other members of Congress available. Again Scott tried to speak, "Paul." Before he could continue, he was silenced and told to be quiet and listen.

"Forget it Scott! We need to have a discussion with this minority group and find out what they want. We've lost our manufacturing business to other countries.

These were good jobs for the poor and immigrants to get them off welfare. We need to impress our business people by tax incentives, and to give their workers decent wages and health benefits. Our immigrants have to become citizens; if they fail we should deport them."

Another member offered, "Most of our poor are Black and Hispanic. For too long, promises given at every election never materialized. They faded away, soon to be forgotten. Let's put our money where our mouths are."

Scott sat there trying to absorb all that was said. He found it difficult to have anything to say; and felt at the moment his world was falling apart in front of him. The frightening thought of the possibility of losing the support of the minority members in the coming election weighed heavily on the minds of the committee. A vote was taken to invite all of the minority members of Congress to a meeting.

Two weeks later the invitation was accepted; but when they met the feeling was strong with the members of the minority group who were determined to make changes. Senator Brown from California spoke first. "We have more minorities coming into this country every year. Some of our citizens will not accept jobs that are available; because of low pay, no health benefits and this is why we need immigrants here. We say everyone is welcome and we'll not discriminate, but we do. We agree that some of them are criminals and bring drugs into the country; but who buys them? Our citizens do!"

"You're right." Another member of the minority group spoke out. "Still there are many good immigrants who look for a decent life for their families. We're open to discuss our proposed candidates, but we want to know what you propose for the poor. We have to discuss education, job availability, a decent place to live and some health benefits."

""I agree we need to change our way of thinking, but time is running out to try and make too many changes in our plans for the White House." Scott replied. "I have no quarrel with a minority as my running mate. There are some already out on the campaign trail. It won't be easy."

Senator Brown spoke again. "Every election we offer the same old agenda; education, jobs and health needs. It gets redundant over and over again. We never solve what we say we will. Winning a war proves nothing. Vietnam, the Gulf war, and two more wars still not completed. These people hate us. We say we won, we didn't. They are ingrained in their tradition and will never change. It's time we take care of our own before we try to change the world."

"Let me interject something here," said one of the Representatives, "We should get Germany, France and other countries to help us. This administration wants it their way."

Our President is listening to the wrong people. Unless we come up with a new program of job availability, health coverage and security we'll still have trouble in getting our person elected. I for one believe we should shut down the space program. The billions of dollars spent affect a few people to have a good life."

"That's right." Another representative said. "There are brilliant people in the space program. I have respect for them, but their efforts, wisdom and focus should be channeled to discover ways to improve people's health and cure the diseases of the world. Don't forget the aids epidemic in Africa. We're wasting their abilities searching outer space. Someone said that place is God's playground and we should stay out of it. Everything we need to cure us is here."

After much discussion between all those who had attended Paul replied, "Why don't we form a committee for each subject we have discussed, especially decent housing and crime which is a real problem here? Does anyone realize how many of our citizens don't take the time to vote?"

"You're right Paul. First we have to get more people to vote. Then we have to impress our poor to be proud to be an American, and I agree we have failed. How can they be proud and be so poor. I have two successful friends who would be pleased to help in the area of unemployment. Their knowledge would be valuable to us. Yes I'm very open to having a minority as my running mate."

"Thank you Senator." One of the minority members a Representative from New York said. "I'm happy to hear you say that; but we haven't come to a conclusion you're the right one for the Presidency. You have worked hard and we do appreciate your loyalty to the Democratic Party; but Scott you haven't convinced us, because we don't know what your platform is."

The meeting ended and no date set for another session. Paul and Scott stood in disbelief and disappointment. Scott finally found his voice. "Paul, what do you think of this?"

Paul remained quiet until one of the members said; "I had no idea this kind of a discussion was going on in Congress with the minority members. Did you Scott?"

"Not in the least. The last time I knew they were in favor of what we had agreed on; the Senator from Alabama and I would be the ones on the ticket for the 2008 election." After leaving the meeting, Scott called Tiffany asking her to meet him at his office. He felt emotionally ill as he sat, cradling his head in his hands. All the plans he had made were coming unraveled. When Tiffany opened the door she knew something was wrong. "Scott, are you having trouble with Philip again? The sound of your voice seemed so sad."

"No honey, it's larger than that. Sit down and I'll tell you what's happened at the meeting. Paul and I thought everything was all set with our plans; but the minority members of Congress have banded together and want a minority person to run for the Presidency position."

Tiffany was stunned. He had felt confident that everyone was behind him. Now this was a new situation causing him concern. Was Grace behind all of this? He remembered when she threatened to withdraw her pledge to give millions of dollars to his campaign. She was so angry at that time.

"But I thought you were selected as the Presidential candidate for the Party?"

"I was, but other people can run as Independents or as a Democrat. We have to wait until we have the Convention to decide who it will be. I had this feeling when I visited the large cities this year. There's been an increase of Blacks and Hispanic young people, especially the college students that are on a mission to get all of their peers to register and vote.

If they can convince young women and college age to join them, I'll have trouble at the Convention to have them vote for me."

"Scott don't stop working; I'll be with you on your campaign and do anything you want me to. You promised."

"Yes I did. Maybe if they see you as a vibrant, intelligent, attractive young woman hopefully it might entice that age bracket to vote for me. Our young high school students should be required to study American history as well as the immigrants.

We can't help the poor nations succeed in having a better life if we interfere politically. We must educate our own young people first."

The following week Scott met with the Leaders of the Democratic Party to reorganize their plans for him. Paul called Senator Brown who seemed to be the spokesman for the minority to ask for a private meeting.

A few weeks later they received a negative answer. "I know this is a shock to you Paul. These are difficult times, and we've waited too long and ignored the college students to inspire them to look for a career in politics. This is why for the past year we have a campaign going into every college in the country; giving seminars, imploring them to get active in politics and be sure to vote themselves."

After a long discussion they agreed to meet at the Democratic Headquarters. Visibly upset Scott stood and said, "How did this ever happen, we had no idea this was going on? I had met with Democratic groups in many states and the enthusiasm was great."

A month passed and both groups met to form a Party Agreement. When finalized it would be released to the press. Paul opened the meeting, asking for all present to have open minds and willingness to participate in discussions.

Before we start I'm going to repeat what I have said for a long time at meetings regarding our party. Another war, billions of dollars leaving this country, and going to other countries around the world. Their leaders are getting rich indulging in their wealthy life style. They want for nothing while their people go hungry. We forget that charity begins at home. We can't be the police force of the world. We need other countries to assist us." Paul took a breath and continued. "Our Space Program can wait. The poor could care less about that. When a man loses his job and maybe his house, and other bills continue to build up: he knows his family needs food, clothing and so on. You know what his first priority will be. We should know when we give our money to needy countries we should have the right to know how it's spent.

Other members from both sides expressed their thoughts and ideas. Then one person spoke up about the minorities in our country. "I believe that all the people that come to this country wanting to be citizens must learn and speak our language. Certainly they should retain their heritage, language and history. When they become American citizens they owe their loyalty to the United States. We should have a commitment from them."

After a long day Senator Brown spoke out. "Once again I will say; I am a minority and you should know I hate the word minority. I'm an American, the color of my skin; my ethnic birth has nothing to do with me as a person. We must have a program we can present to our people. One that will work, and we need their confidence in us. The majority of our citizens are disappointed the way the country is headed. Our promises we have made to them have fallen short. We need the news media to help us get our message out. We've been labeled as the big spending party, and we have to stop giving ourselves raises and more benefits."

There was clapping of hands as he continued. "In closing we have to reform the pension plan in Congress. My plan is to have all members of Congress serve at least fifteen years or more to receive a pension and to start receiving it at the age of sixty. This payment would increase in value if a member serves more than fifteen years. We also should review health programs for all government employees."

"You're right," I also believe the United States Government tries to get too involved in the states affairs. Each state shouldn't be subsidized with their financial problems. Only exceptions should be when they have failed. Then the government should help them. Too many people believe our government should support them."

Paul was getting tired of all the different comments, and no one was coming up with any solid workable solutions. "Let me suggest Senator Brown, your committee appoint three of your members to each of the following subjects. The names of Minorities for the President and Vice President. We need Committees of Education, Drugs and Welfare and Immigrants Programs. Congress and Government Employees on retirements and health benefits. We will do the same if there is no more discussion I now close this meeting. We will meet in two months to discuss our differences."

Before leaving Scott asked Paul, "Could you set up meeting with some of the newer members of Congress and try to get them to go along with us in the plans we had agreed on?"

"I'll think about it Scott."

Tiffany is Missing

One afternoon, as Tiffany left the office, two men grabbed and blindfolded her, pushed her into the back seat of a car. They placed a wet rag over her face. After a brief struggle she went unconscious, never getting a look at them.

It was later that day when Scott returned to his condo. Seeing the blinking light on his answering service he pressed the button. "If you want to see your girlfriend again, it would be wise for you to resign from seeking the Presidency. You have only forty-eight hours to make your decision; you'll find her tied up in your office. Remember, only forty eight hours."

Scott not sure what he would find, broke all speeding laws as he rushed to his office. Bursting through the door he found Tiffany gagged and tied to a chair. He quickly set her free and held her trembling body close to him. It took awhile until she regained her composure. He assured her she would be safe and no harm would come to her.

Still in his office Scott called Paul. "I have to meet with you now. This situation with the minorities is more serious then we think. When I got back from our meeting I had a message that someone had kidnapped Tiffany, threatening me to resign as a candidate for the Presidency. I have forty-eight hours to comply or I will never see her again. She was bound and gagged in my office just as they said."

"Scott stay with Tiffany, we can meet tomorrow to discuss this."

More Plans

"Paul I can't wait. She's in danger; I have to see you now. I've taken her back to her apartment."

"You left her go alone, your crazy?" Hearing the urgency in Scott's voice, Paul said, "Come on over."

It didn't take him long to arrive at Paul's office. "Sit down Scott. I'll call Senator Brown now. Maybe he has an idea what this is all about." Leaving a message on the Senator's answering machine they waited patiently for his call. In a few minutes the phone rang. After a lengthy conversation with the Senator, he had no information about the kidnapping. He knew there was some unrest in the minority groups but knew nothing of anyone banding together to become involved in the process of choosing a candidate for the Presidency,

For a few weeks there were no incidents and everything seemed normal. Scott insisted Tiffany never go anywhere alone. She argued with him to no avail; he insisted he bring her back and forth to work. Tiffany said there was no danger and she would be careful. "No, for the last time I don't want you alone at any time."

Two months had passed and the committees were still in sessions, discussing their assignments of the areas agreed on. About the drug situation it was a recommendation to increase the number of people guarding our borders. Increase the fines and jail sentences for those who smuggle these people into our country; and expel any person involved in this situation.

Companies using illegal immigrants as slave labor will be fined heavily; and refused the right to sell their products. The subject of education was difficult for the members to reach an agreement. Some members had a struggle in their feelings for the poorer student and wanted exceptions for entrances into colleges. Others felt strongly that entrances should be on scholastic ability, and colleges should have the right to make decisions and accept those they wanted and not be harnessed by law.

Any Federal monies should be for a student's education and housing, not for individual pleasures and sports accomplishments. The children must have at least a high school education, and we should enforce a law holding the parents responsible for their children's attendance.

Dress codes should be made by the school committee's decisions, and with the parent's cooperation. Schools are for learning; and to prepare the student to become a viable member of society in sharing their knowledge, making the world a better and safer place to live."

These statements brought strong objection from some of this committee. "Many colleges make millions on attendance at sports events. Some make up subjects to accommodate the sport players so they can graduate. Most of them spend more time in practicing and playing what they enjoy, while the real hard working students struggles hoping they will graduate."

Pension plans and retirement benefits for Congress and Government workers became very heated when some of the members suggested that their salaries and retirement should be based on the recommendations of an impartial committee.

Other members thought the members of Congress should be required to attend a certain amount of time in Washington when in session, and be held accountable if they are absent too many times.

The committee responsible to bring name or names who should be on the ballot for the year 2008 had great difficulty with this responsibility. It was decided not by a majority that they have a Black or Hispanic woman selected to be a nominee for the Vice President position.

This brought murmurings from some members. "What about the Senator from North Carolina we already selected?" A few loud voices echoed from the rear of the hall.

"We have two names from each of the minority groups, and if we agree we'll send a complete list of their backgrounds, party affiliation and what they have accomplished in the political field. Each member should return to their home base and seek out possible candidates."

Finally each member of these committees realized their task would not be easy. It was agreed they would meet in one month and report back to Paul and Senator Brown of their progress. Some the members disagreed and could not come to an agreement. The majority of members in their respective groups out voted them. All of the groups must be ready in a month to present what they believed will be the best program to present at the Convention of the Democratic Party.

One night as Tiffany and Scott were dining at one of the local restaurants she gasped and couldn't believe her eyes when she noticed a man enter the room.

"What's wrong sweetheart?" Try as hard as she could, words would not come. Scott noticing the look on her face, questioned her again. "What's wrong? Do you know that man?" She continued to stare at him. "I noticed he looked over the tables and he stopped looking when he saw us. Is he one of the men that kidnapped you?"

"It is; it must be Justin. I don't really know because I couldn't see, and they had masks over their faces."

Staring back at Tiffany he smiled and left the restaurant. Tiffany knew she was lying to Scott. "He looked different with the heavy black beard, the long hair, but still very tall and muscular. How can I tell Scott he's the Father of Robbie?"

Knowing now was not the time or a place for questions. Scott asked, "Honey, what would you like for dinner?"

Getting her composure back she responded, "I think I'll have a Caesar salad, but I'd like a glass of wine first?"

At Scott's condo Tiffany turned on the television hoping this would delay any further conversation. When the clock struck eleven Tiffany took her shower saying she was exhausted and went to bed falling asleep. Is she really sleeping or pretending, or just wanting to be left alone? Scott wondered as he went to bed. With a resignation in his mind he tried to sleep; but like the sheep, questions jumped over the bed all night.

In the morning Tiffany was waiting for him, but to his surprise she was still in her housecoat. "Scott, I know you are wondering about the man at the restaurant. I promise I'll answer any thing you want to ask but not now."

The Oval Office

The President called Scott wanting to see him. Changing his plans Scott drove immediately to the White House. He was greeted by the secretary and escorted into the Oval office. "Good morning Scott, we haven't seen each other for some time. It looks like you're going to be my competitor in the next election."

Wondering why the President wanted to see him Scott offered, "Yes Mr. President and our party is going to win.. We have some surprises coming the next time. You'll have to wait until the Convention to find out."

"Scott you've a lot of competition this year. There are some pretty good men running against you. Are you sure you can win? I heard your girlfriend was kidnapped; is that true? The FBI is here to assist you."

Stunned Scott stood silent for a moment. He knows about the kidnapping? "Who told you that Mr. President? My girlfriend is fine. Where did that rumor come from?"

"One of the secretaries mentioned it to me. You know how rumors are here in Washington. I'm glad she's okay. The offer still stands if you need help. I'd like you to come to Mexico with me. We need some co-operation from both parties to solve the immigrant problem."

"It's nice of you to ask me sir, but I must beg off this time. I'm sure there is someone in Congress who can help you. I'd like to invite you to my first inauguration. Remember Yogi Berra said; it's never over 'til it's over."

"Okay Scott I understand. You and your girlfriend are invited to my inauguration after the next election. Like they say at a wedding, second best isn't too bad."

Scott left the Presidents office and hesitated for a moment when a tall young man with a heavy dark beard and long hair passed him. Stopping, Scott turned back to see this man looking back and smiling. "It's him, the young man we saw at the restaurant."

Inside the Oval office the President greeted Justin. "It's good to see you again. I'm hoping you can be successful this time, like you were before on that difficult assignment. Have you finished with your education, and ready to come to work with us on a full time basis?"

"What are your plans for me this time sir?"

"Just keep a low profile for now. Later you will get a call. I initially wanted you to come to the next staff meeting at Camp David this weekend, but the timing isn't good. We have our minority person selected; but we have an obstacle and don't know how the person we want to replace will react to our suggestion. Relax and enjoy Washington for the present time. Later you will get a call from someone you won't meet, but he will give you instructions. We want to surprise the Democratic Party with our plans that will knock their socks off. We know the minority groups in their party are planning to have one of their own run for Vice President."

Because of the many commitments Scott had to attend, it wasn't until later he called Tiffany to tell her he had seen the some young man in the Oval office that had been at the restaurant "I didn't like the way he smirked at me as he walked by. How do you know him? I didn't ask you last night because you were upset. The President was smug and self assured he would win the election."

In the evening Tiffany asked Scott to join her. Sitting in opposite chairs nervously she began to speak. "Honey, that young man was my former boyfriend. I know he's changed in appearance. I understand he is going to the poor countries to teach them and hopefully help them become a democratic nation. He's strong and persuasive; he's able to convince any one to change their mind. His name is Justin, and he's Robbie's Father."

For a while Scott remained silent. He didn't know how to respond to her. "Scott, I'm sorry it happened, I was only fourteen years old. You said it didn't matter and now you won't even talk to me." Scott left the room long enough to have a glass of wine, ignoring Tiffany. She finally asked him for wine too.

Finishing their wine in silence, Tiffany quietly rose from her chair and walked out of the room. Picking up her coat she left the condo not knowing what to do. Going down the street she kept looking back hoping to see Scott; but he was not there.

Missing Again

Scott had dozed off, probably the result of the long day and consuming the rest of the bottle of wine.

Waking up he realized how he had reacted to Tiffany's news about Justin and his connection to Robbie. Thinking she was in bed, Scott opened the door and found the room empty. He heard the mantle clock strike and knew four hours had elapsed. "Where did she go?" he wondered? Panic set in, and he called the police station asking for help.

Getting into his car he started to drive around the different streets, even stopping at all night restaurants to ask had anyone seen her; but the answers were always no. Going to his office he saw the light blinking on the answering machine. Pressing the button a voice came on saying, "We warned you to give it up. You have ignored us. Soon you'll receive a letter with instructions telling you what you are to do if you want to see your girl friend again."

Scott called Paul's office leaving an urgent message for him to call back as soon as he came in. Then he left a message for the President asking for his help saying he would explain when the President called him back. Time went slowly until at eight in the morning when Paul called. "What's wrong Scott?" After explaining what had transpired, Paul said he should meet him immediately.

Entering Paul's office he was surprised to see a few members of the Party there." Scott why didn't you tell the President how you found Tiffany tied up in your office? He could have had the FBI involved."

"Paul when the forty eight hours passed I thought it was a prank so I didn't do anything about it. I'm sorry I didn't get the FBI involved. It's been my life long ambition to be the President, and I don't want to lose her."

"Scott! Nothing is as important as your girlfriend and future wife. There'll always be the next time. How can you be so selfish at this time thinking only about yourself?"

One of his associates said in great disgust," Scott; if you don't resign you will lose my help. We'll find out who's behind this. At the present time we have to go along with the minority group and select one of them for the Presidency in your place. We could ask Senator Brown to run?"

"Paul; can't we wait a little while longer. I'm sure the FBI will be able to find Tiffany."

"Scott, we have no time left; we have to change it now. After you sign the letter I'm sure they will release Tiffany. You have no other choice my friend. My opinion is to get back to your office immediately."

When he arrived, Helen handed him a sealed envelope. His heart pounding with fear, and his hands trembling; he read the letter that could change his life forever. He knew he was at a cross road in his life; his desire to be President; or his love for his wife? Will there be another time for him to run for the Presidency? He knew what he had to do; Paul was right. There was no way he could sacrifice Tiffany for his desire.

Leaving the White House Justin got into a cab and told the driver where he was staying. Looking out the window he saw a woman alone, walking slowly. "That's Tiffany," he thought. "Driver stop I'll get out here." Giving him a twenty-dollar bill he left the cab.

He followed her quietly and saw the opportunity to grab her from behind. Placing a handkerchief over her face and sprayed it with a bottle he had with him. In a moment she collapsed on the ground. Hailing another a cab that was passing by, he told the driver she had passed out from drinking and asked him to stop on a deserted street and help him to place Tiffany in a more comfortable position. When the driver bent down to lift her up, Justin choked him until he became unconscious. Quickly he got into the drivers seat and drove until he reached a house he had rented in Maryland. Picking Tiffany up he carried her inside and tied her to the bed. She lay there helpless and quiet.

In the morning Justin left the room just long enough to ask a friend to deliver a rental car to the house he was staying at. Placing her in the car he drove to a second place. He brought her inside and tied her again to a bed. Loosing Tiffany's hands he gave her a pad of paper and a pen and motioned her to sign it at the bottom of the page. Reading it she shook her head back and forth implying a no answer. He grabbed her hand again and motioned for her to sign. Reading it again she became frightened as she read, "We warned you before to give up your candidacy for President.

We have your girlfriend in a safe place. If you don't resign you will never see her again.

The world is a big place and there are many places to hide her. There are men who would be very happy to have her as a wife. Your girlfriend signed this paper to prove we have her. Sign this paper as a final proof of your withdrawal. If the police and FBI people are with you, or any one waiting with you, it's all over. The President is not aware of this, or has anything to do with it." Looking at the second page it said,

"I, Senator Scott Drew of a clear mind and with no pressure am giving up my ambition to pursue the nomination for the President of the United States for the Democratic Party for the year 2008."

Scott Drew   Tiffany Walker

He sat there silently watching her as he meditated as to what he should do, if she continues to not sign? Finally he took her hand and motioned to her once again. She read the paper and once more she shook her head with a negative answer. He was getting frustrated and stood her up shaking her with determination. She knew he would not accept any answer except what he asked for. Finally realizing it was fruitless to continue, she signed. After signing he tied her to the bed once again and said in a muffled voice, "If the Senator signs this paper we will release you. If he doesn't you will never see him again."

With those final words he left the room. She laid there with little hope and all kinds of thoughts racing in her mind, The tears flowed down her face, everything she planned seemed to be fading away.

Inside the envelope Scott found a separate piece of paper. Written on it was his instruction on how he was to return it with his signature. "Return the paper with your signature. Your girlfriend has signed it as you can see. When everything is in order return to your condo; there you will receive a telephone call as to where you will find Tiffany."

He had no sooner entered his apartment than the phone rang. "Hello Senator Drew?" A muffled voice said. "Place the signed paper in the envelope and slide it under the front door. After you have done that, go into your bedroom and close the door. We're watching you; if you don't do this it will be the end of our contact with you. Any move to open the door will result in you getting shot and Tiffany will disappear forever. Right now she is waiting inside a private plane ready to take off if you try anything. Don't be foolish, Senator. We mean what we say."

Scott's nerves were almost out of control. He took the paper, signed it and placed it inside an envelope, sealed it, sliding it under the door. Getting his gun from the closet, he waited listening for footsteps. Thinking he heard a sound he quietly opened the door but no one was there, the envelope was still on the floor.

Immediately the phone rang. Picking up the phone he heard a voice saying, "We warned you and told what to do.

Go into your bedroom, close the door and wait a half hour. This is your last chance. There will be no second one." Scott heard a dial tone as the person hung up.

It was the longest half hour he had ever spent. Thoughts about many things raced through his mind; the possibility of losing Tiffany, his resignation of being a candidate and other changes in his life. Watching the clock the minute hand moved so slowly. By the end of the half hour he frantically opened the door to find the note gone, replaced by a brown envelope. He opened it and inside was piece of paper addressed to him. "Senator if you go to the Washington monument you will find Tiffany waiting for you. Remember we have a signed agreement that you have resigned from seeking the office of the Presidency. If you fail to abide with our agreement we will release this to the news media."

Mixed emotions, and relief knowing Tiffany was safe, he reached the monument in half the time it would normally take and found her sitting on a bench inside the entrance. "I'm taking you home sweetheart, everything's going to be okay. You're safe now. It's over."

The light on the answering machine was blinking when they entered the room, it was a message to call Paul. "Scott, come to the office as soon as you can." Before leaving he contacted Suzy asking her stay with Tiffany.

At Paul's office Scott heard, "I have good news. The FBI has arrested a man named Justin. After some strong interrogating, you know what I mean. He confessed being part of a group that had kidnapped Tiffany. They wanted you out as a candidate. He wanted Tiffany as his wife.

He intended to move to one of the Muslim countries where they wouldn't be found. He agreed to work with them if he could have her as his payment. They reneged so he's talking. This group is an outlawed Muslim group that wants our country out of the Middle East. Mean while the Republican Party is going to ask one of the minorities in the Presidents inner circle to agree to run for the Vice President's office. The Vice president will accept another position in his cabinet."

With this good news Scott called Tiffany telling her the FBI had captured Justin a member of a Muslim group. "He confessed to the kidnapping. They wanted to destroy my campaign. Justin wanted you for his wife and was going to take you out of the country." Relief mixed with laughter and tears of joy, disbelief that the trauma had ended.

"Scott I have more to tell you; we have asked Senator Brown to take your place as the nominee and run for President in the coming election. You can't put your girlfriend in danger again. You have signed the release from being our Parties choice."

"Paul, I can't believe what you're saying. I'll make sure someone will always be with her. I have many friends throughout the country that will back me up. I signed that paper under duress"

."I'm sorry, it's too late. We can't change our plans. We are sure that Senator Brown will accept, and this will satisfy the minorities in Congress."

Kevin's Plan

"Okay Paul, I'll run as an Independent at the Convention and let the people decide." Returning home Scott made a call "Hello Jim, are you ready to come aboard my team?"

"I sure am. See you in a couple of days." Jim replied. Tell me where can I meet you?"

"Give me a ring when you arrive and I'll be there."

"Hello Kevin, Scott here. Are you ready for Washington?"

"Anytime you want. I'll be there in a couple of days." Calling to Katy he said, "Honey, Scott called and I'm going to Washington to help him for a few weeks. Jason can handle everything while I'm gone. I'll go out to California and meet Jim. We can fly together in his plane." I'll call him and let him know I'm coming."

"That doesn't make sense. You can fly from here; but whatever you want."

Arriving in Stockton he took a cab to Jim's house. When Karen opened the door she stood in amazement to see Kevin. "This a surprise to see you. Jim didn't tell me you were coming. He's away for a few days on business."

"I called him and left a message on his office phone and thought we could fly together to Washington. I guess I could get a room in a hotel until he gets back."

"No, that doesn't make sense you can stay here until he gets back. I'll call him to let him know you're here."

After the evening meal Karen and Kevin went in to the living room to watch the evening news. He kept looking at her and would glance away when she turned toward him. Time passed quickly until she said she was tired and had to go to work early in the morning "Stay up as long as you want. I'll show you where the guest room is."

As Karen was leaving the room Kevin walked to her, held her tightly kissing her long and hard. "Stop it! What's wrong with you?" she said, trying to get loose from him.

"Alicia I love you. I can't let you go."

"Kevin you have to leave. You can't stay here. I'll call a cab for you. The driver will take you to one of the hotels down town. Let me know where you're staying. I'll call Jim to let him know you're here. You can't come again unless Jim is here. It's over and has been for a long time." When the cab arrived Karen called Jim to let him know Kevin was here and what happened. He said he had called you. He's staying here in a local hotel."

"He never called me. I'll be home tomorrow."

Leaving Karen and going to a hotel Kevin called Katy. "I'm in a hotel for the night. Jim is on a business trip. I'm flying back tomorrow." Sitting in a chair he came to the conclusion he had to move on as Karen has. Remembering what his Father had said; you don't repeat your mistakes and you build on your successes.

A Change

"Catherine, will you call the Vice President and tell him to come to my office. When he arrives I will not be taking any calls or visitors for some time."

"Come in my friend and sit down. This is not going to be easy for me, but our people in Congress and those who support us with our financial needs are asking that you not run for your position in the next election." With no response an eerie cloud of silence was hanging over the room as the Vice President gazed up at the ceiling.

Finally he said, "Mr. President, you want me to step down; you can't be sincere. We were successful twice and running ahead in all the polls now. We have planned to go for a third term. We have to control Congress. I can't believe what you're saying. That's out of the question."

I'm sorry, but I have no choice. Pressing the intercom button, "Catherine, call my staff members and tell them to meet here as soon as they can. No excuses. Whatever they are doing will have to wait. What I have to tell them is more important than whatever they're doing now."

When all the members arrived the President said, "Listen carefully to what I'm going to tell you, it could affect your future here. The FBI has called to inform me Justin, the young man we had high hopes for failed in finding out what the Democratic Party was doing. He was to find out what they were doing in selecting a minority on their ticket for the Vice President position in the next election."

"They found out he had kidnapped Senator Drew's girlfriend. He knew her in high school and planned to take her to a Muslim Country. We have to make a change. We have no idea what they are doing as far as having a minority on their ticket."

"How can we make a change now?" The Secretary of State asked. "Whoever we ask will have no time to go out campaigning."

"Who said it has to be a man?" questioned one of the women on the staff. "Are you suggesting we have a minority for the Vice President in the next election?'

"Certainly some women are capable of serving in that position. I would be happy if we can find the right one. Yes I said a minority person for the Vice-Presidency."

"Mr. Vice President you're extremely valuable to us, and we can't lose you. I know some people don't appreciate you, but we know what you have accomplished as the Vice President. I have my own ideas who I'd like to have, but I want your input too. I want all of you for the next few weeks to talk to all the minorities you believe are capable to serve in that position. We have limited time to accomplish this. No one knows we're hoping for a third term, and we can get approval if we hold the votes in the next election."

Shocked at what they had just heard, everyone left the office, leaving the President and Vice President alone sitting silent, not knowing how to start a dialogue on this sensitive situation.

Standing up the Vice President walked out of the room. The President slumped down in his chair, his mind filled with unanswered questions. "How do I tell the Republicans in Congress we might be making a mistake? What about the many who have contributed so heavily to the Party? If I get elected and we have a minority as the Vice President, and for some unknown reason I can't fulfill my position before my term is up; we would then have our first minority President. Will people think about this when they vote? Only time will tell if this happens."

While all of this was going on Scott began to formulate his campaign plans with Jim and Kevin for the 2008 running as an Independent candidate. Kevin's son Jon continued his studies at Maryland University. Suzy was waiting until he graduated, remaining true to him. Katy and the twins remained in Wyoming looking forward to the twin's high school graduation.

Jim and Karen are still waited patiently for Tiffany and Scott to tell them when they will be married. Jim senior and Joyce are enjoying the raising of Eric and looking forward to retirement. Carolyn and Jason were married the following spring. Robbie was the best man.